CHANGING LANES

CHOOSING PROVIDENCE - BOOK 3

JILL BURRELL

First edition: July 2023
Library of Congress Control Number: 2023911854

ISBN: 978-1-955507-12-7 (eBook)
ISBN: 978-1-955507-16-5 (pbk)

To my sisters. Your support and encouragement mean the world to me.

CHAPTER 1

*E*den dropped into the chair behind her desk and kicked off her heels.

She looked across the space she shared with her father's executive secretary. Nora wasn't there, so she propped her elbows on her desk and rubbed her temples.

Thank goodness it's Friday.

She glanced at the clock on the wall. Ten more minutes. She couldn't wait to get Chinese takeout and go home and soak in a bubble bath. Thankfully, her father didn't have any social plans this weekend for which he needed her by his side.

The door to her father's office opened and serious, strait-laced Nora walked out, wearing her typical black skirt with a white blouse. She *always* wore black and white. "Your dad wants to see you before you leave today," she said in her no-nonsense tone as she rounded her desk.

Of course he does. He's going to ruin my date with my bubble bath, I just know it.

Eden wondered what her father wanted but she didn't bother voicing the question, because Nora's response would be a shrug followed by, "Why don't you go ask him and find out?" The woman never engaged in what she deemed inane conversation.

For someone who enjoyed interactions with others, it made work stuffy and boring for Eden.

She hadn't always hated her job. When she'd first come to work for her father's company five years ago—yep, nepotism at its finest—she'd enjoyed her job. As the assistant to her father's personal secretary, she'd been tasked with planning team building and social events; the fun things stiff, inflexible Nora hated most.

But Eden had proven herself knowledgeable about the company and the work they did which quickly—thanks to nepotism—earned her the position of Head Market Analyst. Which meant she now spent ninety percent of her workday dealing with complaints from their clients.

She attended countless meetings where she explained to company administrators and CEOs how to improve their marketing tactics and increase their customer base according to market trends. Only to have to explain six months later to those same executives why their company was still in decline; because they'd failed to follow the prescriptive plan DuPont Data Analytics laid out for them.

Boring meetings with egotistical CEO's. Just one reason Eden hated her job.

She let out a sigh and slipped her heels back on. Rising, she entered her father's office with barely a tap on the door.

"Hi, honey. How did things go with Burton manufacturing?"

"Exactly as expected. They still want to blame their loss of revenue on flaws in our analysis."

"Did you set them straight concerning the time and money they'd save by adding additional automation?"

"I did." The words came out through a tight smile. Additional automation meant laying off hundreds of employees. Yet another reason she didn't like her job. Many times, what DuPont Analytics prescribed as the best plan of action for the company turned out to be the worst for their employees.

"The sooner Old Man Burton catches up to the times, the better off they'll be," her dad said.

What Old Man Burton needed to do was retire, but Eden didn't blame him for not wanting to step down, since his son planned to take the company in a totally different direction than what he wanted. Although at the rate things were going, there wouldn't be much left by the time Junior got a shot at it.

They talked for several minutes about some of the other meetings Eden had attended that week. Tense meetings where she pointed out all the things bosses were doing wrong in running their businesses. She tried to get to know the leaders behind the companies and what drove them, but sometimes people were stubborn and unwilling to make changes. Never mind that they paid DuPont Analytics a lot of money to tell them what to do.

It wasn't until Eden pointedly looked at the clock on the side wall of her dad's office that he cleared his throat and straightened the papers on his desk.

"I'd like you to come over for dinner tonight." The words were spoken in his usual brusque, business-like tone and without eye-contact.

There goes my bubble bath.

A sensation of heaviness swept over Eden, leaving her feeling exhausted. "I wasn't aware you planned to entertain tonight."

"It's a last-minute thing, but I have a surprise for you." Still not meeting her gaze, he stood and shifted papers to his briefcase, almost as though dismissing her.

"Surprise?" Eden stood too. "So, is this business or personal?"

"Both."

What kind of surprise could he have for her that was both business and personal?

"Who are your guests?"

Eden lived by the motto: Forewarned is forearmed. And this felt like one of those times when she needed to be armed. For what, she didn't know, but if she refused to go to dinner, her father would give

3

her a lecture about being selfish and how everything he did was for her and her future.

She hoped he didn't plan on bringing up her taking over the company someday. She didn't want this company. Or any other company, for that matter. Honestly, she didn't know what she wanted, but it wasn't this.

She'd never particularly enjoyed her job, but her unrest had been nearly unbearable since her best friend Kennedy got engaged and made her move to the small town of Providence permanent.

He waved a dismissive hand. "You'll see when you get there." Not waiting for Eden to leave, he picked up his briefcase and headed toward the door. "Dress nice."

Eden stood there for several seconds staring after her father. Oliver DuPont was always assertive and decisive in his business and in his personal life. She had never seen him act evasive and cryptic.

That man is up to something.

A heaviness filled her stomach, and her heart rate slowed, as if the effort to dispel the foreboding feeling that swept over her was just too much.

So much for a relaxing Friday night.

Ninety minutes later, when she walked into the sitting room of her childhood home, she echoed that sentiment.

It was all she could do to not cringe when she spotted Tristan Jordain seated on the loveseat in the formal living room, drink in hand. Her heart plummeted. Any surprise involving Tristan was not a pleasant one. No wonder her father wouldn't meet her gaze this afternoon.

Tristan gave her a slow, lingering appraisal, letting his gaze remain on her bust line for far too long. "Looking good, Eden."

A creepy crawly sensation skittered across her skin as it did every time she was around the playboy son of the tech billionaire they often did business with. Everything about Tristan rubbed her wrong.

"Ah here you are, finally." Her dad sprang to his feet.

Eden checked her rhinestone studded watch. She was only three minutes late, but if her father had been entertaining Tristan for more than a few minutes, she could understand why he was so eager for her arrival.

She scowled, first at Tristan then her father, making no attempt to hide her displeasure. "No wonder you wouldn't tell me who your dinner guest was." Although she said the words quietly, she didn't care if Tristan overheard her. It was no secret she didn't like him.

Dad took her elbow and pulled her further into the room. "Tristan and I... Well, *he* has an important matter to discuss with you tonight."

"An important matter?" Eden's voice was flat.

She doubted Tristan could hold an intelligent conversation about anything truly worthwhile that lasted more than five minutes. The man was only ever worried about where the next party was and which woman he'd be taking home for the night.

"A proposal...uh, I mean business proposition." Dad spoke again since Tristan made no effort to.

Eden turned to find the playboy studying her backside. She rolled her eyes.

Letting sarcasm fill her voice, she said, "I can't wait."

She was saved from learning more about the *important matter* when Helen, her dad's housekeeper and Eden's former nanny, walked in to inform them dinner was ready.

Helen wrapped Eden in a tight hug. "How are you doing, sweet girl?"

Eden tensed.

Helen had hugged her many times over the years, but never in front of a guest. Despite being with their family for as long as Eden could remember and living in an apartment over the garage, she always remained proper and formal when her dad entertained.

So why did Helen hug her so tight tonight?

Eden forced a smile. "I get to eat your cooking tonight, so I'm great."

"I made your favorite dessert."

"Mmm..." Eden's mouth watered at the thought of Helen's chocolate mousse cheesecake.

Helen ushered them into the dining room, and Eden's footsteps faltered when she spotted the Waterford crystal and Noritake bone China adorning the table. Usually when her father entertained only a few guests who were close friends they used the everyday Royal Albert China. Not that she considered Tristan a close friend. He was more of an irritating nuisance who just kept turning up.

But why was he here tonight? And without his father.

It wasn't unusual for her dad to entertain business associates at home. He'd invited Tristan's father Laurent Jordain, the tech billionaire, over more than once since they started running performance analytics on his company's software programs two years ago. And even though Laurent often insisted Tristan accompany him to these dinners—probably in the hopes that he'll someday take an interest in the company—Tristan had never come without his father.

She couldn't decide if her dad's fascination with Laurent was hero worship or a bromance. He'd been ecstatic last year when Laurent invited them to what turned out to be the first of many high-society functions that, despite her father's wealth, he'd never been included in before.

And her dad had networked like a master at each one, entrenching himself in the ultra-rich society that his bank account didn't quite measure up to.

"So, I have good news." Her father spoke as soon as Helen left the room after serving the salads.

"Oh?"

"I've been working closely with Laurent. I'm sure you're aware that he sits on the board of half a dozen large companies." He then proceeded to rattle off the names of several Fortune Five Hundred companies.

Eden nodded even though she hadn't been aware that Laurent Jordain was involved with so many big-name companies. It didn't surprise her, though. Laurent was not only brilliant he was also a shrewd investor and businessman. He achieved billionaire status several years ago after inventing and selling some sophisticated, high-tech electronic components. Since then, he'd grown his business

Innovative Solutions by purchasing a software development company formerly known as Andertech Solutions.

"He has promised me he'll seek exclusive data analytic rights for us with each of those companies."

Eden set down her fork and gave her dad a tight smile. "That's great!"

That would mean some high-profile contracts for DuPont Data Analytics and would make the company a lot of money. For some reason, the thought only made her dislike her job more. Mega companies were sometimes the hardest to work with when it came to demanding, know-it-all CEOs.

Eden couldn't help feeling like there must be a catch. If Laurent followed through, he'd expect something in return. Men like him didn't do favors. They always had an agenda.

They talked a little more about what exclusivity rights with these companies would mean for DuPont Analytics then halfway through the main course, her dad changed the subject.

"Tristan is getting ready to step up in his dad's company."

Eden nearly choked on a bite of broccoli.

What exactly did that mean?

Had the playboy ever worked a full day in his life?

She couldn't help recalling the conversation she overheard last year between Tristan and his buddies.

He smirked when he told them, "Oh I have no intention of running Innovative Solutions when the old man hands over the reins or kicks the bucket, whichever comes first. I plan to persuade the board of trustees to let me sell off bits and pieces of the company to the highest bidder until there's nothing left." He threw back his drink before adding, "You dangle enough money in front of someone, they'll do anything you want them to."

Seeing as how Innovative Solutions was worth billions, Tristan could easily spend the rest of his life partying and never run out of money.

"That's nice," she murmured into her water glass as she lifted it to her lips.

I'll believe it when I see it.

She finally let her gaze rest on the man across the table from her. He still ogled her with half-hooded eyes. Most women would find that smoldering look sexy, but Eden had shut it down a long time ago. She repressed a shudder. She'd come to hate that look almost as much as she hated him.

A bitter taste filled her mouth as she recalled the first time she met him at a high-class charity function. Within minutes of being introduced, he'd invited her to his hotel room.

She'd barely refrained from slapping him, regretfully, and told him she'd never sleep with someone she'd just met. So, he offered to wine and dine her for the evening before they got it on in his room.

It was sad. With his good looks and money, he could influence people to do all kinds of good if he only tried. Though she'd never experienced it personally, she'd heard he was smart and could be quite charming.

"Laurent has decided that if Tristan cleans up his act and gets serious about learning the business, he'll let him hold a position within the company."

This time, she choked on her water. Did Laurent seriously plan to hand the business over to Tristan one day?

"Your father wants you to clean up your act?" Eden said, barely repressing a laugh. "What exactly does that entail?" She looked directly at the playboy now with raised eyebrows.

No more parties, benders, and loose women? She doubted Tristan could go without any one of those for twenty-four hours, let alone all three indefinitely.

One side of Tristan's mouth quirked up. "Oh, you know, show up at the office more than once a week and find a good woman to help me clean up my image." He leaned forward in his seat and gave her a smile she supposed he meant to be charming, but to Eden, looked predatory. "So whatta you say, darlin'?"

Eden's humor evaporated faster than dew on an Arizona summer morning, and her stomach rolled. She pushed away her dinner plate and looked at her dad. "What's going on?"

"I've been trying to explain it to you. Laurent is willing to get his companies to offer us exclusivity rights, if we—I mean you—help Tristan clean up his reputation."

Eden pushed to her feet so fast she nearly tipped her chair over. "What?"

Dad gave Tristan a pointed look and a nod.

"Oh right." Tristan gave a lazy grin as he got to his feet. "I guess this is the part where I'm supposed to get down on one knee." He fished a small box from his pocket as he rounded the end of the table.

She backed away, but she was boxed in by her chair and the one beside her.

Tristan dropped to one knee and flipped open a ring box with the biggest, most pretentious diamond she'd ever seen. It was downright gaudy.

"Eden, darling, will you do me the honor of being my wife?"

He can't be serious!

He didn't sound serious. His words sounded insincere and lazy, even insolent. Nor did he look serious. His face reflected boredom rather than happiness and hope.

She turned wide eyes on her father who held up his cell phone, documenting this mockery of a proposal. Was this all part of his plan? Would photos of Tristan's proposal be in the news and all over the tabloids by morning?

"Wait. Wait. Wait." She held up her hand, palm out. "No. No. No."

Great! I sound illiterate.

She always got that way when she was upset or angry. And she was both right now. She couldn't seem to spit out more than one word at a time, so she kept repeating herself.

She sucked in a deep, steadying breath. "This isn't happening. Of course, I won't marry you. I don't love you. I can barely stand you."

"Love has nothing to do with it." Tristan rolled his eyes. "It's about family obligation and responsibility. You know, duty to the company and carrying on the legacy and all that nonsense."

The words he'd laced with sarcasm sounded familiar. Much like the lectures her father often gave her about her responsibility to

9

uphold the family name and how the company was the legacy he'd created for her, never mind that she didn't want it. Just like she knew Tristan didn't want his father's company.

So why was he doing this? Had Laurent threatened to cut him off if he didn't shape up?

Even though she recognized Tristan's words, it didn't make her empathize or sympathize or any other -ize with him. She didn't want anything to do with him. Definitely not anything that involved an engagement ring.

"Nuh-huh. No way. Absolutely not."

Wow! Those words aren't much more articulate.

Tristan stood and turned to her dad. "I told you she wouldn't go for it."

"Of course, I'm not going to *go for it*. No way will I marry you."

"Eden, honey, sit down. Let's discuss this." He gave her the look—the one that said she was acting selfish and disappointing him—until she pulled her chair in and dropped onto it.

She remained perched on the edge, however, because no matter what her dad said, she had a feeling she'd be leaving soon.

"No one expects you to *marry* Tristan, but Laurent thinks if you two get engaged, it will help him clean up his image. Maybe women will stop...throwing themselves at him when they see him out in public with his fiancée."

"Throwing themselves at him? Really?" Sarcasm filled Eden's voice and she shot a scowl Tristan's way. She recalled how not fifteen minutes after she rejected him last year, she saw him propositioning another woman.

"I can't help it if women want a piece of this." Tristan dropped back into his chair and despite the upright back managed to look like he lounged. He always gave off that carefree, blasé attitude. He winked at her and puckered his lips for the briefest of moments.

She shuddered. Tristan may agree to a fake engagement, but he didn't expect it to be platonic.

"No. No. No." There she went again. Why couldn't she just go speechless at times like this?

She pointed a finger at him. "Don't for one minute think I will ever sleep with you, fake engagement or not. Besides the fact that I find you totally deplorable, I refuse to pretend to be your fiancée, because I know there is no way in he—" She sucked in a sharp breath to keep herself from swearing. "I know you will never stop sleeping around. And I won't allow you to humiliate me like that."

"Eden!" Her dad's voice was full of censure. "Nobody is sleeping with anybody. That's what this is all about. Tristan is trying to change his ways."

The eye roll Tristan shot her dad told Eden he had no intention of making those kinds of changes.

Dad put a hand on her arm. "Think of the good of the company, honey."

Heat filled Eden's chest, and every muscle in her body tensed. Her blood pumped hard, creating a drumming sound at the base of her skull.

The good of the company?

When had the company come to mean more to him than she did?

He didn't care at all about her feelings, about what a fake engagement to Tristan would do to *her* reputation. Everyone would think she was as big of a hussy and money grubber as the women who threw themselves at him. Her father didn't care about the humiliation she would suffer when the tabloids sported photos of Tristan slinking around with other women despite being engaged to her.

She looked at her dad. "I'm sorry. I can't— No, I *won't* do it." She stood and raced from the room. She was halfway up the stairs, headed to her old bedroom, before she remembered she didn't live here anymore. Turning back, she hurried out the front door.

She'd just opened her car door when her father's voice reached her. "Eden, wait!" Authority and censure filled his voice as he hurried out of the house. "Why are you doing this?"

She folded her arms and glared at him. "I could ask you the same question. Have you thought about the effect Tristan's reputation could have on *our* company? His own father doesn't even trust him in his company, yet you're pushing him on your daughter?"

He scoffed. "He won't technically be involved with our company. But honey, think about what exclusivity with all these companies could do for us? This will make us rich."

"You're already rich, Dad!"

"Alright, yes, we live quite comfortably, but I'm talking about millions!"

Tears stung her eyes as she looked up at the row of windows in the massive house where she was raised. She'd grown up in the lap of luxury. Yes, she'd enjoyed having anything a girl could want, but these empty halls hadn't rung with laughter like her friend Kennedy's much smaller, more modest home had.

Her dad let out a sigh. "I know you've never liked Tristan, and I can't say I blame you, but I'm doing this for you, honey."

"For me? Like how you insisted I go to business school when I wanted to study interior design? Like how you gave me a job as an assistant to your secretary even though I should have worked my way up in the company?" She blinked away the tears that always came when she faced conflict.

How many times had she heard her father say *I'm doing this for your own good?*

And she'd let him run her life. Because every time she thought about standing up to him, she remembered her mother's final words to her. "Promise me you'll be a good girl for your daddy."

Tearfully, she'd promised her mom she would be a good girl. And she'd done everything her father ever asked because she thought that's what it meant to be a good daughter.

But this is too much.

She'd only ever truly stood up to him once before—when he'd insisted the daughter of a mechanic wasn't a suitable friend for someone of her social standing. But as motherless ten-year-olds, she and Kennedy had shared a bond that few people understood. They couldn't be more different from one another, but Kennedy was the sister Eden never had.

She had refused to stop being friends with Kennedy when she was eleven years old, and she'd refuse to bend to his will tonight. "I'm sorry, Dad. I won't be a pawn in the game you're playing. I won't pretend to be engaged to Tristan. Not for the good of the company, not for your sake, and certainly not for mine."

She climbed into her BMW, but her dad prevented her from closing the door. "Why don't you take some time and think about it?"

"I don't need time because I'm not going to change my mind. And oh, by the way, I quit."

A stunned expression covered his face, and he fell back a step. Eden used that opportunity to close the door. With her breaths coming in rapid succession, and her heart racing, she started her car and drove down the long driveway.

Holy cow! Did I really just quit my job?

A burst of adrenaline shot through her, followed quickly by a sinking feeling. Yes, she'd always hated her job, but how was she supposed to support herself now?

With a shaky hand, she grabbed her phone from her purse and called Kennedy.

CHAPTER 2

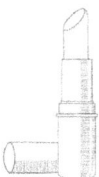

*E*den hefted her last suitcase into the back of her BMW X3
and closed the door. Besides two suitcases and a carry-on,
she'd also packed a duffel bag with cosmetics and toiletries. She'd
probably over packed big time, but she had no idea how long she'd be
gone or where she was even going really, other than to visit Kennedy
for a while.

She looked back at her apartment. As much as she loved it, it
hadn't felt the same since Kennedy moved to Providence last year. It
was quiet and boring without her best friend. If she was being honest
with herself, she had to admit that she was more than a little jealous of
her friend. Not only had Kennedy found love but she'd also gained a
family and part ownership in her own business. The two things her
friend had always wanted.

A sense of melancholy filled Eden as she pulled her eyes away
from her apartment. It's not like she never planned to return, but she
wanted to be anywhere but Spokane right now. If she wasn't here, her
father couldn't show up on her doorstep, asking her to reconsider her
job and Tristan's proposal. He'd already texted three times this morning, and with each text, she'd become more agitated.

The first one read: *Have you cooled down from your tantrum last night?*

Heat had shot through her body at her father's choice of words. She'd finally found the courage to stand up for herself, and he called it a tantrum? She was still so furious with him that she didn't dare respond. She'd only end up saying things that would further damage their relationship.

So, she'd ignored his text, but that hadn't kept him from sending another one thirty minutes later: *You've been under a lot of stress at work lately. I suppose it'll be good for you to take a few vacation days. Hopefully it'll help you clear your head so you can focus on what's important.*

She had no intention of doing what he deemed *important*, so she'd ignored that text too.

When his third text came through, it was all she could do not to throw her phone across the room. Especially when she read his words: *I expect you to keep in mind how hard we've worked to build this company and all the families who rely on its success.*

DuPont Analytics would be fine without her, and they'd still be successful even without exclusivity rights with all those bigwig companies. It's not like it would fold overnight.

For a while this morning, she'd questioned whether she'd done the right thing in quitting her job, but the fact that her father tried to guilt her into doing what he wanted only made her more determined than ever to leave.

She had no idea what she'd do for a job, but she refused to let the uncertainty get her down. She climbed in her car and started the engine.

A little over an hour later, a sign on the side of the road advertising strawberries caught her eye. They were her favorite fruit, and the thought of fresh strawberries had her making a hasty lane change.

Within minutes, she juggled two pints of strawberries and her purse as she opened her car door.

A bee flew into her face. Its buzzing triggered a mini panic attack in her, stealing the air from her lungs. She danced around and swung her arm through the air, causing the strawberries to slip. Correcting her movements, she straightened the small containers before the berries could fall on the ground. It didn't keep her purse from falling and spilling its contents, however.

Frick!

She hated bees and wasps because she was deathly allergic to them. Once she was sure the bee was gone, she set the strawberries on the passenger seat then crouched to pick up the spilled contents of her purse. Panic filled her again when she realized her Epi Pen was missing. Crouching low, she looked under her car.

Spotting the long slender yellow tube, she sucked in a breath of relief. She snatched up the pen and shoved it into her purse before climbing back into her car.

Only twenty more minutes until she reached Providence. Then Kennedy could help her make sense of her messed up life.

RUDY PARKED his patrol car at the notorious speed trap north of town. The locals knew it was there and often adjusted their speed, but it never failed; he always managed to catch at least one motorist speeding down the hill.

He set up his radar gun and pulled out his phone. He wasn't supposed to check his email while working the speed trap, but there was nothing else to do.

The third email in his inbox was a quarterly statement from the investment company his accountant hooked him up with a few years ago after he got that hefty bonus and a raise, thanks to the sizable donation given to the sheriff's department.

He smiled as he scanned the numbers on the statement. With careful planning and continued investing, he could retire comfortably in twenty years.

At twenty-seven, he was too old to still be living with his parents, but it had allowed him to surpass his five-year goals, and he was on track to hit his ten-year goal of owning his own home early. Besides, there was a housing shortage in Providence.

He wanted to be financially secure before he settled down and started a family, so waiting until he had a house built only made sense.

His mind wandered to the call Kennedy received last night as he continued to clean up his inbox. Her phone rang just as they finished the second round of the card game he, Scott, and Kennedy had been playing with their parents—yes, he felt every bit the fifth wheel that he was since Scott and Kennedy became a couple. When she answered her phone, Eden's hysterical voice came through so loud, everyone at the table heard her.

She'd lamented something about her father trying to force her onto some playboy, then said something about quitting her job.

Kennedy had excused herself and talked to Eden for half an hour before returning. When she did, she wrapped her arms around Scott and kissed his cheek before asking, "Is it okay if Eden comes to stay with us for a few days? She's going through some pretty heavy stuff right now."

Of course, Scott nodded. Like he could ever say "no" to Kennedy. That woman had Rudy's big, strong, grumpy brother wrapped around her little finger. He was putty in her hands. It was ridiculous really.

Rudy had heard that love changed people, and his brother was still quiet and surly most of the time, but he'd never known Scott to smile as much as he did since Kennedy turned his world upside down less than a year ago.

Kennedy never told them exactly what was up with Eden, but Rudy couldn't help wondering if she was just being melodramatic and overreacting to something. She struck him as that type when he met her a couple months ago at Scott and Kennedy's wedding.

He'd recognized her high-maintenance type right away; carefully manicured fake fingernails, false but realistic-looking eye lashes, expensive clothing, and even more expensive jewelry. She reminded him of his sister Debbie before she toned down the flashiness and simplified her life.

Knowing she came from money, he assumed she was an over-indulged socialite who threw a tantrum anytime things didn't go their way. That's how Meredith, his girlfriend from high school, had acted.

She was pampered and spoiled by her rich parents, and the first chance she got to leave this small town, she took it.

Scott and Kennedy had been trying to line him up with Eden for months, but things had never worked out, for which Rudy was grateful. Eden was pretty and friendly. She was fun to be around, and he could see himself falling for someone like her. But the last thing he wanted to do was fall for another woman who hated small towns.

The disastrous ending to Scott and Kennedy's wedding should be a reminder enough to keep his distance from Eden DuPont. He hadn't meant to injure her. He was only trying to protect her from her overzealous cousin, like Kennedy asked him to. But he'd seriously underestimated Violet's momentum and determination to catch the bouquet.

Violet took him down, and he took Eden down, giving her a bloody nose and ruining her dress in the process.

The radar gun's noise escalated and rose in pitch. Rudy looked at the speed it clocked on the blue mini-SUV coming down the hill. Only six over the speed limit. He looked back at the car, deciding to let it go. But as he watched, it strayed from the left lane to the right then jerked back again.

He flipped on his lights and pulled onto the freeway.

The car swerved once more before pulling over to the shoulder.

Well, that was easy.

It often took people forever to realize he was behind them. He hadn't even needed to get on the tail of the BMW X3 to let the driver know he needed to pull over. He liked it when they made it easy on him.

Pulling up behind the small SUV, he lifted the radio to call in the license plate. But then he replaced the handset when he spotted the letters on the plate: DADSGRL. He knew someone who drove a metallic blue BMW X3 with that license plate, and she was coming to town today.

Eden DuPont.

His breath hitched at the prospect of talking to her. He hadn't seen her since Scott and Kennedy's wedding. The night he accidentally gave her a bloody nose.

He'd let her off with a warning today, unless he determined she was inebriated or something. He didn't think she drank, but why else would she swerve all over the road? Even as he watched through her back window, she swung her arms around her head.

What's wrong with the woman?

He climbed from his car and approached her window. Just as he opened his mouth to speak, a bee flew through her open window and hit his cheek. He ducked and swatted at the insect.

No wonder she flailed her arms!

He bent to look at Kennedy's dark-haired friend. "Are you—" His words died off when he saw the wide-eyed, panicked look on her face.

She pressed a hand to her bicep. "It stung me!"

"Are you serious?"

He recalled the scene she made at the wedding when two bees swarmed around her, trying to get at her and Kennedy's bouquets of fresh flowers. When he gave her a hard time for disrupting the wedding, she'd informed him she was deathly allergic to bees.

"You think I'm making it up to get out of—?" A tight cough cut off her words, followed by another series of violent coughs that had her nearly hitting her forehead on the steering wheel.

Wheezing, she rubbed at her arm where the bee must have stung her, and an angry red welt rose almost instantly. Red splotches covered her face just as quickly.

Rudy swore under his breath.

Coughing again, she grabbed her purse off the passenger seat and dug through it with frantic motions. "Where is it?" Her words were little more than a raspy whisper.

Finally, after what felt like an eternity, she pulled out an Epi Pen and snapped off the cap.

Rudy cringed when she lifted the hem of her skirt and rammed it into her thigh. He silently counted with her and sucked in a deep breath when he hit five, and she pulled the pen away from her leg.

He gasped when she looked up at him.

Her violent coughing had ruptured blood vessels in her eyes, and her lids were puffy. Her lips looked like they were beginning to swell too. She grabbed his hand that rested on the door. "It doesn't last long," she wheezed. "I need help." Her eyelids fluttered as she forced out the plea.

He swore again.

The pen isn't enough!

He'd read somewhere that they were only meant to buy time. Maybe ten to fifteen minutes. They didn't stop or reverse the effects of anaphylactic shock. Eden needed medical attention. Fast.

They were almost fifteen minutes from town. An ambulance would never get there in time.

He noted the time on his watch then opened her door and scooped her up into his arms. He rushed to the passenger side of his car. Her body hung limp in his arms, and he nearly dropped her before he managed to get the door open and deposit her on the seat. He was already in his own seat when he remembered the first aid kit in his trunk had another Epi pen.

He hated taking precious time to retrieve the pen, but Eden would need another dose of epinephrine before they reached the hospital.

He left his lights flashing as he raced down the highway, driving far faster than he had ever driven, even as a reckless teenager. Picking up his handset, he barked into it, "Dispatch this is Wheeler," He rattled off his badge number.

"Dispatch. Go Wheeler."

"I have a 10-33. Twenty-six-year-old female in anaphylactic shock." He stated his location and ETA to the hospital. He had to suck in a deep breath before finishing. "I need the ER standing by to receive the patient."

He glanced at Eden's face.

Her eyes were now closed, and her normal olive complexion looked pale except for the angry red splotches covering her face and neck. A blue tint surrounded her swollen lips.

He pressed a little harder on the gas, inching the speedometer even higher. Kennedy would never forgive him if he let her best friend die.

He spoke into his radio again. "Janice!" In his panic, he forgot all formality. "Get all available officers to block every possible intersection along main street in seven minutes. I need to get this woman to the hospital fast!"

As soon as he released the radio, he grabbed Eden's hand and squeezed it. "Stay with me, you hear."

Her eyelids fluttered open but then closed again.

His heart raced, and his skin flushed from the adrenaline coursing through his veins, creating a prickly, electric sensation throughout his body. He barely registered Janice's response as he checked the time on his watch. As soon as the exit for Providence came into view, Rudy used his teeth to wrench the lid off the second Epi pen. He didn't cringe this time when he rammed it into Eden's thigh, he just prayed it would be enough to save her life.

He kept dispatch apprised of his location and turned on his siren as he exited the highway and hit the traffic in town. He kept a white-knuckle grip on the steering wheel as he raced down Main Street of his sleepy little town at ninety-five miles an hour.

He sucked in a deep breath when the EMTs, a doctor, and two nurses darted out of the emergency room entrance with a stretcher before he could even bring his car to a stop.

Relief warred with fear as he watched them pull an unconscious Eden from his car. Knowing there was nothing more he could do, he sank back into his seat and prayed.

A knock sounded on his window half a second before his door was wrenched open. Sheriff Robert Winters crouched beside him. "Are you okay? What happened exactly?"

"I saw her car swerving..." Rudy's voice shook as he talked. The more he tried to fight the tremor, the worse it became. Then a stinging sensation hit the back of his eyes. He stopped talking and looked away, not understanding why he felt the urge to cry.

Robert clasped a hand on his shoulder and gave him a little shake. "It's okay. It's just the adrenaline wearing off."

Rudy shook his head. He'd felt the adrenaline drop many times, but something about today's emergency affected him much stronger than ever before.

"You did good work. You saved her."

He looked at the doors to the ER.

Did I? What if I wasn't fast enough? Kennedy will kill me.

Kennedy. He picked up his phone as Robert walked away and called his sister-in-law.

A WARM, calloused hand slipped into Eden's cold one, and a muffled voice said something, but Eden couldn't interpret it through the fog in her head. Her hand wiggled and the voice came again.

"Eden, are you okay?" At least that's what she thought the distant voice said.

She tried to open her eyes because a verbal response felt impossible. Either her mouth had shrunk, or her tongue had swollen to the point that it filled her whole mouth. And it was as dry as a cotton field in bloom.

Her eyes refused to stay open, so she squeezed the hand that held hers.

"Talk to me. Are you okay?"

Recognizing Kennedy's voice, Eden fought a little harder to keep her eyes open. Her fiend's blurry face finally came into focus.

"Oh, thank goodness." Kennedy let out a breathy sigh and squeezed Eden's hand again. "You scared me to death. I was getting ready to call your dad to tell him he needed to come say his goodbyes." Despite the teasing twinkle in Kennedy's eyes, Eden recognized the tension in her voice.

"No." The word rasped out of her dry, swollen throat. "Don't call...my dad."

Kennedy's brow furrowed as she propped a hand on her hip. "I won't yet, but you need to call him. Imagine how upset he'll be when he sees a bill from the hospital come through your insurance."

Eden winced and closed her eyes again. No doubt he'd lecture her on the consequences of her actions and how she should have stayed in Spokane and done as he'd told her.

Like getting stung by a bee is direct punishment for disobeying him.

Kennedy squeezed her hand again before releasing it. "Scott and I brought your car in from the highway, and I brought you an overnight bag." She motioned to a small gray duffel on the chair.

Eden's heart sank, matching the lethargy that encompassed her body. "They're keeping me?"

"Yeah, you were in pretty bad shape by the time Rudy got you here."

Rudy.

The last thing she remembered before losing consciousness out on the highway was Kennedy's good-looking brother-in-law lifting her from her car. Heat filled her chilled body as embarrassment plagued her. He'd truly seen her at her worst.

Twice now. First the bloody nose at the wedding, and now this.

"He's here." Kennedy said quietly.

"My dad?" Eden's mind struggled to keep up.

"No, Rudy?"

"Why is he still here?" It took so much energy to get each word out.

"He refused to leave until he knew you were okay. But because he isn't family, they wouldn't let him in to see you. I'm lucky they let me in. I had to tell them you were my sister." Kennedy laughed. "Like we look anything alike."

Except for the fact that they both had brown eyes, they looked nothing alike. Where Kennedy was blond and fair-complected, Eden was dark-haired with an olive complexion, thanks to her mother's Italian ancestry. And where Kennedy was tall with curves to die for, Eden barely reached five six when she wore three-inch heels and could never be mistaken for curvy.

"You're the closest thing I have to family, Ken. Especially now." Tears pricked behind her eyes, and she quickly blinked what felt like puffy—and no doubt bloodshot—eyes to keep them from falling.

Kennedy patted her leg. "You and your dad will work things out.

You'll see. He just needs time to realize how ridiculous this scheme of his is."

Eden wasn't sure she believed Kennedy. For a long time now, her father had been more concerned about money and his social standing in the community than he had her or the fact that she hated her job. She didn't have the energy to argue with her friend though, so she kept her mouth shut.

She just wanted to close her eyes and take a long nap. Wouldn't it be wonderful to wake up and find out that the last twenty-four hours had all been a dream? But then she'd have to quit the job she hated all over again.

"So can he come in?"

"Who?" Eden's brain felt so heavy and sluggish.

"Rudy. He's been pacing the halls since you came in. He wants to see for himself that you're alive."

Oh, him. Do I want him to see me like this?

She'd only ever gone into anaphylactic shock once before, but it left her face swollen and her eyes bloodshot, puffy, and bruised. She owed him a sincere thank you though. If it wasn't for him, Kennedy really would have had to call her dad. But they wouldn't have had the opportunity to say goodbye. Her breath caught at that thought, but she still wasn't ready to talk to him. They were at too big of an impasse to bridge that gap just yet.

"Send him in."

"Okay." Kennedy leaned over and gave her a tight hug. "I'm so glad you're okay. I'll be back in the morning to pick you up."

"Thanks."

Kennedy had barely walked out the door before Rudy Wheeler, her knight in shining armor—well, in uniform anyway—walked in. He was one good-looking man with his auburn hair, a little lighter and redder than his brother's and his striking blue eyes. The man looked amazing in uniform, and even though he wasn't as tall and bulky as Scott, he was strong. He proved that when he carried her to his car.

He froze at the foot of her bed, and his gaze searched her face before skimming over the rest of her body and returning to her face again. His usual jovial smile was absent, and tension created little lines that fanned out around his eyes. "You're really okay?"

She pressed a hand to her cheek that grew warm under his scrutiny. "Yes. I'm sure I look awful, but I'm okay. Thanks to you." She gave him the sincerest smile she could muster.

"You nearly died. You have the right to look like he— I mean, garbage."

"Jeez, thanks. You sure know how to make a girl feel good."

He finally cracked a smile. "Sorry, that sounded pretty bad, didn't it." His posture relaxed a little. "Honestly, I'm just glad to see you alive. I thought for sure when they hauled you from my car, that I'd never see you again. Alive, anyway."

"Well, thanks to your quick action, here I am." She spread her arms in a "tada" motion. The action took more energy than she expected, and she dropped them again.

His cheeks reddened, and he shook his head, obviously uncomfortable with the praise.

She let her eyes drift closed for a long moment. They remained closed when she spoke. "It was amazing how you went into rescue mode and scooped me out of my car like that." Hopefully, her voice didn't reflect the breathlessness she felt at the memory of being in his arms. Unfortunately, that memory was fuzzy and very fleeting. Maybe she'd have to ask him to repeat his rescue.

Stop flirting with him.

"What did you say? You're flirting with me?" Humor filled Rudy's voice.

Frick! I said that out loud.

She didn't know what to say, so she just shook her head and gave a half-hearted wave of her hand. When she opened her eyes again, it was with monumental effort, and she looked everywhere but at his face.

No, she shouldn't flirt with Rudy. Sure, he was good looking and fun to be around, but he was a small-town boy. She had no intention of ever moving here. They didn't even have a spa and a decent bakery, so there was no point in getting to know Kennedy's brother-in-law better.

Rudy laughed. "You obviously don't remember the part where I almost dropped you."

"You almost dropped me?" She scowled at him now.

"Well yeah. You're not all that heavy but your whole body was limp, so you were dead weight."

Eden gasped and searched for something—anything—to throw at him.

He must have noticed her frantic search because he stepped to the side of her bed. "What's wrong? Are you having trouble breathing? Do you need me to get a nurse?"

Finding nothing but her IV tubing and the remote for the TV that was attached to her bed, she reached behind her head and pulled her pillow out. Before Rudy could guess her intent, she swung it and hit his shoulder.

His eyes widened and he flinched even though she was sure she hadn't hurt him. "What did you do that for?"

"That's for calling me dead weight."

"I didn't mean it like that. You're actually kind of skinny. Too skinny if you ask my mom."

"What?" She swung her pillow again. "Just stop talking. Right now."

Rudy pressed fingers to his lips, but his eyes crinkled, and his cheeks lifted.

Totally spent, Eden flopped back onto the bed with her pillow on her stomach. She didn't have the stamina for a pillow fight right now.

"Hey, you okay?" Concern once again deepened Rudy's voice. He leaned over her but remained tense. As though wary to get too close in case she decided to swing her pillow again.

"I'm fine. Just exhausted." Her eyelids suddenly felt too heavy to hold open.

He grinned at her, flashing perfect white teeth.

Nice smile.

Even her voice sounded dreamy in her head. Was she about to pass out on him again? That would be twice in one day. Okay, she wasn't going to pass out, but she felt like she could fall asleep any second, and it was a little disconcerting to have him leaning over her, watching her as she did so.

"Do you need me to help get your pillow under your head?"

Her eyes fluttered closed, but she forced them back open. "Yes, please." Her voice was little more than a whisper.

Her eyes drifted closed again as his strong arms wrapped around her. She caught a scent of his cologne—a perfect mix of woodsy, smoky, and spicy. Warm. His scent made her feel warm and comfortable. Or maybe that was because he adjusted her blankets too.

Smells nice.

A chuckle sounded near her ear. "Thank you."

Frack! I did it again.

She should be embarrassed, but she was just too tired to care. She couldn't even find the energy to vocalize the groan that wanted out.

"I'm glad you're okay." His husky words stirred the hair by her ear, sending a little tingle of awareness through her that quickly fizzled into exhaustion.

CHAPTER 3

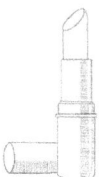

*T*he young waitress who looked like she was still in high school laid the check on the table and smiled at Scott. "I'll be your cashier when you're ready."

Eden snatched up the check before Scott could reach for it, startling the girl. "It's my treat tonight." And because she reached for her purse right away, the waitress waited for her to hand over her credit card.

Across the table, Kennedy dropped her napkin on her plate. "Thanks for dinner, Eden."

Scott grunted something that could have been, "Thanks," or something else entirely.

"You're welcome. It's the least I can do for letting me crash at your place all week." She'd like to tell them she'd be leaving soon, but that wasn't the case. She wasn't ready to return to her empty apartment in Spokane yet. And she hadn't found a new job, so she didn't have plans to leave Providence anytime soon.

Now there's something I thought I'd never say.

Scott gave another indiscernible grunt, and Kennedy waved a hand in dismissal. "It's been fun. Kind of like old times, huh?"

It had been like old times. They'd stayed up late every night watching all their favorite romantic comedies and talking for hours. Kennedy cooked, and Eden pretended to help since she wasn't all that skilled in the kitchen, despite Helen's attempts to teach her how to cook when she was a teenager.

But things had changed too. Scott was always there, quiet and brooding. Kennedy kept calling him the strong silent type, but Eden couldn't see him as anything other than grumpy.

And having to walk through his and Kennedy's bedroom to get to the bathroom was awkward with a capital A. With no lock on the bathroom door, it had taken less than twenty-four hours for Scott to walk in on her. Fortunately, she was ready to walk out, but it still made things uncomfortable. Judging by Scott's surliness he thought so too.

The young waitress fiddled with the hem of her apron and chewed on her bottom lip as she returned to the table. She gave Eden an apologetic look. "I'm sorry, but your card was declined."

Eden's eyes widened, and her head jerked back. "What? That's not possible."

Her credit card had never been declined, and she'd used it a lot! Had she maxed it out with her frequent shopping sprees over the last six months?

Scott leaned forward and reached into his back pocket, but she held up her hand. "No, I promised it was my treat, and I meant it."

Heat filled her face as she fished out her debit card and handed it to the waitress with a tight grin.

Half afraid her debit card might be declined as well, she fiddled with her napkin, unable to make eye contact with Scott and Kennedy. She'd never been so embarrassed and confused in her life. Why on earth had her card been declined?

She was tempted to pull out her phone and check her balance.

No. There's plenty of money there.

She was sure of it. But what was up with her credit card?

Maybe she'd actually have to talk to her dad, since her credit card was still attached to his account, at his insistence.

When she called him last week from the hospital, he'd acted

concerned, but once he knew she was out of danger, he'd insisted she stop this foolishness and come home.

She'd ended up hanging up on him. And she'd ignored the half dozen texts he'd sent her this week. They were all various iterations of the same thing: *remember your responsibilities* and *think of the good of the company.* The only one she'd responded to was his: *I look forward to seeing you back at work on Monday.*

She'd let him know she had zero intentions of returning to work at DuPont Analytics. Ever.

The waitress returned with a smile on her face. "That one went through."

Oh, thank goodness.

Eden breathed a sigh of relief and let herself sag back against her chair. Tension continued to build between her shoulder blades, however, as they crossed the street to return to the apartment above the garage. She needed to figure out what was up with her credit card. It had worked fine when she paid for her manicure yesterday at *In Style.*

She'd been surprised to find such a quaint little salon in this town and couldn't resist getting a manicure. Susie, the nail tech, and her beautician mother, Naomi, were friendly women, and she'd had a blast visiting with them.

When they entered the apartment, Scott disappeared into the bedroom, but Kennedy plopped down on the couch beside Eden.

"So, are things really that bad?" Kennedy asked, looking her square in the eye.

"No, they're fine. I don't know what's up with my card, but I have plenty of money."

Kennedy's eyebrows rose. "Define plenty."

Eden squirmed, pulling the throw pillow beside her into her arms. She hugged it against her chest like a shield. "Well, I haven't exactly been careful with my money lately, but I know I still have plenty in savings." That last part sounded every bit as defensive as she felt.

"I thought you made good money working for your dad?"

"I do. I mean, I did. But since you moved out last year..."

"Go on."

Eden played with the fringed edge of the pillow. "I haven't cooked much."

"Yeah, because you're a lousy cook."

Her friend was right, but Eden swung the throw pillow at her face anyway.

Kennedy snatched it from her hand. "You ate out every night?"

Eden shrugged. "Sometimes, I just got takeout."

Turned out eating out alone wasn't that enjoyable. Sure, Eden had other friends besides Kennedy, but they were often busy with their own lives. Kennedy wasn't the only one to get married in the past couple years. Two of them even had babies. It seemed everyone had a life lately, except her.

"So, you spent a considerable amount on food each month, but what about the rest of your money?"

With no pillow to fiddle with anymore, she stroked her thumb over her glossy fingernails, admiring the curvy emerald design across the pearly surface.

"I've been on a few...shopping trips over the last several months," she admitted in a quiet voice.

She'd been on more than a few, but she didn't want to admit that she'd gone through a serious depression after Kennedy got engaged back in January. It meant her best friend was never coming back to Spokane, and Eden had struggled with that.

It might not have been so bad if she'd had a man in her own life to distract her, but thanks to all the social functions she'd attended with her dad lately, Tristan and his buddies were the only single men around. And she'd rather become a nun than to get into a relationship with one of them. All the social events had really helped boost her Instagram followers though. She'd surpassed ten thousand followers a few months ago.

She'd also had standing monthly hair, nail, facial, and massage appointments. But she didn't mention that to Kennedy. She knew she led an extravagant lifestyle, but she'd always been able to afford it, so why not?

Eden's stomach hardened as she realized how self-centered and spoiled she was. She tried to be generous too, but that didn't really make up for her indulgent lifestyle. She admired her nails for another long moment, thinking this might be her last manicure for a while. If she didn't find a job soon, she'd have to make some lifestyle changes.

Even though the thought left her feeling a little anxious, it didn't fill her with disappointment, like she thought it would.

Maybe it wasn't only my job that I've been unhappy with lately.

"So, how much do you actually have in savings?" Kennedy asked, pulling Eden from her thoughts. "Do I need to help you find a job here in Providence?"

"Goodness, no." Eden grimaced. The last thing she wanted was to feel obligated to stay in this tiny town indefinitely. It was nice for a relaxing visit, but she couldn't live here long term. She'd die of boredom. "I'll be fine. I have enough to support myself until I find a job."

Worst case scenario, she could pay rent on a new apartment for a few months, if she needed to. Not that she considered moving. That would be too drastic of a move. Especially since she'd never paid her own rent. Like so many other things in her life, her dad took care of it. Yet one more thing that bothered her. She'd appreciated the gesture when she first moved out on her own, but it was past time she took responsibility for her life.

"Just until you get on your feet," he'd said, but years later he still insisted on paying her rent. "It's the least I can do for my only child," had always been his response.

A heaviness settled in her chest, creating a sinking feeling throughout her whole abdomen. Did he insist on paying her rent and credit card as a means to control her?

Control might be a strong word, but his providing for her kept her indebted to him and made her feel obligated to do the things he asked. She'd been bending to his will for years just to please him, from her education to her career. Even her social life was wrapped up in him and the company.

For all his talk about her taking responsibility, he sure hadn't allowed her to do so in her own life.

Pulling herself from thoughts of her father, she smiled at Kennedy. "I have a long-term savings and some investments, so don't worry about me. I'll be fine until I find a job." Not that she wanted to have to pull from either.

Scott walked out of the bedroom. "Ready?"

Kennedy stood. "We sure are. Aren't we, Eden?"

"Ready for what?" Eden asked.

"We're going over to Scott's parents' house to play games. Remember I mentioned it yesterday?"

That's right. Eden did recall her mentioning it, and she had cringed the same way she wanted to right now. Even though playing games sounded more enjoyable than watching TV, she felt weird inserting herself into their life any more than she already had.

It was bad enough she slept on their couch, with her suitcase shoved into the corner of the living room because there wasn't room for it anywhere else. She hadn't even been able to bring in all her stuff.

I'm practically living out of my car.

Kennedy must have seen the hesitation on Eden's face because she bent and slapped her leg. "Come on, it'll be fun."

Eden scrunched up her nose. "I don't know. I'm not feeling very social tonight."

"Rudy will be there," Kennedy said in a teasing voice.

Eden groaned. She loved her friend, but she wished she'd stop pushing her and Rudy together. Sure, her brother-in-law was good looking, and he had a fun personality, but Eden just couldn't see a future for the two of them.

He was a country boy through and through, and she was a city girl. Power suits and high heels were her norm, whereas Rudy was boots and a pickup truck. At some point, she would leave Providence and return to the city again. She didn't need any romantic entanglements to complicate things.

"Ugh, don't remind me."

She hated the thought of facing Rudy again. She'd be eternally grateful to him for saving her life, but she was so embarrassed that he'd seen her at her worst. When she finally got out of bed and went to the bathroom last Saturday, she looked even worse than she thought when she agreed to see him. No wonder he said she looked like garbage.

Kennedy waved Scott out the door then sat back down on the couch by Eden. "Come on, you've done nothing but sit around the apartment all week."

"Not true. I went for a run twice this week, and I got my nails done." But there really wasn't much else to do in this small town, so she really had sat around the apartment all week.

It wasn't like she wasted all her time watching Netflix, though. Okay, she had watched an awful lot of Netflix, but she'd also done some job hunting online. She just hadn't found anything that felt right. She was only qualified to work in the business field, but she wasn't sure she wanted that anymore.

The thought of sitting in a stuffy office where she attended endless meetings and only communicated with people who had problems made her cringe. She needed a change, but what kind of change, she didn't know.

"Hey," Kennedy grabbed her arm. "Are you okay?" Concern filled her voice.

"Of course, I'm okay. Why do you ask?"

"I'm worried that maybe you're slipping into a depression. You know, with quitting your job and this thing with your dad."

Eden let her head fall back on the couch and stared at the lion head she'd found in the texturing on the ceiling. "It's not like I have a broken heart or anything. I don't regret quitting my job at all. And yeah, I'm still upset with my dad, but I think once this thing with Tristan blows over, we'll have a better relationship if we aren't working together."

"I'm sure you're right. Your dad really is a good man, even if he is kind of controlling. I'd hate to see you lose him from your life forever." Sadness filled Kennedy's voice.

Eden's heart hurt for her friend. Kennedy had lost her dad a little over a year ago. It was obvious she still missed him.

"Me too."

The thought of losing her own dad tightened Eden's chest to the point she could hardly breathe. But she was still so upset with him right now, there was no point in trying to make amends. Especially because she feared he was the reason her credit card was declined.

Giving Kennedy another reassuring smile, she said, "Don't worry about me. Go have fun with the Wheelers. I'm going to take a bubble bath and read a book while you're gone."

Kennedy stood. "Okay, but for the record, I feel bad leaving you alone on a Friday night."

"Noted, but seriously, I'm fine."

After Kennedy walked out the door, Eden pulled out her phone. She stared at the screen for a full minute before texting her dad: *Did you put a block on my credit card?*

She could understand him cutting access to her business visa, since she no longer worked for him. But blocking her from using her personal credit card felt like an attack. She'd been using that card since she was sixteen. Sure, he was the one who paid it off each month, but she would have taken responsibility for it if he'd let her.

I should have put my foot down years ago.

She would have been a lot more careful with her spending if she'd been the one paying off her credit card each month.

Her phone pinged in her hand, and she looked at it warily. *You wanted your independence, so I'm giving it to you.*

Although the words weren't particularly harsh, she heard her father's clipped and judgmental tone as she read them.

Gee, thanks, Dad, she thought.

He picked a great time to let her finally take responsibility for herself when she had no job.

Her phone pinged again. *I refuse to foot the bill for your rebellion.*

Rebellion?

Heat filled Eden's chest, and tears stung her eyes. Her father viewed her standing up for herself as rebellion? If he thought cutting her off financially would make her come back and agree to his hair-brained plan, he was wrong.

She was more determined than ever to stay away from Spokane a little longer. She'd just have to be careful with her money and find a job. Soon. Maybe she should look for a job in the Tri-Cities area instead of Spokane.

Deciding it was best not to respond to his last comment, she left her phone on the couch and laid her suitcase out on the floor. She rummaged around it in for a minute before remembering that she'd packed her bubble bath in the other suitcase.

She slipped on her flip flops and hurried down the back stairs to get her favorite gardenia and jasmine bubble bath. She'd packed more than one bottle, but there wasn't enough space in Scott and Kennedy's shower for her hair care products and body wash as it was, so she only brought in one bottle of bubble bath and the romance novel she packed last minute.

Relaxing in the bath, she let herself get lost in her book. Too bad men in real life weren't the amazing compassionate heroes she read about in her romance novels. Sure, there were plenty of great men out there, but there were also plenty of Tristan's in the world too.

Her thoughts drifted to Kennedy's handsome brother-in-law. He was nice and could even be considered compassionate with the way he saved her life. But what kind of a name was Rudy? It sounded like a little boy's or even a dog's name, not a strong leading man like Gavin or Roman.

When she first met him a couple of months ago, she quickly realized that he liked to joke around and had a friendly personality, but he certainly wasn't suave and debonair, like the heroes in her romance novels. No, he was just a small-town boy who enjoyed a simple life. There wasn't anything wrong with that, but he definitely wasn't her type.

When her bathwater grew cold, she shifted back to the sofa to continue reading about the fake relationship the main characters had gotten themselves tangled up in with their lies. Two hours later, she set her book aside and rubbed her tired eyes as the third yawn of the evening hit her.

It was only ten o'clock on a Friday night, and she was exhausted. She hadn't been sleeping well thanks to the uncomfortable bar that ran through the middle of the hide-a-bed. Scott and Kennedy would probably be home soon, but she felt weird about pulling out the bed before they went to their own room for the night.

She had just popped a bag of microwave popcorn and started one of her favorite romcoms when they walked through the door.

"You're watching *When in Rome* without me?" Kennedy plopped down on the couch beside Eden.

"You're welcome to join me." Eden passed the popcorn over.

Scott cleared his throat and gave Kennedy a pointed look. "You're starting a movie now? It's after ten." His usually gruff voice sounded deeper and more growly than usual.

"I know, but this is one of my favorites." Kennedy popped a few kernels into her mouth.

"I have to get up early to go work on the house." Again, tension filled his voice.

"Don't worry, we'll keep it down. You should definitely get a good night's rest." She stood and gave him a quick kiss before plopping back down on the sofa.

Scott stood there for a moment scowling before walking to the bedroom and closing the door much more forcefully than necessary.

Eden wouldn't call it a slam, but Scott's scowl had felt like it was directed at her.

She looked at Kennedy. "Is everything okay between you and Scott?"

Kennedy looked at her wide-eyed. "Of course. Why do you ask?"

Because I heard you two arguing last night.

Eden bit her tongue to keep from saying the words aloud.

This wasn't the first night Kennedy had stayed up late with her. But each time Kennedy stayed up with Eden instead of going to bed with Scott, he became a little grumpier.

Eden gave Kennedy a tight smile. "No reason."

As they watched the movie, Eden pondered her predicament. She wasn't ready to go back to Spokane yet. Yes, she could afford to stay at a motel to get out of Scott and Kennedy's hair, but that would be lonelier than her apartment. Besides, she'd blow through her savings in no time if she did that.

And her biggest dilemma: she had no idea what she wanted to do with her life.

~

RUDY CLIMBED from his truck and stretched. Not for the first time, he questioned why he was up early on a Saturday morning helping someone else build a home. He looked at the foundation of Scott and Kennedy's house, then he turned and surveyed the empty lot next door. His lot.

That's why he was here. Because when they finished Scott's house, they'd start building his.

It'd be much quicker to hire contractors to knock it out, but with his dad's and his brother-in-law Austin's skills there was no point in hiring someone to do what they could do themselves. He'd save a ton of money. Besides, there was a sense of pride in being able to say you built your own home.

Debbie and Austin bought this entire tract of land and gifted a lot to Scott and Kennedy as a wedding gift. And when Rudy approached her about buying a lot to someday build on, she gifted him one too, even though he wasn't getting married.

He wasn't in a hurry to build or marry, for that matter. He had plenty of time. Those things were part of his ten-year plan.

He didn't like accepting the gift from his rich sister any more than Scott did, especially when he could afford to buy the land outright. But Debbie had always been generous with her money, and now that she was married, it felt like a slight to Austin to refuse to accept a gift from them.

Austin had such a hard time accepting Debbie's money that the whole family agreed he needed to let go of his pride if he wanted to be worthy of their sister. So it felt dumb to be prideful and refuse to accept a gift from them.

Especially when Debbie and Austin were only trying to do good with their money. This was the third tract of land they had purchased. They'd already started developing the first with apartment buildings. The second was still in the design and planning phase and would contain small homes with equally small lots intended for low-income families. This tract would have larger lots and homes. All three projects would meet a great need for the little town of Providence that had been experiencing a housing shortage for years.

Austin drove up as Rudy walked over to help Scott unload the trailer full of lumber their dad had picked up in Pasco yesterday. He gave his newest brother-in-law a wave before clapping Scott on the shoulder. "Want some help? I know you can carry four boards to my one, but I could use an upper body workout, so save me a few, okay?"

Scott's only response was a scowl and a grunt as he wrapped his arms around a stack of five two-by-fours and walked away.

Rudy turned toward their dad, who stood nearby unwrapping an extension cord. "What's up with him today?"

Dad looked at Scott's back. "Dunno, but he seems especially broody, doesn't he?"

Sleep obviously hadn't improved Scott's disposition from last night. At first, Rudy thought his quiet brother was grumpier than usual because he was losing the card game they played, but even after Scott's luck turned around, and he ended up winning, he was still as surly as ever. And when Kennedy suggested they play another round, he refused and insisted they go home.

It was the first time Rudy had ever heard Scott tell his wife no.

When they'd arrived last night, Rudy had half expected Eden to follow them through the door. But she didn't, and his chest constricted, trapping the air in his lungs, and his stomach plummeted.

"Is she okay?" The words had rushed out before he could stop himself.

He'd worried all week about her. He couldn't help it. She looked so beaten and fragile in that hospital bed. Her heart-shaped face had been so pale.

Kennedy had grinned at him with a knowing gleam in her eyes as she answered. "She's fine. She just wanted a quiet evening at home."

So Rudy had been the fifth wheel again, but it was probably a good thing Eden hadn't come. He found her extremely attractive, and even though he tried to deny it, he was interested in her. Getting to know her better would only make him fall for her though, and he couldn't do that, because falling in love wasn't in his plans right now. Besides, he'd be crushed when she returned to Spokane.

As he helped unload the two-by-fours, he contemplated asking out one of the few single girls in town. Maybe it would distract him from Kennedy's pretty friend. He'd given up dating a while ago, because he simply couldn't see himself settling down with any of the local girls. He'd known most of them since they were in diapers. They either felt like a sister to him, or they had personality quirks that turned him off big time.

Scott let out a string of swear words thirty minutes later when he accidentally hit his thumb with a hammer. And when the nail gun jammed up, he threw it on the ground and swore again.

Rudy let out a swear word of his own as he jumped out of the way.

"Hold up, son." Dad put a hand to Scott's chest to keep him from walking away. "What's the matter?"

Dad tolerated a little language better than mom did, but throwing the nail gun on the ground was not only mistreatment of the tools, it was also dangerous. Rudy would have been nailed if the jammed gun had decided to fire. He chuckled at his own pun.

"What do you mean?" Scott's voice was as gruff as it had ever been.

"I mean you're ornerier than a bear with a sore paw after someone stole his berries."

Rudy snickered at his dad's ridiculous analogy.

"Not only that, but you're putting us all in danger by throwing the nail gun around like that."

Scott's mumbled, "Sorry," was barely audible. He shook his head and looked toward what would be the backyard. "Eden's been staying with us for a full week."

"Yeah, so?" Dad set to work unjamming the nail gun.

"So that's a full week that Kennedy and I haven't spent any time together outside of work." Scott cast a quick glance at Rudy before lowering his voice. "And it's been a whole week without...you know what."

Rudy attempted to stifle a laugh but ended up snorting. He turned to find Austin's lips pinched together.

Scott's voice took on a whiny tone as he continued. "Kennedy has stayed up late every night talking to Eden or watching a movie with her."

Rudy couldn't help himself; he busted out laughing. Dad and Austin joined him.

Apparently, the only thing worse than a grumpy Scott was a sexually frustrated Scott.

His brother pulled off his glove and swatted him on the shoulder which only made Rudy laugh harder.

Dad was the first to recover. He scratched his stubbly jaw for a moment before putting a hand on Scott's shoulder. "Let me talk to your mother."

Rudy's brows furrowed. What was mom supposed to do about Scott's dry spell? She loved helping people, sometimes to the extent of meddling, but she was so sweet about it, you couldn't get mad at her. He sure hoped Dad didn't intend on Mom taking Kennedy aside and explaining her "wifely duties" or something else equally as antiquated.

As much as he didn't want to get involved with Eden, maybe he needed to take her out for an evening so his bear of a brother could lose this bite-your-head-off, grizzly-bear attitude he had lately.

CHAPTER 4

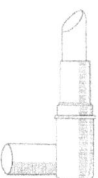

*E*den had just settled down on the couch with her book after another frustrating morning of job hunting when a knock sounded on the door. Before she could even get to her feet, it opened, and Alice Wheeler breezed in.

"Hello, dear. How are you doing? All healed up after your unfortunate accident last week, I hope."

"Yes, I'm fine, thanks for asking."

She'd repeatedly assured Rudy's sisters who expressed concern at Sunday dinner yesterday that she was fine. She'd received so much attention, she almost regretted accepting Kennedy's invitation to join all the Wheelers for family dinner.

She'd only tagged along because she was starving, and Kennedy took the chicken Alfredo that smelled so amazing with her. It had been awkward enough sitting by Scott's parents at church yesterday morning, showing up for family dinner as well felt like she was integrating herself a little too deeply into their lives.

"That's good." Alice looked at the sofa and tutted. "I imagine it's not very comfortable sleeping on that old sofa bed every night. You need to sleep in a real bed." She walked to the corner where Eden's suitcase sat. "Is this yours?" When Eden nodded, she made a tsking sound. "It's kind of in the way, isn't it? I'm surprised someone hasn't tripped over it and gotten a bloody nose."

She gave Eden a friendly smile, but her reference to a bloody nose carried bad memories for Eden ever since Rudy accidentally gave her a bloody nose at Scott and Kennedy's wedding. A bloody nose that wouldn't stop bleeding.

Alice wheeled the large suitcase out of the corner and into the middle of the room. "This apartment is just too small for three people." She grimaced at Eden. "I bet it's rather uncomfortable to have to share a bathroom with Scott."

Now there's the understatement of the year!

Alice snapped her fingers. "You know what? I have just the thing. Scott's old bedroom is just sitting empty. I even painted and redecorated it after he moved out. It would be perfect for you." As if that decided it, she pushed the suitcase toward the door. "You'll be much more comfortable in a bedroom of your own with a real bed."

"But—" Eden was so stunned she struggled to find words. She wasn't sure how to form an argument because everything Alice said was true. The bed, the bathroom, all of it. She loved the idea of sleeping in a real bed again, but she wasn't sure she wanted that bed to be across the hall from Kennedy's good-looking brother-in-law.

"Oh come, dear." Alice put a gentle hand on Eden's arm. "If I'm ever going to get more grandkids these newlyweds need a little privacy."

If Eden wasn't speechless before, she was now. Her eyes widened, and her jaw dropped at the casualness with which Alice brought up her son's sex life. Or lack of. Was that why Scott had been so grumpy lately?

Kennedy had talked a lot about what an amazing woman her mother-in-law was. So much so, that Eden had grown jealous that her friend once again had a caring mother when she herself didn't. She recalled Kennedy's words. "She's so giving and selfless. Some people might consider her a busybody, but she's so kind you can't get offended when she helps you. I've never met anyone quite like her."

Neither had Eden. Still, it felt strange taking Alice up on her offer to stay with them. "I couldn't impose on you."

Alice scoffed. "You'd hardly be imposing. We have plenty of room."

And with that, Alice picked up Eden's very heavy suitcase and carried it out the door.

"Wait! Wait! Wait!"

Alice stopped on the landing and looked expectantly at her.

"I need...to grab my...toiletries," Eden said in a meek voice. "And I'll carry my suitcase down. It's really heavy." She couldn't seem to tell the woman no.

As she drove behind Alice to her house, she kept telling herself that she should return to Spokane and her job and face her life there, but she couldn't bring herself to stop or point her car toward the highway.

Did she really want to live under the same roof as Kennedy's handsome brother-in-law though?

She had a feeling he was as hesitant to get involved with her as she was him, since he hardly talked to her yesterday at Sunday dinner. Or maybe he just saw her as an inept woman who was always in need of rescuing.

Before she could think of a valid reason not to stay with the Wheelers, she arrived at their house. The modest ranch-style home was older, but it looked well kept. White siding with navy blue shutters created a striking facade. Colorful flower beds and a white picket fence bordered the immaculate front yard.

A picket fence.

Who had those anymore? She stared at the humble home that looked much more inviting than the veritable mansion she grew up in. If it hadn't been for Helen, her housekeeper-turned-nanny, the large empty house in the gated community would have felt like a mausoleum.

A sudden, powerful stirring behind her ribcage had her pressing her palm to her chest. The feeling continued to ripple through her abdomen, creating a fluttering sensation.

I want a house like this.

The thought that filled her head surprised and confused her. She tried to dispel it, but it wouldn't leave. It pulsed there, keeping rhythm with the pounding in her chest.

A knock on her window startled her. She shook her head and gave Alice a smile as she stepped out of her car.

"You can just leave your luggage for Rudy to carry in when he gets home from work, if you'd like," Alice said.

"It's okay, I can get it." She really didn't want Rudy to know how much stuff she'd packed.

Back at the garage, when she opened her trunk to put her suitcase in, Alice had let out a startled gasp at the sight of her other suitcases.

"Well, you really were intent on getting out of the city, weren't you?"

Embarrassed, Eden had shoved her suitcase in and closed the trunk.

Alice insisted on helping her carry her luggage into the house, so Eden gave her the carry-on and duffel before stumbling to the house with her two large suitcases. She had no doubt Alice was a strong woman, but she hated to impose on her any more than she already was.

The room Alice showed her to was decent sized with a small walk-in closet and another door that Eden assumed led to a bathroom.

Nice!

She hadn't expected to have her own bathroom. Even though the room still smelled faintly of paint, it was attractive and inviting, with a queen-sized bed covered in a beautiful, embroidered, floral print quilt in cream, peach, and olive green with coordinating decorative pillows. Matching curtains hung on the window.

Eden put her suitcases down and ran a hand over the bedspread. "This is pretty."

Pink tinged Alice's cheeks. "Oh, thank you, dear."

"Wait. Did you make this?"

"Yes. Well, I had help from my friend Sarah and her quilting machine."

"It's beautiful."

Alice waved away the praise and opened the second door. "This is the bathroom. You'll be sharing it with Rudy." She pointed to an open door on the other side of the bathroom. "His room is just through there."

Eden looked in the other room to see a queen-sized bed covered in what looked like a patchwork quilt in blues and grays with splashes of yellow. A computer with multiple monitors filled a large desk that sat against one wall.

"I have to share the bathroom with Rudy?" It was bad enough she'd be living in the hot deputy's house, but she had to share a bathroom with him too?

"Yes, it's called a Jack & Jill bathroom," Alice explained as though she were talking to a child. "Of course, it's usually shared by siblings, but at least you don't have to traipse through Scott's bedroom anymore." Alice chuckled then waved a hand. "Don't worry, he cleans up after himself quite well."

"But..."

Sharing a bathroom with Rudy made her all kinds of uncomfortable. What if she forgot to lock the door? Or left her bra hanging over the shower rod? Yes, it was better than traipsing through Scott and Kennedy's bedroom to go pee, but the thought of Rudy showering behind this door made her skin flush. The bathroom still smelled like him—masculine with a hint of woods and spice—even though he probably showered hours ago.

At least it's a nice smell.

A riotous fluttery sensation swept through her abdomen. She wanted to blame it on anxiety over sharing the bathroom with a man, but she had a feeling it had more to do with who the man was. A good-looking guy that she'd like to get to know better but shouldn't since she wasn't planning on sticking around.

Alice showed her around the rest of the house that looked just as neat and tidy as the exterior. It had a lived-in feel, but it was also cheery and inviting. And comfortable.

It felt like a place where Eden wanted to linger. The furniture was neither over-the-top expensive nor cheap and worn, but everything looked clean and well cared for.

She followed Alice downstairs where she pointed out a spacious family room with a sectional sofa and a large-screen TV. A few decorative pillows and throw blankets made the sectional look cozy and inviting. Yet another space that made Eden want to curl up and relax.

Alice led her down the hall, to first her sewing and craft room then to a home gym.

Eden stepped into the room and breathed in the scent of rubber mats and steel weights. She half expected the room to smell like stale body odor since Scott had come over here twice last week to work out with Rudy. But the faint scent of Rudy's body wash and pleasant masculine scent lingered in the air.

The room was almost as large as the master bedroom upstairs. A Bow flex machine occupied the center of the room with a treadmill to one side and a bench press with a rack of weights on the other. In the corner sat additional padded floor mats and a yoga ball.

Would Rudy and Scott mind if she made use of their exercise room? She hadn't seen anything remotely close to a gym here in Providence, and even though she'd gone for a run a few times, the inactivity wasn't helping her decide what she wanted to do with her life.

"Make yourself at home," Alice said as she left Eden to unpack. "Feel free to come and go as you wish and help yourself to anything you'd like."

Before opening her first suitcase, Eden sent a quick text to Kennedy, thanking her and Scott for letting her crash at their place, then she explained that Whirlwind Alice had kidnapped her.

Kennedy's initial response was a laughing-face emoji. Then she sent another text: *I'm sure you'll be much more comfortable at the Wheelers. At least I'll still get to see you often. Have I mentioned what a great cook Alice is?*

Before Eden could put her phone down, another text came through: *Don't have too much fun with Rudy.* A winky-faced emoji followed the taunt.

Eden shook her head and tossed her phone on the bed. What will it be like living under the same roof as the handsome deputy?

As she hung up wrinkled clothes from her suitcase in the closet, she kept asking herself what she was doing.

I'm moving in with people I hardly know just to avoid going home and facing my dad.

Finished unpacking, she sat on the edge of the bed wondering what to do now. She felt strange searching out Rudy's mother for the purpose of entertainment, so she decided to do some more job hunting.

An hour later with her head swimming with words like performance, expertise, implement, and collaborate, she set her laptop aside and rubbed her eyes. She slumped back against the pillows, more depressed than ever.

Sure, there were plenty of jobs in Spokane for which she was qualified, but she cringed every time she read a list of responsibilities that included things like: development of processes and services, interpreting policies and metrics, and problem identification and solution mapping.

They were all things she'd done at DuPont Analytics for years, and she'd come to hate them. She toyed with the idea of pursuing one of her childhood dreams of being an event planner or interior designer. But she wasn't sure she wanted to take that drastic of a turn, especially if it required more schooling.

Pushing it all out of her mind for now, she filled the tub with water and poured in some bubble bath. She had a novel to finish. After making sure she locked both doors, she undressed and slipped into the tub.

RUDY PARKED his cruiser behind the sheriff's office and hurried inside. He went straight to the break room and pulled both a water bottle and a Gatorade from the fridge. He chugged the water down without stopping then took the Gatorade back to his desk.

He was supposed to be off shift already, but he still needed to file the paperwork for an accident out on the highway before he left for the day. As far as injuries go, it wasn't a bad one, but the driver of a truck pulling a trailer full of porta potties fell asleep at the wheel. He panicked when he ran off the road and over-corrected. He ended up jackknifing the trailer, tipping it over. A dozen Honey Buckets were scattered alongside the highway.

Sheriff Winters assigned Rudy to stay on the scene until it was all cleaned up. He'd waited three hours for the company to get another truck and trailer there plus the equipment to reload the portable outhouses.

Three hours of standing out in the blazing sun with sweat trickling down his back beneath his bulletproof vest, soaking every inch of his body, was bad enough, but being surrounded by porta Johns made him gag repeatedly. He'd had to help lift many of them upright. They were supposedly clean, but...

Rudy shuddered. He couldn't wait to go home and take a shower.

Half an hour later, he finally called it a day and grabbed another Gatorade on his way out of the office. The ride home passed quickly, and he had his tie loosened and the top two buttons undone before he hit the porch.

As soon as he closed the front door, his mother called from downstairs. "Rudy, is that you? Come here for a minute, will you?"

He groaned. He didn't have time to help Mom with some task right now. He just wanted to get out of his sweaty uniform and wash off the stench that clung to him.

"I'll be down in a minute, Mom. I need a quick shower."

He continued undressing as he walked down the hall and into his bedroom. He tossed his gun belt, uniform shirt, and vest on the bed then stripped off the t-shirt he always wore under his vest. Opening the bathroom door that he didn't recall closing this morning, he froze.

Humid, floral-scented, warm air hit him nanoseconds before a feminine scream.

He turned to see Eden covered in bubbles in the bathtub. His bathtub.

She jerked upright, pulling in her arms and a shapely leg from the edge of the tub to shield herself. Her rapid movements sent bubbles flying out onto the floor.

Oh snap!

Much more colorful words flitted through his mind, but his mom taught him to watch his mouth around women, so he bit his tongue to keep them from flying out his mouth.

"What are you—"

"Get out!" Eden shrieked.

Squeezing his eyes shut, Rudy stepped back, pulling the door closed with him. Heat filled his body, as hot as if he stood out in the afternoon sun again.

Mom rushed into his room. "That's what I was trying to tell you. Eden is staying here now in Scott's room." She motioned to the door. "And sharing your bathroom, obviously." She stepped closer to the door and called, "Sorry, Eden dear, I forgot to warn you that the locks on the doors don't work."

She turned and swatted Rudy's shoulder.

"Ow. What's that for?"

"That was a warning." She pointed a finger in his face. "I expect you to be a perfect gentleman. I know it's a little awkward for the two of you to share a bathroom, but you'll just have to make the best of the situation."

A little awkward?

She walked to the door but turned back before exiting his room. "You can flirt with her, date her, you can even kiss her and cuddle on the couch with her..." Her finger pointed again. "But don't you even think about doing anything inappropriate with her in this house."

"Mom!" Although the idea of kissing and cuddling with Eden sounded mighty tempting.

"Or any other house for that matter." She gave him an innocent smile with fluttering lashes and all. "Don't forget the way you were raised and the things you were taught." Then she was gone, leaving Rudy feeling like the rug had just been yanked out from under him. She called back from down the hall, "And take a shower. You stink!"

The bathroom door flew open, and Eden stepped into his room, wearing nothing but a towel and soap suds. She had her hair piled on top of her head in one of those messy buns women always wore nowadays. "The locks don't work? What is it with this family and no locks?"

Rudy's mouth went dry as his gaze roamed over her. She must have grabbed one of the older, smaller bath towels from under the sink, because it barely came to the middle of her thigh, leaving an enticing slit near her hip.

Realizing he was staring, he quickly blinked and averted his gaze. To her bare shoulders.

Gah. That's not any better!

Her eyes darted around his room. "Oh, I thought your mom was still here." A flush covered her cheeks as she stepped back into the bathroom. Her voice took on a defensive tone when she spoke again. "You need to learn to knock."

"Why would I need to knock? I've been the only one to use this bathroom for the last two months."

"Well, not anymore." She reached for the door.

"Wait," Rudy said. "What are you doing here?"

"I was taking a bath before you so rudely interrupted."

"No. Why are you in my house?"

Her nose scrunched and her brows creased. "You know, I'm not really sure. Your mom showed up at the apartment and went on about newlyweds needing their space and rambling stuff about wanting more grandkids. Then she grabbed my suitcase and walked out the door. The next thing I knew, I was here." Eden waved an arm behind her. "In Scott's room. In *your* bathroom." A delicate flush colored her cheeks.

Rudy watched a cluster of soap suds slide from her shoulder down to the edge of the towel around her chest. Warmth filled his body.

Great! Why couldn't mom have just had a talk with Kennedy about her "wifely duties"?

How long would he have to share a bathroom with Eden?

Instead of closing the door, Eden's gaze swept across him. Color flooded her cheeks when her gaze hit his chest.

A perverse sense of pride spiraled through him as her gaze lingered there. But then the realization hit him that they were both half naked, and he grew hot all over again. When her gaze shifted to the scar on his shoulder, he shifted his body away from her and searched for something to break the awkward silence that surrounded them.

"We should get rid of that towel."

Eden's jaw dropped. "Excuse me?"

Heat once again filled his face, only hotter this time.

Gah. I'm as awkward as Scott.

He suddenly had a new appreciation for how his brother felt when he tried to flirt with Kennedy last fall. Not that he was trying to flirt with Eden, because he wasn't. Not at all. But the words coming from his mouth sounded about as ridiculous as Scott telling Kennedy he liked her hammer.

He cleared his throat. "I mean, you don't need to use the small towels. There are much bigger, nicer ones in the bathroom closet."

Eden looked down at her body, causing the slit at her hip to widen and expose more skin. Her eyes widened and she let out a noise that sounded like a combination of a gasp and a shriek. Then she slammed the door.

Rudy sure hoped she didn't plan on getting back in the tub, because he needed a shower. A cold one.

EDEN RETREATED into the bathroom then to her bedroom before stopping to take a breath. She knew the towel she'd grabbed from under the sink was rather small, but she'd been so intent on giving Rudy and Alice a piece of her mind that she hadn't realized how skimpy it was.

Then when she saw Rudy standing there shirtless. Her mouth went dry, and her mind short-circuited. To hide how flustered she felt at the sight of his sculpted bare chest and tones abs, she went on the defensive by accusing him of rudely interrupting her bath and telling him he should learn to knock on his own bathroom door.

Rudy wasn't as bulky as Scott—that man was just plain big—but he had muscle. Lean and toned muscle. He also had a sizable scar on his shoulder.

She wracked her brain, trying to remember whether Kennedy had ever mentioned Rudy being in an accident. She couldn't recall anything, but judging by the size of the scar, it must have been a bad accident.

He had every right to question her presence in his bathroom. She didn't belong here, in the Wheeler's house or in this small town. There wasn't anything for her here. But there wasn't anything back in Spokane for her either.

Before she could get depressed by her situation again, she shook the thoughts from her head and quickly dressed.

Now what?

She wasn't eager to leave her room and face Alice or Rudy, but when she heard the water turn on in the bathroom, she didn't want to stay there and think about him showering on the other side of a door that didn't lock.

Eden found Alice bustling around in the kitchen, putting final preparations on a dinner that smelled amazing.

The older woman pressed a hand to her cheek. "I'm so sorry. I forgot to warn you about the locks or lack thereof. I tried to catch Rudy but..." She finished with a shrug.

Eden waved away the apology even though she was still a little breathless from the whole ordeal. Although she wasn't sure if it was because Rudy walked in on her in the bath or because he was shirtless.

"Can I help with dinner?" Eden held up a finger. "Although I should warn you that I'm mostly inept in the kitchen."

"Good thing I'm a firm believer that anyone can learn then." Alice smiled. "We'll start you off with something easy like tossing a salad."

Alice pulled a flowered apron from a drawer and handed it to Eden, then she guided her to the counter where she had the makings for a green salad. She gave Eden a few instructions then went back to stirring something in the pot on the stove.

The older woman engaged Eden in conversation as they worked together by asking her questions about herself. Thankfully, she didn't broach any touchy subjects like her job—or lack thereof—and her relationship with her dad.

Eden shared a little about how her nanny had tried to teach her to cook, but as a boy-crazy teenager, she'd had little interest.

Just as she finished the salad, Bill Wheeler walked through the door that led to the garage. "Well, hello, Eden." He was a tall, lanky man, who always wore a smile.

Rudy resembled him. He and Debbie seemed to get their slender figure from their father, whereas the rest of the family was curvy—or in Scott's case, bulky—like Alice.

Eden gave Bill a friendly smile. "Hello, sir."

"What did I tell you? I'll have none of this 'sir' stuff."

He'd insisted back at the time of the wedding and again at Sunday dinner yesterday that she call him Bill.

"Sorry, Bill."

He gave an approving nod then turned and swept Alice into his arms and planted a lingering kiss on her lips. After a little squeal, Alice wrapped her arms around her husband and returned the kiss.

Warmth filled Eden's cheeks at the display of affection. She couldn't recall ever seeing a mature couple kiss so passionately before. They were obviously still very much in love.

She tried to think back before her mother died. Did her dad ever greet her mom like that when he came home from work? A pang of sadness filled her when she couldn't dig up a single memory of her parents kissing.

Rudy entered the kitchen while Bill still held Alice and called, "Get a room!"

Eden's heart stumbled then sped up a little at the sight of him in well-worn jeans and a snug blue T-shirt that brought out the blue in his eyes. A five o'clock shadow still covered his jaw, and his damp hair only added to his attractiveness.

She couldn't make herself meet his gaze and judging by the way he grabbed plates from the cupboard and started setting the table, he didn't intend to meet hers either.

Bill finally released Alice and grumbled something about annoying kids. "Just wait until we're empty nesters, then we can run around the house in our birthday suits all day, if we want."

This elicited a chuckle and a swat from Alice. "Hush, you're going to scare Eden away."

Bill turned and winked at Eden, letting her know he was teasing.

Well, I guess I know where Rudy gets his easy-going, joking nature from.

Before long, they were seated at the table, and Eden did her best not to stare at Rudy across from her. When she did happen to glance at him, he quickly looked away. Despite the mouth-watering roast beef that sat in the middle of the table, she could smell Rudy's shower gel, and it did funny things to her insides.

Light-hearted conversation flowed around the table as they ate, and Eden joined in the laughter when Rudy recounted how he spent his afternoon.

He shook his head and waved his arms as he talked. "I swear that forklift operator had no clue what he was doing. He knocked the first porta potty off the trailer when he put the second one on. Then it took him three tries to get the last one seated properly."

No wonder he was so eager to take a shower when he came home.

Bill then told them about the massive wasp nest he uncovered as he took down siding in preparation to build an addition onto an older home. His voice was animated, and he waved his arms almost as much as Rudy did when he told his story, but Eden didn't laugh this time. There was nothing funny about bees and wasps.

Rudy must have noticed her lack of a reaction because he looked at her until she made eye contact with him. Twin lines formed between his eyebrows as he regarded her.

Was he remembering her going into anaphylactic shock a little over a week ago? She couldn't decipher exactly what his look meant, but she recognized the empathy and compassion in his eyes.

"It's a good thing you weren't there, Eden," Alice said. "Can you imagine if you'd gotten stung again?"

"I would have freaked out at the first sign of a wasp." Eden shuddered. "I'm constantly on the lookout for them and bees, believe me. And nuts. I'm allergic to nuts too."

"I'll be sure to remember that," Alice said.

Eden half expected Alice to share her day next and explain how she dragged Eden home like a lost kitten. Thankfully, Alice said nothing of the sort, and no one asked Eden what she did that day.

"I took a bath," would sound extremely lame after stories of battling wasps and porta potties. Unless she included the part where her bath got interrupted by a shirtless man.

Rudy was the first to finish his dinner. He rinsed his plate and loaded it in the dishwasher, then he grabbed a set of keys off a hook and looked at his parents. "I'm going to run down to the hardware store and see if I can find some new locks for the bathroom doors." The tips of his ears reddened when his gaze slid to Eden.

She almost burst out laughing. Yes, she was still miffed about what happened this afternoon, but she found Rudy's embarrassment humorous.

Alice nodded. "Good idea. We don't want any more mishaps." As soon as Rudy walked out, she proceeded to tell Bill that Rudy had accidentally walked in on Eden when he came home from work. Alice brushed off the whole ordeal with a laugh and a wave of her hand.

Eden wished she could do the same. She wasn't sure Alice realized she'd been in the bathtub when Rudy walked in. And because she left Rudy's room so quickly, she didn't know that Eden confronted Rudy in his room wearing nothing but a skimpy towel.

Warmth flooded over her at the memory, and she picked up her water glass and drained it.

Once dinner was put away and the dishes were done, Alice followed Bill to the back door. "Would you like to come see our garden, Eden?"

"Um...sure." Eden had never taken much interest in gardening, but Kennedy had told her how she'd helped plant all kinds of fruits and vegetables in the massive plot behind the Wheeler's house. Her friend was anxious for the watermelons and cantaloupe to grow and ripen.

Eden's footsteps slowed as she followed Bill and Alice across the backyard that was every bit as colorful and beautiful as the front. She let her gaze roam over bushes, rows, and circles of greenery. This garden was huge!

While Bill pointed out all the different fruits and vegetables that they grew each year, Alice crouched near a large bushy, foot-tall bed of green leaves with little white flowers and began picking strawberries.

Eden followed Bill, listening for fifteen minutes, more amazed by the second. They grew such a large variety of produce, and the garden was immaculate. It's a good thing Eden had just eaten, or all this talk of fresh fruits and vegetables would make her hungry.

After her tour of the garden, Eden walked over to where Alice still picked strawberries. "Can I help?"

The older woman sat back on her heels and smiled. "I'd love some help." She pushed a bowl toward Eden. "Only pick the ones that are all red. And be sure to move the leaves aside so you can get the ones that are hiding down low." She demonstrated how to shift the leaves, revealing three fat, red strawberries.

Eden crouched then hesitated, remembering her last experience with fresh strawberries. She searched the leafy bed for bees.

"It's okay," Alice said softly. "The bees are most active in the mornings. That's why we pick berries in the evenings. Of course, we'll be fighting mosquitoes in about an hour."

"Okay." Eden nodded her head and reached for a ripe berry.

Her mouth watered at the sight of the red fruit. Was it as sweet and juicy as it looked? With monumental effort, she resisted the urge to pop the berry in her mouth, but the temptation only grew stronger with each one she picked.

"What a beauty!" Alice held up a perfectly shaped, ruby-red strawberry. Then she stuck it in her mouth and bit it off below the leafy top. She tossed the stem into the middle of the strawberry patch then grinned at Eden as she chewed. She held up a finger. "The rule is: for every strawberry you eat, you have to put five in the bucket."

Eden's face split into a grin. She liked that rule.

Who knew picking strawberries could be so fun.

True to Alice's words, the mosquitoes came out as it turned to dusk and drove them into the house, carrying multiple overflowing bowls of strawberries. Eden didn't know what Alice planned to do with so many strawberries, but she looked forward to eating more, even if she did have to pick them first.

While Bill and Alice used the kitchen sink to wash up, Eden headed to the bathroom to do the same. She couldn't remember the last time she'd played in the dirt and with plants.

Have I ever?

She walked into her bedroom and through the open bathroom door and slid to a stop.

Rudy knelt on the floor, fitting a new knob into the door on his side. "Sorry, I'll be done in just a minute."

"It's okay. I'm just washing my hands." The whole time she scrubbed her hands she was aware of Rudy only a few feet away and his clean masculine scent that hung in the air. Would she always feel so attracted to him? If so, living here would be torturous.

She leaned her hip against the counter and studied him as she dried her hands. Maybe she just needed to familiarize herself with him. Then he wouldn't make her so uncomfortable.

"What?" he asked with a laugh.

She should have felt embarrassed for staring, but she was too fascinated by the way his t-shirt stretched across his bicep and the flexing of his forearm as he tightened the screws into the shiny new doorknob.

She lifted her gaze to his and gave a small smile before narrowing her eyes and tilting her head. "Why didn't you ever replace the locks before now?"

Rudy shrugged. "Didn't need to. It's not like Scott and I required that much privacy." He dropped his hands and his gaze for a moment before looking at her. "I don't think I ever apologized for walking in on you this afternoon. I'm sorry. I should have respected the closed door. I just wasn't expecting..." Rudy's ears grew red again.

Eden tried to imagine how shocking it must have been for him to find a naked woman in his tub.

Probably as shocking as having a man walk in on you when you're in said tub.

"I know," Eden said. "I'm sorry too. I shouldn't have gotten snippy with you."

Rudy pushed to his feet and jiggled the new knob. "Well, now our only problem will be remembering to unlock the other door before we leave the bathroom. I may as well apologize now for forgetting. Because I can't ever remember a time in my life when the locks worked."

"I'm not sure I'll remember either. I've never shared a bathroom with anyone other than Kennedy." Like Rudy and Scott, she and Kennedy hadn't bothered locking the door. It never failed that one of them needed to get in to brush their teeth or do their hair while the other was in the shower.

Rudy's gaze flitted over her then jumped around the bathroom. "Okay, well... I'll... I've got things to do." He motioned over his shoulder with a thumb before stepping back into his room and closing the door between them.

Eden grinned. She recalled Kennedy telling her how awkward Scott was when they first met. But the first time she met Rudy, he was cheerful and talkative. The opposite of his quiet brother. He usually acted so confident and self-assured. Until tonight.

Was he uncomfortable because they'd seen each other half naked, or did he feel the same powerful magnetic attraction she did anytime they were in the same room?

Deciding she was better off not pondering that topic, she returned to her room and changed into pajamas. The cow-print shorts and tank top with the word "Mooody" across the chest were her favorite pajamas. After a whole week of sleeping poorly, she looked forward to an early night.

She returned to the bathroom, locked the door on Rudy's side and started her nighttime routine. She'd been too self-conscious to do a facial mask in front of Scott last week, so she took time to apply one tonight.

Soothing and hydrating avocado. Exactly what I need.

She returned to her room and slipped her ear buds in before selecting her ambient music playlist. Then she laid down on the floor to do some stretches and meditation. The muscles in her back ached after bending over picking strawberries for so long.

Several minutes later, a knock sounded on her door, breaking her concentration and relaxation.

She pushed up off the floor and pulled the ear bud from one ear before opening her door.

"You forgo—" Rudy jerked back, wide eyed and shuddered. "Ahh!"

"Wha—" Belatedly, Eden remembered that she wore a green face mask. Would the heat filling her cheeks be visible behind the green? This was exactly why she hadn't done a face mask while she was at Scott and Kennedy's.

Rudy composed himself. "Okay, that's just scary."

"Very funny." She scowled at him. "What do you want?"

"You forgot to unlock the bathroom door." His gaze raked over her, taking in her cow-print pajamas, and his eyebrows shot up.

Feeling suddenly exposed by the shortness of her shorts and the thinness of her tank top, she turned defensive again. "I didn't forget to unlock the door." She totally had, but she'd never admit it. "I'm not finished in there."

"Obviously."

Eden sucked in a sharp breath. "How rude!"

Now he scowled. "I'm just stating facts. You obviously need to wash off..." He pointed to her face. "...whatever that is."

Eden lifted her chin and squared her shoulders. "It's avocado and oatmeal. It hydrates my skin."

He snorted. "If you say so."

"I do." She glared at him, daring him to argue with her.

"Whatever." Rudy raised his hands palms out before sighing. "When are you going to be finished in the bathroom?"

She gave him a cheeky grin and said, "When my mask is dry, and I'm done getting ready for bed." Then she closed the door on him.

"Mooody?" Rudy's voice came through the door in a perfect imitation of a cow. "I can think of a more appropriate word."

"Humph!" Eden scowled at the door.

Why did she always get so defensive around him? And would there ever be an end to the awkward situations between them?

CHAPTER 5

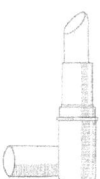

*E*den rolled over and stretched. A beam of sunlight hit her face, and she grimaced before rolling back and opening her eyes. She checked the bedside clock.

Is it really nine already?

She hadn't expected to sleep so well when she climbed into bed last night and felt its firmness. She'd quickly concluded that Alice had bought a new bed for the guest bedroom when she redecorated it. There was no way a big man like Scott slept in this bed for years without leaving a dip in the center.

Although she'd slept great and much longer than she'd expected, she was tempted to roll over and go back to sleep since she had nothing to get out of bed for. But with the way the sun streamed through the curtains, she doubted that would happen.

Once again, she questioned what she was supposed to do with her life. She didn't regret quitting her job, but she felt aimless. She looked up at the ceiling.

Lord, tell me what you want me to do with my life.

After waiting several long moments for a lightning bolt of inspiration to hit, she climbed out of bed and knocked on the bathroom door. When no answer came, she tried the knob.

Locked, of course.

She went down the hall to Rudy's room only to find his door open. Of course, he was gone to work already. She took a moment to look around his room as she made her way to the bathroom.

Alice was right; he cleaned up after himself. His bed was made and there didn't seem to be a single thing out of place. No shoes or dirty socks on the floor. No shirt laying over the back of his desk chair. Even the little notepad and pen on his desk seemed to be in perfect order.

She studied his computer setup. Why did he need two monitors in addition to his laptop? Was he a gamer? A geek at heart?

Realizing she was being nosy, she hurried into the bathroom where the scent of his body wash hit her. She loved the powerful masculine scent. It fit Rudy perfectly.

Last night, she'd thought that if she familiarized herself with his good looks, she'd be more comfortable with him. Then maybe her fascination with him would subside, but that didn't appear to be the case. Every little thing she learned about him only ramped up her attraction to the man.

She took the time to hand wash her favorite bra. It was long overdue for a cleaning, but she'd been too embarrassed to wash it at Kennedy and Scott's apartment. She doubted her friend's surly mountain man of a husband wanted to find it hanging to dry in his bathroom any more than she wanted him to.

She faced a similar dilemma here, however. She didn't want Rudy to walk in and find her unmentionables hanging in his shower. She tried to convince herself that she would remember to take it down before he came home, but she tended to be forgetful when it came to things like that.

For lack of a better place, she finally decided to hang it on the bathroom doorknob in her bedroom. That way, if she forgot to take it down in a few hours, she'd be the only one to see it.

After she dressed in denim shorts and a white tee, she found Alice in the kitchen.

"Good morning, dear." Alice looked up from the large lump of dough she kneaded. "Did you sleep well?"

"Very well, thank you." Eden looked at the dough. "Are you making...bread?"

"Yes." Alice wiped her forehead with the back of her wrist. "I've gotten lazy over the years and don't make bread near as often as I used to. But fresh strawberry jam tastes best on fresh homemade bread."

"You're making jam with the strawberries?" Eden rocked forward on the balls of her feet.

Naturally, strawberry jam was her favorite, but so many of the store-bought brands didn't taste good. Her favorite brand was only sold at a cute little boutique in Spokane. Because it was so expensive, she only bought it on special occasions.

"Jam and pies." Alice dropped the dough into a large bowl and spread a dish towel over the top. "Would you like to help me? My daughters often come to help, but they're all busy today."

"I've never made jam before, but sure, I'd love to help. It's not like I have anything else to do."

"Job hunt not going so good?" Alice asked, her voice full of sympathy.

"No, because I'm not sure I want to work in the business field anymore."

"So, what do you want to do?" Alice pulled a covered plate from the fridge and put it in the microwave.

"I don't know." Eden shrugged. "I don't want to feel like I'm wasting my business degree, but..." Eden let her words die off.

"But you don't want to use it the same way you did while working for your father."

"Exactly."

Alice understood her better than she understood herself right now.

The older woman pulled the plate from the microwave and set it on the table. She motioned for Eden to sit. "If you're going to help me, you need to eat a good breakfast first. We have a lot of work to do."

Eden wasn't a big breakfast eater, but the smell of bacon made her stomach growl, and she slid into the chair without complaint. Her eyes widened as she took in the pancakes and eggs that accompanied the bacon.

Alice unloaded small jars from the dishwasher as she talked about the jam-making process. The woman seemed to always be in motion. Kennedy had once said her mother-in-law was happiest when she was serving others, and Eden believed it.

Surprisingly, Eden finished her whole breakfast. She'd have to make it a point to work out more often if she was going to eat like this.

As soon as Eden loaded her plate in the dishwasher, Alice handed her an apron. This one was black and red and said *Kiss the Cook* across the front. "I'd hate for you to stain that white shirt." As soon as Eden had donned the apron, Alice continued. "We'll start with the pies. Which means we need to wash two quarts of strawberries."

Eden followed Alice's instructions washing and trimming the tops off the strawberries, while the other woman pulled out ingredients for the pie crust.

When Eden had enough strawberries trimmed, Alice motioned for her to join her at the counter where she showed her how to cut the butter into the flour until it created a clumpy yet crumbly powder.

"Good, now stick your hands in there and mash it all together," Alice said as she poured in the water. When Eden hesitated, she stepped closer. "It's okay, dear. Just stick your hands in like this." Alice's hands disappeared into the dough, and she demonstrated how to mix and knead for a minute before cleaning her hands. "Now it's your turn."

The wet dough clinging to Eden's hands made her stomach feel a little funny. Every time she moved her hands, it seemed more dough stuck to them, and she doubted she was doing any good. Alice continued to sprinkle more flour in until the dough was smooth and barely tacky.

After dropping the dough on the counter and kneading it a little more, Alice broke the clump of dough into two balls. Eden did her best to mimic Alice's actions and follow every step, but her crust ended up shaped like Africa, instead of round.

"You're doing fine. Now roll the other direction," Alice patiently coached Eden. "That's the way. Push a little harder."

Eventually Eden achieved a mostly round crust that didn't fall apart when she lifted it into the pie pan. She felt like cheering at her accomplishment, small as it was. She settled for giving herself a mental pat on the back.

While the crusts baked, they made the pie filling. Fresh strawberry pie was Eden's favorite, and her mouth watered the whole time she stirred the glossy, delicious-looking filling.

"Don't they look beautiful?" Alice said twenty minutes later, as she closed the refrigerator door on the pies. "Now the real work begins."

She set Eden to work at the sink washing and trimming more strawberries, while she punched down the bread dough and pulled out the biggest pots and pans Eden had ever seen.

If Eden thought her back hurt last night after picking strawberries, she was mistaken. Leaning over the sink was ten times worse than picking. She had muscles aching in areas she'd never been aware of before.

When Alice suggested Eden take a break from washing and trimming, she eagerly agreed, until she found herself wiping away beads of sweat from standing over the stove stirring sugar and crushed, bubbling strawberries next to a massive pot that held steaming water. It didn't help that the bread now baked in the oven, heating the kitchen up even more.

Eden had no idea making jam was so much work. Washing, trimming, crushing, and cooking—that was just making the jam. Then they still had to process the jars in the big pot of boiling water to seal the lids, only to start all over with a new batch.

Alice gently corrected Eden every time she did something wrong and patiently explained why every step of the process was important. She had a lot more patience than Helen, Eden's former nanny.

When Alice declared it was lunch time, Eden sighed in relief. She needed a break. She looked at the clock on the stove, expecting it to be mid-afternoon, but it only said twelve-thirty. It felt like they had been making jam for five hours, not two and a half.

Lunch consisted of leftover roast and potatoes from last night, but the highlight was watching Alice slice into a loaf of warm bread. She placed a slice on a saucer and pushed it toward Eden along with the butter and the jar of jam that hadn't been full enough to process in the hot water bath.

Eden was hesitant to bite into the jam covered bread. It couldn't possibly taste as good as it smelled and looked.

Alice took a bite then watched her expectantly, waiting for her to try the fruits of her labors. So Eden took a big bite. An explosion of flavor filled her mouth. Delicious, sweet, and amazing. The jam easily rivaled the gourmet jam she often bought at the boutique in Spokane, and the bread was equal parts chewy and airy.

It had been a lot of years since Helen had made homemade bread, opting instead to buy it at a high-end bakery. But even when she used to make it, Eden didn't recall it ever tasting this good.

She forced herself to stop after devouring a second slice. Thank goodness Alice put the remaining half loaf away. Eden hadn't eaten this many carbs in one setting for months. She'd have to go for a run this evening.

That is if she had the energy after helping turn the rest of the strawberries into jam.

A WALL of heat and humidity hit Rudy along with the most amazing smells when he walked into the house after work. Homemade bread, sweet strawberry jam—and hopefully, pie—and the rich savory scent of mom's beef stew. Mom always threw something in the Crockpot in the morning before she started canning.

He rounded the corner into the kitchen intent on stealing a slice or two of bread but skidded to a stop at the sight of Eden in a red apron that added some curve to her slender figure. She stood near the stove stirring a large pan that no doubt held more jam. He'd never taken her for the domestic type, but she looked like she belonged in the kitchen.

Wow, that sounds sexist.

He slowed his approach, letting his gaze move around the kitchen. Dozens of jars of ruby-red strawberry jam filled all of one counter and judging by the bubbling and hissing of the massive, unsealed pressure cooker, another batch was being processed.

Eden looked up from the pot she stirred. He hoped for her sake it was the final batch of the day. She looked exhausted, yet she also had an attractive glow about her.

She gave him a hesitant smile as she swiped the perspiration from her brow.

"Where's my mom?" His gaze went back to roaming the kitchen.

"She went down to the storage room for more canning rings."

He nodded his head in acknowledgment as he took in the four loaves of fresh bread already tied up in bags. Mom would kill him if he cut one of those. Knowing her, she probably planned to give a loaf or two to a neighbor. "Aha, there it is!"

Eden jumped and let out a little squeak.

"Sorry. I was looking for this." He grabbed the partial loaf he assumed his mom and Eden had snacked on at lunchtime. He rotated, studying the kitchen again. "Is there an open jar of jam?"

"Your mom put it in the fridge."

With the jars of jam taking up so much space on the counters, the average-sized kitchen felt small and crowded. Rudy was hyper aware of Eden standing at the stove beside him while he sliced himself a piece of bread and slathered it with butter and jam.

"How do you do that?" Eden asked.

"Do what?"

"Slice the bread so it's even and perfect?"

Rudy shrugged. "I don't know. Practice, I guess. Mom got tired of us kids mangling the loaf, so she insisted on teaching us to slice it properly." He motioned to the serrated-edged knife that he'd used. "The right knife makes a big difference."

Eden studied the knife for a moment before she went back to stirring.

Silence settled in the kitchen except for the bubble and hiss of the pressure cooker and the scrape of her wooden spoon against the bottom of the pan. Rudy knew he should try to make conversation, but he was still so surprised to see her in the kitchen, that he figured it would be best to keep his mouth shut. With his track record, he'd probably say something offensive.

Besides, he was way too distracted by the words on her apron to think clearly.

Kiss the Cook.

When mom wore that apron, dad *always* kissed the cook. Of course, she didn't need to wear a special apron for dad to show his affection. He was good about that.

And even though the current cook looked very kissable, Rudy couldn't go there with someone who was only here temporarily. That didn't keep his mouth from salivating in a way that had nothing to do with the delicious bread and jam though.

He'd just stepped farther away from Eden to remove himself from the temptation when his mom returned from the storage room with her hands full of canning rings. "I see you found the bread. Don't eat too much. Dinner will be ready soon."

Rudy finished his snack just as the timer signaled the end of the hot-water bath. He lingered in the kitchen for a moment, watching his mom and Eden work together to pull the hot jars from the cooker. Watching her work alongside his mom made it all too easy to picture coming home to her every day.

Whoa! I shouldn't be entertaining thoughts like that about Eden.

He hurried to his room to change his clothes and clear his head. When he tried to go into the bathroom, he found the door locked. He gave a quick knock to see if Eden had gone in there in the last few minutes. Hearing no response, he went to her room and paused outside the open door.

His mom's voice traveled down the hall. "Careful, dear. Don't burn yourself."

Eden was busy. There was no point making her come unlock the bathroom door for him. He could just go into her room and on to the bathroom and she'd be none the wiser. He stepped in, intent on beelining straight to the bathroom, but stopped when he saw a pink lacy bra hanging from the knob of the door he needed to open.

His hand froze outstretched.

It wasn't like he hadn't seen a bra before. He had older sisters, but they were all considerably older than him and had left home years ago. It was more the fact that this piece of under clothing belonged to the woman he hadn't been able to get out of his mind all day.

He was still in the process of convincing himself it wasn't a big deal to grab the knob where Eden's bra hung when she walked into the room and saw him standing there with his hand reaching for her bra... erm, the doorknob. He was reaching for the doorknob!

"What are you doing?"

"I...uh..." Heat flooded Rudy's face, making the tips of his ears burn.

Her eyes widened. "Oh my heck!" She snatched her bra off the door and quickly turned away, hiding it from his view, but not before color filled her own cheeks.

"You...uh...forgot to unlock the door on my side." Rudy tugged on the collar of his shirt. Why was it suddenly so hot in here?

"As did you this morning."

"Right. Sorry. I guess that makes us even."

"Except you didn't leave your...you know what...hanging on the doorknob." She flung her hand—bra and all—through the air. Then gasping, she shoved it behind her back again.

Rudy couldn't help himself; he busted out laughing. He was glad he wasn't the only one who was rattled by this whole situation. Thankfully, she joined him instead of getting offended or angry.

"I guess this is just as big of an adjustment for you as it is for me," she said, still smiling.

His gaze dropped to her lips. Had they always been so red and full?

"You can say that again." The words came out deep and husky.

An insane urge to pull her into his arms and kiss her hit him as an awkward silence settled between them. He sucked in a sharp breath and reminded himself why he was in her room in the first place. He reached for the doorknob then quickly jerked back.

Eden wasn't directly between him and the door, but she stood close enough that if he continued to reach for the knob, it would look like he intended to grab her hip.

"Um... do you mind?" He looked pointedly at the door.

"Sorry."

She sidestepped, and he wasted no time going into the bathroom and closing the door between them. He couldn't believe he'd wanted to kiss her. He blamed it all on his mom. She told him he could kiss and cuddle with Eden, and he may have imagined doing just that a time or two today. It didn't help that she still wore that ridiculous apron.

Would things always be this awkward and tense between them?

Yes, as long as I continue to fight this attraction for Eden.

But if he decided to stop fighting, and she reciprocated—like he suspected she might—then things would be tense in a whole new way.

He jumped when a knock sounded on the door behind him. Bracing himself, he opened the door and peered at Eden. "What?" His voice came out gruffer than he intended.

"Sorry, I...um. I need some burn cream."

"Why didn't you say so?" He held the door open and beckoned her in. He looked at the hand she held out in front of her. An angry red mark marred the side of her thumb.

The bathroom that had always felt rather roomy suddenly shrank to the size of a clothing-store dressing room as Eden rifled through her cosmetic bag.

"You keep burn cream with your makeup?"

"I can't count the number of times I've burned myself on a curling wand or straightener." She glanced at him in the mirror before continuing to dig in her bag. "Aha, found it!" She shot him a triumphant smile before disappearing from the bathroom.

A smile that made his heart pound so hard in his chest, he feared he might have a heart attack.

CHAPTER 6

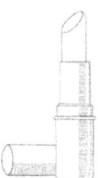

*S*itting across the table from Eden again for dinner was only slightly less uncomfortable than last night. Just as he'd guessed, Mom had made a rich and savory stew, and between the four of them, they devoured another loaf of bread with jam, of course.

He grinned when Mom brought out the strawberry pie and topped it generously with whipped cream. Rudy loved this time of year. His mom's fresh strawberry pie was almost as good as her fresh peach pie in the fall. Oh, and her apple pie...

She was the best cook.

She placed a big slice in front of him, and he took a bite. Delicious, as always. He closed his eyes and savored the sweet and buttery taste. "Mmm... Mmm..."

Dad's hum of approval joined his, and Eden started giggling.

Rudy looked at her. "What? It's good."

"You're both so expressive, so..." She waved her hand in the air as she searched for a word. "So dramatic."

"Passionate, Eden, girl," Dad said with a wink. "It's not drama. It's passion."

Eden stopped laughing, and her gaze skittered away from Rudy's.

Rudy lowered his own gaze to his pie. Passion was not a word he should be thinking about. Not after he had that insane urge to kiss Eden less than an hour ago.

After scraping the last morsel from his plate, he stood. "Delicious as always, Mom."

"Don't compliment me. Eden made the pie. Not bad for a first attempt, huh?"

Again, Rudy stared at Eden, stunned. If someone had told him when he first met the rich Daddy's Girl that he'd be eating her home-made pie and jam a few months later, he would have laughed. Eden had joked about what a lousy cook she was while they made home-made pizza two days before the wedding, and Kennedy had seconded it. Either the two of them had been exaggerating, or Eden had had a change of heart when it came to the desire to acquire culinary skills.

At any rate, he'd misjudged her.

He met her gaze and gave her a big smile. "It tasted great. Thanks."

Several minutes later after helping clean up the kitchen, he was about to head downstairs to work out—anything to get away from Eden—when his mom stopped him.

"Rudy, will you and Eden walk a loaf of bread and a jar of jam down to Miss Georgie?"

He groaned inwardly.

"Walk?" It was one thing to drop off a loaf to the elderly neighbor, but why did Mom want him to walk it to her house?

Mom scoffed. "It's only a mile. Eden has worked so hard today, I think she'd enjoy a little fresh air."

A little chill swept over him despite the still sweltering heat of the kitchen, and a knot settled in his stomach.

Mom's playing matchmaker.

If it were with any other woman, he wouldn't mind. But he could easily fall for their house guest, and it would kill him when she returned to the city. And she would leave, just like Meredith, his high school sweetheart, did.

Besides, falling in love wasn't in his plans. Not for a few more years anyway.

His gaze jumped to Eden who dried her hands on a dish towel. She looked exhausted, but she still had that glow of excitement and accomplishment about her. He didn't want to spend more time with her, and he had no desire to choke down Mrs. Georgie's rock-hard shortbread cookies, refusing to go would be rude to Mom though, and Dad had never tolerated that.

"Fine." He gave Eden another smile. "Would you like to meet one of Providence's worst cooks?"

"Be nice, Rudy," Mom chided. Then she turned to Eden. "Seriously though, don't eat her cookies. You're likely to break a tooth."

Within minutes, Rudy found himself walking beside Eden. He carried a jar of jam, and she carried a loaf of bread.

"Do you think it's going to rain?" She asked, looking up at the sky.

Rudy studied the scattered clouds in the sky. Although there were quite a few of them, they didn't look like they carried rain. "No. We'll be lucky to get a sprinkle, if we get any moisture at all."

Despite their numerous awkward interactions and Rudy's fear he'd say something that might come out wrong, they managed to make small talk on the walk to Miss Georgie's house as he shared stories about his neighbors.

When he spotted Chase Williams out in his driveway in his wheelchair shooting baskets, a sense of guilt swept over him, as it did every time he saw his neighbor. He wasn't responsible for the accident that paralyzed Chase, but he was responsible for the accident that took Chase's older brother.

He turned to Eden. "Do you mind if we stop and visit Chase for a few minutes?"

"Not at all."

EDEN SAT on a short retaining wall to the side of the driveway and watched Rudy and the young man he called Chase.

The young man's eyes lit up when Rudy dashed in and grabbed the rebounding basketball. Chase's smile grew when Rudy feinted then darted around him to go in for a layup.

Rudy grabbed the ball and threw it to Chase. "Let's see what you got, Williams," he challenged as he crouched in front of Chase, who looked to be in his late teens.

Chase bounced the ball a few times before dropping it on his lap and rolling himself first to one side then the other, causing Rudy to dart back and forth across the driveway. When it looked like he might zip back a third time, Rudy shifted, and Chase lifted the ball and shot.

Eden couldn't help herself, she clapped when it went through the net.

Rudy shot her a scowl. "I see how it is."

Clouds continued to gather in the sky as the two continued to play, each round becoming more and more aggressive. There were times when Eden was sure Rudy let Chase score, but then there were other moments when she could tell the younger man surprised him.

And Rudy surprised Eden.

She knew he was friendly to everyone and an all-around good guy, but the fact that he took time out of his day to play basketball with Chase touched her. It was obvious he'd had other plans when his mom insisted he take bread to Miss Georgie, yet he wasn't rushing through the unpleasant task. Instead, he took time to make his neighbor's day. And it only made him that much more attractive.

Both men had worked up a sweat and shared a lot of laughter before Rudy finally clapped Chase on the shoulder. "Okay, man. One last shot before I go." He grabbed the back of Chase's wheelchair. "It's all you. I'm taking you in for a lay-up. You ready?"

Without waiting for an answer, he pushed Chase from the back of the driveway, circling to the right and allowing Chase to dribble the basketball as he glided across the concrete. The young man shot just before rolling under the basket, bouncing the ball off the backboard and through the net.

Eden cheered, and Rudy gave Chase a high-fived.

Both men made their way to where she sat.

"You gonna leave without introducing me to your girlfriend?" Chase asked Rudy as they made their way toward her.

Eden froze in the process of standing, and Rudy gave an uncomfortable chuckle.

"She's not my girlfriend. She's uh... just a friend." Rudy shuffled his feet. "Didn't you meet Kennedy's friend Eden at the wedding?"

"Nah, man. I was back in the hospital again with that infection, remember?"

"That's right. You obviously feel better with the way you smoked me tonight." Rudy motioned to her. "Eden DuPont, this is Chase Wheeler. He's like a little brother to me."

Chase extended a hand then pulled it back. "Sorry, my hands are dirty."

Eden smiled and shrugged as she extended her own. "I don't mind." She waited for Chase to take her hand. "It's nice to meet you."

"You too." Chase eyed the bread and jam. "You guys must be headed to Miss Georgie's."

"How did you know?" Eden asked.

"All the moms on the street send food to Miss Georgie because she's a terrible cook, and they're worried about her health." Chase laughed. "That's the best thing about being in a wheelchair, Mom can't make me deliver food to Miss Georgie anymore, because she doesn't have a ramp."

"I think you should join us." Rudy grabbed the back of Chase's chair and pointed him down the street. "I'll find a way to get you up her steps."

"Oh, no you don't." Chase locked his wheels and swatted over his shoulder at Rudy's hands. "I don't need to visit her to be subjected to her cookies. She drops by with a plateful way too often." He wheeled backward when Rudy let go of his chair. "Enjoy your visit. Oh, and Eden, don't eat her cookies."

She laughed as she and Rudy walked away. She was more than a little terrified to face Miss Georgie and her cookies now.

Rudy turned and walked backward. "Chase! Did you check out those online classes I told you about?"

"Not yet, man," Chase called back. "But I will. I promise."

"You better." Rudy pointed a finger at him before turning back around.

"What happened to him?" Eden couldn't keep the curiosity out of her voice. He seemed like such a nice young man.

Rudy's jaw clenched and his gaze dropped to the sidewalk. He kicked a small stone into the road. It was several long moments before he spoke. "He and his buddy Ryan were in a terrible car accident almost a year ago." Rudy's voice was so quiet, she had to strain to hear him. "Ryan didn't make it."

"How horrible." She blinked back tears. "Survivor's guilt coupled with paralysis must be horrible."

"It is." Rudy's voice was so husky, Eden studied him.

All joviality had disappeared. His rigid posture radiated tension, his jaw clenched, and his fists doubled. His right hand gripped the jam in a white-knuckled grip. She had a feeling that if she could see his eyes clearly, she'd find dark shadows in their depths created by painful memories.

Did Rudy have to investigate Chase's accident? Or was he thinking of another accident altogether? Perhaps the one that left the scar on his shoulder?

Trying to diffuse the tension radiating off him, she said, "He's a great shot. Did he play before the accident?"

"He had a scholarship to play college ball." Again, Rudy's voice was low and strained.

"I assume he lost it?" When Rudy nodded, she asked, "And you're trying to get him to start his education by taking online classes?"

Rudy found another pebble to kick at. "I'm trying to get him to do something. Anything. He's been depressed since the accident, understandably. But I worry that if he doesn't do something, his depression will only worsen."

"He sure perked up while you played with him."

"I enjoy it." He shrugged. "When we were younger, he was just one of the pesky younger neighborhood kids, but now as an adult, he's alright."

Eden's stomach churned a few minutes later when Rudy led them up the front steps of a small cottage-style home and rang the doorbell. "Are her cookies really that bad?"

Rudy pulled a face that made her laugh. "Besides tasting like salt, lard, and flour, they are hard as a rock. Seriously. I tested it once. They're like that salt dough my third-grade teacher had us put our handprints in before baking it. Miss Georgie always has cookies on hand, but the problem is, you never know how long ago she made them. Could be days, weeks or even months."

Now Eden was the one who grimaced. "So how do we say 'no' if she off—"

The door opened to reveal a stooped, blue-haired woman who looked to be in her late seventies. Her face split into the biggest grin Eden had ever seen, lighting up her pale blue eyes.

"Good evening, Miss Georgie," Rudy said with a smile of his own. "My mom thought you'd like some homemade bread and fresh jam."

"Rudy! What a nice surprise. It's been ages since I've seen you." She stepped back and beckoned them in. "Have you grown again?"

"Not since you saw me last week," Rudy said under his breath. "No, ma'am. I stopped growing about eight years ago."

Miss Georgie peered at Eden. "Who is this lovely young woman? Is she your girlfriend?"

Again with the girlfriend thing?

Eden's eyes widened. Was that why Alice insisted Rudy take her for a walk? Was she trying to force a relationship between them? Alice, with her cheerful smile and friendly attitude definitely seemed like the meddling matchmaker type.

"Uh...no. Eden is just my friend."

Once again Eden sighed in relief. Not that there wasn't a certain appeal to being the girlfriend of a good-looking man who respected his mom, washed his own dishes, and took time to play basketball with a neighbor. Someday, some lucky woman would be fortunate to have Rudy call her his girlfriend, but it wouldn't be Eden.

It couldn't be her because she wasn't planning on sticking around this little town. It was just a pit stop while she figured out what she wanted to do with the rest of her life.

"That's too bad. You're such an attractive couple." Miss Georgie closed the door. "Isn't your mother the sweetest woman? I do love her fresh bread, and no one makes jam quite like Alice." Miss Georgie waved them toward a floral loveseat. "I haven't had visitors in ages. Have a seat. Have a seat. Let me get you some tea. I just made fresh cookies yesterday. Or was it the day before?" She bustled off into the nearby kitchen.

"It was probably the week before last," Rudy said under his breath as he took a seat.

Evidently Miss Georgie didn't *offer* her visitors cookies, she simply insisted on feeding them. Eden had expected Rudy put up some resistance, but knowing the kind of person his mother raised him to be, taking time to visit with a lonely old woman seemed to be par for the course.

Miss Georgie chattered from the kitchen while she heated water and laid items out on a tray. Eden only heard half of what she said and was unable to make sense of the words she did hear. Her gaze roamed the small living room that was lined on both sides with stacks of boxes and totes, leaving a narrow path down the center to the TV. A fancy lace doily lay atop each stack of boxes.

What on earth is in the totes? Is the woman an organized hoarder?

As if reading her mind, Rudy pressed his shoulder to hers as he whispered, "They're full of yarn."

Trying to ignore the warmth that raced through her at the contact and his warm breath against her cheek, she asked, "All of those boxes," she pointed around the room, "are full of yarn?"

"Well, it's actually crochet string." He pointed to a bulky spool of thick thread nestled on a brown stand near a recliner that Eden assumed was Miss Georgie's usual seat.

"Is that..."

"A toilet paper holder? Yes. It holds the thread quite nicely, don't you think?"

Eden nodded. It did indeed. The spool of string was the same size and shape as a roll of toilet paper. If it spun as smoothly as toilet paper it probably made crocheting a lot easier.

Before long, Miss Georgie carried in a tray and set out a teapot, cups, and a plate of shortbread cookies.

Eden's stomach tightened. After Alice and Chase's warnings, Eden had no desire to try the infamous cookies. How did she refuse without offending the woman?

Miss Georgie took the decision out of Eden's hands by plopping two cookies onto her small plate with a thunk.

Rudy gave her a tight grin and mouthed, "Hard as a rock."

Determined not to offend their hostess, but also not interested in breaking a tooth, she decided to follow Rudy's lead. When he made no move to pick up a cookie or sip his tea, she felt the need to at least pretend. She picked up a cookie and tried to break it. The biscuit truly was as hard as a rock. Crumbs didn't even flake off in her hand.

Rudy rolled his eyes and gave a subtle shake of his head beside her.

Before she could set the cookie, or rather hockey puck, back down, Miss Georgie picked up a cookie and dunked it in her tea, so Eden figured she'd do the same. Maybe it would soften it up.

Rudy grabbed her arm before she could get her cookie to her cup. He leaned toward her and whispered. "It won't help, trust me. The tea doesn't taste any better than the cookie."

"Well, what am I supposed to do with it?" Her whispered words sounded like a hiss.

Rudy winked and shot her a grin that made him look like his dad but also made her heart stop for a moment. "Miss Georgie, Eden would love to see your doilies."

The older woman's eyes lit up again as she dropped her cookie into her tea and stood. For the next fifteen minutes, Miss Georgie guided her around the room pointing out the pretty lace-like decorations with beautiful, intricate patterns.

As Eden admired and oohed and aahed over each one, she watched Rudy out of the corner of her eye. He used his napkin to scoop up his cookies and tuck them into his pocket. Then he tucked hers into his other pocket.

Note to self: make sure I wear pockets when I visit Miss Georgie.

Not that she'd ever have an occasion to visit Miss Georgie again, but knowledge was power. Or in this case, protection. Eden bit back a grin when Rudy dumped first her tea then his into a nearby potted plant.

When she finally returned to her spot on the loveseat so Miss Georgie could demonstrate how she made the pretty doilies, the older woman's cookie still sat propped in her tea, whole and not at all dissolved.

"How long does it take you to crochet a doily?"

"It's called tatting, sweetie, not crocheting. I can do a small one in a day as long as my arthritis isn't acting up." She picked up a small silver, fish-shaped tool called a shuttle and wound the string around the fingers of both hands. With surprising speed, she shifted the shuttle back and forth between her fingers making a series of knots.

Eden was fascinated by the delicate design that formed. It wasn't until a clap of thunder sounded outside that she realized they'd been there for the better part of an hour.

Rudy stood. "We'd better head home."

Eden rose too and thanked Miss Georgie for sharing her talent with her. She caught sight of the cookie the old woman left in her tea before she stepped to the door. It was still whole. Not one bit dissolved.

She grimaced. She thought everyone had been exaggerating about Miss Georgie's cookies, but she really could have broken a tooth if she'd tried to eat one. Wouldn't her dad love that? It would confirm everything he believed about this hick town.

Rudy sucked in a deep breath as soon as they stepped out onto the front porch. "Doesn't that smell great?"

Eden inhaled deeply. The moisture in the air created a heady and fresh scent. "It does. But I thought you said it wouldn't rain." Light rain drops landed on Eden's head and shoulders as they started their walk home.

"I said it would probably just sprinkle, which is what it's doing."

Another clap of thunder sounded, and either the percussion of the sound ripped the heavy rain clouds open or Mother Nature needed a laugh, because the sprinkle became a downpour. A deluge of cold water.

"Ahh!" Eden shrieked at the same time Rudy said, "What the—"

Without discussion, they both took off running. Rudy's legs were longer than hers, and he could easily out distance her, but he slowed his pace enough to stay by her side, for which she was grateful.

It was full dark now, and even though she was sure she could find her way home, she appreciated that she didn't have to watch for landmarks while keeping her head down against the pelting rain. Instead, she focused on Rudy's tennis shoes beside her.

They were both drenched and shivering by the time they reached the Wheeler's house. The moment they set foot on the porch the downpour stopped. Sudden silence surrounded them.

"Huh?" Rudy turned and looked out across the yard before opening the door. "That's odd."

"I'll say." Eden held out a hand, checking to see if rain still fell.

Nothing. Not even a sprinkle.

"That was some *sprinkle*." Scowling, she followed him inside and kicked off her shoes.

Rudy snorted as though trying to hold back a laugh but then gave up and busted out laughing.

Rolling her eyes, Eden joined him. It seemed to be one mishap after another with them.

Still laughing, Rudy shook his head, sending more water droplets flying her way.

"Hey! Keep your water to yourself. I'm wet enough."

"Are you sure about that?" His gaze roamed over her, and his laughter died when his eyes hit her chest.

Eden looked down and gasped. She'd forgotten she wore a white T-shirt. A T-shirt that now clung to her body, showing off the light blue bra she wore beneath it. She wrapped her arms around herself.

Frick! That's the second time he's seen my bra today.

Rudy cleared his throat. "You...uh... You can have the shower first."

"Thank you!" Eden darted down the hall.

She kept shaking her head as she made sure both bathroom doors were locked before stripping.

Will there ever be an end to the embarrassing situations between us?

As the hot water warmed her chilled body, she tried to ignore the warmth growing in her chest. Every time she turned around, Rudy was either saving her life or doing something incredibly thoughtful. It made it hard to keep telling herself she shouldn't get mixed up with him.

When she turned off the shower, she heard his voice on the other side of the door. "Where are you, Chase? They're killing me! You gotta come help me!"

So he is a gamer!

Eden didn't know why but that knowledge pleased her. Probably because he was the exact opposite of the kind of man her dad expected her to date. Not that she planned to date Rudy, but all of a sudden, she wasn't as opposed to the idea as she was a week ago.

CHAPTER 7

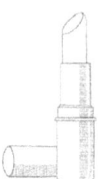

*E*den woke to the sound of the shower running.

Rudy must be getting ready for work.

A small smile spread over her face as she remembered the events of last night. Everything from watching Rudy play basketball with Chase to hiding Miss Georgie's cookies in his pockets made her laugh. Even the way his wet t-shirt clung to his pecs and abs made her smile, until she'd realized her own wet shirt had become see-through.

Hearing her phone vibrate on the nightstand, she grabbed it, fearing she'd find a text from her dad—it had been a few days since he'd hounded her to come home and do her duty. She turned it on to find tons of Instagram notifications. Her eyebrows rose.

For the first time in a long time, she'd posted a picture last night before going to bed. The dozens of jars of jam were simply too pretty not to share. She'd captioned it with: Yes, it tastes as good as it looks.

She was proud of herself for sticking with the hard work even though she'd wanted to quit on Alice many times.

Who knew making jam could make me feel so worthwhile?

Her Instagram feed was mostly selfies, showing off her cute—meaning expensive—clothing or pretty food pictures—prepared by someone else, of course—and pictures of her manicures.

Can't get much shallower than that.

Now that she had stepped away from her old life, she was beginning to see it in a whole new light, and she wasn't sure he liked the person she'd been.

She was by no means an influencer, but she had a significant number of followers. Followers who liked her jam post. Last night's post had hundreds of likes and dozens of comments ranging from *Yum!* and *So pretty!* to *Where can I buy some?*

Even as she scrolled through the comments, new ones came, many of them expressing interest in buying jam. She laughed when a comment saying, *Seriously, where can I buy some?* popped up.

She'd only helped Alice make the jam, but she'd never felt quite so popular. And happy. Being recognized for something other than her connections, brand-name accessories, and her business acumen felt good.

She waited until long after the shower shut off before getting out of bed and dressing. If she waited long enough, Rudy would leave for work, and she wouldn't have to cross paths with him. She'd embarrassed herself in front of him enough to last a lifetime.

When she finally made her way out to the kitchen, it was empty. While waiting for her toast to pop, she spotted Alice in the garden, pulling weeds. That woman was the hardest-working person Eden had ever met.

More likes and comments continued to show up as she nibbled on her jam-free toast. It had taken every ounce of her willpower not to slather the bread with the sweet berry concoction, but if she wanted to continue to fit into her clothes, she couldn't continue to indulge like she did yesterday.

Her gaze drifted to the dozens of jars of jam they'd made yesterday. She knew Alice intended to give some to her children for their families, and it wouldn't surprise her if she gave more away to neighbors and friends, but there were a lot of jars on the counter, and they'd be making more in another day or two when more strawberries ripened. Would Alice be interested in selling some of her jam to strangers from the Internet?

Alice came through the sliding back door, wiping her brow, as Eden finished her light breakfast. "Phew, it's muggy out there this morning after last night's rain." She smiled at Eden. "Did you manage to dry out sufficiently after your soaking?"

Eden laughed. "I think so."

After discussing the weather for a few minutes, Alice asked what her plans were for the day.

"I don't know. I should probably do some more job hunting." Although there wasn't likely to be anything new posted since she looked two days ago.

"Would you like to help me with something a little more entertaining?"

"Sure." Eden was all for avoiding the job search.

Within minutes the table was littered with red checkered fabric, funny-looking zigzag scissors that Alice called pinking shears, and a spool of thin brown twine.

Alice talked as she demonstrated how to cut a square of fabric and tie it over the top of the jar of jam. "Every summer, I take a few dozen jars to Miss Hattie's craft boutique to sell."

Alice sells her jam?

Should she tell her there were people on the Internet that would love to buy it? She mulled it around in her mind as she helped Alice. She still hadn't decided how to broach the subject by the time they finished tying the fabric squares to the tops of the jars.

"Would you like to come down to Miss Hattie's with me to drop these off?"

Eden tapped her lips. "Let me see. Go to a craft boutique or look for a job. Tough choice."

Alice laughed. "Well, help me carry the rest of these jars down to the storage room, then I'll get showered, and I'll take you to meet Miss Hattie after lunch."

When they reached the storage room, Eden stared in shock, her eyes growing wider by the second. She rotated and surveyed the small but full room. Jam wasn't the only thing Alice canned. Just about every fruit or vegetable that could be bottled sat on Alice's shelves.

Eden had heard about people who lived off the land and canned everything themselves, making themselves almost completely self-sufficient, but she'd never met one until now.

So this is how Bill and Alice managed to support a big family on a carpenter's and a school lunch lady's income.

Alice pulled two dozen jars of jam from last year off the shelf. "I always divide out the older jars among my kids every year. They eat a lot more than we do nowadays, especially now that Scott has moved out."

Eden laughed. "I don't know, I think I gave Scott a run for his money yesterday when it came to the homemade bread and jam."

"You did seem to enjoy it." Alice chuckled. "Next time I make bread, I'll teach you how."

"I'm not sure that's a good thing."

After she finished helping Alice, Eden went to get ready. She finally had something to dress up for. A trip to the boutique hardly warranted dressing up, but she was so excited to be going out, that she changed from her yoga pants and t-shirt to a cute, striped, short jumpsuit.

Surveying herself in the bathroom mirror, she decided the outfit justified a little make-up and more than a messy bun. She plugged in both her straightener and curling wand to heat up. Her hair wasn't curly, but it had enough body that she usually had to smooth out her waves before putting in loose curls.

She was almost done when Alice knocked on her door.

Eden opened it to find Alice had changed too. She looked nice in her tan capris and floral button-up blouse.

"We have a change of plans," Alice said. "Debbie needs me to watch the little ones this afternoon while she goes to the dentist. So if we're going to make it to the boutique today, we need to leave right away."

"Okay, I'll hurry and finish getting ready."

Eden hurried back to the bathroom to finish her last two curls while she considered which of her sandals would go best with her outfit. She'd just slipped her shoes on and was about to put her stuff away in the bathroom—minus the still hot wand and straightener—when Alice called her name.

I'll do it when I get back.

The last thing she wanted was for Rudy to find his bathroom a mess.

~

EDEN KEPT TELLING herself not to have too high of expectations about Hattie's Boutique. Especially when she saw that it was only a small shop in a strip mall, two doors down from *In Style* where she got her nails done last week. A For Rent sign sat in the corner of the window of the neighboring shop.

Places like this were usually stocked by local artisans after all. How many crafty women could there possibly be in this small town?

An awful lot, Eden realized a few minutes later as she walked the narrow aisles of Hattie's little store after meeting the owner. Hattie was much older than Eden had expected. The woman had to be in her late seventies.

Many of the handmade crafts on the shelves were simple and a dime a dozen like crocheted hot pads, place mats, matching baby blankets, bibs, and burp cloths, but the majority of the items that filled the shelves could easily rival the home decor one would find at Pottery Barn, Wayfair, and Crate & Barrel.

She could decorate her apartment, or even a whole house, by shopping here. Sure, the layout could be improved to create better aesthetics, but there were so many beautiful and amazing items here, she couldn't believe people weren't coming from miles around to shop at this quaint store. Okay, so there weren't many towns for miles, but still...

It wasn't only decor though. One corner of the store was dedicated to perishables like homemade fudge, caramels, cake pops, hot chocolate bombs, and organic honey, as well as Alice's jam. Another corner held personal care items like soaps, lotions, lip balms, body butter, and cupcake-shaped bath bombs that looked good enough to eat.

Encouraged by all the likes and comments she'd received on last night's jam post, Eden began snapping pictures, occasionally shifting items around to get a good shot. She spotted doilies that she was certain had been made by Miss Georgie, quilts and decorative throw pillows, crocheted afghans, and wall hangings with humorous or inspirational sayings—some hand painted and others in vinyl lettering.

The women in this town are talented!

Their talents were going to waste though. The population of this small town wasn't nearly big enough to support this store. If the only patrons who frequented the store were the same ones who provided the wares, it's no wonder Hattie's shelves were overflowing, and she and Alice were the only ones in the store.

Eden paused her perusing to post a few pictures on Instagram. After searching the Internet for Hattie's website so she could tag it and coming up empty handed, she went to the back of the store where Alice and Hattie visited.

"What do you think?" Alice asked.

"This place is amazing!" Eden shifted her gaze to Hattie. "What's your website? I'd like to tag you in my posts."

"Oh, I don't have a website." Hattie chuckled and waved her hand. "I don't have a clue about how to do that sort of thing."

Eden frowned. "How are people who aren't from Providence supposed to find you? You have so many beautiful things here."

Hattie shrugged. "I rely on the locals mostly and a few faithful customers from neighboring counties."

"That's it?" Eden looked around her. The full shelves made sense now. "Well, do you mind if I create a hashtag for your store to share on my story?"

"A what?" Horizontal creases lined the older woman's forehead as she stared at Eden like she'd sprouted an extra head.

Eden wasn't sure how to explain how social media worked to the older woman who didn't seem to have much of a grasp of technology.

"It's just a way for followers to know where my pictures originate from."

"Followers?"

"My friends."

"Oh sure, go ahead and share all the pictures you want with your friends."

Hattie had no idea that giving Eden permission to share her pictures online would put her crafts in front of thousands of people.

"Thank you." Eden turned away and continued to wander as she posted photo after photo.

Then she took even more pictures of ceramic table vases in coordinating colors, shapes, and sizes—some holding small flower arrangements—and beautiful framed watercolor prints. She paused and studied a pretty beach scene that had a familiar style. It reminded her of a couple pieces of art at the Wheeler's house. Examining the print more closely, she found a small S.R. in the corner.

"Beautiful, isn't it?" Alice said from behind her.

Eden jumped.

"Sorry, I didn't mean to startle you." She pointed at the picture. "My granddaughter is talented, don't you think?"

Eden's eyes widened as she stared at the picture and tried to remember the names of all of Alice's granddaughters. Besides the twins, who were only two, there was a six-year-old and four teenage girls. Then she recalled the massive mural on the wall in Debbie and Austin's house.

She looked at the initials again. "Savannah painted these?"

"Yes. Her high school art teacher and mentor, Jessie Winters, encourages her to sell her art. I just wish there was more of a market for it around here." Alice pointed to other paintings that had a different style—but were no less incredible—with the initials J.S.W. in the bottom corner.

"Me too." Eden said quietly. "She's very talented."

They both were, and they deserved to have their work seen and appreciated.

On the ride home, Eden finally asked Alice if she was interested in selling her jam online. She explained how she'd posted a picture of the jam they'd made last night and the overwhelming responses she was still receiving.

"You mean people want to buy our jam?" Alice asked as she parked the car in the garage but made no move to get out.

"There are people out there who avoid the big conglomerates at all costs and are willing to pay top dollar for organic, homemade products."

"But...my jam?"

Eden opened her phone and leaned an elbow on the center console to show Alice all the likes and the string of comments requesting jam. As she did so, likes and comments started showing up on the other posts she'd made while at Hattie's.

"See, people love this kind of thing and want to support the little guy."

Alice sat back and stared though the front windshield for a long moment. Finally, she shrugged. "We have a lot of jam right now, and it's still early in the strawberry season, so we'll be making more. I suppose we could sell some, but we'd have to figure out how to ship it."

"Don't you worry about that. I'll figure it out."

Eden's mind raced as a lightness filled her chest. She couldn't wait to get her computer and start doing some research.

"I'd have to buy more canning jars. That could get pricey."

"We'll price the jam accordingly. Maybe we could offer some sort of discount on the next jar if they ship the first one back." The idea sounded crazy even as she said it, but Eden loved the challenge of figuring out how they would make this work.

"Do you really think we could meet that kind of demand?" Alice looked at her with wide eyes.

"Probably not year-round, no. But..." Eden hesitated, fearing she was pushing Alice to do something she didn't want to do.

"But every jar we sell would be one less jar sitting on my shelf, collecting dust."

Eden grinned. "I don't want your family to go without. Maybe we should figure out how many you can afford to sell, then I can say that it's a limited time offer and when supplies are gone, they're gone."

"That's a good idea." Alice finally pulled the keys from the ignition.

They talked as they went into the house and fixed sandwiches for lunch.

"Do you think there would be a similar interest in raspberry jam next month and maybe even blackberry? Of course, they are a lot more work, because of the seeds. I try to get out as many as I can." Alice turned to Eden, her face thoughtful. "Would people like jellies and syrups?"

"I think I've created a monster." Eden laughed. "I can post pictures of some of your jars from last year and see what kind of response we get."

They continued to discuss the possibilities as they ate, and a steady stream of notifications continued to hit Eden's phone. Hundreds of likes streamed in within an hour and once again, people wanted to know where they could buy these things. Several asked for the link to her Etsy shop.

"Do you think the artisans who bring their wares to Miss Hattie's Craft store would be interested in selling them online?" she asked Alice as they tidied up the kitchen.

"Artisans?" Alice laughed. "That's a fancy word for people who craft." Then she tilted her head, and a slow smile covered her face. "I think if someone is willing to help them figure out how to go about it, they should be given the chance."

Eden's heart rate kicked up a notch, and her breathing came a little faster. She had never sold anything online, but she was a smart woman, she could figure this out. It couldn't be much harder than buying things online, could it?

"I can help them figure it out, but do you really think they'd be interested?"

"Let me tell you a little secret." Alice paused in the process of wiping off the counter. "People from small towns have big dreams, just like everyone else. Whether it's making money, finding a little fame, or creating a name for themselves. If you're willing to help do the hard work, I think you'll find a lot of people interested in selling their goods."

Eden wanted to do a little dance, but she settled for rocking up on her toes. She didn't know why she was so excited, but she loved the idea of helping these people recognize their potential.

As she drove back to Miss Hattie's, she realized helping these artisans find success wasn't all that different from what she used to do working for her dad. But it felt different. And for some reason, it was extremely important to her.

Now all she needed to do was get Miss Hattie and the crafty people in this town on board.

THE KITCHEN WAS empty when Rudy walked into the house on Wednesday afternoon. His stomach sank when he didn't find Eden in the kitchen.

Why am I disappointed?

He should be relieved Eden wasn't standing there wearing an apron that begged him to kiss her.

If she's not in the kitchen, does that mean she's in the bath again?

That thought caused tension to coil in his midsection.

Instead of heading to his room to change, he went downstairs in search of his mom. He found her in the downstairs family room with Debbie's little ones.

"Where's Eden?" He tried to keep his voice casual.

"I'm not sure at this point." Mom's shoulders bounced.

"What do you mean?" Rudy asked.

She hadn't left already, had she? That should please him, but it didn't. Did she leave because of him? Had he made her feel unwelcome?

Mom shifted little William away from the entertainment center. "Last I saw her, she was headed to Hattie's."

"The store?" Rudy cocked his head. "What's she doing there?"

He'd had a hard time picturing Eden as the domestic type, but Eden and crafts? That just didn't compute.

Mom raised an eyebrow as she regarded him. "I guess you could say she went to apply for a job."

"She wants a job at the boutique?" Rudy shook his head. "I wasn't aware Miss Hattie was hiring."

Was the boutique even that busy? Why on earth would Eden want to work there? It seemed so beneath her. Beneath her skills anyway.

Mom chuckled. "Hattie wasn't hiring, but I have a feeling she'll have a hard time saying no to Eden."

"What are you talking about?"

"Why are you so concerned about her?" Mom gave him a sly grin.

"I'm not. I just...don't understand."

She waved him away. "I'm sure she'll tell us all about it during dinner."

Still bewildered, Rudy went upstairs and changed his clothes. He stepped into the bathroom to wash his hands and froze. It looked like a hurricane had swept through the room. Makeup and hair accessories lay strewn across the counter along with funny looking V-shaped and pointy curling iron things that looked like dangerous weapons.

It was bad enough that her bottles of pretty-smelling body wash and hair care products in the shower—yes, he'd given into temptation this morning and smelled them—practically crowded his out, but now she'd invaded the rest of the bathroom along with her coconut scent.

He propped his hands on his hips and pressed his lips together. Scott used to always call him a neat freak, to which Rudy responded by calling him a slob—which he wasn't. But even Scott hadn't been this messy.

How long do I have to put up with this woman in my bathroom? In my house? Stuck in my head?

As soon as the thought filled his mind, he regretted thinking it. He didn't know exactly what Eden was going through, but he figured it must be major to cause her to leave her father and her job the way she had. He still wasn't sure it wasn't some sort of tantrum, but was she desperate enough to need a job at Hattie's?

He doubted Eden liked this situation any more than he did, but he wouldn't make her feel unwelcome. When she chose to leave, it wouldn't be because he drove her away.

Bending, he opened the drawers and cabinets. Even though she had totally invaded his life, there was plenty of room in the bathroom for both of them. He just needed to condense and organize the odds and ends in the drawers and maybe throw a few things away, then there would be room for her stuff.

An hour later, he stared across the table at the beautiful, raven-haired beauty with the heart-shaped face. There was something about her that made last night's glow of accomplishment after making jam look pale compared to her radiance tonight. Her hair was curled, and she wore makeup today, but her beauty tonight radiated from within.

Mom kept Eden talking so much she hardly had a chance to eat her food.

"So Miss Hattie decided having a website couldn't hurt as long as it didn't require any extra work from her, and she agreed to let me start selling the crafts online after I get permission from all the artisans." Eden met his gaze for a moment before pushing her fingers into her hair and flipping it to partially block her face from his view.

He probably made her uncomfortable with his staring, but he couldn't help wondering who this woman was. What had happened to Kennedy's snooty friend who turned her nose up and said, "That's it?" the first time they took her on a drive through Providence?

"I'll have to reach out to some of my old contacts to find someone who can build a website," Eden said before taking a bite of her chicken and rice casserole.

"Rudy can do that for you," Mom smiled at him. "Can't you?"

Rudy's chicken stuck in his throat. Sure, he could do it, but why was mom encouraging Eden at all, let alone trying to get him involved in her craziness? People like Eden didn't stick around small towns like this. This little pet project was probably just to keep herself from getting bored.

"He created the new website for the repair shop a few months ago."

Eden turned wide eyes on him. "You know how to build websites?"

He shrugged. "It's not that hard. There are plenty of tutorials online."

Some were even created by him.

Her lips turned up in a slow grin as she stared at him. "So, you're a geek too?"

"What's that supposed to mean?"

"Nothing." She gave a slight shake of her head, but her smile remained. "Would you mind helping me build a website for Miss Hattie's Boutique?"

He gave her a lazy smile. "I never mind, just ask my parents."

"Of course, he'll help you," Mom said, giving him the look that said behave and obey.

I haven't seen that look for years.

The smile he gave Eden tightened. "I'd be glad to help you."

That's how he found himself twenty minutes later secluded in his room with Eden. No, they weren't secluded, because Mom never allowed them to have the door closed when they had a member of the opposite sex in their room. So, not only was the door open, Mom had already walked into her bedroom across the hall twice and back out again.

Eden sat right next to him, however, in a dining chair. Close enough he could smell her coconut shampoo mixed with a subtle floral perfume.

Rudy listened to Eden talk for a few minutes about what she had in mind for Miss Hattie's website before opening a browser.

When it came time to pay for a domain, Eden cringed. "I forgot to talk to Miss Hattie about that part. I'll just pay for it for now." She got to her feet then froze. "I um... I don't have a credit card anymore."

Rudy's brows rose. "Why not?"

She dropped back into her chair. "My dad uh...froze my credit cards."

He leaned back in his chair and studied her face. "He cut you off, so you quit your job and left town?"

Sounds like a massive tantrum to me.

"No, he...cut me off *after* I refused to...compromise myself and bend to his will. Quitting my job was something I should have done a long time ago."

Compromise herself? What was her dad trying to get her to do?

He continued to stare at her until she flipped her hair from the left side to the right, shielding her face from him.

"And you have no intention of going back to work for him again?"

Her gaze dropped to her hands. "No."

"So you're going to work for Hattie? You realize working there won't even come close to replacing your corporate income, don't you?"

"I'm not getting a job at Hattie's. Well, she did say I could have ten percent of the online sales, but I'm not doing it for the money."

"Then why are you doing it?"

She shrugged one shoulder as she ran her thumb nail along the edge of his desk. "I don't know. These people are really talented, and I guess I just want to help them recognize their potential."

"Their potential? You think these people need help recognizing who they can become? Who do you want them to be exactly?" Rudy was trying hard not to take offense.

"No. I don't want to change them. Maybe potential was the wrong word." She waved a hand through the air. "I want everyone out in the world to realize how talented these people are. But no one is ever going to know if all they do is sell their goods in Hattie's little store."

Are her motives really that selfless?

She locked gazes with him. "Believe me, I don't understand my desire to help these people any more than you do. All I know is this is the first thing that has felt right in a really long time."

"Okay, then." He pulled his wallet from his pocket and fished out his credit card. "I hope you know what you're getting yourself into and won't let them down."

And I hope I don't regret trusting you.

CHAPTER 8

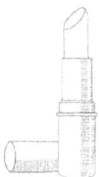

"This is what the website will look like." Eden leaned forward on the settee and placed her laptop on the coffee table and rotated it toward Hattie.

She clicked on one dropdown after another, giving Hattie a feel of how the website was organized: Art & Decor, Kitchen, Living, Bedroom, Bath & Body.

"Right now, I only have a handful of pictures in each of these categories. They'll expand as I get more pictures uploaded."

Even as she spoke, more ideas kept filling Eden's head for additions to the website and organizational changes that could be made here in the store that would create greater appeal and aesthetics.

"Wow. You did all this last night?"

"There's still a ton of work to do, but Rudy is great at this stuff." Eden pulled a notepad from her oversized purse. "I also talked to Ben Young. He should have some contracts written up for the vendors by Monday."

"This feels like a lot of work." Horizontal worry lines creased Hattie's forehead. "Are you sure it's worth it?"

Eden picked up her phone. "Look at these comments. People want to buy the things you're selling."

Hattie propped the glasses that hung from a chain around her neck on her nose and eyed Eden's phone. "Those photos you took turned out pretty good."

She'd had to apply a filter to some of them because she just couldn't get the lighting right, but they had turned out pretty good.

"I need to take more. In fact..." Eden pressed a finger to her lips for a moment. "I'd like to rearrange some shelves, if you don't mind, so we can create displays that combine mediums in appealing ways."

And lessen the inventory. People are more apt to buy when they think the beautiful vase is the last one.

"I suppose that would be okay." Hattie looked around the store. "It's been years since I changed things around here. It could definitely use a facelift." She rubbed her gnarled hands. "I'm afraid I can't provide much muscle, but I have a grandson who could help."

"That would be great. Let me do a few sketches of new layouts and we'll see what you think. Then I'll see if I can find some boxes, both for shipping the orders that are coming in and for emptying the shelves so we can rearrange them."

So many ideas floated through Eden's head as she studied the high ceilings and considered new lighting options. She wasn't sure what to focus on first.

"I have plenty of boxes." Hattie pushed to her feet and motioned for Eden to follow her.

Eden followed the older woman to a storage room in the back of the store. Her eyes widened as soon as she stepped through the door, and she fell back a step. She thought Miss Georgie was a hoarder. But her boxes full of yarn had nothing on Hattie's...stuff.

The chaos out front all makes sense now.

Eden let her gaze roam the storage room that was much more spacious than she first thought. Yet baskets, bins and boxes filled almost every square foot. Some of it was clearly old marketing and promotional stuff, some holiday decorations, along with excess inventory, and some were just plain junk.

A mountain of cardboard boxes of all shapes and sizes filled one corner. Extra furniture filled another. And a ladder and tool shelf filled a third.

"I used to have a space back here where I kept my kiddos when they were little." Hattie motioned to the corner that held an assortment of furniture. "Then several of my grandkids came here in the afternoons until Naomi finished cutting hair for the day."

"Naomi is your daughter?"

"Yes, and Susie is my granddaughter. They're the reason I kept this shop open and hung onto this monstrosity of a building this long. I wanted to make sure they had a place to run their business." Hattie's face fell as she looked around. "When I stopped having little ones coming here, I let the clutter take over."

"You own the entire building? As in all the shops?"

There was only one other shop—a photo studio—besides the salon since the space next door was currently vacant.

"Yes, and the apartments above them. Although one is empty right now, because it needs repairs I can't afford to make. My late husband was a businessman and real estate developer. This is the only investment he hung onto because I had my store here. Thank goodness, because I'm not near the businesswoman he was."

"I've heard you've kept this place open for over thirty years. That takes some business smarts."

"I've only been able to keep it open because of all the crafty women in this town. If it wasn't for them..." She let her words die off as she shook her head and looked around again. "It's not flourishing like it once did, back in the day."

Eden wrapped her arm around Hattie. "Well, we're going to change that. It's time to take this business into the twenty-first century."

EDEN HEAVED a sigh as she dropped onto the loveseat in the family room.

What a week!

She didn't think she'd ever worked so hard. Or felt so accomplished, even though she still had a ton of work to do.

Alice walked into the room. "How did your morning go?"

"It was quite productive." Eden brushed her hair back. "I've made substantial progress at Hattie's, both out front and in the back." Thank goodness Hattie agreed to let her throw some things away. "And more than half the artisans have signed their contracts already."

"That's great!"

They chatted a little longer about how excited the artisans were to sell their stuff online. Word had spread, and people were reaching out to Eden now, letting her know they wanted to be included. She'd started making a list of people to follow up with once she had everything in place.

She was a little concerned that some of the interested parties wouldn't make the cut with their simple little crafts. But she had a plan, and it included going through Miss Hattie's—well-kept but hand-written (of course, because nothing can ever be easy)—books to find the bestselling crafts and vendors. Those would be the first products available on the website. In the meantime, she'd do her best to fill orders from her Instagram posts as quickly as possible.

"Are you sure you don't want to take a break from all of this and go shopping in Pasco with me?"

Alice had a list a mile long of things she planned to shop for, including fabric, more canning supplies, and groceries. She'd be gone all afternoon, and Eden had things to do. So many ideas buzzed around in her head. She needed to get them out so she could make sense of them and organize them into a productive plan.

"I'd better stay home. I have a lot I need to do."

If Eden went shopping, she'd be tempted to spend money, and she couldn't afford to do that. Especially since she'd made it a point yesterday after helping Alice make more jam to go to the bank and withdraw the money to pay Rudy back.

She decided to just pay for the domain herself for now. If this venture was as successful as she hoped, then she'd discuss the expense with Hattie. Judging by how slow the store was the few days when she'd been there, the older woman didn't have a lot of extra money.

Eden considered it an investment. One she hoped would pay off. Even if this venture was successful, it would be a long time before she earned back the money she'd put into it already. That was one thing she needed to brainstorm this afternoon; how to advertise and market on a tight budget to ensure success.

"Okay, I'll see you in a few hours then," Alice said before walking out.

Eden curled her legs under her and pulled her computer onto her lap. Before bringing it to life, she tore open the bag of chocolate-covered cinnamon bears she'd splurged on. They were her weakness, but she felt less guilty if she thought of them as brain food.

She'd taken more photos over the last few days as she reorganized, and now, she needed to get them added to the website in a visually appealing way. As she worked, she couldn't help thinking about the time she'd spent working with Rudy. The man was as smart as a whip. Not only did he have the know-how to build the website, but he also had great ideas.

When he started manipulating the html code in the website's template to make it do what he wanted it to, she asked how he knew all this stuff. He shrugged and said he enjoyed learning and reading. Eden had a feeling he was being modest and that he knew even more than he let on about computers, websites, search engine optimization, and coding.

She was still surprised he'd agreed so easily to his mom's request to help her. She often saw a hint of hesitation—laced with annoyance—on his face when his mom asked him to do something that involved her, but he never said anything negative toward her or his mom. In fact, he cleaned up the mess she left in the bathroom the other day, making room for her in the drawers. Rudy had been nothing but patient with her despite the way she'd disrupted his life.

Four hours later, her chocolate covered cinnamon bears were gone, and she'd made substantial progress. She was excited about the plans she'd made. It still surprised her that Hattie had given her carte blanche to reorganize the store and run the website and online sales the way she wanted.

The woman either knew it was the only chance to increase the store's revenue, or she recognized it was time to take her business into the twenty-first century and felt overwhelmed trying to do it by herself. Maybe both. At any rate, Eden was excited to have a worthwhile project to do.

She jumped when a knock sounded on the front door. Rudy and his parents weren't home, and she wasn't expecting anyone, but not answering the door felt rude. Her leg muscles protested as she rose and made her way to the door. Her phone dinged with a text notification as she opened the door to find the last person she expected to see here in Providence.

"Dad? What are you doing here?" She fell back a step.

"It's time to pack your bags and come home," her father said in his demanding business voice. The one that commanded respect and obedience.

Eden shook her head and took another step back. "How did you find me?"

He shrugged as he stepped into the house. "I went to Kennedy's, and she told me you were staying here." He was far enough inside now that he closed the door behind him.

The text must be from Kennedy.

Why couldn't it have arrived a little sooner? Then she wouldn't have opened the door.

Her dad shook his head in disgust. "What are you doing here, Eden? You don't belong here with these people."

These people?

The Wheelers were amazing people. Some of the best she'd ever met. They were genuine and caring. She loved how Bill always kissed Alice when he came home from work and how they worked together in the garden.

His gaze drifted around the family room, and judging by his frown, he wasn't impressed.

"Who says I don't belong here?" she asked in a burst of courage.

"I raised you better than this." He swept his arm, motioning around the room.

Eden bristled. The Wheeler's house and furnishings were modest, sure, but they were comfortable and inviting. She liked it here.

Sucking in a deep breath, she squared her shoulders. "You raised me to be egotistical and vain."

"Stop being dramatic. I raised you to take pride in who you are and what you have. You were born into privilege, and with—"

"With privilege comes responsibility," Eden finished, her voice heavy with sarcasm.

It's the same old song and dance.

Dad showed up and said the words to remind her who she was, and now he expected her to dance.

She'd hoped when she saw her father again, he would have forgotten the whole nonsense with Tristan and exclusivity for the company. Apparently, that wasn't the case.

Exhausted already, yet knowing she had a battle ahead of her, she sank onto the loveseat.

Her father sat opposite her on the end of the couch. "Laurent is growing impatient."

"Then you'd better make it clear to him there won't be an engagement." She folded her arms and stared him down.

"He's decided you two would only have to be engaged for six months. He thinks that would be long enough—"

"Dad, I won't do it. I detest pretty much everything about Tristan, and I won't let him—or Laurent—use me and make a fool of me."

"You can have whatever you want, if you'll just come home and do this one thing." He leaned forward. "I won't hound you to come back to Dupont Analytics anymore. I'll unlock your credit cards."

"Just stop—" Eden's voice caught as emotion clogged her throat.

Her dad was still worried about the company more than he was about her, and it hurt. She used to think she was the center of his world, but that changed somewhere along the line, and now she questioned when that had happened.

How long have I been a pawn for him?

This time when she folded her arms, it wasn't an attempt at defiance, but rather as a shield. She swallowed back the emotion and attempted to keep her voice steady. "I'm sorry you feel like I've failed you and the company, but I need to do what's right for me." She lifted her chin and met his gaze, even though she didn't feel nearly brave enough right now to face her father down.

"Which is what? Play perpetual house guest to Kennedy's in-laws, and throw away your skills and education?"

Eden didn't answer because he was right. She didn't know how long she planned to stay here. She hadn't even looked for a job in the past week. She'd been too busy. Sure, she was using her experience and business skills to help Hattie, but it wasn't something she planned to do long term.

Her father leaned back and scrubbed his hands over his face. A sure sign he was losing his patience, but Eden refused to give in. She couldn't. She'd sacrificed too much to win the independence that she had.

"If you were involved with someone else, I'd be willing to let this rest, but you're acting as irresponsible and careless as Tristan."

How dare he compare me to Tristan?

Eden ignored the last part of her dad's comment, despite the heat burning in her chest. Instead, she latched onto the first thing he'd said.

If there was someone else, he'd let it rest.

There wasn't anyone else, except...

Her mind jumped to Rudy. To the way he played basketball with Chase, replaced the bathroom locks, and cleaned up the mess she'd left in the bathroom. Then an image of him shirtless filled her mind, and warmth flooded her midsection.

She'd tried to keep herself from thinking too much about him—which was a constant struggle—because she'd realized he was as much a hero as the men in the romances she read. In fact, with all she'd learned about him in the last few days, she could easily see herself falling for him.

She couldn't let that happen though, because even though this little town wasn't as bad as she'd first thought, she couldn't see herself staying here forever.

"Is there someone else?" Dad straightened up and narrowed his gaze on her.

Eden resisted the urge to fidget. If she had time to discuss her dilemma with Rudy, he might agree to help her out, but... Could she sell it on her own?

Just as she opened her mouth to fabricate a big fat lie, the front door opened, and in walked her knight in a uniform.

Hopefully, he wouldn't hate her for what she was about to do.

CHAPTER 9

*R*udy shoved the last bite of the cookie he'd snatched from the break room at work into his mouth as he turned down his street.

He let out a long low whistle at the sight of the shiny Chevrolet Corvette Stingray parked in front of the house. They had a visitor. A rich one.

He climbed from his truck and strolled to the house, admiring the pearly white car sitting in his usual parking spot.

Torn between wanting to know who their guest was and remaining on the porch admiring the sleek lines of the sports car, he finally pushed open the front door.

Eden shot up off the couch as though she'd been burned. She rushed over to him wearing a stiff smile. "I'm so glad you're home. I missed you today."

Her intense, wide-eyed, pleading expression triggered a warning bell in his head. When she rocked up on her toes and planted a soft kiss on his cheek, his internal alarm went haywire. It didn't help that she wrapped her arms around his neck and hugged him.

"Please, play along," she whispered with a note of desperation.

He stiffened, then slowly placed his arms around her back and whispered, "What's going on?"

"I'll explain later, but please pretend you're my boyfriend." Her warm breath tickled his neck sending all kinds of pleasant sensations skittering across his skin. And the smell of her coconut-scented...

Wait! Boyfriend?

"*This* is why you didn't want to get engaged to Tristan?" Oliver Dupont rose from the couch almost as fast as Eden had. Disapproval filled his deep voice.

Rudy had only met Eden's dad once before, at Scott and Kennedy's wedding. Even though he'd seemed like a nice enough man, there had been an air of disdain and condescension about the polished man. Today was no different.

So he's the owner of the stingray.

Rudy wished he'd lingered outside a little longer. Or better yet, loitered at work.

Eden remained tense as she released Rudy and stepped to his side. The closer her father got, the more her shoulders rounded, and she shrank against Rudy.

Oliver stood directly in front of them now, his face hard and his gaze probing. "How long has this been going on?" He pinned Rudy with his glare.

Rudy had no idea how to respond, so he didn't. He simply held the other man's gaze, unflinching—even though that's exactly what he felt like doing.

When Oliver shifted his glare to Eden, she leaned closer and fisted a hand in the back of his shirt.

Whether as a plea or an anchor, Rudy wasn't sure. He didn't know what was going on between Eden and her father, but he didn't like how she shied away from him.

She shot him another pleading look before leaning her head against his shoulder, giving him another whiff of her coconut shampoo. The same scent that drove him crazy every time he walked into the bathroom. It made him imagine things he had no business thinking about.

It didn't help that his mom kept pushing them together.

Rudy slipped an arm around Eden, pulling her a little closer to his side. Squaring his shoulders, he looked Oliver in the eye. "A while now."

Even if Oliver believed him, which judging by his furrowed eyebrows, he didn't, Rudy had only met Eden two months ago, right before the wedding. There's no way the two of them could be serious.

Oliver's heavy brows lowered, and his eyes narrowed. "How serious are you two?"

Not. Not serious at all.

Eden wrapped her other arm around his waist. "I like Rudy, Dad."

Rudy's heart beat a furious staccato against his ribcage.

She doesn't mean it, of course. She's just trying to get her dad off her case.

That knowledge did nothing to dispel the strain between his shoulder blades. Ever since Eden moved in last week, a tension he couldn't shake had consumed him. Even the late-night workouts he'd done after working side by side on the website with her hadn't eased the tension that permeated the air any time he was near her.

Eden loosened her hold, and sidestepping her dad, she led Rudy to the loveseat.

He usually went to his room and took off his gun before relaxing at home. It was a mental exercise he'd learned to do, like shaking off all the bad things that happened that day and letting them go. Today, looking at Oliver's lowered brow and pinched lips, he appreciated the extra confidence the gun and badge gave him as he settled in beside Eden.

When he put his arm along the back of the sofa, she leaned into him, but her posture remained stiff. He lowered his arm to rest on her shoulders and pulled her a little closer, hoping to make her appear less tense. The position felt strange, yet perfect.

Wouldn't mom love to see me snuggling with Eden already?

Was it considered snuggling with her dad staring at him like he'd love to filet him?

Oliver shook his head as he sat on the couch again. "Are you sure this is what you want?"

Eden was quiet for so long Rudy wondered if she intended to ignore her father's question.

Finally, in a quiet voice, she said, "I want to see where this goes."

A surge of electricity sparked in Rudy's chest and spread outward, making him suck in a deep breath.

She doesn't mean it. She's only saying it for her father's benefit.

Oliver shook his head again. This time, the look he gave Rudy was one of disgust rather than disbelief. His gaze shifted back to Eden. "You really intend to turn your back on everything you've worked so hard for... for this? For a mediocre life in an inconsequential town."

Heat filled Rudy's chest at the way Oliver talked down to them.

What an arrogant prick!

He opened his mouth to throw a few big words of his own at Oliver, but Eden beat him to it. "This town is not inconsequential, and neither are the people in it. They just have different priorities. Not everyone has to live up to your expectations to be happy, Dad."

Rudy stole a sideways glance at Eden as he tightened his arm around her. A light flush colored her cheeks. She'd never looked quite so beautiful. If her father wasn't sitting right in front of them, he'd be tempted to kiss her. He hoped she meant the words she said. Her defense of his family and their small town raised his esteem for her.

Resignation tinged Oliver's voice when he spoke again. "You're right. I'm sorry." He shot Rudy a quick apologetic glance, but then his brows lowered again, and he waved a hand at them. "I just don't believe this."

Eden cleared her throat and scratched her neck. "Believe what?" Her voice sounded unnaturally high, and tension lifted her shoulders again.

Was it the lie they were trying to sell that made her agitated? Or was it her father's disapproval?

"The two of you. Although you make an attractive couple, I have a hard time believing you've fallen for a simple sheriff's deputy from some two-bit town."

Rudy wanted to bristle. To defend himself and his beautiful little town. But he'd known people like the DuPont's before. He'd seen the look on Eden's face when she first visited Providence. It had looked a lot like her father's did now.

Despite her words of defense, Rudy struggled to believe Eden would fall for him and want to stay in a small town like Providence. That's why he'd tried to keep his distance from her.

Eden pitched forward. "Right, because it's so much more *responsible* of me to fall for a billionaire playboy who will publicly humiliate me when he cheats on me. Or maybe you'd rather me fall for a boring investment banker who only ever talks about capital, dividends, and stocks? Or how about a narcissistic, morally gray, criminal defense attorney?" She punctuated her words with a small cough.

Rudy wasn't sure where her burst of courage came from, but if those were the kind of guys Eden dated, no wonder Oliver couldn't believe she'd fall for a small-town sheriff's deputy.

Oliver's piercing gaze jumped back and forth between them, pinning first Eden then Rudy. Once again, his gaze narrowed as he shook his head. "I'm not buying it."

"What do you mean?" Eden scratched her neck again before putting her hand on Rudy's thigh and stroking his leg.

She was only trying to convince her father there was something between them, but warmth immediately penetrated his polyester pants. The desire to pull her even closer ricocheted through him.

Would Oliver be convinced if he hauled Eden onto his lap?

"I don't think the two of you are in love." His eyes locked on Eden. "I think you're just trying to get out of coming home and doing your duty."

"When did duty become more important than love?" A hard edge filled Eden's words.

Rudy coughed this time. "It's still early. I'm not sure we're at the love stage yet."

Oliver's gaze pinned him now. "I thought you said this has been going on for a while now. Are you toying with my daughter for your own amusement?"

"No, sir!"

I'm not doing anything with your daughter. At least I wasn't until a few minutes ago.

Eden cleared her throat and scratched her neck, leaving a red mark there. "What do we have to do to prove to you we're serious?"

Oliver leaned forward and propped his elbow on his knees, his gaze never leaving Eden. This time he pinned Eden with his stare. "Kiss him."

"What?" The word burst out of her so fast, her father was sure to know this was all fake.

Rudy stroked her upper arm to calm her down.

"You have kissed, haven't you?" Oliver's expression was a sneer now.

Kissing?

Rudy had all kinds of qualms about going there with Eden. He feared that once he cracked that door open, a flood of passion would sweep in, ripping it right off its hinges. There would be no way to shut out the constant desire to pull her into his arms and kiss her until they both gasped for air.

Eden's hand gripped his thigh a little tighter. "Of course we have." Her voice was half an octave higher than usual. She looked up at Rudy with another pleading expression—or maybe this one was an apology. "Haven't we, honey?"

Rudy's throat tightened as he looked into her brown eyes, noticing for the first time the golden flecks in her irises. He pushed a strand of hair back from her face and cupped her cheek. "All the time. I mean, I can hardly keep my hands off you." Did his voice betray the tremor that reverberated through him?

Maybe that was laying it on a bit thick. Eden apparently thought so because her eyes widened, and her fingers dug into his leg.

He doubted a quick peck on Eden's lips would satisfy Oliver. No, this needed to be a genuine kiss. The kind Rudy had dreamed about giving Eden. The kind that would drive him crazy, leaving him wanting more.

Eden's tongue darted out, moistening her red lips, and Rudy's breath hitched. He took a moment to stroke his thumb across her cheek before slowly lowering his mouth to hers. Her eyes drifted closed, and he closed his own.

I can't believe I'm doing this.

Her lips were every bit as soft as he'd imagined, and the moisture that remained there only ramped up his desire. He did his best to tamp it down by reminding himself this wasn't real and that they had an audience.

First kisses were often awkward and hesitant as each participant wondered whether the other one truly wanted this, and how deep did each expect the kiss to be? First kisses in front of an audience were even worse.

Did Oliver—or Eden for that matter—expect this kiss to be close lipped or open-mouthed? He doubted either of them expected tongue action. But when Eden's grip on his leg tightened, and she leaned into the kiss, he found his lips applying enough pressure to encourage hers to part. When they did, he couldn't help himself; he claimed her mouth in a kiss that could be classified as anything but sweet.

His hand slid from her cheek into her thick hair of its own volition and with gentle pressure against the back of her head, he guided her mouth more firmly against his and deepened the kiss. He was vaguely aware of her gripping his tie and tugging. A rush of sensations swept through him. The foremost was a surge of warmth and electricity that consumed him, making his whole body feel tingly and aware.

The hint of chocolate and cinnamon on her breath only made him eager to taste more. The moist warmth of her mouth yielding to his, her lips shifting and moving under his, amplified his hunger. And her smell... Not just her coconut shampoo, but the subtle scent of her floral perfume mixed with her natural feminine essence created a fragrance that he wanted to surround himself with forever. Like snuggling up under a fleece blanket on a cold winter day.

Except today wasn't cold. It was hot outside. And it was roasting in here, despite the air conditioning that his dad kept at sixty-nine degrees. Heat continued to build in him as his blood pumped harder and faster in his veins, and his breath grew ragged.

It was exactly as he'd feared; he never wanted to stop kissing Eden.

A loud guttural sound filled the room when Oliver cleared his throat, reminding Rudy they had an audience.

He broke the kiss and sucked in a deep breath. His gaze darted to Eden's eyes before he pulled his hand from her hair. Her wide pupils suggested she felt the same desire that coursed through him, but he feared he'd been too intense with the kiss.

She gave him a faint smile before turning her head and coughing twice.

As the fog of their kiss lifted from his brain, he registered pain in his leg where Eden's hand had previously burned a hole. He looked down to find her fingernails digging into his thigh. He covered her hand with his and discreetly pried her nails away, holding her fingers captive with his.

"You obviously have chemistry and have done that more than once."

Guess we fooled him.

Oliver's eyes again bore into Eden. "You're sure this is what you want? I raised you with wealth and financial stability." He waved a hand at Rudy. "You'll never have that with him."

A different type of heat rushed through Rudy now. He was about to lean forward and give Eden's pompous father a piece of his mind when her movements distracted him.

She scratched her neck again and tugged at the collar of her T-shirt. "I want to make my own choices." She said the words firmly before clearing her throat again.

Rudy studied the woman beside him. Her neck showed angry red marks, and the edges of her eyelids appeared red, maybe even a little puffy. It reminded him of how she looked after the bee stung her two weeks ago.

Something's wrong with her. This isn't just agitation from lying to her father.

Oliver stood and made a scoffing sound before Rudy could ask Eden if she was okay. "Fine, but don't expect financial help from me." He walked straight to the door.

Rudy rose too. He was torn between wanting to smack Oliver for not noticing his daughter's dilemma and getting the man out of the house as quickly as possible. After making sure the door was closed tightly behind the man, he spun to face Eden.

"Are you okay?"

"No." Clearing her throat, she pushed to her feet and headed to her room. "I'm having an allergic reaction." Her cheeks now sported small red splotches.

With his heart lodged in his throat, Rudy followed her, fearing she might go into full-blown anaphylactic shock again. He watched from her doorway as she pulled her inhaler from her purse and inhaled a puff, followed by another. She sat on the end of her bed before opening a tiny box and slipping something into her mouth.

He stepped into her room. "Are you going to be okay? You kind of look like you did after that bee stung you." He dropped onto the other corner of her bed.

"I feel like it." She cleared her throat again and fanned her face. "I'm not sure what's causing it." Her eyes narrowed on him. "Did you eat something with nuts this afternoon?"

Rudy's stomach bottomed out, and he tugged on his collar as heat rushed to his face. "Um... I ate a cookie as I left work. I think it had walnuts in it."

She smacked his arm. "You knew you were coming straight home, and you know I'm allergic."

"Yeah, but I didn't know I'd be kissing you."

Or that I'd enjoy it so much.

"You're right." Sighing, she shoved her fingers into her hair and flipped it to the other side of her head. "I'm so sorry about all of that." She waved a hand toward the living room. "When I asked you to play along, I had no idea he'd force us to kiss."

"What was that all about, anyway? What's going on between you and your father?"

When he met them both at the wedding, he thought they had a good relationship, but there was certainly tension between them today. Her father was the reason she was here and avoiding her life in Spokane indefinitely.

"Kennedy didn't tell you?"

Rudy shook his head. "She just said you were going through some stuff."

"That's putting it mildly." Eden snorted, then flopped back on the bed and stared at the ceiling. "Have you ever heard of Laurent Jordain?"

"The tech guru who's worth a bazillion dollars?"

"That's him. Have you heard of his son, Tristan Jordain?"

Rudy's brow furrowed as he searched his memory. "Can't say that I have."

"He's a major playboy, living it up with daddy's money. He shows up in the tabloids occasionally, but he's all-over social media, always with a different woman and usually at a party or on a bender."

When Eden stopped talking, Rudy responded with a drawn out, "Okaaay?" to prompt her to continue.

"Laurent wants Tristan to shape up and step up within his company." She rolled her head to the side to look at him. "Laurent and my dad have decided I'm the one who needs to help him clean up his act."

"And how are you supposed to do that? He's a grown man, he's going to do what he wants to do."

Although with a woman like Eden in his life, Rudy had a feeling he could be persuaded to do a lot of things he might not otherwise do.

"Exactly. He's not going to suddenly change his ways just because we pretend to be engaged."

"Engaged? Wait, what?"

Eden let out a sigh that sounded like a huff. "Our dads are in cahoots. Laurent will help Dupont Analytics get exclusivity rights with some bigwig companies, if I pretend to be Tristan's fiancée."

"Meaning you have to be seen out in public with him at all the right places?"

She stared back up at the ceiling. "Yes, Laurent's hoping if Tristan is engaged, he'll stop messing around with every woman he sets eyes on. But I know Tristan, and it would only be a matter of time before he's caught slinking around with someone else."

"And your dad is not concerned about how that will reflect on you?"

Eden blinked rapidly, as though fighting tears. Her voice was quiet when she spoke again. "No, he's only concerned with how much money this deal could make the company."

"Is that why you quit your job? To spite him?"

She looked at him again. Weariness covered her face, and sadness filled her eyes. "I quit because I'm tired of being his puppet."

"How so?"

Was Eden not the shallow, selfish Daddy's girl he thought she was?

EDEN SAT up on the bed and tucked one leg under her. She pulled lip gloss from her purse and rubbed it on her lips that still tingled from their kiss. Then she took the cinnamon-flavored breath mints from her purse and put one in her mouth. It wouldn't erase the memory of that incredible kiss, but maybe it would distract her mouth a little.

"Would you like one?" She held them out to Rudy.

He chuckled. "Was my breath that bad?"

His breath had been pleasant, except for the part where it irritated her throat. And the taste of his kiss...

Warmth filled her face and abdomen at the memory. Eden had never been kissed quite like that; tender yet assertive and gentle yet passionate. And the firmness of his thigh under her hand...

Holy smokes! Talk about hard as a rock!

Just sitting beside him had warmed her in a way the summer sun never could. He smelled so good, which was odd, since it had been hours since he'd showered. He had a spicy and earthy scent to him, a natural male musk that she found very pleasant. She'd heard of people who were attracted to their spouse because of pheromones, but she'd never experienced it until now. Of course, that wasn't the only thing about Rudy that attracted her.

With great effort, she pulled her thoughts from their kiss. "No. I just hate the aftertaste the inhaler and Benadryl leave in my mouth. However, your breath was, and still is, tainted with walnuts."

"Right, sorry." He took a mint and popped it into his mouth. He sucked on it for a moment before opening his mouth and exhaling heavily. "That's hot!"

She laughed. "It's got a strong flavor, but it's not *that* hot."

He rolled it around in his mouth for a minute, then stomped his foot and shook his head. "How do you enjoy this?"

"You are *so* dramatic." She laughed again, harder this time.

She thought about what Bill said the other night about being passionate, and now, after kissing Rudy, she agreed. He was passionate, but he was still dramatic.

"I'm not dramatic." He quickly chewed the mint, breathing with his mouth open. "I don't know why you like those things."

"Cinnamon is my favorite." She shrugged as she tucked her mint into her cheek. "Listen, I'm sorry again for pulling you into my family drama." She flipped her hair over her head again as agitation built in her. "My dad refuses to let this thing with Tristan go. It's driving me crazy. When he said he'd understand if there was someone else..." She let her words die off and made a rolling motion with her hand so Rudy would understand why she'd acted the way she had.

"You needed a scapegoat." He nodded his head in understanding. Fortunately, he didn't seem to be angry. "Will he let it go now that he thinks we're together?"

"I hope so." She let out a heavy sigh. "All my life, he's dictated what he thinks I should do. I haven't always been happy about it, but I've done what he wanted. However, this... This is all too much."

"Why have you always done everything he asked, if it wasn't what you wanted too?"

She lowered her gaze to the bedspread and traced the stitching with her thumbnail. "I thought that's what I had to do to be an obedient daughter."

"Respect and obedience to a parent doesn't mean total acquiescence."

"I know, but..."

How did she explain something that no longer made sense to her either?

"But what?"

She continued to study the bedspread as she talked. "When I was ten, my mom and I were in a car accident. A truck ran a red light and broad-sided us in the driver-side door."

Rudy inhaled sharply, then swore under his breath.

Eden lifted her gaze to find his eyes hooded and his jaw set. His hands balled into fists, much like they had the other night when he talked about Chase's accident.

"I'm so sorry." His voice was as strained as the rest of his body.

"Thank you." Eden blinked back tears as she struggled to find the words she'd never told anyone before, not even Kennedy. "It was my fault."

"What? No. You said the truck ran a red light."

"I know, but... If I hadn't been distracting my mom, she might have seen it coming and been able to avoid it somehow."

"Not likely."

Eden lost her battle against the tears. "I was throwing a fit about stopping for ice cream after my dance class. She kept insisting it was too close to dinnertime, but I wouldn't let it go." She swiped at her cheeks as guilt and regret filled her.

"She was in bad shape, but she was conscious for a bit and insisted on talking to me before they took her away in the ambulance. She must have known she wouldn't make it, because she made me..." Eden ran a shaky hand through her hair again. "She made me promise I'd be a good girl for Daddy."

Rudy reached over and wrapped a large hand around hers. "And you thought that meant you had to do everything he asked?" His voice was as gentle as his touch.

Eden nodded. "When we left the cemetery a few days later, Dad wrapped his arm around me and said, 'It's just you and me now. I promise I'll take care of you, but I need you to be a good girl for me, okay?'" She stared at their hands as she continued to talk. "So, I tried to be the perfect daughter. I received love and acceptance from him when I did what he asked. But when I went against his wishes, I got lectures about how I'd disappointed him and needed to act more responsibly."

"I think all kids, especially teenagers, get those kinds of lectures, but I imagine you took it more personally than most kids."

"I did, and I let it dictate my life, my schooling, my job. I did everything he wanted. I didn't realize until a few years ago how unhappy I was, and I asked myself how I'd gotten here. I'm not sure if he even realizes he does it. I know he loves me. I'm just not sure he knows how to show it."

"I'll say." Rudy snorted as he withdrew his hand.

"Anyway, thanks for saving me out there and not throwing me to the wolves." She gave him a tight smile.

"So, was that a one-time thing? Or will we need to continue this charade for his benefit?" Rudy rubbed his hands against his thighs, and Eden couldn't help remembering how firm that muscle was beneath her hand.

"I don't know. I'd love to hear him say he's dropping the whole Tristan thing, but I'm not sure he really believed us. And if Laurent continues to pressure him..." She left her sentence hanging and shrugged.

"Well, at any rate, it might be best to keep this between us." He motioned back and forth between them. "The last thing my mother needs is more ammunition to work with."

Eden chuckled. "She seems pretty intent on pushing us together, doesn't she?"

"Yes, but you and I both know that's not a good idea."

Eden's smile faded. She kept telling herself falling for Rudy was a bad idea, so why did hearing him agree with her feel like a rejection? Was he really that averse to a relationship with her?

She scrambled to hide her hurt. "Right, because I'll be leaving soon."

"Will you?" His gaze narrowed on her.

Was that disappointment on his face?

"I don't know. I love what I'm doing for— I mean *with* Hattie, but you said it yourself; it won't replace my corporate income. Eventually, I'm going to have to find a serious job. We both know that won't happen in Providence."

When had she started to think that maybe she could stay in Providence if only there was a real job for her here?

CHAPTER 10

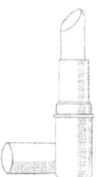

*E*den climbed from Alice's car and studied Debbie and Austin's house. It was a little larger than the house she grew up in. But she knew from having attended Sunday dinners here it was much warmer and more inviting than her childhood home.

Not only was it filled with love and laughter, but it was also filled with acceptance. Debbie didn't get angry when one of the kids made a mess, instead she took them by the hand and helped him clean it up, all the while discussing what they could have done to be more careful.

Austin and Debbie's blended family was far from perfect. They certainly had their share of challenges, but there was no doubt in Eden's mind that Debbie loved Austin's kids, and he doted on her adopted daughters. And the little boy they adopted right after they got married was the chunkiest and cutest baby Eden had ever seen.

"Eden, dear, would you carry this basket?" Alice lifted a laundry basket full of food and supplies from the trunk of her car.

Who knew laundry baskets could be so versatile?

Alice handed it to Eden, then grabbed a second one. "Oh, shoot! I forgot to grab the bacon from the fridge." She set her basket back into the trunk and pulled out her phone. "I'm going to call Rudy. Maybe I can catch him before he heads over to work on Scott's house."

"Okay, I'll take this stuff inside."

Kennedy opened the door for Eden. "You've come to join in the craziness, huh?"

"Well, you know Alice. She's a hard person to say no to."

"She is, but believe me, you're going to have a blast. These ladies are a hoot. I look forward to this every month. Each of us brings all the ingredients to make one meal for everybody. We get to visit while we work together to assemble the freezer meals, and then I get to take five meals home. They're great for really busy days."

Eden had enjoyed getting to know Rudy's sisters when she worked with them to help plan Kennedy's wedding. They were all friendly and talkative—apparently, Scott was the only quiet one in the family. Despite this, she braced herself, certain, she'd feel like an outsider.

"Oh, Eden, we're so glad you came!" Sheila was the first to greet her.

"It'll be so great to have an extra set of hands." Joy gave her a brief one-arm hug.

Debbie's greeting was less enthusiastic as she pressed a hand to her stomach, mumbled, "Excuse me," then hurried down the hall.

All eyes followed the oldest sister.

Joy looked at the others. "Have Debbie's kids been sick? Should we have scheduled this for another day? I can't afford to come down with something. We're taking the kids on vacation in two weeks, and I have way too much to do between now and then."

"I hope there's not something going around." Sheila shook her head. "We're planning to go out of town around the same time, too. If my kids are sick, I won't dare take them to Mason's Grandma's eight-ieth birthday party."

Alice came into the kitchen and looked around. "Where's Debbie?"

Three of the five women in the room pointed down the hall, but it was Sheila who spoke. "She just hurried to the bathroom, looking like she was going to puke. Has her family been sick?"

"Not that I know of." Alice shot a concerned look down the hall. "Should I go check on her?"

"Let's give her a minute," Joy said.

"Good idea." Alice clapped her hands. "Okay, who's going first?"

"My recipe has chicken in it," Sheila said, "so we should probably get them made up and in the freezer right away."

The women shifted baskets and coolers around, so Sheila could lay out the ingredients for her chicken cordon bleu casserole. They were almost ready to assemble when Debbie returned to the kitchen.

"Are you okay?" Alice asked. When a pale Debbie nodded, she put an arm around her. "How long have you been sick?"

"A couple of weeks now." Debbie slid onto a bar stool.

"A couple of weeks!" Alice exclaimed. "Why haven't you seen a doctor?"

"I did last week."

"Yet you're still sick? Did he say what's wrong with you?"

"I lied when I asked you to watch the little ones while I went to the dentist." Debbie gave Alice a sheepish look. "I actually went to go see my OB/Gyn."

"Are your ovarian cysts bothering you again already?" Sheila asked.

A small smile lifted Debbie's lips. "No. Turns out it's morning sickness."

All the women in the room gasped except for Eden. She saw nothing surprising about Debbie being pregnant. Sure, they already had a big family with six kids, but if Austin and Debbie wanted children of their own, it was best not to wait, since Debbie was in her late thirties.

"I thought you said you couldn't have kids?" Joy sat down on one side of Debbie at the same time Alice sat on the other.

No wonder they're all shocked.

"The way my doctor in Seattle put it years ago, 'my chances of ever getting pregnant were slim to none.' And after two failed IVF treatments, I believed him."

"But how?"

"That's what I asked my new doctor. He explained that having the cysts and scar tissue removed and the endometrium cleaned out last fall most likely aided in my ability to conceive."

"Did you have the surgery hoping you'd be able to get pregnant afterward?" Sheila leaned across the counter to look at Debbie.

"No. I had the surgery because it had all become so painful I could barely care for my little ones."

"And now you're going to have another little one to care for." Joy hugged Debbie. "This is so exciting! Does Austin know?"

"Yes. He's the one who insisted I go to the doctor last week. He was as shocked as I am, but he's happy about it."

"So, why didn't you tell us sooner?" Sheila asked.

Tears filled Debbie's eyes. "Well, I'm only nine weeks. But also, because my old doctor told me if I was fortunate enough to get pregnant, having PCOS would likely cause me to miscarry."

Joy snorted. "I think we've all figured out that your old doctor was an idiot."

"Dr. Madden, my new doctor, plans to watch my hormones carefully, but he's optimistic I'll be able to carry the baby to term." Fresh tears ran down Debbie's cheeks.

Eden sensed a presence behind her just as Rudy whispered. "What's going on?"

His warm breath tickled her ear, sending a tingly shiver down her spine.

"Debbie just announced that she's pregnant."

"Seriously?" His brows shot up. Then a gorgeous grin split his face. "I figured it must be something big. I didn't know my sisters could be this quiet."

She gave a soft laugh and turned so he could see her roll her eyes.

His gaze held hers for a long moment before dipping to her lips. They felt suddenly dry under his scrutiny, so she licked them.

He sucked in a sharp breath. "I'd better go." He turned away, then quickly pivoted back. "Here." He thrust two packages of bacon into her hand.

Sucking in a sharp breath of her own, she tuned back into the conversation. The women were still discussing Debbie's pregnancy, and a sense of despondency swept over Eden. A powerful feeling of loss settled low in her abdomen, causing it to clench. It was all she could do to keep from pressing a hand to her stomach.

The emotion surprised her. It wasn't like she'd ever lost a baby. So why did she suddenly feel so melancholy?

She'd always dreamed of living close to Kennedy and having babies together someday, but that dream had always seemed so far in the future. Until her best friend moved away and got married, leaving Eden behind.

With no prospect of marriage, Eden had thrown herself into her work, determined to be a career woman. But she'd only grown more discontented over time.

Was a baby, or rather a family of her own—what she'd been longing for?

She shook the notion from her head before shifting her gaze to her friend. Kennedy wore a radiant smile that looked almost secretive, and Eden had to wonder what it meant.

Was she just happy for Debbie? Or was she dreaming of having her own babies?

The women soon got to work trimming and cutting meat, chopping vegetables, and adding seasonings to assemble casseroles and Crockpot freezer meals. There seemed to always be at least one conversation going on, sometimes two. Amid the banter and gossip, bits of advice for Debbie kept popping up from her sisters and mom, concerning what to expect with her pregnancy.

And with each one, Eden's melancholy grew. Even though she hadn't enjoyed her job in recent years, she loved what she was capable of as a businesswoman. The satisfaction she felt when she helped someone save their struggling business was unparalleled. But now she wondered if she'd been missing something.

Were children in her future? What would that mean for her career?

What career?

"So, Austin and I have a minor dilemma." Debbie's words pulled Eden from her musings while they all worked on layering lasagnas.

All eyes darted to her. Did their dilemma have something to do with her pregnancy?

"His ex-wife, Cheyenne, wants us to send Savannah, Dallas, and Cody to Florida the week after next for a family retreat with Tucker's work."

"The ex-wife who bailed on taking the kids last year when her husband got the new job without needing to present a family?" Joy asked with a scowl.

"Yep, that one," Debbie said. "She's been making a bit of effort lately, so we want to give the kids a chance to get to know her, but we're not comfortable just shipping them off to Florida. We figured we'd take the whole family, but I'm not sure how I'll entertain the little ones the older kids do activities with Cheyenne and Tucker. Austin and I feel like we need to stick close to the resort, in case things go south with Cheyenne."

"They're too young to appreciate a trip to Disney World." Sheila said.

"Orlando is over five hours away from the resort in Panama City." Debbie grimaced. "I definitely wouldn't feel good about going that far away from the older kids."

Eden didn't envy Debbie having to entertain the three little ones in a hotel room, regardless of how nice the room may be.

Joy and Sheila continued to throw out ideas that weren't at all helpful.

"Might be best if you left them here," Alice finally said.

"I'd offer to tend them," Joy said, "but that's the week we're taking the kids to Disneyland."

Sheila wrinkled her nose. "We'll be out of town that week too, or I would offer as well."

"Leave them here with me," Alice said. "You and Austin go enjoy a little alone time while Savvy and the boys are with their mom. It may be the last chance you get before the baby comes."

"That sound fun, but I'd hate to leave William and the twins."

Joy and Sheila both scoffed.

"They'll be fine with Mom," Sheila said.

"Go, enjoy it while you can," Joy added.

Just then, Savannah walked through the door to the garage, followed by all her younger siblings, and the noise in the kitchen intensified. Little dark-haired girls hugged their mom's legs as Savannah passed the baby off to Debbie. "Is it okay if I hang out with Rainey this afternoon?"

"Sure. Thank you for taking the kids to the park. Will you stick around long enough to help get the kids lunch first?"

Savannah nodded and headed to the refrigerator.

Work in the kitchen shifted as everyone chipped in to make sandwiches and cut up fruit.

Eden soon found herself sitting at the breakfast nook with Debbie, baby William, and the twins.

"So, Eden, how are you liking Providence?"

"I like it. It's definitely a change of pace."

A little slow sometimes, but at least she'd kept busy enough not to notice the lack of a nightlife.

"A change of pace. That's a good way to put it." Debbie laughed. "One thing I love about small towns is that everyone is so friendly."

"They are." Eden couldn't walk down the street without a dozen people waving at her.

One of the twins—Eden thought it was Lucia—reached out and wrapped a fist around a lock of Eden's hair. Then she held out a handful of her own and leaned closer to Eden.

In a family with so many redheads, the little girls probably felt like an anomaly with their black hair.

Eden leaned closer. "We match, don't we? Your hair is so pretty."

Mia watched Lucia and Eden.

Eden he touched the other girl's head. "I love your hair, too."

"Pretty." Lucia said, and Mia looked at her own hair before echoing her sister.

"I hope that hand wasn't sticky." Debbie grimaced when Lucia released her hair.

"It's okay. I don't mind." The words that came out of Eden's mouth surprised her, but they were true. She used to be the first to shy away from kids with sticky hands, but apparently, that had changed.

She and Debbie continued to talk while Debbie coaxed her little ones to eat. Then someone flipped an invisible switch.

All three kids started whining at the same time.

"Oh dear. It's naptime. I missed the window to get them down peacefully. Now it's going to be a battle."

Eden watched as Debbie quickly fixed a bottle for baby William and cleaned up all three kids.

When Debbie lifted the baby from his highchair, the girls bounced from their seats and wrapped themselves around her legs.

"I need to put William to bed. Do you girls want me to see if Grammy will read you a story?"

"I'll read to them." The words were out of Eden's mouth before she could stop them.

Surprising herself for the second time in less than fifteen minutes, she jumped from her seat and crouched in front of the twins.

"Can I read you a story before you go night-night?" she asked.

The whining momentarily stopped, and both girls looked up at their mom.

"I bet Eden is fantastic at reading stories!" Debbie infused excitement into her voice. "How about you let Eden read you a story, then I will come read you one after I get William down? That means you'll get two stories today." She gasped and covered her mouth in true dramatic Wheeler fashion.

"Can I please read to you?" Eden gave the girls her friendliest smile. She put her hand to the side of her mouth and whispered, "I'll read you two stories, if you don't tell your mom."

Finally, Lucia let go of Debbie's leg and took Eden's hand. After a lengthy hesitation, Mia took Eden's other hand.

An odd sense of anticipation and elation filled Eden's stomach and chest, taking her breath away as she walked down the hall with two small hands in hers. She felt like she was in someone else's body, or at the very least, a dream, as both girls snuggled into her with their favorite books.

Warmth, comfortable and pleasant, enveloped her when first Luci —then Mia—laid her head against Eden, and she decided she could be happy like this for the rest of her life. She didn't realize what she'd been missing until now, but suddenly she wanted this more than anything.

CHAPTER 11

*B*oth Rudy's and Bill's trucks sat in front of the Wheeler's house when Eden came home after another busy day of helping Hattie reorganize and follow up with vendors.

She gathered her purse and laptop from the passenger seat and hurried into the house.

"There you are," Alice said. "We just sat down, so hurry and wash up and come join us."

"I'm sorry I'm so late getting home." A twinge of guilt tightened Eden's chest. She'd promised Alice she'd help with dinner so the older woman could teach her how to make chicken Alfredo.

She'd texted Alice when she realized she was going to be late, but she still felt bad for letting her down. Even worse, she was disappointed she'd missed today's lesson. Eden doubted she'd ever make a great cook, but she enjoyed learning from a master like Alice more than she ever thought she would.

When she took a seat at the table across from Rudy—always across from Rudy—she couldn't keep her gaze from roaming over him. He looked amazing in an olive-green short sleeved Henley that made his eyes look more green than blue today.

She was constantly aware of his presence; whether it was across the table from her or sitting beside him at his computer, where she could smell his pleasant masculine scent. It made her mouth water. Or maybe that was the kiss that replayed all too frequently in her mind with shocking clarity.

"So, you had a busy day today?" Alice said, pulling Eden out of her thoughts.

"I did. I spent the morning at Hattie's like usual, then after taking today's orders to the post office, I drove all over the county, visiting some of the people who are interested in selling their goods through our website."

A little twinge of guilt squeezed her chest. Everyone she talked to was interested in selling their goods through Hattie's website, but Eden feared that what she was doing wasn't sustainable if she didn't stick around Providence. Hattie would never be able to do all that Eden was doing alone.

When the time comes for me to leave, I'll make sure I find someone who can help Hattie.

It was the least she could do, considering she was the one who pushed Hattie to take her business online.

"Who did you visit today?" Alice asked, pulling Eden from her thoughts.

Eden talked about all the people she'd met and their amazing talents. Even though the Wheelers already knew everyone she mentioned, they pretended to be a rapt audience. When she said she'd gone to visit Miss Georgie again, both Rudy and Alice said in unison, "You didn't eat her cookies, did you?"

Eden laughed as she shook her head. "I panicked on her doorstep when I realized my dress didn't have any pockets, so I hurried back to my car and grabbed my purse." She looked toward the front door where she'd deposited her purse. "They're still in there." Then she grimaced. "I was lucky enough to divert her attention long enough to hide the cookies, but I couldn't find a big enough distraction to pour my tea into the plant."

"Please tell me you didn't drink it." Rudy cringed.

"I didn't have a choice." Eden shuddered as she recalled the bitter taste of that horrible tea. "I didn't think it could be as bad as you said."

"But it is."

"It really is."

"You dump your tea in her potted plants?" Alice glared at Rudy, then she grinned. "Is that why they look so amazing? Maybe I'll have to try that with my plants." She turned her attention back to Eden. "Who else did you visit?"

When Eden mentioned meeting a cute old white-haired wood crafter who reminded her of Geppetto from Pinocchio, Bill got a twinkle in his eyes. "Aren't Harold's puzzle boxes...puzzling?"

"They are." Eden grinned. "Very puzzling and very beautiful."

She'd never seen such smooth wood that gleamed like Harold's hand carved pieces did. He had everything from animals with elaborate details to intricate flowers and interlocking hearts and chain links. The man was brilliant with a blade.

Already, her mind was spinning with ideas for a display that would combine one of Harold's wood pieces with one of Jessie Winter's ceramic vases and Savannah's smaller paintings. Maybe she could even add one of Miss Georgie's doilies. If she could get the colors and designs to complement each other just right, people might be interested in buying each piece.

I need to talk to Hattie about offering a discount for sets.

Ever since she first stepped foot into the little craft boutique last week, ideas had filled her head. Not all of them were good, but most of them took her breath away with the best kind of adrenaline rush.

"Did you see his wife's homemade jewelry?" Alice asked.

"I did. It was beautiful too." Eden grimaced. "I'm a little concerned about how to feature jewelry on the website with most of it being focused on home decor and crafts."

"Well, if you figure out a way, you should see if Elsie Evans is interested in selling her t-shirts. She does both screen printing and vinyl iron-on. She already has an Etsy shop, but she might like the additional exposure as things pick up with Hattie's."

"What's her address?" Eden pulled her phone out to make a quick note.

Alice and Bill gave her blank stares for a moment before they both spoke at once.

"Take the second left after the sheriff's office," Alice said.

"East on Elm," Bill said. "Then it's the third house on the right."

"No, the fifth house on the left."

Eden bit her lip as Bill and Alice argued about which house Elsie lived in. She looked at Rudy who rolled his eyes and shook his head.

He set his phone that he'd pulled out at some point down on the table and shot her a smile.

Almost instantly, her phone vibrated in her hand. She looked down to find Elsie's name and address on the screen. She aimed a smile in his direction and tucked her phone away.

Apparently done arguing, Alice asked again. "Are you going to sell Trina and Trudy's lip balms, body butter and bath bombs?"

Alice seemed to be oddly interested in the success of Hattie's new website. Or maybe she was just glad Eden wasn't sitting around doing nothing.

"I want to. I think they'll be a hit. I just need to figure out how I'm going to feature those as well."

"Maybe you need to change the name of the website to something like Hattie's Home Decor and More," Rudy said.

"I like that idea!" She chewed a forkful of noodles while she repeated it in her head. "I'll have to discuss it with Hattie. I also need to figure out how to drive more traffic to the store that's not just locals."

"You know," Alice pointed her fork at Eden. "Charity's diner gets a fair amount of traffic from the interstate. I wonder if you could talk to Amy Young, Ben's wife—she owns the diner now. Maybe she would let you put up a sign there or something."

Adrenaline warmed Eden's veins as more ideas filled her head, and she snapped her fingers. "Maybe I could see if she'd give diners from out of town a coupon for five dollars off their first purchase. That might draw people to Hattie's."

"Good idea." Alice's brow scrunched as though she was deep in thought. Then she leaned forward in her seat. "Has Hazel Evans reached out to you yet?"

Eden mentally reviewed all the texts she'd received over the past few days before shaking her head. "I don't think I've heard from a Hazel."

"She makes beautiful wind chimes. I'd bet she'd be interested in selling them on your website." She pointed her fork at Rudy. "You should take Eden for a walk to meet Hazel after dinner." Alice speared a bite of broccoli and put it in her mouth as if that was that.

Again with a walk?

Rudy's eyes widened and his throat bobbed twice as though the food he swallowed stuck there.

Eden waited a heartbeat before speaking to see if he would refuse to take her, even though she knew he'd never talk back to his mother. "Rudy doesn't need to take me. If you'll give me her address, I can stop by and visit her tomorrow."

Alice waved her hand in dismissal. "Nonsense. Rudy always loved visiting Hazel's gardens. I'm sure he hasn't seen them in ages."

Even though he didn't say a single word, his eyes narrowed on his mom, and his lips pressed into a tight line. He wasn't any happier about his mom's interference than she was.

Eden suspected Alice would have suggested a lot more *walks* over the past two weeks if they hadn't spent so much time huddled around Rudy's computer working on the website most evenings.

She'd been so grateful last night when Scott and Kennedy showed up. Judging by the speed Rudy bolted from his chair when Scott asked if he wanted to work out, he was just as anxious to get away from her as she was him.

Ever since they kissed, the tension between them had been thick and palpable. That's why she'd dragged Kennedy to her room and told her everything. From her dad's visit to the lie they'd told, and the way he'd forced them to kiss.

Kennedy had howled with laughter that didn't make Eden feel one bit better. When she finally sobered, she clapped her hands. "I'm so excited for my best friend to become my sister-in-law!"

"What? No way!"

Kennedy grinned. "No matter how hard you fight it or how wrong you think Rudy is for you, you two are bound to fall in love with each other now."

"Nope. Nuh-huh. Not happening."

Now that she knew Rudy better, she no longer felt he was all wrong for her, but she couldn't let herself fall for someone she had every intention of leaving.

"Come on, you've read it dozens of times in your romance novels. A couple fakes a relationship to get an inheritance or get a parent or grandparent off their backs. Then when they are forced to spend time together and show some affection, they can't help falling for each other."

Eden thought about how incredible the kiss was that she and Rudy had shared. If they were forced to do much more of that she'd have a hard time keeping herself from falling for him alright. They spent way too much time together working on the website as it was.

Her brow furrowed as she realized Alice was the reason Rudy was helping her with the website. The woman had an agenda.

Kennedy laughed again. "You know that's how Debbie and Austin got together, don't you. And now look at them. They have six kids with another one on the way."

Eden felt the color drain from her face. "Wait. What are you talking about?"

She knew they were a blended family and that they hadn't been married all that long, but she didn't know they had been in a fake relationship before falling in love.

"When Austin's ex-wife showed up last year threatening to take custody of the kids, he convinced Debbie to pretend to be his fiancé, hoping it would discourage his ex from starting an ugly custody battle. It worked, and now look at them."

Debbie and Austin did look ridiculously happy, but she and Rudy were so drastically different, she just couldn't see the same kind of happy ending for them.

So why did she hold her breath now, waiting to see if Rudy would agree to take her on another walk?

"Sure, I'll take her to meet Hazel." The smile Rudy gave his mother didn't reach his eyes.

Even though Eden knew she shouldn't be disappointed, she couldn't keep her stomach from sinking.

THE MOMENT EDEN walked out of the kitchen to change her clothes, Rudy spun on his mom. "What are you doing?"

She gave him an innocent look as she dried the salad bowl. "What do you mean?"

"You know what I'm talking about. It was bad enough you subjected us to Miss Georgie's cookies and tea. Last time you made me take Eden for a walk, we got soaked in a rainstorm."

Mom looked out the window. "Looks like clear skies this evening."

"That's not the point. Why are you pushing Eden to get all these people involved in her little venture?"

Mom propped her hands on her hips. "Would it be the worst thing in the world if it succeeded?" When he stared at her in confusion, she went on. "If this website is successful, then maybe she won't feel like she needs to return to the city to find a job."

"Aha! I knew it!" Rudy pointed at his mom. "You're trying to push the two of us together."

"Well of course I am. Eden is a sweet girl and pretty too."

Rudy blinked a few times. He'd expected his mom to deny playing matchmaker, but she hadn't. "Yes, she is," there was no denying Eden was pretty, "but...what if she's not interested in sticking around here?"

She'd told him herself last week that Providence didn't have the kind of job she wanted.

"Well, of course she won't be interested in sticking around if we don't give her a reason to stay."

Rudy could think of lots of reasons to make her stay, and most of them had to do with her being wrapped in his arms.

He moistened his suddenly dry mouth. "What do you mean by that?"

"I mean, we need to show her all the charming parts of our little town and make her fall in love with Providence." She patted his arm and gave him a placating smile. "Then you can work on making her fall in love with you." She walked out of the kitchen leaving him with his mouth hanging open.

Eden walked out of her room to find him still gaping.

"Are you ready?" She shot him a smile that made his heart do that hard thumping thing.

He snapped his mouth shut and nodded.

She stopped as soon as they stepped out onto the porch and looked at the sky. "Is it going to rain on us again?"

Rudy examined the cloudless sky. "Doubtful."

When they hit the end of the driveway, she paused again. "You really don't have to take me to meet Hazel. If you want, we can just go see if Chase is out playing ball."

"Mom will want to know what you think of Hazel's garden, so we'd better go. Besides, I stopped and threw the football with Chase this afternoon on my way home from work."

"Football? I thought he played basketball?"

"This is a small town. Every serious athlete plays at least two sports in high school."

Her gaze raked over him from head to toe. "You have a home gym, so I assume you're a serious athlete. Which sports did you play?"

"Guess."

"Hmm..." She looked at him again in a way that made him flush. "You made a lot of baskets the other night, so I'm going to say basketball and...baseball."

"Close. I played basketball, although I was never as good as Chase. I also played football as a running back. And I ran track."

"Three? You must have been a serious athlete."

"Not really. In small towns like this, pretty much everyone who tries out makes the team." He shoved his hands into his pockets. "My parents insisted I participate in sports to keep me busy and out of trouble."

"Are you saying you were a hellion when you were a teenager?"

"Not really, I was a major geek, who was bored with school and became fascinated with hacking for a while."

"Hacking?" She looked at him wide-eyed. "Did you hack into something you shouldn't have?"

"The school computers." He grinned. "But don't worry, I didn't do anything bad. I knew there'd be serious consequences from my parents if I did. So I informed the principal of the weakness and let it go."

"If you were that big of a computer geek, why did you go into law enforcement? I'm surprised you're not a programmer or something."

He didn't want to talk about what caused him to make such a major lane change eight years ago.

"Sometimes plans change." Clenching his jaw, he shoved his hands a little deeper into his pockets. "Did you play any sports in school?"

"No, just dance. I did ballet when I was young then shifted to contemporary dance when I got older."

They continued to talk about their high school and college years as Rudy turned them down another road near the outskirts of town.

When a rustle sounded in the underbrush to Eden's right, she gasped and stepped in front of him and grabbed his shirt in both hands. "What's that?"

Instinctively, he wrapped his arms around her. He didn't care what it was, if it pushed Eden into his arms, it couldn't be anything bad. He held her tight as he studied the bushes. He laughed when he spotted two long white ears followed by a black and white body, sporting a fluffy white tail.

"It's only a bunny. Mr. Jackson had a couple of rabbits escape last year, and he never caught them."

She didn't release her hold on his shirt as she peered at the animal. "Is it dangerous?"

"It'd probably put up a fight if you tried to catch it, but otherwise, it's harmless."

She let go of his shirt as she bent to catch a glimpse of the rabbit scurrying into the bushes again, and his stomach dropped as he lowered his arms. He shouldn't be disappointed about letting her go, but he was.

Before long, they reached Hazel's house where the middle-aged woman greeted them from her front porch and beckoned them into her backyard.

Mom must have called and told her we were coming.

Hazel's garden had been one of his sisters' favorite places to hang out when they were young, so he had come here often when he wasn't playing soccer or football with his friends, but he hadn't visited Hazel's gardens in years. Everything looked much smaller than he remembered.

Rudy leaned close to Eden and whispered. "Be careful not to touch anything and stay on the painted decorative steppingstones. If you don't obey the rules, Hazel will ban you from her gardens." Then he hung back and watched her fascination with the fairy garden where Hazel had created villages on and around a series of five tree stumps.

The tiny homes consisted of an assortment of upside-down flowerpots covered in pebbles and sticks. One home was made from an old teapot. Miniature deer and woodland creatures graced small yards outlined with tiny picket fences, and little ladders and bridges led from one stump to another. Tiny, winged fairies and rocks painted to look like colorful mushrooms dotted the villages.

"They're incredible!" Eden exclaimed as she bent low to get a closer look. She looked up at Hazel. "Did you paint all of these by hand?"

Hazel beamed. "Yes, and I have to touch them up every few years, because the sun and weather take a toll on them."

"I can't believe this. They're adorable. And so detailed."

Eden continued to ooh and ahh, and Hazel continued to beam as they moved from the fairy garden to the butterfly garden.

Here the paving stones were mosaics made of colored rocks and broken tiles. Some even had colorful pieces of broken glass set into the cement. This was where Hazel's vegetable garden sat. Interspersed between the plants sat groupings of garden stakes with a variety of butterflies, bees, and dragonflies in a variety of colors and sizes. Clusters of small rocks painted like ladybugs and other creepy crawlies filled in open patches on the ground.

Hazel had even attached a series of hand-painted aluminum butterflies to the inside of her back fence.

Moving on, Rudy noted that Hazel had cut down a few trees from the cluster on the right side of her garden and added a gnome village amidst the stumps and hollowed-out logs. Here the decor mimicked the fairy garden but on a larger scale with a bolder color scheme. Garden gnomes of all shapes, sizes, and colors worked miniature garden plots, played in the stream, slept in hammocks, and read under mushrooms.

The soft tinkling of wind chimes sounded throughout the garden, adding to the magical feel of the place.

"I just can't get over how cute it all is!" Eden said when she finally pulled her attention away from the gnomes.

She wore the biggest smile he had ever seen, and her brown eyes sparkled in the evening sun. The urge to kiss her hit him like a punch in the gut, stealing his breath. It's a good thing Hazel followed them, or he might have given into the urge. He didn't think she had ever looked more enthusiastic and passionate. The wonder on her face only made her more beautiful. Which was saying something because Eden DuPont was a beautiful woman. One who was quickly worming her way into his heart.

He liked her. More than he'd wanted to admit. And that disturbed him because falling in love and getting married weren't a part of his plans. Not for a few more years anyway. Because when he got married, he wanted kids, and to raise a family, he needed a home for them. Besides, Eden would never be content to settle down in this small town with a country boy like him and live in a modest home.

Eden turned her attention to Hazel's wind chimes. They'd seen several throughout the gardens already, but the bulk of Hazel's creations hung along her back deck. Everything from the traditional chime pipes to small bells and old-fashioned keys to cut glass and gemstones from chandeliers made up the fascinating wind chimes.

As if just for Eden's benefit, a breeze picked up, stirring the dozens of chimes, creating a symphony; a combination of light, tinkling music mixed with low, deep tones. The chimes with crystal beads and broken pieces of glass glimmered and twinkled in the light of the setting sun.

They admired the creativity and beauty of the chimes for some time before Eden brought up the reason for their visit. She told Hazel about the website she was setting up for Hattie and her social marketing efforts.

"Would you be interested in selling your incredible chimes through Hattie's website?"

"How did you get Hattie to agree to that? She's been resistant to change for decades now."

Eden lifted one shoulder. "I just helped her see the potential. Once she realized how it would help all of the talented crafters in this town, she was interested."

Hazel smoothed back dark hair that sported strips of gray. "I used to sell my chimes years ago." She rotated, studying her deck. "Ralph keeps telling me I have too many. He insists I either need to sell some or give them away." Then her lips turned up in a wicked grin. "If I sell some, then I can make more, right?"

Eden laughed; a light, cheerful sound that put the windchimes to shame. "Right."

"Then I'm game." Hazel held up a finger. "As long as I don't have to do anything other than make the chimes."

"I'll take care of everything," Eden assured her, and while the women talked business, Rudy continued to study the chimes.

Hazel's creativity never ceased to amaze him. She used anything and everything to make beautiful wind chimes: wooden beads, seashells, buttons, crystals, old hangers, and even wooden spoons.

Eden amazed him as well. She had great ideas when it came to presentation and layout, within her photos as well as on the website.

And she was great at building people up with compliments and flattery.

"I'll come back tomorrow when the light is better and take some pictures," Eden said, making Rudy realize how dark it had become.

It would be fully dark by the time they got home. For some reason, he didn't mind at all. A moonlight stroll down a country road would give him plenty of opportunity to convince Eden to stick around.

Thanks a lot, Mom, for planting ideas in my head.

CHAPTER 12

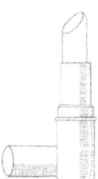

"*A*ren't her chimes amazing?" Eden asked as they started their walk home. When Alice suggested Rudy take her to meet Hazel, Eden had no idea she would enjoy the evening so much. "I loved the vintage keys and the rainbow of crystals. Oh, and did you see the one with the miniature hummingbirds?"

"My favorites were the tea pot pouring out the strings of clear and blue crystals and the horseshoe with bronze and turquoise beads and charms hanging from it."

"She's so creative. Are all the women in Providence crafty?" Eden shot Rudy a sideways glance.

"What makes you think the women are the only ones who are talented around here?"

She grinned at his defensive tone. "Right. I'm sure there are plenty of skilled men like Harold. But seriously, why is it that everyone here can create such amazing things?"

"I suppose it's because we have fewer distractions than you do in the city, so we spend more time developing our talents." He lifted one shoulder in a shrug. "And probably because it's too expensive to drive to the city every time we want something, so we learn how to make things ourselves."

"It's no wonder you have a lot of free time. There's nothing to do around here." Her voice was teasing, but he bristled just like she expected.

"Hey." Rudy stopped walking, and she turned to find him with his hands on his hips. "There's plenty to do. You just need to have a little creativity."

"Okay, besides playing games with your family, what do you do for fun?"

"Camping, hiking, and fishing." He started ticking off activities on his fingers as they started walking again. "Barbecues, picnics, football, soccer, and baseball." He paused for a moment before continuing. "Bonfires, riding horses, and four-wheelers—"

"Oh, riding horses and four-wheelers sound fun."

"Out of everything I listed, that's the only thing that sounds fun to you?"

She scrunched her nose. "I'm not much of a camper or fisher. Hiking sounds fun though."

"Maybe I'll have to talk to Jake Winters and see if I can take you to the Double Diamond to ride sometime."

Was he making plans to take her on a date?

The idea thrilled her, but they couldn't start dating. The future was too uncertain for her. She shouldn't encourage a relationship when she wasn't planning on sticking around. That knowledge didn't stop little tingles of electricity from racing up her arm, however, every time their hands or arms brushed as they walked.

A part of her wished Rudy would just take her hand and hold it in his. But he knew, as well as she did, that getting involved with each other would only be asking for heartache when she left Providence.

"Maybe while we're at the Double Diamond we could do some target practicing." Rudy pulled her from her thoughts.

"Like shooting guns?"

"Yes." When she gave him a wide-eyed look, he went on. "And the next time we get a good rain, I'll take you mudding."

"Mudding?"

"Yeah, we take our four-wheel-drive trucks off road and drive in the mud."

"Why?"

"Because it's fun. Your stomach drops a little when it feels like you might get stuck, but then when your tires catch, you get this burst of adrenaline that's kind of addictive. Plus, you get bragging rights when you get to be the one to pull the other trucks out of the mud."

Rudy's childlike enthusiasm was contagious, and Eden found herself laughing. "What about if you're the one who gets stuck?"

"Then you'd better hope that whoever pulls you out doesn't rub it in your face too badly."

"You think getting covered in mud is fun?" Eden shook her head and gave him a "you're-crazy" look before she started walking again.

"We also do normal, boring things like go for bike rides, watch the sunset, and stargaz—"

"Stargazing isn't boring. Especially in the country." Eden stopped walking again. Her hand brushed his when she lifted her face to look at the millions of stars in the night sky. Her mind told her to pull away, but she couldn't seem to make her body obey.

The sky looked like a glitter bomb had gone off. She'd never seen so many stars. Nor had they ever looked this bright. Was that white swirly stuff the Milky Way? And when was the last time she'd heard crickets?

From the corner of her eye, she could tell that Rudy stood unmoving beside her. He didn't look up, instead he appeared to be studying her neck. The skin under his scrutiny heated, but she kept her gaze lifted, waiting to see if he would pull his hand away from hers.

He didn't, so she pressed her index finger against his knuckles. She was playing with fire, but she needed to know if he was as interested in something more as she was, never mind that nothing could come of it. She hadn't been able to stop thinking about the feel of his lips on hers all week. She was such a hypocrite for knowing she shouldn't kiss Rudy again but wanting to anyway.

His hand twitched then he hooked his index finger around hers.

"You can't see the stars like this in the city," she said reverently.

His shoulder pressed against hers as he lifted his head. "The best way to stargaze is lying on a blanket in the back of a truck. Away from the lights of town."

The husky timbre of his voice sent shivers racing down her spine. She slowly lowered her head and looked at him. "Sounds...romantic.

"It is." His gaze shifted to her. He laced his fingers through hers.

If he was watching for a reaction from her, he wouldn't get one. Other than total compliance.

Warmth raced up her arm at the feel of his cool, strong, calloused fingers wrapped around hers.

His hooded eyes looked captivating and a little dangerous in the darkness. When his gaze dropped to her lips, her mouth moistened. She shouldn't but wanted his kiss. A voluntary kiss that wasn't forced by her father. A kiss that she'd fantasized about for a whole week.

"Country folks are more romantic than city slickers." The words were barely more than a whisper.

Eden gave a small smile and leaned toward him a little. "Is that so?"

He squeezed her hand a little tighter, pressing it against his thigh as he leaned in and tilted his head. Mere inches from her lips, he paused, and the breath she'd sucked in in anticipation stuck in her chest.

He was giving her an opportunity to pull away, but she wouldn't. She couldn't if she wanted to. Which she didn't. All she wanted was his mouth on hers.

She rocked up on her toes and closed the gap between their lips.

His mouth twitched, and she felt him smile before his lips softened and pressed more firmly against hers.

The contact was light and feathery like the butterfly wings in Hazel's garden until Eden leaned into him and slid her free hand to the back of his neck. Parting her lips, she invited him to deepen the kiss.

Rudy took the hint and wrapped his arm around her waist, pulling her tighter against him. Warmth flooded over her as his mouth caressed hers. Both giving and taking in a dizzying rhythm.

Stars exploded behind her eyelids, brighter than those in the sky. The dopamine and oxytocin cocktail that surged through her veins at the contact made her giddy. Happy and elated. Like someone had just given her a shot of feel-good anesthesia. No way could mudding be more exciting than this.

After several long moments, his lips stilled against hers. "You taste good." His whispered breath blew hot against her lips.

She giggled, recalling the cinnamon breath mint she'd thrown in her mouth when she changed clothes. "I thought you didn't like cinnamon."

"Mmm... I love the taste of it on your mouth."

And then his lips were on hers again, more possessive this time. Passionate and urgent. And Eden was all too eager to participate in the heated kiss. He released her hand and wrapped both arms around her, holding her so tight, she struggled to breathe. Or maybe that was the way his mouth covered hers so completely that she lost track of where her lips ended and his began.

A loud rustling and chittering sound came from the bushes behind Eden, and she pulled away from Rudy with a gasp. She couldn't believe she'd lost herself so completely to his kiss. They were practically making out on the street.

She turned when another sound somewhere between a snort and a squeal sounded behind her.

Spotting the movement of a fluffy white blob in the moonlight, she peered closer at the bushes. "Is it another rabbit?" She caught a flash of what looked like a long tail as Rudy leaned in beside her. "Is it a cat?"

A second shape, this one with even more white, joined the first.

"Look, there are two cats." She pointed toward the animals.

Three things happened almost simultaneously. So fast that Eden was incapable of movement. Yet time seemed to slow, allowing her to take in every excruciating detail of the nightmare.

The second animal moved into the moonlight, revealing two white lines on a black body before turning and lifting its tail.

Rudy shouted, "Eden, no! That's not a cat!"

Then the first animal's tail shot up too.

"Oh snap!" Rudy grabbed her arm and jerked her back, but it was too late.

The foulest stench she'd ever smelled permeated the air, and a putrid taste filled her mouth.

"Agh!" She stomped her feet and waved her hands in front of her face. "What is tha—" Her words were cut off by violent coughing and gagging.

"Skunk," was all Rudy managed to get out before choking right alongside her.

Eden's stomach roiled when the horrid stench and taste persisted. She'd never experienced anything so vile and all-consuming on the senses. Her eyes, nose, and throat burned. Even her bronchial tubes and lungs protested. A prickly, stinging sensation covered her face and arms, permeating her skin.

"My mouth was open!" She managed to choke out between coughs that grew so violent she vomited on the ground at Rudy's feet. She was too miserable to even be embarrassed about it.

Another rustle sounded behind him, and he grabbed her arm and pulled her away from the bushes and her vomit. The skunks, victorious in having defended their territory, waddled back into the underbrush, leaving the two of them in a putrid fog that threatened to suffocate them.

The burn in Eden's throat eased a little after throwing up, but the vile taste in her mouth persisted, and tears flowed down her face almost as rapidly as snot streamed from her nose. "Tastes like rotten eggs and raw garlic."

"Burning tires and sulfur." Rudy added as he fidgeted, no doubt fighting the urge to wipe away the snot and tears that streamed from his nose and eyes. "And very intense marijuana."

Eden gave him a questioning look through teary eyes.

"Police academy," he explained. "Gah! This burns even worse than the mandatory tear-gas training."

Covered in tears and mucus, Rudy looked as miserable as she felt. He pointed a finger at her and croaked, "No judgment," before doubling over, pressing a finger to one side of his nose, and blowing out hard and fast. He repeated the action with the other side.

It was the grossest thing Eden had ever seen anyone do, but it was brilliant. Blowing snot out in front of Rudy couldn't be any worse than vomiting at his feet, so she mimicked his actions.

Avoiding his eyes, she straightened and wiped the back of her hand across her nose and mouth. The prickly sensation on her skin intensified. "Frick! I can still taste it!"

"Don't touch your face! Makes it worse." He gagged then cleared his throat. "It's on your clothes, too."

"Now you tell me." She spit on the ground then blew raspberries.

Still sniffling and gagging, they both turned and headed toward home at a much quicker pace than they'd taken on the way to Hazel's. The revolting stench followed them like a persistent stalker.

And the relentless horrid taste lingered in her mouth. She shuddered and groaned as she stomped her feet. "Ugh! I can still taste it!"

Rudy shook his head. "And you call me dramatic!"

Scowling at him, she started walking again. She couldn't wait to get home. She needed a shower or three. That is if Alice even let them in the house.

Another rustling sound came from the bushes, and Rudy squealed like a little girl. "Aah!" He darted to the middle of the road where he continued to walk.

Eden would have laughed if she wasn't so miserable. She couldn't even give Rudy a hard time, because talking only irritated her throat more.

Then she aimed a second scowl heavenward.

Really? This is how you punish me for giving in to temptation?

CHAPTER 13

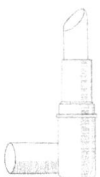

"You've got to be kidding!" Rudy watched his mom pull the kiddie pool she kept for his nieces out from under the back deck.

She held her nose as she scowled at him. "There's no way you're coming into my house smelling like that." She puffed out her cheeks and held her breath as she dragged a laundry basket full of bottled tomato juice over to the pool. "Well, what are you waiting for? Get in."

"But—"

Eden stepped out of the back door of the garage, and Rudy's protest died on his lips. The air rushed from his lungs at the sight of her in a hot-pink, floral swimsuit, a striking compliment to her dark hair and eyes. The tankini, though modest by most standards, displayed a tantalizing swatch of midriff. It also emphasized her slender curves and accentuated her feminine assets.

She wrapped her arms around herself, and Rudy suddenly felt just as self-conscious. It's not like she'd never seen him shirtless before, but now, with his mom expecting them to sit together in this little kiddie pool and bathe in tomato juice, he felt...exposed and vulnerable.

They'd hardly stepped foot into the house before Mom shooed them back outside. "Get out! You stink!" Then she yelled over her shoulder. "Bill, get down to the grocery store and buy all the tomato juice you can."

The next thing Rudy knew, he'd been banned to the shed and ordered to strip. Mom cracked the door open enough to throw in his swimsuit and a garbage bag then quickly slammed it again.

"Throw everything in the bag! It's all going in the trash!"

Eden was ordered to wait in the garage. Mom must have found her swimsuit too. And what a swimsuit it was! She looked incredible in pink!

Eden appeared as skeptical and hesitant to get into the pool as he was. Although this wasn't Rudy's first tomato juice bath. At least when he got sprayed by a skunk at the age of seven, mom let him bathe in the tub. He'd grown a lot since then, though, and he didn't have a pretty woman join him for that tomato bath.

"Okay, in you go." Mom waved her hand toward the pool. "The sooner you neutralize the stench, the sooner you can go take a shower."

Mom's use of the word shower in the singular had all kinds of inappropriate thoughts racing through Rudy's mind. Thought's that took up residence there more often than he'd like to admit since Eden started sharing his bathroom. He wasn't typically one of those men who fantasized about women, but it was becoming increasingly harder not to the more time he spent around her.

It was all too easy to imagine sharing the rest of his life with her, including his bathroom and his bed. He loved the idea of waking up next to her each morning. But as long as she planned on leaving, daydreaming about a life with her was a foolish thing to do.

Kissing her was even more foolish.

People who kissed each other in the passionate way he and Eden had were usually in a committed relationship. Could he commit to her? Was he willing to give up this little town that he loved and move away from his family to be with her when she decided to go back to the city? A move like that would sidetrack all the goals he'd set for himself.

With Mom's repeated nudging, he and Eden both found themselves sitting in the pool. She pulled her knees up to her chest and wrapped her arms around her legs. He wanted to mimic her posture, but Mom handed him a canning jar with a tight lid.

He caught Eden staring at his biceps as he twisted off lid after lid, and a surge of satisfaction shot through him. Not that there was any doubt after their kiss, but it was nice to know she was as attracted to him as he was to her.

Mom held out an open jar to Eden.

She took it and raised it to her lips.

"No. You're supposed to pour it over your body and rub it in," Mom said.

"But I still have that nasty taste in my mouth." Eden took a small swallow then looked at the bottle and shrugged. "I don't think I've ever had straight tomato juice before, but it's not bad." She took another couple swigs then filled her mouth. Her cheeks bulged first on one side then the other as she swished. She tipped her head back and gargled.

Rudy busted out laughing. He still had a lingering foul taste in his own mouth, but Eden seemed to be blowing this whole thing out of proportion.

Tomato juice suddenly hit his head and splashed onto his bare shoulders, dousing his laughter. "Geez, Mom, that's cold!" A shudder shook his body.

"Sometimes you need to learn a lesson the hard way for it to really sink in."

"What's that supposed to mean?"

"Figure it out," she said as she walked back into the house.

Rudy shook his head. It's not like he asked to get sprayed by the skunk.

Maybe Mom referred to the way he'd stared at Eden in her swimsuit. He hadn't meant to ogle her, at least not so overtly. But he couldn't help himself where she was concerned. He found her incredibly attractive.

Or maybe Mom meant the way he laughed at Eden. It wasn't like he intentionally mocked her. There was just something about her naiveté that was refreshing.

"You're right, that is cold." Eden's words pulled his mind away from his mom's confusing words.

He watched mesmerized as she slowly poured juice on her shoulder and let it run down her arm in tiny red rivulets before stopping to rub at her skin. He did the same, trying in vain to ignore the cold chills that rose on his skin. His gaze repeatedly darted to Eden as she poured one bottle after another over her body.

Would she want to talk about the kiss? Didn't women always need to define the relationship?

A twisting sensation tightened his stomach. They didn't have a relationship. Except the fake one they'd tried to sell her father. So he shouldn't have kissed her like that.

Would she demand to know what he was thinking? Technically, she'd kissed him first. Maybe he should insist on an explanation from her.

When she lifted her chin and angled the bottle against her collar bone, he realized she intended to pour it over her chest. He jerked his head in the other direction and angled his body away from her. Her swimsuit already exposed a fair amount of cleavage, he didn't need to see tomato juice pooling there.

"What happened?" Her quiet question came a split second before surprisingly warm fingers touched the scar on his shoulder.

Rudy froze.

He'd rather talk about their kiss than the accident that took his friend.

He rarely talked about the accident, just like Scott didn't talk about the one that killed his girlfriend. Of course, Scott didn't talk much at all. Grief was funny that way, though. Sometimes it helped to talk, but when guilt accompanied grief, talking rarely helped.

Eden continued to trace the scar from the back of his shoulder to the front, and he rotated his body toward her, allowing her to study the scar despite hating what it represented. A scar was a small price to pay for what he'd done though.

When he didn't answer, she changed tactics. "How long have you had this?"

Rudy poured a slow, steady stream of tomato juice from the last jar onto his palm. "Nine years."

"What caused it?" Her voice was gentle, encouraging.

He ground his teeth together. She'd shared with him the accident that took her mother, so why did he find it so hard to talk to her?

Because unlike her accident, mine really was my fault.

"Off road vehicle accident." His voice sounded as tight as his chest felt.

"Off road as in...?" She left the question hanging.

"As in a side-by-side, all-terrain vehicle."

"Like a dune buggy?"

"Yes, except we weren't driving it in the sand dunes."

If they had been, Parker might still be alive.

"We?"

Rudy set down the jar and plunged both hands into his hair. They trembled just like the rest of his body did on the inside. He blew out a deep breath. "Two weeks before starting our freshman year of college, my buddy Parker and I went camping. I talked my dad into letting us take our new Polaris RZR along, so we could ride the trails."

Eden shifted, leaning toward him a little. Her somber brown eyes —filled with tenderness and compassion—compelled him to keep talking.

"I wasn't supposed to let anyone else drive, but Parker kept begging, so I gave in." Now he tugged at his hair. "He drove too fast for the kind of terrain we were on. I kept telling him to slow down, but he was on some kind of adrenaline rush or something and wouldn't listen." Rudy shook his head, again and again, as if doing so could erase the memories.

Eden's hand rested on his arm, and he stared at the swirly emerald design on her nails as he continued to talk. Now that he'd started talking, he couldn't seem to stop.

"He hit a big rock and rolled the side by side." He pressed his fingertips to his forehead and choked back the boulder lodged in his throat. "H-he ended up impaled by a dead tree branch."

Eden gasped, then her arm encircled his shoulders, and she pressed her cheek to his scar. "I'm so sorry. That must have been horrific."

"It was, and it was all my fault."

Eden lifted her head. "Rudy, no—"

"The whole camping trip was *my* idea." He practically shouted now. "*I* convinced my dad to let us take the Polaris. *I* should never have let him drive. *I knew* he didn't have any experience driving in that kind of terrain."

She rubbed his arm. "But you couldn't have known what would happen."

"Maybe not, but I promised my dad when he agreed to let me take the side-by-side that I wouldn't let anyone else drive. I broke that promise and it...it cost Parker's life."

"You can't carry all the responsibility. You told him to slow down."

"I did. Again, and again. And I insisted he buckle up and wear his helmet. But it wasn't enough." He pressed the heels of his hands to his eyes, trying to combat the pressure there. "I couldn't face Chase's family for months after the accident."

"Chase?" Eden lifted her head.

"Parker was Chase's older brother." He forced the words out of a tight throat.

"That must have been very difficult for his parents to have a second son involved in such a serious accident." Eden repeatedly stroked his back, consoling him like a mother would a child. But he wasn't a child, he was a grown man who had made mistakes. Ones he'd pay for for the rest of his life.

More than once, he'd had to remind Scott that the accident that took his girlfriend years ago was just that, and it wasn't Scott's fault.

His family had repeatedly told him the same thing, and Parker's family didn't blame Rudy, but he couldn't stop blaming himself.

Forcing the images of that horrible day from his head, he focused on Eden's touch. The warmth Eden generated against his skin made him feel like anything other than a child. He was all too aware of her body pressed against his. He never knew sitting in a kiddie pool surrounded by tomato juice could feel so sensual and romantic.

Rudy used his hand to scoop up juice and dump it over his legs. "Parker had his whole life planned out. He knew exactly what he needed to do to reach his goals. His five-year plan included getting a criminal justice degree then the police academy. The ten-year plan was to save up for a house and get married."

"Isn't that what you did?" Eden asked.

"Yeah, but I floundered for a while after he... Before I decided to follow the path that Parker had laid out."

"You mean you weren't always planning on going to the police academy?"

"No, I was going to go into computers. Programming or something."

She leaned away from him to look at his face, and he missed the contact immediately. "You became a law enforcement officer because it was what Parker wanted to do?"

Rudy lowered his gaze. "He had better goals than I did. I just wanted to play video games all day."

"You probably could have made more money working with computers."

It was his turn to study her face.

Is money the only thing that matters to her?

A month ago, he would have said yes, but she'd lived as simply as any other small-town resident these past few weeks. She was even canning jam with his mom and cooking from scratch.

"I decided serving others was more important than making money."

"But you shouldn't have given up your dream to follow his."

"I didn't really have any specific dreams. And yeah, I guess I made a lane change and adjusted my priorities, but I feel like it was all for the better." He shrugged. "Besides, I've since completed a computer science degree online. I do some programming and even game development on the side occasionally, but I like the social interaction that comes with being a deputy."

"No wonder you knew how to build the website." Her brow furrowed and she cocked her head. "You've completed two degrees plus the police academy? And you're only twenty-six?"

"Twenty-seven. And the computer science degree wasn't a four-year program. It was really more of a series of certificates."

"Still." The incredulous look remained on her face as she shook her head. "Are you a genius or something?"

Heat filled Rudy's face. He hoped that with the porch light behind him she wouldn't see the color in his cheeks. He cleared his throat before admitting, "I have a higher-than-average IQ. I tend to remember things really well."

"A deputy, a computer geek, a gamer, and a basketball and football player. You're the complete package, aren't you?" Her gaze dipped to his chest and abs.

A warm flush enveloped Rudy's body under her appraisal. "What's that supposed to mean?"

"It means you're...an all-around good guy. I don't understand why you're still single."

Rudy laughed. "Well, if you haven't noticed, there aren't a lot of single girls around here. Besides, I don't plan on getting married for another three years or so."

"Why not?"

He shrugged. "Marriage is part of the ten-year plan."

"Ten years? You're following Parker's plan for your personal life too?"

He stiffened. "I want to be prepared financially to raise a family."

"Don't you think that's taking things a little too—"

"Okay, I have more tomato juice." Mom walked out the back door of the house, carrying another laundry basket full of large cans of tomato juice. "Phew! You guys still stink. I think I'll let you guys open these yourselves." She handed Rudy a can opener and disappeared back inside.

Grateful for the diversion so he didn't have to defend his life plans, Rudy opened a can and handed it to Eden. They continued to bathe—or rather juice—in silence for a time.

"Ugh! I can still smell it. I can't tell if it's in my nose or just still stuck to my skin." She pulled her hair to one side. "Every time I move my head, it grows stronger." She poured a can next to her head, but much of the juice missed her hair.

"Here, let me help you." Rudy shifted to his knees and gathered her hair into his hands. He slowly poured half a can over her hair then worked it in with his fingers before adding the rest of the can.

He'd dreamed many times about running his fingers through her thick, silky hair, but none of those fantasies had included tomato juice. Even the thoughts he'd had earlier about this scene being romantic had dissipated, and he decided there was nothing sexy about tomato juice.

It made Eden's hair clump in his hand and even though the juice had a strong odor, it still hadn't masked the smell of the skunk that seemed to encompass them. Add to that the chill of the night air, and Rudy was ready to take a hot shower. Or at least pull Eden into his arms again.

Just thinking about their kiss warmed him all over.

Once her hair was thoroughly soaked, he shifted to sit beside her again. "So, are we going to talk about...that kiss?"

Her brows shot up, and pink tinged her cheeks. "Do you *want* to talk about it?"

"Not really."

"So, why did you bring it up?"

He let his gaze drift to her bare shoulder before returning to her face. "Because I'd like to do it again." He angled toward her then waited for her to lean in.

She pulled away. "I'm not sure we should."

He straightened. "Why not. I thought you enjoyed it as much as I did."

"I did." More color flooded her face. "But I don't think it's a good idea." She pushed her fingers into her hair to shift it to shield her face, but the clumps didn't move. "I think God is trying to tell me something."

Rudy snorted. "You think God is trying to tell you not to kiss me?"

"Stop laughing." She shoved his shoulder. "I'm serious."

"I'm sorry." He sobered. "Of course, I believe in God. And I know he sends signs and messages. I just don't see why you think he wouldn't want us to kiss."

"Think about it. What happened the first time we kissed?"

Was this a trick question? Was she wanting him to admit how much it affected him? How he'd almost gotten carried away.

She nudged him with her elbow. "I had an asthma attack. I can't believe you've forgotten already."

Oh that.

"I remember *everything* about that kiss, Eden." He wasn't one bit embarrassed about the husky quality of his voice.

Her eyes flashed open wide before she ducked her head. "Well look what happened tonight. We let ourselves get carried away, so God sent skunks to break us up."

Rudy pressed his lips together to keep from laughing again. Yes, their kiss had gotten a little heated, but he didn't regret one minute of it. "I think it was more a case of being in the wrong place at the wrong time. Sure, we were kissing rather passionately, but it wasn't like we were being inappropriate. I don't think God would punish us for wanting to get to know each other better."

"To what end? We both know I'm not going to be here forever. Should we really be getting involved like that?"

Her words doused the embers that had been burning in him since their kiss. "So why did you kiss me then?" A hint of anger tinged his words.

She wrapped her arms around her knees. "I don't know. I guess I just wanted to know if you'd kiss me willingly, without my dad forcing us. I was curious if there would be the same spark as last time."

Hearing her talk about the sparks when they kissed fanned the embers to life. He leaned toward her and in a low voice whispered, "Did it feel like I was a willing participant?"

"Yes." The word came out breathy.

"Did you feel sparks?"

She licked her lips and nodded.

He leaned closer, brushing his lips to her temple. "Will you give me one more chance. If God sends down a bolt of lightning, I promise I will never touch you again."

She gave a shuddering chuckle. "One more chance."

Rudy wasn't about to wait for her to change her mind. He cupped her shoulder as he feathered several light kisses along her jaw before claiming her lips with his. They were much warmer than he expected considering the chill in the night air and even softer than the silky skin of her shoulder.

Her lips moved with his, effectively elevating his heart rate. The electricity arcing through his veins triggered a passion so strong he feared it would sweep him away, but he was prepared for it this time. He tamped it down, refusing to get carried away.

He didn't know what the future held for him and Eden, but he didn't want to mess this up. He wouldn't drive her away and give her a reason to leave by coming on too strong.

He'd just slid his arm around her shoulders and deepened the kiss when it hit him!

The vile, acrid taste of sulfur and raw garlic.

"Gah! You taste awful!" He pulled back. "I thought you were kidding when you said it got in your mouth." The last of his words came out a splutter as a scowling Eden dumped a can of tomato juice on his head.

"Rudy? Is that you?" Mr. Jackson called, poking his head over the fence. "Why are you playing in the kiddie pool?" The older man's head tilted to the side. "Is that...blood?"

"No, it's tomato juice. We got sprayed by a couple of skunks."

"So you're the ones who stunk up the neighborhood." Disgust deepened Mr. Jackson's voice. "Don't you know that's just an old wives' tale? Tomato juice doesn't get rid of the skunk stench."

"It doesn't?" Rudy lifted his chin and yelled, "Mom!"

～

"YOU WANT US TO DO WHAT?" Eden shivered despite the old towel wrapped around her shoulders and stared at the garden tub. In most circumstances, it would be considered plenty big, but not tonight. Not with what Alice was suggesting.

Rudy huddled next to her in his parents' master bathroom, looking as horrified as she felt. He shivered too, thanks to Alice insisting they spray each other off with the hose to wash off the tomato juice before coming into the house.

"I'd make you use your own tub, but with Rudy's long legs, the two of you would never fit." Alice huffed when they both just stared at her. "You're going to keep your swimsuits on, and I'll leave the bathroom door open, so this won't be deemed *too* inappropriate." Despite her words, her voice held a warning tone. She gave each of them a narrow-eyed glare.

Had she seen them kissing in the kiddy pool?

The situation that had felt rather intimate despite being public now felt perfectly acceptable compared to the idea of sharing the tub with Rudy.

"But Mom—"

"But nothing. The grocery store is closed, and I've rounded up all of the peroxide I can from your sisters and the neighbors." She held a large bowl containing a mixture of hydrogen peroxide, baking soda and dish soap; the magic recipe that Mr. Jackson promised would do the trick. "This is all there is."

Eden sure hoped it worked because the stench clinging to her body made her nauseous. She was surprised Alice even allowed them into the house smelling like they did.

She eyed the bowl. "We're supposed to wash our bodies with that?"

Alice put the bowl in the tub and grabbed two washcloths from under the sink. "I suggest you just dip the cloths in the stuff and rub it on, instead of trying to pour it. There's not that much, so use it sparingly." She walked out of the bathroom, flipping on the fan on her way out.

And just like that, Eden was once again alone with Rudy in yet another awkward situation.

Couldn't Alice have divided the peroxide-soda solution and let her wash in a different bathroom? Why was the woman so intent on pushing her and Rudy together at every turn?

She looked at Rudy, but he wouldn't meet her gaze. He just stared at the tub; his brow furrowed, and his lips pressed into a tight line.

Eden was ready for this night to be over already. Heaving a sigh, she stepped into the tub and sat on the edge. She dipped her washcloth in the bucket. Dumping tomato juice over herself was one thing, but rubbing a washcloth over her body while Rudy watched made her more self-conscious than she'd ever been in her life.

Nope. I won't let myself watch him wash his body. And I'll pray he doesn't watch me.

Watching the tomato juice drip off his biceps and well-sculpted pecs had been torture enough. This would be even worse. Especially after sharing a couple of amazing kisses.

God hadn't sent down a bolt of lightning, but the way their last kiss ended so abruptly told Eden they shouldn't be kissing at all.

Alice versus God. Who will win?

The persuasive woman was a powerful force of nature, but God doled out hefty punishments.

The peroxide mixture wasn't any warmer than the tomato juice had been, and goosebumps raised on her skin as she rubbed the cloth over first one arm then the other.

Rudy finally joined her, staying perched on the edge of the tub, like she was. He dipped his cloth and rubbed it over his arm. He let out a long and loud shudder that shook his whole body.

Eden couldn't help herself; she burst out laughing. Never in a million years would she have thought she'd get sprayed by—not one, but two—skunks, bathe in tomato juice, and then share a peroxide scrub with an overly dramatic, handsome sheriff's deputy.

Wouldn't her Instagram followers love to see him now? She'd

made the mistake of posting a picture of them working on the website a few days ago, and they had gone wild, begging for more photos of him ever since.

The more she thought about the ridiculous events of this night and the fact that she and Rudy—both nearly naked—sat so close to one another, yet doing everything they could to keep from touching and looking at each other only made her laugh harder.

Rudy joined her, and when he laughed so hard, he started to hiss, she hit the point where she could no longer breathe. Tears streamed down her face which only made him hiss louder.

Finally, they both gasped, struggling for air. It still took several minutes for their laughter to die away completely.

After wiping down her legs, she dipped her cloth yet again and shifted to wipe at her back the best she could.

Rudy cleared his throat. "I'll wash yours if you wash mine."

Eden froze. That sounded way too intimate and almost inappropriate.

He's only offering to wash my back. Nothing else.

But then he'd want her to wash his. She'd been all too aware of the taut muscles in his back when he told her about the accident that killed his friend, and this situation was even more intimate.

He turned toward her. "Come on, you might be able to reach all of your back, but I know I can't reach all of mine."

Yeah, because you have too many muscles.

Fortunately, she managed to keep the thought from coming out of her mouth. Instead, she said, "Okay," and handed him her cloth before pulling her hair to the side.

She focused on taking deep even breaths as he rubbed the washcloth over her back, because every innocent brush of his fingers against her skin sent a series of shivers racing through her.

"Listen, Rudy. I don't think...we should kiss anymore."

He let out a heavy sigh as his hand dropped away. "You're probably right." He shifted, rotating away from her. "Not going to lie, I'm disappointed, but it's probably for the best."

His quick agreement only amplified her own disappointment.

"It is."

When he turned his back to her, broad, sculpted shoulders beckoned her to touch them. It was obvious he made good use of the home gym downstairs. Something she hadn't found time to do yet. She drew in a deep breath and braced herself for the task at hand.

She dipped his cloth, soaking up the last of the peroxide mixture, and focused on not touching his skin as she wiped over his taut muscles. Every time her mind began to fantasize about dropping the washcloth and caressing his back with her hand, she reeled it in. She shouldn't be thinking about him like that after telling him they couldn't kiss anymore.

"Okay, I'm done." she said as she tossed his washcloth into the empty bowl.

Did her voice sound as breathless as she felt?

Rudy surveyed his arms and chuckled. "We're going to look like a couple of albinos."

"Why?"

"Because peroxide is like bleach, it takes the color out of your hair. Why do you think there are so many blonds in the world?"

Eden would have laughed at the joke if her body wasn't slathered in a solution that would lighten her hair. At least she'd shaved her legs this morning. She looked at her arms where small clumps of the goopy mixture clung to the fine hairs.

Then a thought hit her, and she felt the color drain from her face.

Oh no, have I touched my hair? What about my eyebrows?

Her face was one of the first places she washed.

Rudy must have seen the horror on her face because he laughed again. "Relax, the hairdressers always leave the peroxide stuff on for like thirty minutes, if you shower soon, I'm sure you'll be fine."

Eden didn't know how long they'd been perched on the edge of the tub, but she wasn't taking any chances. She turned on the water, stood, and tugged the lever to turn the shower on.

Cold spray struck Rudy's body and bounced off, hitting her.

"Oh snap! That's cold!" He bolted upright and pulled the shower curtain closed before cowering at the back of the tub. "You could have at least let the water warm up before turning the shower on."

"Sorry." She really wasn't, though. If it wasn't for Rudy agreeing to take her to meet Hazel then talking about stargazing, they wouldn't be in this crazy predicament, where as the shower grew warmer, the temperature in the bathroom skyrocketed.

CHAPTER 14

*E*den jumped when her cell phone dinged beside her. She'd been so intent on inputting Hattie's ledgers into a spreadsheet so she could analyze the state of her business that the noise startled her. With Alice spending the week at Debbie's house tending the three youngest children while Debbie and Austin were in Florida, the house was quiet.

She picked up her phone to find a text from her father. *I'd like you to bring Rudy to dinner on Friday evening.*

Eden's breath caught in her throat. She and her dad had only exchanged a handful of menial texts over the past two weeks since his visit, so this request surprised her. If she took Rudy home for dinner with her dad, they would have to pretend he was her boyfriend again.

Despite agreeing they shouldn't kiss anymore, something had shifted between them. Mutual acceptance and respect seemed to strengthen the bond they shared. The tension was always there though. She wished they could just stop fighting what was happening between them and enjoy a real relationship. Maybe they could if she'd ever figured out what she wanted to do with her life.

She finally applied for two jobs yesterday, leaning more toward marketing and branding rather than analytics. Part of her hoped that one particular job panned out, because she felt she'd enjoy working for Avant-Garde Home Decor. The rest of her hoped neither did because it would mean she'd have to leave Providence. And she wasn't sure she wanted to do that.

Even though she and Rudy hadn't kissed again, there had been more across-the-room eye contact accompanied by smiles and an occasional wink. They'd shared a few casual yet lingering touches. And every time he touched her, her heart skipped a beat.

Every. Single. Time.

Her phone buzzed in her hand, and the screen showed another text from her dad. *If you really like this guy that much, I figure I should get to know him.*

Did she really like Rudy enough that she wanted her dad to get to know him?

Yes! Her heart screamed.

Could she convince Rudy to have dinner with her dad, knowing she'd be taking him into a lion's den full of condescension, judgment, and piousness.

Other thoughts flooded her mind. Did her father really want to get to know Rudy or was this just a ploy to get her close enough to try to force the whole engagement to Tristan thing?

If so, she'd rather not subject Rudy or herself to dinner with her dad. She'd love to see Helen, but she'd be more than content to spend her Friday night playing games with Rudy's parents and Scott and Kennedy.

After several long moments of internal debate, she typed out a response. *I'll invite Rudy if you promise not to mention Tristan while we're there.*

Eden's phone rang in her hand, causing her to jump again. The noise echoed through the quiet house for several long seconds as she regarded her father's face on her screen. Her stomach tightened at the thought of speaking to him, especially if he intended to talk about Tristan. But she couldn't ignore his call, since he knew she was near her phone.

She pressed talk. "Hello." She kept her voice low and hopefully, steady.

"I was afraid you might not answer." Her father's voice was equally quiet and hesitant.

"I almost didn't."

"I guess I can't blame you." He let out a heavy sigh. "I owe you an apology."

"What?" Eden didn't think she'd ever heard her father apologize.

"I was...rather hard on you."

"Uh...which part are you referring to?"

Her dad gave a small cough. "I behaved quite deplorably, letting this thing with Laurent and the prospect of exclusivity turn my head. I was aware of Tristan's reputation, yet I tried to force you into the engagement anyway. In light of recent developments, I'm glad we didn't tie ourselves to him."

We? Ourselves?

Eden had no idea what recent developments her father referred to, but he made it sound like he was the one who'd refused involvement with Tristan.

"Uh... I'm... What?"

Eden stared at the flashing cursor on her computer screen as she attempted to make sense of her father's words. He was a proud man and not one to apologize easily. Yet, he'd done it twice now. Sort of. And he was dropping the whole Tristan thing? Just like that? What recent developments was he referring to?

"I'm sorry my insistence that you get engaged to Tristan drove you away from work and from Spokane."

Did he just apologize a third time?

"Wait. Wait. Wait." She shook her head, hating her inability to articulate words sometimes. "What recent developments are you talking about?"

"Haven't you seen the tabloids?" Incredulity filled her father's voice. "Tristan's latest...indiscretions are all over social media."

"I haven't paid much attention to Instagram lately." Other than to post pictures and process the online orders for Hattie, that is.

"That's probably a good thing. I won't bore you with all the details that you can easily look up. Let's just say that Laurent is furious with Tristan and threatening to disown him altogether now that a second woman has come forward claiming to be carrying his child."

A second woman? Eden wasn't aware there had been a first.

Wait, that's not true.

She did recall some woman claiming to be pregnant with Tristan's baby a few months ago, but Laurent insisted it was all a ploy for money and demanded a prenatal paternity test. The woman was quiet after that, so Eden assumed the results were negative.

What if they were positive? And Laurent paid her off.

Then he tried to force Tristan to shape up by forcing an engagement with her, treating them like puppets on a string. A shudder rippled through her body. She'd definitely dodged a bullet there. She'd never cared much for the narcissistic billionaire, but she'd held him in a little higher regard than she did his playboy son.

Not anymore.

Eden must have been quiet for too long because her father asked, "Are you still there?"

"I...uh...yes. I'm just confused. Are you okay? You're not acting like yourself?"

He chuckled. "I suppose I deserve that." Then he cleared his throat. "Helen and Nora both chewed me out for driving you away."

Eden's jaw dropped. She could understand her former nanny defending her, but Nora? Her dad's strait-laced, stoic secretary stood up for her?

"Wow. I was not expecting that."

What had he said? He'd behaved quite deplorably. That sounded like a phrase Nora would say, alright.

Silence again filled the line.

"So, will you bring Rudy to dinner on Friday?"

Eden had to admit that she'd missed Helen and even her father, in a way. She didn't miss his judgment and criticism, but maybe having dinner with him could start to heal this rift between them. He'd certainly extended an olive branch today.

"I'll have to see if Rudy is available. If I bring him... No, if *I* come home for dinner, there's something else I refuse to discuss." Silence hung heavy on the line while Eden waited to see if he'd protest. When he didn't, she said, "I don't want you to try to talk me into coming back to work at DuPont Analytics."

He let out another sigh, but this one sounded like it was tinged with a growl. "You never did like it here, did you?"

She gave a rueful grin as she looked at Hattie's ledgers spread across the table in front of her. She certainly didn't enjoy having to enter all this data, but it was necessary to see the bigger picture and ensure success for Hattie.

Eden didn't understand why she felt so strongly about helping the aged store owner, but she did. And the most important thing was she enjoyed it. She hadn't made much money yet, but that wasn't as important to her as helping Hattie, who was so appreciative of her help.

She needed to find a job soon though, because she couldn't take advantage of the Wheeler's hospitality forever. Nor did she want to be at her father's mercy again.

Eden didn't bother answering her dad. She'd made it no secret in recent years that she didn't like her job. She just wished she hadn't waited so long to finally take a stand.

"Fine," he said with a huff. "If I promise not to mention coming back to work for me, will you give me a chance to get to know this Rudy kid, so I can figure out what you see in him?"

Her father must really be lonely to push this hard for her to bring Rudy home.

"He's not a kid, Dad."

He's a man. A strong, attractive one.

"I prefer the idea of my baby girl having a crush on a boy rather than falling in love with a man."

Falling in love? Was she falling in love with Rudy?

Warmth filled her abdomen as she thought about their kisses and the hours they'd spent working together on the website. Just thinking about him made her heart beat a little harder against her ribcage.

Holy smokes! I'm falling for him.

She'd insisted they avoid a relationship, thinking that if they weren't involved romantically, she wouldn't fall for him, but she hadn't expected him to sneak under her skin like he had. Every time she turned around, she discovered something about him that endeared her to him. Whether it was the way he so respectfully did the things his mother asked, played basketball with a disabled neighbor, or built a website for her. It all made her fall a little more.

She cleared her throat and fanned her face. Thank goodness her father couldn't see her. "I'll see if Rudy is available this Friday and let you know. But Dad, you'd better be nice. No talking down to him and treating him like he's beneath you just because he's from a small town."

"I'll be on my best behavior."

"I'm not sure that's good enough," she joked in a dry tone. It had been a long time since she'd been able to joke with her father like this.

"Probably not." He chuckled. "I promise I'll try not to be too hard on him for taking my daughter away."

"He's not taking me away." Then because she feared he might guess she and Rudy weren't actually in a relationship, she added, "At least not yet."

"Until you marry him," he grumbled. "Then you'll move to that godforsak—" He cleared his throat. "I mean to that small town, and I'll never see you again."

Eden caught her breath at the thought of marrying Rudy. Never in all her life had she thought she would be content to settle down in a small town, but if it were *this* small town where she'd already met so many amazing people, and with a certain handsome sheriff's deputy... Well, the thought no longer appalled her like it did a little over a month ago.

"It's not like I'd be moving across the country. You'll only be an hour and a half away."

"Yeah, but will you come to visit?" Her dad's voice was quiet, serious.

"If we can put our difference of opinions behind us, and I don't feel like I'm constantly being judged for my life choices, I'll make it a point to visit on a regular basis." Eden shifted in her chair, uncomfortable with the lie she was perpetuating. Even though the thought of marrying Rudy appealed to her, she still wasn't sure they belonged together. She wasn't convinced God wanted her to be with him.

She ended her call with her father and tried to focus again on Hattie's ledgers, but her mind kept drifting to Rudy. Had she really admitted to herself that she was in love with him?

No, I may be falling, but I'm not there yet.

It was only a matter of time though. If she kept spending time with him, she'd be so deep that she'd never find her way out.

Her phone rang again.

Thinking it was her dad again, she answered without checking the caller ID. "Hello."

"Oh Eden, thank goodness you answered!" Alice's panicked voice was so loud, Eden had to pull the phone away from her ear. "Bill was in an accident. Can you come to Debbie's and watch the little ones so I can go to the hospital?"

"Absolutely." Eden sprang to her feet the moment Alice said Bill had been in an accident. "I'm on my way!"

The drive to Debbie's house couldn't have been more than three miles, but Eden struggled to take a deep breath the whole way. She hoped whatever accident Bill was in it wasn't like her mother's.

Eden had planned to go over in an hour anyway to help Alice fix dinner just as she had for the last three nights.

Her stomach remained clenched as she parked in Debbie and Austin's expansive driveway and raced to the front door. Alice opened it before she could even knock.

"Is Bill okay? What happened?"

Worry filled Alice's tear-stained face. "I don't know other than he fell off the roof at Mrs. Jacob's house."

"Oh no."

She waved behind her into the house. "The kids are eating a snack right now, if you want to, you can just fix mac & cheese for dinner.

They'll probably eat that better than the chicken parmesan I planned to make."

"Don't you worry about a thing." She caught Alice's arm as the distraught woman went to step off the porch. "Are you sure you should be driving?"

Just then Scott dove up in his truck.

"I'm not driving. Rudy sent Scott to come take me to the hospital."

"Good. I'll be praying for Bill." Eden wasn't sure Alice heard her since she was already opening the door to climb into Scott's truck.

Eden pressed a hand to her chest as she sent up a prayer for Bill. Then she sent up another one for Rudy's family.

CHAPTER 15

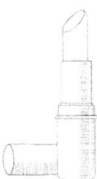

*E*den pasted on a smile as she walked into Debbie's house. Just as Alice had said, baby William and the twins sat at the kitchen table eating cheese and apple slices. An applesauce packet sat on the table near William.

Eden did her best to infuse enthusiasm into her voice as she greeted the children. "Hi, guys. Are you having a yummy snack?"

A pout formed on Lucia's face—at least she thought it was Lucia. She hadn't been around the girls enough to tell them apart yet. But she recalled Debbie telling her she used to always put a pink bow in Lucia's hair and a purple bow in Mia's hair to help Austin learn who was who and now, the girls always chose those colors.

The little girl, who now had tears forming in her eyes, wore a pink bow in her curly black hair. "Gamma?"

Eden sat down between the baby and the twins. She reached out to stroke Lucia's cheek. "Grandma had to go bye-bye for a while, so I get to play with you. Do you remember me? I'm... Auntie Eden."

Calling herself their aunt was a stretch, but they had three aunts that they knew well and trusted. If they could think of her as another aunt, maybe it would make them more comfortable with her.

Little Mia's eyes also filled with concern, so Eden gently stroked her cheek next. "We're going to have so much fun. Why don't you hurry and finish your snack, and then we can go outside and play."

Eden's chest remained tight with worry for Bill while she fed William his applesauce. She was more than a little anxious for herself as well over the responsibility that had been heaped upon her.

Panic repeatedly clawed at her throat making it difficult to breathe as she cleaned the children up. She had no idea what she was doing. Hopefully, Debbie's kids didn't suffer irreparable damage from her inept care.

She recalled the childcare class she took in high school, where the students helped care for the kids at the school's day care. It was the easiest A she'd ever earned, and she'd loved playing with the children. Her teacher had always emphasized the importance of keeping the children safe and busy. When they got bored was when they cried for their parents or made messes and got into trouble.

Before letting the kids down from the table, she pulled out her phone and sent Rudy a text.

I'm so sorry about your dad. I'm praying for him. Please let me know how he's doing as soon as you can.

She looked down at the twins as they prepared to go outside. "Should we blow some bubbles?"

"Yay!" they cheered while bouncing on their toes.

"Can you show me where the bubbles are?" She'd seen one of Rudy's nieces blowing bubbles for them a couple weeks ago, but she didn't see where they came from.

They both raced across the kitchen and pointed up to a cupboard.

With William on her hip, she searched the cupboard, spotting the bubbles right away. She also found sidewalk chalk and finger paints. The chalk might help entertain the kids, but Eden wasn't brave enough to attempt finger paints with two toddlers and a baby. William would probably try to eat it.

She managed to keep all three children entertained for all of fifteen minutes with the bubbles before their interest waned, and the girls wandered off to the play gym.

She bounced back and forth between pushing a child on the

swings to standing nearby as they went down the slide again and again. Her heart clawed its way up to her throat every time one of the twins climbed the steps. In a rare moment when they were all three on the ground or in a swing, her phone rang, sending her heart to her throat again.

It was too early for news of Bill's condition already, wasn't it? Unless...he didn't make it.

No. He has to be okay.

She pulled her phone from her pocket to find Kennedy's face on her screen.

Please don't let this be bad news.

"Hello?"

"Eden, I just closed up the shop. Are you sure you're okay with Debbie's kids?"

"Yes," she lied. "I'll be fine."

Kennedy let out a sigh. "Good. I can come help you if you need me to, but I feel like I should be with Scott. At least until we know how Bill is doing?"

"Have you heard anything at all?"

"Only that he hurt his back and couldn't move without terrible pain."

"Oh no."

Her thoughts turned to Chase whose back injury left him paralyzed. Pain was a good thing, wasn't it? If Bill didn't have any pain after a fall off a roof, then that would mean... No, she refused to consider that for the larger-than-life man.

"You go be with Scott and Alice. I'll manage just fine here."

"Thank you. I'll let you know when I hear something." Then the line went dead, leaving Eden wondering who would be there for Rudy.

When it got too hot outside, Eden brought the kids in and played with them, doing her best to keep them entertained, but she couldn't help feeling more than a little stressed when it came time to fix dinner. After what felt like forever, she finally managed to figure out how to work the TV in the family room and turned on a cartoon.

With William frequently following her, she bounced back and forth between the kitchen and the family room to check on the girls while she made mac & cheese and heated chicken nuggets. It had been a long time since she'd eaten the simple fair that was a children's favorite. She'd forgotten how much she liked the fake cheese flavor on the macaroni.

After dinner, all three kids grew restless and whiny while Eden hurriedly cleaned the kitchen. Mia and Lucia kept asking for Gamma, and William seemed to feed off their anxiety and became increasingly fussier.

Eden found herself near tears a time or two. She wasn't sure if it was because she felt overwhelmed by responsibility or if it was worry for Bill. She hadn't heard anything yet from Kennedy or Rudy and her fears ran rampant.

All three children hit meltdown mode at the same time, and desperation drove Eden to the lengthy list of instructions that Debbie had left on the fridge, but she hadn't had a chance to read yet. Bouncing William on her hip and alternately patting the heads of the toddlers who clung to her legs, she scanned the pages.

Her eyes caught on the word bath, and she recalled how much the children at the daycare had enjoyed playing with the water table. There was something about the element that calmed children.

"Who wants to take a bath?" she asked.

The tears stopped immediately.

"Bath?" Lucia repeated.

"Yay!" Mia let go of Eden's leg and darted down the hall.

Eden faced a moment of panic as she realized she had no idea how to bathe one child let alone three. Did she put them all in at once or one at a time? She knew she couldn't possibly dress all three at once, but it would be dangerous to leave the girls in the tub while she dressed William and vice versa. So, even though William fussed and clamored to get into the tub, she put the girls in first.

He eventually settled down and was content to play with the girls over the edge of the tub, squealing each time the girls flicked water at him. Because they were all so happy, she let them play until the girls' hands and feet looked like raisins.

She repeatedly found herself smiling at the children's joy in such simple little things. As stressful as taking care of these little ones was and even though she felt out of her element, she couldn't help thinking that she would make a good mom given the opportunity. Preferably with one baby at a time.

A twinge hit her low abdomen, and she pressed a hand to her stomach. She'd heard of women feeling like their biological clock was ticking, but she'd never experienced this kind of yearning before. It mimicked that powerful feeling she had the day she learned Debbie was pregnant.

I'm only twenty-six, for goodness' sake. My biological clock is not ticking.

Besides, she wasn't ready to give up her career just yet. Well, when she found another career.

The next forty minutes as she got all three kids bathed and into pajamas were hectic and exhausting. Eden made a mental note to come back and clean up the bathroom after she put the children into bed, which she hoped was soon. She needed a break.

Concern for Bill stayed with her as she fixed the girls sippy cups of milk and William a bottle of formula. She couldn't believe no one had bothered to let her know how he was doing. Surely, they'd heard something by now. If not, that didn't bode well for Bill.

Of course, she wasn't actually a member of the family, so she'd be the last person they would bother notifying. Hopefully, they had let Rudy's sisters know. Would they all end up cutting their family vacations short?

She turned off all the lights except for the one over the kitchen sink and a lamp in the family room before settling on the couch with the children to read stories. Unsure of the children's actual bedtime routine, she let the girls look at more books in their beds while she rocked William for a few minutes.

The way he laid his head on her shoulder and put his chubby arm around her neck triggered that urgent feeling low in her abdomen again. Trying to ignore it, she gently kissed his head and tucked him into his crib.

When she returned to the girls' room, she was grateful to find them still in bed already half asleep.

When she bent over Lucia to take her book and tuck her in, a concerned look crossed the toddler's face. "Gamma?"

Eden knelt on the floor beside the toddler bed and stroked her cheek. "It's okay, sweetie. Grandpa got an owie and Grandma needs to be with him for a while. She'll come back as soon as she can. I promise."

Eden hoped her promise wasn't in vain and again prayed that Bill's "owie" wasn't so serious it prevented the children from seeing their grandparents again soon. But the longer she went without hearing from anyone, the heavier the feeling of foreboding that settled over her became.

After pressing a soft kiss to each girl's forehead, she left their door open a crack and hurried to clean up the mess they'd made in the bathroom.

When she rushed over here this afternoon, she didn't know she'd be spending the night. It didn't look like Alice would be returning tonight, so she hoped she would hear if one of them woke up in the middle of the night. Maybe she'd have to ask Kennedy to come over in the morning, so she could run home and take a quick shower and pack a bag.

Speaking of Kennedy... Eden couldn't believe her best friend hadn't bothered to let her know about Bill's condition yet. She pulled out her phone as she picked up the pile of wet towels to take to the laundry room. She was halfway down the hall when she saw a dark figure looming where the front hall met the kitchen.

"Aah!" She dropped the towels and pressed a hand to her racing heart, freezing with indecision.

Did she lock herself in the girls' room to protect them from the intruder or did she go to William's room? Could she rip William from his bed and hurry to the girl's room before the prowler attacked?

The figure turned to face her, and the dim light over the kitchen sink illuminated the side of his face. A familiar, rugged, handsome face covered in a heavy five o'clock shadow.

"Rudy?" She dropped the towels, slipped her phone back into her pocket, and hurried toward him.

The closer she got the more pronounced the tortured expression on his face and in his red eyes became. He looked so exhausted and beaten. Again, she asked herself who had been at the hospital for Rudy?

Without hesitation, she wrapped her arms around him. "How's your dad?"

He clung to her, holding her in a vice-like hug and let out a lengthy sigh. "He's in serious condition and heavily sedated, but he'll survive, thank goodness. Hopefully with no lasting damage."

The band that had been around Eden's chest all afternoon and evening loosened and she sucked in a deep breath. Well, as deep as she could with Rudy hugging her so tight. She relaxed her hold, but he showed no inclination of releasing her, so she kept her arms around him, giving him the comfort he seemed to so badly need.

He sniffed a few times, and Eden's heart constricted. This afternoon and evening must have been a nightmare for him. Knowing Rudy, he had probably been the pillar of strength his mother needed and now he relied on her strength.

Except she didn't feel very strong. She didn't know how to comfort this man that she cared an awful lot about with something so difficult.

Eventually, his hold loosened, and he stepped back but didn't meet her eyes. "Thank you. I needed that."

She put a hand on his arm and ducked close to meet his gaze. "Anytime. I want you to tell me everything. But first...have you eaten?"

"Yes, Mom refused to go home for the night, so Scott and I insisted she go to the cafeteria. We all choked down sandwiches and soup."

"Probably a far cry better than the mac & cheese I made for the kids." The quip didn't trigger a smile on Rudy's face like she'd hoped. She took his hand and led him into the family room. "Tell me what happened to your dad."

Rudy sat on the couch next to her and propped his elbows on his knees. He scrubbed his hands over his face. "I was mobile when I heard the call for an ambulance come through. So I headed straight to the address. I beat the ambulance there. As soon as I turned onto Aspen Lane, I knew the call was for Mrs. Jacobs' house, and I knew my dad had been injured." Rudy tugged at his hair now. "I found him on the ground behind the house with Mrs. Jacobs standing nearby, wringing her hands. He was in such excruciating pain he couldn't move at all."

Eden rubbed Rudy's back much like she had in the kiddie pool when he told her about his friend Parker. He still wore his brown uniform pants, but he'd shed his uniform shirt, Kevlar vest, and gun belt, leaving him in a tan t-shirt.

"It took the ambulance forever to get there, and I felt so helpless. Other than lifting the ladder off him, I couldn't do a darn thing for him." Rudy rocked a little as he continued to talk. "He'd been in the process of climbing from the ladder onto the roof when he slipped. He wasn't sure exactly what happened, but the next thing he knew, he was on the ground with the ladder on top of him."

"Oh no." Eden's words were soft.

"Because he kept complaining of pain in his back and ankle, they x-rayed those areas first. He has a fracture in the L1 vertebrae—that may need surgery—and an ankle that's broken in two spots. He'll almost certainly need surgery on it." He scrubbed his hands over his face again. "Just as the doctors were preparing to send him to the Tri-Cities to be seen by an orthopedic surgeon, his blood pressure plummeted. So they rushed him in for an MRI."

The hands Rudy now raked through his hair trembled as badly as his voice. Eden scooted a little closer and leaned against him, wrapping an arm around his back.

"They found a tear in his spleen. Probably caused by the ladder falling on him. They took him in for emergency surgery. It ended up being worse than they originally thought, and they almost lost him."

"Oh, Rudy, that must have been horrendous for you and your family."

He nodded and leaned back, pulling her into his arms as he did so.

She leaned her head against his shoulder and wrapped her arm around his stomach.

"I just kept praying that he would be okay. I'm not ready to lose my dad yet." His voice caught, and she held him a little tighter.

Eden thought about the conversation she had with her dad today. It felt like an eternity ago, but they'd made a little progress in mending their relationship. At this point, she couldn't ask Rudy to go to dinner with her father. Not with everything that was going on with his dad.

"I've been praying all day too." She lifted her head to see his face. "Is he really going to be okay?"

"I hope so." Rudy tucked a lock of hair behind her ear. "He'll be transported tomorrow via ambulance to the Tri-Cities to see an orthopedic surgeon. He'll likely undergo surgery on his ankle and maybe even his back. Either way, he's looking at a lengthy recovery."

Alice would want to go with Bill, so Eden needed to assure her she was fine to take care of the kids until Debbie came home. The thought both thrilled and terrified her. Hopefully, she could figure out how to keep the little cuties occupied.

Rudy gently guided her head back to his chest. "The down time is going to kill him. He was such a bear last year when he had hernia surgery."

"He's such an active man. It will be hard for him."

In the time that she'd been staying with the Wheelers, she'd never known Bill to sit still for longer than it took to eat a meal. When he was home, he was always working in the garden or on one home improvement project or another.

They sat in silence for a long time, and Eden couldn't help feeling like she was right where she belonged. Rudy's masculine scent wove a tantalizing web around her. The hint of his soap was so faint, she determined the essence she loved was all him. His pheromones were like a heady fragrance to her. And the hand that caressed her back warmed her in a way no words of reassurance could.

She tried not to think about the amazing kisses they'd shared and how much she'd like to repeat them. With their luck, something might go horribly wrong for Bill if they kissed again. It was silly to think that God didn't want her and Rudy together, but she still wasn't convinced it was a good idea.

They lapsed into silence and remained locked in each other's arms for a long time.

When her eyelids grew heavy, she finally sat up and left the circle of Rudy's arms.

He startled and opened his eyes.

"You should probably go home and get some sleep." Although she wasn't sure he should be driving with how drowsy he looked.

He stared across the room. "I can't go home to that empty house, knowing how close we came to losing Dad tonight."

"Then, go sleep in Debbie and Austin's bed." She'd sleep on the couch so she could be close in case one of the children woke up.

"No, you should sleep in their bed. I could probably go upstairs to Savannah's or one of the boy's beds."

When he made no attempt to move, she put a hand on his arm. "Are you okay?"

He ducked his head and shrugged. "I just don't want to be alone right now."

"Then let's stay right here for a while." Eden grabbed another throw pillow off the other side of the sectional and tucked it behind her. "Take off your boots and lay your head on my lap."

That's how Helen had comforted her on those nights that she had been inconsolable after her mother's death.

"No I..." He shook his head. "You don't need to..."

"Come on." She tugged his shirt. "I've been so worried about your dad and your mom and you all day. I don't really want to be alone either."

With a little more coaxing, Rudy pulled his boots off and laid his head on her lap. The offer was meant to soothe and comfort him, but as she ran her fingers through his thick hair and caressed his shoulder, something warmed deep inside her. She couldn't recall ever comforting someone like this.

"Thank you." A deep sigh escaped Rudy. "You know, I misjudged you when we first met."

"What do you mean?"

"I thought you were just a spoiled little rich girl who didn't care about anyone but herself."

Eden's stomach tightened as she waited for further insult from Rudy.

"I'm glad I was wrong about you."

Was he though?

Eden reflected on how self-centered she used to be. She'd never been as demanding as her father and many other rich people, but she'd loved her conveniences. And she'd paid a lot of money for people to spoil and pamper her, thinking she deserved it. All because she had money.

It sickened her to think about how self-indulgent she had behaved. If she hadn't had the influence of Kennedy, the daughter of a humble mechanic, most of her life, Eden would likely have turned out as uppity and snooty as many of the people she detested in her father's social circles. Surprisingly, she hadn't missed the indulgences as much as she thought she would. They seemed so frivolous and insignificant in comparison to the life she now lived.

A life she liked. A lot.

THE RINGING of a cell phone pushed its way into Rudy's consciousness. He shifted, trying to figure out where he was and why his neck hurt so bad.

A soft groan sounded from somewhere above his head, and something shifted under his cheek. His eyes flew open.

Pink filled his vision, blurry and soft. The same pink of the t-shirt Eden wore yesterday.

Oh snap!

He bolted upright, sending mini lightning bolts through his head that was stuffed full of cotton. Yesterday's nightmare flooded his mind followed by last night's events.

Eden had comforted him in a way no one ever had, not even after the accident that killed Parker. Her gentle touch had been so soothing, he'd been loath to lose contact with her. He should have insisted on going home or upstairs and let her go to bed, but he'd been selfish and continued to hold her.

He recalled them shifting at some point so she could lay down, but he still hadn't wanted to let her go, and when she'd encouraged him to snuggle with her and lay his head against her stomach, he did.

All. Night. Long.

He'd slept with his arms wrapped around Eden for the entire night.

His stomach knotted as Eden disentangled herself from him. He'd never slept with a woman before. He and Eden hadn't done anything inappropriate, but his mother would freak out if she knew he'd spent the night with her.

Eden finally managed to fish the annoying, ringing phone from her back pocket. "Hello."

"Eden, thank you for being such a lifesaver!" Rudy's eyes widened at the sound of his mom's voice coming through the phone. He scrambled away from Eden, but he could still hear his mom. "How are you? How are the kids? Did Rudy stop by last night to check in on you?"

Rudy made frantic motions with his hands, trying to signal to Eden not to tell his mom he was still there.

Her brow furrowed and she shook her head in confusion. "Um yeah. I had just gotten the kids to bed when he showed up."

"So everything's okay then?"

"Yes, yes the kids are fine. Don't worry. How is Bill doing this morning?"

"He's still in a lot of pain, so they're keeping him pretty heavily medicated, but he's out of trouble, thank goodness." Despite the good news, his mom's voice still sounded weary.

"I'm glad to hear that," Eden said.

"They'll be transporting him to the Orthopedic Surgical Center in Kennewick in an hour or so. I won't be allowed to ride in the ambulance with him, so I'm going to call Rudy to come take me home for a quick shower, and so I can pack a bag."

Eden looked at him. "Well he's—"

Rudy waved his arms in a frantic motion and whispered, "Don't tell her I'm here."

"I'm... I'm sure he'll be happy to come get you," Eden said.

The call ended and before Rudy could explain, his phone rang.

He stood and moved away from Eden before answering. "Hi, Mom. How's dad?" He listened to the same report she'd given Eden then quickly agreed to hurry over to the hospital.

When he hung up, he almost didn't dare meet Eden's gaze. He felt bad for imposing on her all night long.

"What were all the theatrics about?" she asked.

"My mom would freak out if she knew I slept with you last night."

Eden's cheeks turned rosy. "We didn't sleep together. Well, we did but not like...you know?"

"I know, but I feel bad for taking advantage of you all night."

More color tinted her cheeks, and heat crept up his neck at his choice of words.

"If you think that was taking advantage of me, you're more of a naive country boy than I thought."

"You know what I mean. I should have let you go to bed, rather than selfishly use you as a pillow all night."

She stepped close to him then, and it was all he could do not to pull her into his arms again. "You needed a friend. I enjoyed being that friend."

Friend. Right.

Except at some point, when he'd finally been able to block the nightmare of the evening from his mind, the thoughts he'd had concerning Eden had gone way beyond friendship. It's amazing he'd managed to keep his hands from wandering and not make out with her half the night.

I'm such a selfish jerk.

He could never take advantage of her like that again. She deserved more respect than what he'd given her last night. He needed to put some distance between them.

He took her by the shoulders and pressed a quick kiss to her forehead before pushing her away. "Thank you for being my friend."

Did he imagine it or did a flash of disappointment flit through her pretty brown eyes?

Or maybe he was just projecting his own disappointment.

CHAPTER 16

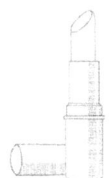

*R*udy's dad heaved a sigh as he helped him settle on the couch. "Thanks, son."

He carefully lifted his dad's broken ankle onto the sofa and propped it on a pillow. "You're welcome, Dad. Do you need me to get you anything else?" He made sure the TV remote and a water bottle sat within easy reach.

Sheriff Winters insisted Rudy take some time off, so he'd been here all week to help his mom care for his dad, for which he'd been grateful. His mom was a strong woman, but he feared she'd wear herself out before his dad fully healed.

"I'm fine." Dad waved Rudy away. "Stop fussing over me."

Grinning, Rudy backed toward the door. "Well, Mom's out grocery shopping, so holler if you need something."

"I won't." This time his grumble made him sound like Scott. "Stop trying to smother me."

He took one more lingering look at his dad before leaving the room. Bill Wheeler was not a patient man, but his whole family was so glad he was still with them, they couldn't help smothering him.

Rudy's sisters stopped by daily with treats and things to help entertain him. His brothers-in-law and some of the grandkids had shown up to help in the garden several times, and this Saturday, all the men had decided to forgo working on Scott's house to help finish up the addition at Mrs. Jacobs' house.

Fortunately, his dad didn't need to undergo back surgery. Thanks to modern medicine, the surgeon had been able to inject bone cement into the cracked vertebrae to help it heal. He still needed to wear a brace that limited his mobility for six weeks, however. And he wasn't so lucky when it came to his ankle. He now sported a metal plate and numerous screws, which only limited his mobility even more and made him further dependent on others, and he hated it.

Rudy stopped at the entrance to the kitchen and studied the beautiful dark-haired beauty at the table, pouring over Hattie's ledgers. Things were running smoothly with the website nowadays and that disappointed him. He missed working side by side with Eden in the evenings.

She had amazed him this past week. Even though she'd admitted to being overwhelmed, she'd patiently taken care of Debbie's kids for forty-eight hours.

Debbie had arranged to come home immediately once she heard about their dad's accident, but a canceled flight dragged the journey out for two days.

Eden had helped tirelessly with his dad and around the house too, lifting the burden placed on his mom. She spent more time in the kitchen than his mom did lately, and she seemed to be the only one who could tease his dad out of his grumpy moods. Every little act of kindness Eden did made him fall a little deeper for her.

He kept reminding himself marriage was not part of the plan for a few more years, but his reasoning was beginning to sound faulty.

Her phone rang while he stood there admiring her. After checking the screen, she set the phone down again. But she must not have felt like she could ignore it, because she snatched it up again.

"Hi, Dad." Her voice was quiet, but not nearly as annoyed as he'd expected, considering her father was on the other end.

Had she mended the rift with her dad sometime in the past month?

"He's doing better, but he'll be laid up for some time."

They're talking about my dad.

"I don't know. I hate to ask him to come, because that leaves only Alice to take care of Bill."

Come where?

"No, I haven't mentioned it to him yet. He's been pretty stressed with everything that's been going on." She paused for a moment, listening to her father. "I know. I promise I'll talk to him soon, but next week might be better." She paused for a moment. "I miss you too, Dad."

Rudy's eyes widened. Had she really told her father she missed him?

She ended the call, and he suddenly felt guilty for eavesdropping. He shifted his weight, trying to decide whether to fess up or walk away. The floorboard creaked under his foot, and Eden looked over her shoulder.

When she shot him one of those grins that made his heart race, he decided walking away wasn't possible.

"Was that your dad I heard you talking to?" He strolled into the kitchen and got himself a drink of water he didn't need and carried it to the table. He sat across from her.

"Yes."

"You didn't sound nearly as irritated as I expected."

"Things have changed. We've talked some things out." She lifted one shoulder in a shrug. "I guess you could say we're trying to mend our relationship."

"That's good, right?"

If it was so good, why did his stomach clench at the thought of Eden getting along with her father?

Because if they get along too well, she might go back to working with her dad.

"What's changed?"

Was she planning to leave already?

"The whole Tristan thing imploded. He's surrounded by all kinds of negative press lately, and my dad realized we dodged a bullet there. Thankfully, he's no longer pushing me to get engaged to him."

"Good." But if that was the case, Eden no longer needed a fake boyfriend. He should feel relief, but instead his stomach tightened a little more.

"I'm glad that ridiculous engagement is behind us, but there's still plenty of tension between us. He's still sore that I refuse to return to DuPont Analytics."

His stomach finally relaxed.

Eden's not leaving. Yet.

Why did he have to tack a *yet* onto the end of that thought? It sat there like a ticking time bomb. As content as Eden seemed here, deep down, Rudy knew she'd leave Providence someday.

"I'm glad things are improving." Did his voice sound as tight to her as it did to him?

"Speaking of my dad..." Eden grimaced. "He wants me to bring you to dinner Friday night."

Now he needed a drink of water. He picked up the glass and drained it.

"Why?" His voice squeaked on the single word.

"He wants to get to know you." She pushed her fingers into her hair and flipped it from the left side to the right. "He still thinks you're my boyfriend."

Rudy's heart surged upward in his chest, cutting off his air supply. "You didn't come clean now that the Tristan thing is behind you?"

She slumped forward. "I know I should have, but I... I just couldn't admit that I lied to him. He'd be so angry and disappointed with me."

He ducked his head a little to meet her gaze. "At some point, you need to stop trying to please your father and live your life on your terms."

"I know. I'm trying. I really am. But until he accepts that I'm not coming back to work for him, I don't want to cause more waves. It's just easier to pretend you're my boyfriend." She wrinkled her nose a little. "That is, if you don't mind going along with the charade a little longer."

Mind? Why would I mind?

He'd been wanting to fill that role for real for a while now, despite all the misgivings he had about a relationship with Eden. Would Oliver DuPont force them to kiss again?

"Let me see..." He pretended to put serious thought into it. "Do I mind facing your father so he can grill me about how I intend to support his daughter."

She grimaced again. "You're right. It's a bad idea. I warned him he'd better be nice, but I'm sure he'll find a passive aggressive way of telling you you're not good enough."

Meaning I'm not good enough for his daughter.

Rudy had to agree. Eden hadn't turned out as spoiled as he'd first thought and hadn't once looked down her nose—that he'd seen—at his family, but that didn't change the fact that she was raised with wealth and privilege and was used to a certain lifestyle. One he wasn't sure he could afford.

The classy summer dress she wore today, like most days, attested to that. Even her jeans and T-shirts had designer labels.

"He asked me to bring you for dinner last week, right before your dad's accident." She looked over her shoulder toward the family room. "Needing to be here to help your dad has been a convenient excuse to avoid him, but I should probably just tell him the truth about us and face the music." She lowered her gaze and picked at fingernails that were overdue for a manicure.

"I don't mind going with you," Rudy heard himself say. If it meant spending all of Friday evening with her, he could suffer through dinner with her judgmental father.

Her head shot up, and she smiled. "Really?"

He loved how her smile reached her eyes and lit up her whole face. If she kept smiling at him like that, he'd be hard pressed to ever say no to her.

He gave a nonchalant shrug. "I'm a police officer. I've dealt with a lot worse than passive aggressive comments."

"Are you sure?" When he nodded, she went on. "We should probably make sure Scott and Kennedy will be around, in case your mom needs help."

Yet another reason he looked forward to an evening with Eden away from here. When Kennedy came over, she and Eden usually disappeared into her bedroom where they talked for hours. Rudy suspected a good chunk of their conversation centered around him. Or maybe that was just wishful thinking.

He was tempted to talk to Scott about the push and pull going on between him and Eden and his contradictory feelings, but besides the fact that guys didn't discuss stuff like that, he wasn't sure his quiet brother would be any help.

RUDY CAUGHT back the low whistle that clawed at his throat as soon as Eden pulled into the circle driveway of her childhood home. The house was massive. Easily as big as Debbie's, if not bigger.

There's no way I can compete with this.

A stark awareness of the humble circumstances he'd grown up in hit him. With a carpenter father and a mother who was a school lunch lady, they'd always lived frugally. Simply. They'd never enjoyed great luxuries, yet Rudy had never felt like he'd missed out on anything. And they'd never wanted for the necessities of life.

But this...

He'd pegged Eden for a rich girl the first time he met her due to her fancy manicure, brand-name clothing, and expensive car. But he had no idea exactly how wealthy her father was. The Stingray Oliver DuPont drove to Providence a couple of weeks ago should have given him a clue.

He tugged on the collar of his blue button-down shirt, cursing his decision to wear a tie and a blazer. It felt even more restrictive than the Kevlar vest he donned every day for work.

As they walked up the lengthy sidewalk to the front door, Eden repeatedly smoothed the front of her red silk dress that fit her like a second skin and made his pulse kick into overdrive. After flipping the hair she'd curled so nicely from one side to the other and back again, her hands fidgeted as though she intended to smooth her dress again.

Apparently, I'm not the only one who's nervous.

Eden had every right to be anxious.

Her relationship with her father was on the line. She said they were trying to mend things, but there was still a lot of tension between them. If things went badly tonight, she might never return.

Rudy only had to worry about Eden's dad being judgmental and condescending toward him. Failure to meet Oliver DuPont's expectations—which he knew he never could—wouldn't have the lasting consequences for him that it would for Eden.

Unless he decided to pursue a relationship with her.

The urge grew stronger every day.

Rudy's only hope to impress Oliver was to be honest and frank. And respectful.

They stepped onto the porch and Eden raised a hand to her hair again.

He caught it in his and laced his fingers with hers. "Relax. It's going to be okay."

He wasn't sure how strongly she intended to sell their relationship, considering the Tristan threat was no longer an issue, but he liked having an excuse to touch her and hold her hand.

"Easy for you to say. You've only ever been around my dad for a few minutes at a time."

"Do we need a code word? That way if things get to be too much, you can say the code word, and I'll make an excuse to get you out of there. We could go with something like skunk."

"Anything but that!" Eden laughed like he'd hoped she would. "I never want to hear that word ever again, nor do I want to see another one of those vile little creatures for the rest of my life."

"Okay, we could go with something like wind chimes." He recalled the joy on her face as she admired Helen's handiwork. "Although that could be awkward to work into conversation."

"And skunk isn't?" She held up her hand when he opened his

mouth to try again. "No need for a code word. When I decide I've had enough, I'll announce that we're leaving."

Her face didn't look as confident as her words sounded.

"When? Not if?" Still gripping her delicate hand in his, Rudy pressed the doorbell.

"Believe me, there's no doubt there will come a point *when* we're both ready to leave."

The door opened and Oliver DuPont aimed a frown at Eden. "You didn't need to ring the bell. This is still your home. You can just walk in."

"My fault, sir." Rudy held out his hand. "I guess I was a little eager."

Oliver took it in a solid handshake, and Rudy remembered the lesson his dad taught him before allowing him to go on his first date. Always look her dad in the eye and shake his hand like a man.

That's exactly what Rudy did, and when Oliver's gaze narrowed on him, he stared right back, unflinching.

When Oliver finally released his hand, Rudy smiled. "Thanks for having me, sir." If Oliver detected the hint of challenge in Rudy's voice, he hid it.

He refused to cower to this wealthy businessman. He'd stand up to Eden's father, and if she needed him to, he would defend her and back her up.

Oliver turned to Eden and hesitated with his arms half extended, as though unsure Eden would welcome a hug. Evidently Eden was determined to do her part to mend their relationship, because she stepped into his embrace.

"I'm glad you came. I've missed you." Oliver whispered in a husky voice.

"I've missed you too, Dad."

Oliver beckoned them in and waved them toward the sitting room.

Rudy sat on the loveseat and put his arm along the back, an invitation for Eden to sit beside him. The knot that took up residence in his stomach the moment he stepped out of the car loosened when she not only sat beside him, she leaned into him.

They would face her father together. As a team.

"How's your father doing?" Oliver asked him.

"He's still in a considerable amount of pain, but he's slowly improving, thank goodness."

They continued to discuss his dad's accident for a few minutes then Oliver said, "Such accidents are part of the job in construction, I suppose."

"They happen occasionally, but they really aren't all that common," Rudy said. "All jobs come with risks of one kind or another though."

"Blue collar jobs especially." Oliver's chin lifted a little. "I mean *you* strap on a bullet-proof vest every day for work."

And there it was. Oliver's first dig. Subtle, but full of disdain all the same. Judging by the way Eden's hand gripped his thigh, she'd caught it too.

Rudy refused to be ruffled. For Eden's sake, he'd do his best to avoid conflict with her father. He grinned at the older man. "Isn't it great that there are people willing to take the risks, so others can sleep in their warm comfortable homes in peace at night?"

Eden's face split into a broad grin. The kind that made his heart beat a little faster.

Rudy couldn't quite let her father's dig go. "Even the business class suffer from the stress of their jobs though. I recently read an article about how most businessmen and women are sleep deprived and consequently suffer from depression and anxiety in addition to addiction and heart disease. Heck, we're all probably walking around with an ulcer that is only one stressful day away from rupturing."

Oliver laughed at this. If he heard the criticism in Rudy's words, he chose not to react.

A tall, slender woman who looked to be in her mid-fifties walked into the sitting room. Her simple navy-blue dress with a white lace collar matched her stiff posture. A smile softened her features when she spotted Eden. "There's my girl."

Eden rose from the couch and let the woman wrap her in a tight embrace.

"I've missed you, sweetheart."

Rudy heard a soft sniff from Eden before she whispered, "I've missed you too, Helen."

The older woman, who was considerably younger than Rudy had expected, continued to hold Eden tight. "I chewed your father out for that ridiculous scheme he tried to force you into." She shot a scowl in Oliver's direction over Eden's shoulder. "I made him fend for himself for a whole week."

Eden giggled. "Good."

"Don't let that stubborn fool chase you away again, you hear?"

"I won't."

On the drive here, Eden had talked a great deal about Helen, her dad's housekeeper and Eden's former nanny, explaining that she had often acted as a buffer between her and her father. Even though Helen was rather strict and impatient, according to Eden, she'd smothered her with love.

Eden finally pulled back from the embrace. "Helen, I'd like you to meet...my boyfriend, Rudy Wheeler."

Hopefully, neither Helen nor Oliver caught Eden's hesitation before saying boyfriend. They might need to work a little harder at selling their relationship.

Rudy sprang to his feet and held his hand out to Helen. "It's nice to meet you."

The older woman took his hand and pulled him into an embrace, tugging his head down to her level. "I know eleven different ways to filet a fish, so don't even dream of hurting my girl, you hear?"

"Helen!" Eden exclaimed.

And Eden had been worried about the threats her father might make.

"Mmm...I love seafood," Rudy said with a grin.

Helen chuckled as she released him. She eyed him up then back down before squeezing his bicep. She winked at Eden. "He's got the trifecta; tall, strong, and handsome. Don't let this one get away."

A flush of warmth filled Rudy's face, matching the color that tinged Eden's cheeks.

"Helen, stop harassing the boy." Oliver rose too. "I assume dinner is ready?"

"It is." Helen hooked her arm through Eden's and led her toward the dining room. "I made all of your favorites. And this time, don't you dare leave without eating your chocolate mousse."

"I won't." Eden shot an apologetic look over her shoulder at Rudy.

He smiled and waved her on, glad she had Helen in her corner. His footsteps faltered, however, when he entered the dining room that was furnished just a lavishly as the rest of the house with satin draperies and a lace tablecloth—every bit as delicate as Miss Georgie's tatted doilies—covering a massive cherry-wood table. Crystal goblets, fancy China, and more forks than Rudy knew what to do with marked three place settings at the table. One at the head and two to the right.

At least I get to sit by Eden.

They were still getting settled into their seats, when Helen tapped Oliver's shoulder, pointed a finger at him, and mouthed something Rudy couldn't read. Then she was gone, disappearing through a door on the other side of the room. The whole thing happened so fast, he wondered if he'd imagined it.

Rudy had barely taken a bite of his salad when Oliver brought up his job again. "So, Rudy, how much do you make a year as a sheriff's deputy?" His words sounded cordial enough but there was an unmistakable challenge in his voice.

"Dad!" Eden scowled at her father.

Rudy put a hand on her leg under the table to calm her. Even though he couldn't possibly feel more out of place in this monstrosity of a house, he would do whatever it took to keep the peace between Eden and her father tonight. Which meant he would fall back on the motto he'd adopted for himself at the police academy.

Faux confidence and false bravado.

Fake it 'til you make it.

It didn't matter how intimidating your opponent, a.k.a the perpetrator—or in this case, Eden's dad—was, if he saw your weakness, he'd pounce.

He met Oliver's gaze. "Nowhere near as much as you do, sir." He let his gaze wander around the opulent dining room for a moment before returning to the older man. "But I don't have near the expenses you do either."

"Of course, you don't. You still live with your parents." Oliver didn't even attempt to mask the disdain this time.

"Dad, stop it! You promised me you'd be nice." Eden's whole body tensed as though she intended to spring to her feet.

Rudy gave her leg a gentle squeeze. Was silk always this thin? It was all he could do to not caress the slender yet firm muscle of her thigh.

Focus!

A look of regret flashed across Oliver's face. His jaw clenched as he gave Rudy a tight smile. "Forgive me. Your living and financial situation are none of my business."

"On the contrary," Rudy said. "A father should be concerned about how the man his daughter marries intends to support her." Rudy held up a finger. "Although, for the record, Eden and I haven't discussed marriage yet." He locked gazes with Oliver again. "Honestly, sir, I have no hope of being able to support your daughter in the manner she was raised. But I guarantee you if I marry your daughter..." At Eden's sharp intake of breath, Rudy let the sentence hang for a moment. "If I marry Eden, I promise she will never go hungry or without a roof over her head."

Heat sparked in his chest. Speaking of Eden and marriage in the same sentence, triggered all kinds of fantasies in Rudy's head, and not just ones that took place behind closed doors. It was all too easy to picture a life with her as his wife.

Until he looked around at this extravagant house. Then all his insecurities came rushing back.

Despite the images racing through his head, Rudy continued to hold Oliver's gaze until the other man's right brow arched and his lips quirked.

Had he earned a measure of respect? Or was that look masked disapproval?

Rudy gave a curt nod before breaking eye contact and picking up his fork again. He speared a cucumber as if he wasn't sweating bullets under his blazer. "Besides there being a housing shortage in Providence, I've chosen to live with my parents this long because it has put me on track financially to build my own home next year."

Eden's brow shot up right along with her dad's. She turned to face him. "Really? You're building a house? Where?"

He grinned. "I'll give you one guess."

"The only new homes being built in Providence are in the development Austin and Debbie own." She grabbed his arm and gasped. "Are you building in the same subdivision as Scott and Kennedy?"

"Next door." He nodded.

She let out a little squeal. "That's so exciting! I can't believe you haven't mentioned it before."

"Well, we have to finish Scott's house first. My dad's injury will probably slow the whole process down."

"You're building your house yourself?" Oliver asked in a flat tone.

Rudy couldn't tell if the lack of inflection in his voice meant disgust, surprise, or respect—it was difficult to tell with the man—but he decided he didn't really care. Eden's excitement for him was all that mattered.

Helen brought out the main course, consisting of salmon and stuffed bell peppers, and again, she gave Oliver a look that Rudy couldn't interpret, but she definitely conveyed a message when she locked gazes with Eden's dad.

Rudy wasn't all that concerned about impressing Oliver anymore, but he figured this would be a good chance to pick the wealthy man's brain concerning the investing he'd done over the past few years.

"I could use your advice on something, sir," Rudy said with his fork hovering over his salmon.

Once again, Eden's brow rose right along with her dad's.

"I've been wondering if it's time to diversify my investments."

"You have investments?" Oliver coughed into his napkin.

"Nothing like you do, of course, but in addition to the low-risk investments I have through my broker, I've been considering dabbling in penny stocks.

"Wait." Oliver's brow furrowed. "How can you afford to invest? Let alone dabble in penny stocks—which can be risky, by the way—on a deputy's salary?"

"Well, I do some coding and software development on the side in my spare time."

Eden put a hand on Rudy's arm. "He has a computer science degree as well as a criminal justice degree, Dad."

"Software development? I should hook you up with my friend Laurent at Innovative Solutions."

"No, you shouldn't!" Eden pitched forward in her seat. "I do not want Laurent Jordain anywhere near Rudy."

Rudy smiled at her vehemence, until her hand dropped possessively to his leg. Warmth immediately seeped through his dress slacks, and he found himself wishing Oliver would demand they kiss to prove they were committed to each other.

He cleared his throat. "Thanks for the offer, sir, but I'm quite content being a deputy. I'm afraid if I coded full time, I'd find it tedious and boring."

Oliver regarded him for a long moment before shaking his head—in disgust if the frown on his face was anything to go by. "You can stop calling me sir. Now, what kind of questions do you have about your investments."

Rudy shared with Oliver how he'd been investing for the past few years in low-risk, medium-yield stock options but that he was ready to take a little greater risk, and Oliver gave him advice on several different fronts, including corporate bonds and fixed indexed annuities. He listened intently to the older man's counsel and even pulled out his phone to take a few notes.

Eden cleaned her plate then fiddled with her napkin, folding it first one way then another. She must have been bored because she put her hand on his leg and drew little circles on his thigh. Visions of the more intimate fantasies he'd tried to block out earlier filled his head as warmth flooded through his body.

Did the woman have any idea of what her touch did to him?

He caught her hand midway through the third stroke. "Careful, darling, you're playing with fire," he said in a low voice. Then he lifted her hand to his lips and pressed a lingering kiss to the back.

Eden's gaze jumped to his, and she watched wide-eyed as he kissed her hand. Her tongue flicked out to moisten her lips, and Rudy groaned inwardly.

He wanted to haul her onto his lap and kiss her until they both forgot their own names. Instead, he cleared his throat and smiled at Oliver. "I'm afraid we're boring Eden. Perhaps we should talk about something else."

Oliver's easy-going demeanor vanished, and he laid down his fork. His narrowed gaze locked on Eden, his jaw set. "There *is* something I would like to discuss with Eden."

The authoritative tone in his voice instantly cooled Rudy's ardor.

Oh snap!

Was it too late to change the subject back to stocks and bonds?

CHAPTER 17

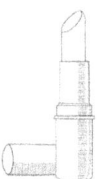

*E*den's stomach plummeted, and she braced herself.

Her dad always used that tone when he intended to control and micromanage her life.

A cold chill swept over her, and she gripped Rudy's hand tighter.

She'd hoped her dad's affable—yet boring—conversation with Rudy meant he'd truly changed. But she should have known he had ulterior motives when he invited her to dinner. Had his insistence that she bring Rudy only been a front to get her to agree to come home?

"I have a job lined up for you," her father said in his no-nonsense, I-expect-to-be-obeyed tone.

"Don't!" She held up a hand and scowled at him. "You promised you wouldn't bring up Dupont Analytics." Heat coursed through her body, hardening her stomach and tightening her chest. She couldn't believe how quickly he'd shifted gears, slipping right back into the same controlling person he'd always been.

"I'm not talking about you coming back to work for me." Bracing his elbows on the table, he leaned forward. "My friend Tad McAllister at Equity Health is looking for an executive secretary and personal assistant."

Those two titles tacked together were code for run-the-bulk-of-my-company and oh, by the way, I-need-you-to-pick-up-my-dry-cleaning-and-take-my-son-to-his-soccer-game-this-weekend.

No thank you!

"Dad, I'm not interested in working for Tad or any of your other colleagues."

"So, you plan to remain aimless and freeload off friends indefinitely?" His tone was full-on disapproval now, matching the deep V between his brows and the thin line of his pinched lips.

It was all Eden could do not to squirm in her seat as perspiration pricked between her shoulder blades. She was well aware she had been mooching off the Wheelers for far too long. She'd asked Alice once if they'd like her to pay rent, but the older woman had shooed her away, saying her helping with the canning was payment enough.

Rudy laid down his fork and covered their clasped hands with his right one.

"No. I'm looking for a job." She forced as much bravado as she could into her words, wishing she had Rudy's confidence from earlier.

"Good. In the meantime, why don't you come back to DuPont?"

"Dad—"

"Now hear me out." He waved away her protest. "You don't have to come back as Head Market Analyst. You can have any job you want. You could even work as a consultant, if you want."

Any job I want. As long as I'm working for you.

He still wanted to control her life, while making it look like it was on her terms.

Eden shook her head and fought back angry tears. Would she ever be free of his interference and micromanaging?

Rudy must have sensed her frustration because he cleared his throat. "With all due respect, sir—"

"Who's ready for dessert?" Helen burst through the door carrying three servings of chocolate mousse cheesecake.

Normally, Eden's mouth started watering about now, but tonight she feared the salmon and stuffed bell peppers might make a reappearance. How could she possibly enjoy the rich dessert while her father continued to criticize her and attempted to control her life?

Eden debated how she could throw out the word skunk without sounding stupid. She'd told Rudy she'd announce when she was ready to leave, but she'd forgotten how difficult it was to stand up to her father who expected her to do everything he demanded.

Helen placed a piece of cheesecake in front of Eden, then rested a hand on her shoulder. She looked up as the older woman bent and whispered, "Hold your ground, honey."

Then Helen turned, blocking Eden's view of her dad. She seemed to take her time setting his dessert down. Eden heard her whisper something to him, but she couldn't make out the words.

She released Rudy's hand to pick up her dessert fork and missed the contact immediately.

Silence, tense and heavy, hung in the air after Helen walked out.

Finally, her dad let out a sigh. "I'm sorry. I know I promised not to push you to come back to Dupont. I just hate to see you throw your life away."

The loud clearing of a throat came from the other side of the door Helen had just exited through, and Eden bit back a smile.

Her dad scowled at the closed door. "I mean—" He sucked in a deep breath and held it for several counts. "Is it me? Am I too critical? Is that why you don't like it there?"

"No, Dad." She let out a sigh of her own.

He seemed willing to listen—as long as Helen stayed near—so how did she tell him she never wanted to follow in his footsteps?

Rudy put his hand on her knee again, lending her his strength and driving her more than a little crazy with the contact.

"I've never enjoyed business analytics," she blurted. "Data collection and analysis are tedious and boring. It's maddening to have business owners argue with my insights and predictions for their company when I'm only trying to help them improve their growth and sales." She bit her tongue to shut herself up.

How ironic that she'd spent the past two weeks inputting Hattie's ledgers so she could run analytics on them. She needed to be able to see the bigger picture to develop a successful business plan for Hattie's Craft Boutique.

"I know." Her dad let out a sigh as he shook his head. "You wanted to go into interior design. And before that, event planning." His voice still held a note of disappointment, but it lacked the sharp tone of disapproval that had been there when they butted heads over her college curriculum.

The tone that eventually made her capitulate and take the business classes he pushed at her. She was an adult by then and should have been able to stand up to her father, but she'd still longed for his approval, so she'd done what she'd needed to please him.

Interior design still interested her, especially when it came to creating eye-catching displays using a variety of mediums at Hattie's. But she also understood why her successful businessman father, who had built his business from the ground up, hadn't thought those professions worthwhile.

"But you wouldn't let me go either of those routes." Her voice was quiet as she picked at her cheesecake with her fork.

Rudy squeezed her leg. She wasn't sure what message he tried to convey, but his silent support meant the world to her. He understood that she needed to stand up to her father on her own, but that she didn't want to do it alone.

"You were so smart, I felt like you were destined for bigger things than planning weddings and birthday parties."

The passive aggressive compliment triggered Eden's defenses. She folded her arms and lifted her chin as she met her dad's gaze. "Maybe, but I should have been allowed to choose for myself." She held her breath after saying the words.

It had been a long time since she and her father had spoken so frankly with one another, and she expected him to blow up any second now and tell her how ridiculous and immature she was acting.

But he didn't blow up. Instead, he looked at the kitchen door, the muscle in his jaw repeatedly flexing.

Helen must have threatened him with something big, to make him hold his tongue like this.

He let out another sigh, but this one sounded more resolved. "I suppose you're right." After a brief pause, he went on in a firmer tone. "I know I was hard on you and pushed you to do things you didn't want to do, but I figured I knew what was best for you and that some-day, you'd thank me."

Eden bristled and dropped the fork she'd just picked up. It landed on her plate with a clatter. "You want me to thank you for pushing me down a path I never wanted to go?"

She felt Rudy tense beside her, no doubt waiting for her to yell skunk. And boy, did she want to. Why couldn't her dad trust her to run her own life without criticizing every little choice she made?

His features hardened as he squared his shoulders. "I hate to see you not living up to your full potential."

"Why do you get to decide what my potential is?" She couldn't help raising her voice in response.

The sound of pans banging together in the kitchen had all three of them looking at the closed door.

Her dad scrubbed a hand over his face. He'd tempered his tone when he spoke again. "But you're wasting your education and your years of experience in the business field. You're just walking away from everything you worked for."

"No, I'm walking away from everything *you* worked for." Eden tried to keep her voice even. "I'm not wasting anything. My education and experience are valuable in all areas of business. In fact, I'm doing some marketing for a small craft boutique in Providence to increase sales and take their business online."

"A craft boutique?" The blank look on his face said he was far from impressed. "You can't honestly expect to support yourself on a fifteen percent cut from...an *Etsy* shop." The emphasis he put on Esty was full of disgust.

Eden squirmed. She didn't want to admit to her father that he was right, especially since she'd only asked Hattie for ten percent.

"It's more than an Etsy shop. It's brick and mortar and not solely online." But it was pretty much the same thing. "Besides, it's only temporary, until I find a real job."

Rudy's fork scraped against his plate, sounding like nails on a chalkboard, and she sensed him tensing again. Except this time, she doubted it was in anticipation of defending her.

Is he upset that I might be leaving soon?

Or did her use of the words "real Job" sound as condescending to him as it did to her? Working for Hattie was a respectable job, it just wasn't the corporate job she was used to.

She shot him an apologetic look before turning back to her dad. "I applied for some jobs last week. Here in Spokane."

Only two actually, but the use of the plural sounded better than the singular.

Rudy stared at her now, but she couldn't bring herself to meet his gaze. She felt so torn.

Please my dad and disappoint Rudy, or please Rudy by staying in Providence forever and disappoint my dad.

Her father's opinion shouldn't matter so much to her, especially since she'd fought so hard to gain her independence, but it did. She'd never had the unconditional love and acceptance from him that Rudy had from his parents, and she wanted that. If her dad was willing to meet her in the middle, she needed to do her part.

Yet less than twenty minutes ago, she'd been ready to kiss Rudy for the way he'd faced her father with pride and confidence. Her heart had swelled with emotion when he promised that if he married her, she would never go hungry or without a roof over her head. Then when he said he planned to build a house next door to Scott and Kennedy, her daydreams of sharing that house with him had run rampant, complete with images of a white picket fence around the yard where their children played.

"Great! Where did you apply?" Her dad's question pulled her thoughts away from a future with Rudy. "Maybe I can put in a good word for you."

"No, Dad. My next job will be one I get on my own." She doubted her father had connections with the home decor stores where she'd applied to be a brand manager.

He gave her a tight smile, but that didn't keep the muscle in his jaw from tensing and the grip on his fork from tightening. Eden had never known him to show this much restraint. This time, she was the one who stared at the kitchen door.

What did Helen do to my dad?

Was her real father tied up in the pantry?

"You're right. You're a grown woman with many talents." His words sound stilted, as though he had to force them out. They also sounded like something Helen would say. "You're capable of finding a job on your own."

"Thank you." Relieved, Eden shoved a big bite of cheesecake in her mouth, relishing a feeling of freedom along with the rich chocolate mousse.

"You're also capable of paying the rent on your apartment, so I won't interfere there anymore either. By the way, your lease runs out in three days."

Eden nearly choked as she tried to swallow the cheesecake. Her stomach plummeted, leaving her feeling light-headed. Her chest tightened again, and the temperature in the room climbed.

Was he trying to cut the final apron strings? Or was he trying to force her hand? She couldn't afford to pay her rent for more than a few months without a decent job. And to get a decent job, she'd need to return to Spokane. Even if she did get a job with one of the home decor stores, she wasn't sure she'd make enough to pay her rent without the help of a roommate.

Bill and Alice would let her stay with them as long as she wanted, she was sure of it. But was that wise? She still didn't know if she belonged in Providence. Nor was she certain she was meant to be with Rudy.

There was undeniable chemistry between them, but she couldn't discredit all the bad things that happened every time they kissed. Besides, if he felt that strongly about her, he wouldn't have been so quick to agree that they shouldn't kiss anymore after the whole skunk ordeal.

Rudy leaned toward her and whispered. "Did you say skunk?"

Had she said that out loud? Or could he tell she was upset and ready to go home?

She nodded, more than ready to get off this emotional roller coaster.

Rudy set his napkin on the table and rose. "Thank you so much for having us, Mr. DuPont, but I'm afraid we need to head home."

A look of disappointment flashed over her father's face, but he quickly hid it. "Of course. I'm glad you were able to come." Her dad stood too. "It was nice to get to know you a little, Rudy."

"You too, sir— uh Mr. Dupont."

"Call me Oliver." Her dad held out his hand to Rudy as if they were old friends.

The evening had gone so much better than Eden expected, so why did she feel so drained and confused?

Because I have big decisions to make. And I need to make them soon.

No more sitting around learning how to be a homemaker from Alice and playing craft boutique assistant. She needed to decide what she wanted to do with her life. The only goal that had filled her mind the last few weeks was to be a mother.

But if she chose motherhood and all the craziness that came with it, she really would be wasting her degree and years of experience. Many women were mothers *and* maintained demanding careers, but was that what she wanted?

They said stilted goodbyes to her father, and Eden hugged Helen again before walking out the door.

Rudy caught Eden's arm as they approached her car. "Are you okay? Do you want me to drive?"

Without meeting his gaze, she nodded and pulled the key from her purse. "Thank you."

She remained quiet as he drove. She was tempted to ask him to stop at her apartment so she could pack up a few more things. But they would only be things she didn't need. Things she hadn't thought about for the past month. Besides, she might be returning to her apartment sooner rather than later. Why haul more stuff out, only to have to bring it back?

As if sensing her turmoil, Rudy asked. "What are you going to do about your apartment?" When she didn't answer, he went on. "Scott and I can bring our trucks on Saturday and help you move out, if you'd like."

Move out?

Although she didn't have a desire to go back to her apartment right now, did she want to move out of it altogether? And did she detect a hint of hopefulness in Rudy's voice? Could she move to Providence with so much uncertainty about the future still hanging in the air?

"You and Scott are supposed to be helping at Mrs. Jacobs' house this Saturday."

"Austin and the others can get along without us for a few hours."

Eden shook her head. "I'll just pay the rent for a month or two, I guess, until I decide what I'm doing with my life."

Rudy's lips pressed into a tight line and the muscle in his jaw tensed. She took in his tight grip on the steering wheel.

Is he angry with me? Or just disappointment?

"Did you really apply for jobs here in Spokane?" His voice was quiet and tense.

"Yes, but I'm not sure I'll get either one. They don't exactly fall within my area of expertise." She shifted her hair from her left to her right. "The one I'm interested in could end up being partly remote work."

"Remote? That means you could stay...in Providence, if you wanted to." That hint of hope filled his voice again.

"Yes, but I'm not sure if I should."

And the disappointment returned to his face. She hated letting both her father and Rudy down on the same evening, but she needed to make these decisions on her own. Without letting herself be swayed by a handsome face.

Rudy shot her a smile. "Looks like I need to up my game and convince you to stay in Providence."

"Up your game?" She gave a laugh, grateful for the distraction. "Have you really been trying to convince me to stay in Providence?"

"My mom seemed to think it was a good idea." Color flooded his cheeks.

"That's why she keeps insisting you take me for walks and help me with Hattie's website?"

He nodded.

"Is your mom the only one who thinks it's a good idea?"

He winked as he reached over and took her hand in his. "Well, she hasn't had to twist my arm too hard yet."

Warmth crept up her arm, slowly spreading throughout her body. Every time he'd touched her tonight, her insides went haywire, sending fluttery feelings from her core throughout her limbs.

"Tell me, were the skunks part of your plan? Or the freak rainstorm?"

"No, on both accounts."

"Are you sure you've got game?" She grinned and quirked a brow at him. "How will I know when you up it?"

His mouth dropped open in a dramatic show of offense. Then a twinkle lit his eyes, and he grinned. "That sounds like a challenge."

She bit her lip. Did she want to encourage this? Would it help her make the hard decisions she needed to make, or would it only complicate things more?

Would God make it clear she wasn't meant to be with Rudy? Or would everything miraculously work out?

"So, what's the deal with Helen and your dad?" Rudy changed the subject.

"I don't know what's going on there, but she sure seemed to be hanging something over his head. I wonder if she threatened to quit if he didn't patch things up with me."

"I think it was more personal than that."

"Personal? What do you mean?"

"Didn't you see the way she touched his shoulder when she gave her little warnings—or whatever it was—she said to him? And the eye contact?"

"No, I didn't. She always blocked my view of him when she spoke to him." She turned wide eyes to Rudy. "Are you saying you think there's something going on between the two of them?"

"This probably could be interpreted a dozen ways, but I looked over my shoulder as we walked out. Just before the door closed, I saw her lean into him and slip an arm around his waist. And your dad put his arm around her shoulder."

Eden gasped. "Are you sure?"

"I'm a cop. It's my job to notice details and read body language. Trust me, there was a lot of communicating going on tonight between the two of them."

"I can't believe it. She's always been so strict and proper, and my dad... Well, appearances are everything to him. He's not the type to get mixed up with his housekeeper."

Although Helen was one of the few people who could put him in his place without him getting angry. Was that why he was trying so hard to change? For Helen?

For the rest of the ride home, she talked, analyzing every interaction she'd seen between Helen and her dad, going back to before her mother died. "She was my mother's best friend. Mom convinced her to come work for us shortly after I was born to get her away from an abusive husband. She's always lived in the apartment over the garage. Never moved out, even after she got on her feet financially. After my mom died, I know my dad was grateful she was there to help with me.

"I'm not sure she ever dated. My dad has a little, but he hasn't been in a serious relationship since my mom died. I do recall walking in on Dad and Helen in the kitchen in deep conversation a few times over the years, but it wasn't like they were holding hands or anything." Eden let out a huff. "I wonder how long this has been going on. Will they continue to keep it hidden? Or will they eventually come out in the open with their relationship?"

Surprisingly, the thought of them being in a relationship didn't bother her as much as she thought it would. They'd both been alone for a long time and deserved to be happy. If they found that with each other, then so be it. And Helen seemed to be helping her father make changes for the better.

Eden only hoped it would last.

THE HOUSE WAS dark when they arrived home, but Alice had left the porch light on for them. Disappointment filled Eden when Rudy pulled his hand from hers to get out of the car. She'd grown so used to the connection that she missed it immediately. She half hoped he'd take the opportunity to give her a good night kiss on the porch, but that was ridiculous since they would both be going inside.

Evidently the thought never crossed Rudy's mind because he opened the door and walked right in, holding it open for her.

"Thanks for going with me tonight. It was nice not to have to face my dad alone."

"You're welcome." He locked the front door and turned off the porch light, throwing the entry into almost complete darkness. "Things probably could have gone better, but I suppose they could have gone worse too."

"Yeah." She left it at that because she didn't want to rehash the evening right now. She wanted Rudy to take her in his arms and kiss her, but waiting for him to make a move was torture. She couldn't bring herself to make the first move though, because she'd been the one to insist they not kiss anymore.

She turned to go down the hall, but Rudy caught her hand and tugged her back to the dark entryway. She bit her lip to hide the smile that tried to take over her face. Not wanting to appear too eager, she took a small step back but met the wall.

"What are you doing?" she whispered.

"What do you think I'm doing?" He stepped closer, and her breath stalled in her lungs. His rugged, woodsy, masculine scent teased her nose.

She leaned into him and inhaled, filling her lungs with his intoxicating smell.

"Did you just sniff me?" Grinning, he pulled back a little.

She cursed herself for not fighting the urge to smell him, but she refused to be embarrassed.

"Maybe." She couldn't hide her smile any longer. "Are you trying to up your game?"

He grinned and shifted closer still, bracing his arms on the wall on either side of her head. "Depends. Is it working?"

Her heart rate kicked into overdrive, and her lungs seemed to have stopped working altogether. She grew lightheaded from the lack of oxygen to her brain. Or maybe it was his proximity that made her lightheaded. He didn't touch her, but he stood so close she couldn't think straight. His heady scent wreaked havoc on her senses, not to mention the warmth emanating from his body.

"If I say no?" Her words sounded as breathless as she felt.

"Then I'm just taking a moment to express my disappointment in your dad this evening."

Eden frowned. Her dad was the last thing she wanted to discuss right now. "I'm sorry he grilled you about your job and finances. He promised to be nice, but I should have known—"

"That's not what I'm referring to."

"Do you mean how he tried to ambush me with that job with Tad McAllister?"

Rudy pressed a finger to her lips to quiet her. His warm breath caressed her cheek, and her mouth went dry.

"I'm disappointed he didn't ask us for a public display of affection."

"Oh." The word came out breathily and rushed. "I-I guess he's accepted that we're in a relationship."

"Have *you*?" He pressed a feather-light kiss to the hollow below her ear.

She sucked in a sharp breath. "Have I what?"

"Accepted that we're in a relationship?" He dipped his head to kiss the pulse that raced at the base of her neck near her collar bone.

She couldn't help herself; she tipped her head back, granting him better access.

Are we in a relationship?

She shouldn't let him kiss her neck like this if they weren't. She shouldn't kiss Rudy at all, not until she had her screwed-up life figured out.

Trying to strengthen her resolve, she said, "It's not s-supposed to be real." A shuddering sigh escaped her as he slowly worked his way back up her neck.

"It feels pretty real to me." He pressed soft kisses along her jaw. "No matter how hard I try to fight it, I can't deny I'm attracted to you, Eden."

Holy smokes!

She loved the way her name sounded when his voice was husky like that.

"Same." The single word was barely more than a whisper. Her purse strap slipped from her shoulder and fell to the floor, but she ignored it.

He paused with his lips mere millimeters from hers. "Unless you have an objection, I plan to kiss you like I did under the stars a couple weeks ago."

"But..." the word came out weak, barely more than an exhale.

"But what?"

"What if God doesn't want us together?" Her voice lacked conviction, and Rudy only grinned.

He leaned in until his body was flush against hers. An electrified vibrating thrum filled her in anticipation of his kiss.

"Then he'd better strike me down now because I want to be with you. I want to be your *real* boyfriend. I want to make out with you late at night. Under the stars. In my parent's—"

"You talk too much." Eden grabbed his face with both hands and pressed her lips to his. Her last thread of resistance snapped when he said he wanted to be her *real boyfriend,* and she needed his lips on hers. Now.

Rudy didn't hesitate to gather her in his arms and pull her tight against him as he accepted her invitation.

She slid her fingers into his hair and reveled in the feel of its thick waves slipping through her fingers. Again, and again. When she played with the tendrils at the back of his neck, a low moan escaped him, fueling her confidence. She gave herself to the kiss wholly and completely.

His lips continued stroking hers in a rhythmical motion, evoking a rush of emotions in her: elation, happiness, and desire. He slid his hands up her back, spreading warmth through her body, and Eden couldn't help thinking this was what she'd been waiting for all her life. She'd never been kissed like this. And deep down, she knew she'd never feel this sense of wholeness and fulfillment with any other man.

She felt silly for thinking God didn't want her to kiss Rudy. How could something that felt so right be wrong? When her knees grew weak, she clung to him, keeping tempo with his mouth even though her lungs screamed for oxygen.

His lips finally released hers only to drift to that sensitive spot below her ear again. "You drive me crazy." His ragged breaths tickled her neck, sending shock waves of pleasure shooting through her body.

"Likewise," she whispered, but she wasn't sure any sound came out because she still struggled to breathe with his lips caressing her skin.

"You smell almost as good as you taste."

She wanted to tell him he smelled good too, but she couldn't seem to form coherent thoughts, let alone words.

"Have you caught your breath yet?" His mouth was dangerously close to hers again.

"No."

"Too bad."

Then his lips were on hers again, his hands now gripping her hips. He made her feel alluring and desirable, yet at the same time, carefree and light-hearted. If he hadn't been holding her, she feared she might float away. Lights, far brighter than the starry sky, exploded behind her eyelids, lighting up her world.

No, wait. The light's above us!

Eden's eyes sprang open to blinding light in the entryway.

"Oh, it's only you two," Alice's voice came from near her shoulder.

Rudy released Eden so fast she would have fallen if it wasn't for the wall behind her. Instantly, he stood four feet away on the other side of the entry, face beet red.

Wide-eyed, Eden turned away from Alice and covered her face with her hands as similar heat filled her cheeks.

"I must say, it took you two long enough." Satisfaction filled Alice's voice. Then the entry went dark again. "Carry on. But I'm warning you..." Her voice faded as she walked down the hall. "I'll be back out in two minutes to make sure you're keeping it appropriate."

"Geez, Mom. Way to kill the mood."

Eden would have burst out laughing if she wasn't so mortified. She'd never been caught kissing her boyfriend—or any guy, for that matter—by a parent before. No way would she let it happen again. She spun and hurried to her room so fast her door clicked closed milliseconds after Alice's.

"Eden, wait!" Rudy followed her, but she already had her door closed with her back pressed to it.

She jumped when a soft knock sounded behind her.

"Eden, come out and talk to me, please."

She turned until her temple pressed against the door. "I can't. Not tonight."

If she faced Rudy, she'd probably end up kissing him again because the fire he'd sparked in her still burned hot. Or maybe that was the embarrassment of having his mom tell them to carry on.

"Fair enough." His quiet voice sounded like his face was as close to the door as hers was. "But we need to discuss what's happening between us."

Yes, they did, but Eden wasn't sure she wanted to. She was more confused now than ever. She wanted to live out her daydreams with the man who'd stood up to her dad and earned his respect. With the man whose kisses drove her crazy. But she couldn't help feeling that if she chose marriage and a family that she'd be settling and burying the talents God had given her and she'd worked so hard to develop.

She could have a family and a career, she knew that. Women did it all the time. But she wasn't sure she could divide her time and attention like that, without neglecting one or the other.

Speaking of God... Was Alice's interruption a message that she shouldn't kiss Rudy? Or would Alice consider tonight a victory?

After Rudy's door closed, Eden tip-toed back out to the entryway to pick up her purse that she dropped at some point during their kiss. Once safely back in her room, she pulled out her phone. She hesitated a long moment before typing out a text to Rudy.

Remember how I asked if you were upping your game?

Then she hesitated a little longer before hitting send.

His response came almost immediately.

Yes.

Out of curiosity, what would you have done if I'd said it was working?

This time, his response wasn't so fast. In fact, he took so long to respond that she'd changed into pajamas before her phone vibrated again.

Lock your door tonight or you might find out.

CHAPTER 18

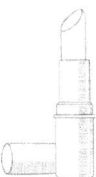

*R*udy laid out traffic cones in front of and behind his patrol car that blocked the intersection of Second South and Main Street. He looked to his right beyond the city offices and spotted most of his family. Everyone was there except for his parents and Eden.

He wasn't sure when he'd started thinking of Eden as family, but it just felt right.

He continued to search the group looking for her as the crowds grew. Scott and Kennedy promised to bring her to the Independence Day festivities, and they were here, but he couldn't see Eden anywhere.

He wished he could spend the day with her, but unfortunately, it was all hands on deck today. For such a small town, Providence celebrated their freedom in a big way. Even if Eden didn't find the plethora of small-town activities impressive, he hoped she still had fun.

"Excuse me, deputy, is it okay for me to park my chair in the middle of the street here?" The dark-haired beauty that he'd been searching for appeared by his side.

Grinning, he resisted the urge to pull her into his arms. "I think you'd be a lot more comfortable in the shade with my family."

Eden shrugged. "I put on sunscreen."

"You don't want to sit by Kennedy?" He leaned against the fender of his car, crossed his ankles, and folded his arms as she settled into her chair.

Eden grimaced. "I'm afraid she'll grill me about us."

"Us?" Rudy laughed. "Is there an 'us?'"

"I don't know. We haven't had a chance to have that talk, have we?" Shielding her eyes from the sun, she looked up at him.

With the way they kissed in the entryway of his parents' house a few nights ago, Rudy sure hoped there was an "us." But he was afraid he might have come on too strong and scared her away.

He straightened and shifted until he cast a shadow across her face. "You've been so *busy* the last few days, I thought maybe you were avoiding me."

They'd hardly had a chance to talk, let alone kiss again, since Eden had spent the last two evenings following up with vendors who worked day jobs to fill the orders that continued to pour in thanks to her social media efforts. She was also still recruiting new artisans from all over the county.

She gave him a knowing look. "And you were the one who avoided me on Sunday by playing soccer with your nephews all evening."

Despite the confidence with which he'd kissed her and his intentions to convince her to stay in Providence, he couldn't help recalling the magnificence of the house she grew up in, of the life she'd led before coming here. Would she really be content to settle down in this little town with him?

Rudy took his time scanning the surrounding area for potential problems or threats before turning back to Eden. "I admit I'm... concerned about how our 'talk' might play out."

She got to her feet now and looked him in the eye. "Why are you concerned?"

He scanned the noisy, growing crowd again before looking at her.

"I don't want to hear that you're not planning on sticking around." His voice was low and vulnerable.

She lowered her gaze for a moment before lifting her face again. "I can't make promises I'm not sure I can keep."

The sheen of tears in her eyes pricked at his heart. Eden felt as torn as he did. Both of them wanted something they weren't sure they could have.

"I know." Despite being on duty and in front of hundreds of people, Rudy wrapped an arm around her and pulled her close. He pressed his lips to her temple. "We do need to have a serious talk, but I think we can both agree that this isn't the right time or place."

A police siren signifying the start of the parade punctuated his words.

Eden gave him a small smile and nod as she stepped out of his embrace.

Rudy looked across the street to find Sheriff Winters, arms folded, staring at him. Without looking at Eden, Rudy said, "You'd better sit in your chair, or you'll get me fired."

Eden's gaze followed his. "Is that your boss?"

"Yes, that's the sheriff, and he doesn't look happy."

Eventually Sheriff Winters' attention shifted elsewhere, and Rudy did his best to remain alert while enjoying the parade.

Eden was every bit as excited about the little things that set this small-town parade apart as he'd hoped she'd be. She put her hand over her heart and said, "How precious," when the preschool dance group stopped in front of them and performed their little routine. Then she tapped her foot with the music when the older groups did their dances.

She commented about how cute or pretty each float was and laughed out loud when the lawn-chair brigade stopped in front of them and did a hilarious dance routine with their folding lawn chairs. They were followed by four motorcyclists who rode in formation, making figure eights and tight circles. Then local ranchers did a similar drill with their horses, followed by a harried teenage boy scrambling to pick up the horse droppings.

Eden chuckled when an assortment of old tractors in pristine condition passed by, and grimaced when a float full of taxidermy animals appeared, displaying deer, elk, coyotes, and even a mountain lion.

She got to her feet and pointed at the sign on the side of the truck that pulled the trailer full of animals. "Wait. Ralph Walker taxidermies animals?"

Rudy nodded. "Have you met Ralph?"

"Not yet, but he sent me a text yesterday inviting me to come check out his animals. He wants me to sell them on Hattie's website." She pulled a face and shuddered. "He can't be serious. No one wants that in their house."

"You'd be surprised. There's more than one avid hunter around here."

"Ugh, I feel sorry for their wives." A frown lingered on her face as her gaze followed the trailer. "How would you even ship something like that?"

"It might be best to ignore Ralph's texts."

"Yeah, I think so." She nodded and dropped back into her chair.

When the fire station's old tanker truck brought the parade to a close by repeatedly opening its pump onto the crowd that followed it down Main Street, Rudy grinned at a wide-eyed Eden. "You should get wet. It'll help cool you down for the afternoon's festivities."

"Um...hello, I'm wearing a white t-shirt."

Rudy let his gaze wander over her. How did she make khaki shorts, a white T, and sandals look so good and classy? He couldn't help remembering how see-through her white t-shirt became the last time she got soaked in the rain. And even though it was totally inappropriate of him to think it, he couldn't help wondering whether she wore her pink bra or the blue one today.

"Right. Probably not a good idea this time."

Would there be another time? Or would Eden leave Providence soon?

As the crowd thinned around them, making their way to the activities at the park behind the city offices, Eden stood and gathered her camp chair. "I guess I'll see you around this afternoon?"

He stepped close to her, but a quick glance across the street told him Sheriff Winters watched him again, so he kept his hands to himself. "I wish I could hang out with you today."

"Me too, but don't worry, I understand you have a job to do."

Rudy gathered up the traffic cones as the crowd continued to flow toward the park. After depositing them into the trunk of his car, he looked up to find Sheriff Winters crossing the street.

Rudy's gut tightened, and he braced himself for a public dressing down for letting himself be distracted while on duty.

"Who's the pretty brunette?" Robert Winters asked.

Rudy fought the urge to fidget. "Eden DuPont, Kennedy's friend."

"The city girl who's working with Hattie?" Robert still wore his sunglasses, so Rudy couldn't see his eyes. Couldn't tell what he was thinking.

"Yes."

"Isn't she staying at your house?"

Rudy nodded.

"You dating her?"

"Um...no... Not yet." Rudy scratched his ear. Was dinner with her dad considered a date?

"Why not?"

"Excuse me?"

Robert pulled off his sunglasses and pinned Rudy with a stare. "Don't make the same mistake I did. Make your move or you'll lose her."

Rudy sucked in a sharp breath and fell back a step from the intensity in Robert's words.

Robert had finally married his high school sweetheart eighteen months ago, eleven years after they graduated, and after she'd nearly been killed by an abusive husband.

Rudy didn't want to lose Eden, but could he really keep her happy in this small town?

"Well, what are you waiting for?"

"What do you mean?" Rudy took off his own sunglasses and locked gazes with Robert.

"Go win your girl over. Don't wait until it's too late."

Rudy had no idea the sheriff was such a romantic. Had his mom been talking to Robert?

"But I'm on duty all day."

"Not anymore. I'm moving you to on-call." Robert started to walk away then turned back and pointed a finger at him. "Show up for your shift at the dunking booth this afternoon and make sure you're at your assigned spot to direct post-firework traffic tonight. Otherwise, you're free to show your girl a good time."

My girl.

Rudy liked the sound of that. Could he convince Eden to make her move to Providence permanent and become his girl?

KENNEDY NUDGED EDEN'S SHOULDER. "You should go race."

"No way."

They'd been watching foot races grouped by age and gender for the last forty-five minutes on the grassy field at the northeast corner of the park. Eden enjoyed cheering on first Rudy's nephews and then a couple of his teenage nieces, but she had expected the MC to stop after announcing the eighteen and nineteen-year-olds. However, he'd just called for the twenty to thirty-year-old men to line up at the end of the field. The women would be next.

"But you're a runner," Kennedy said. "I bet you'd win."

Eden wiped the perspiration from her brow. It was hot enough already, the last thing she needed was to work up more of a sweat.

"I'm not a sprinter."

Unless I'm getting soaked in a freak rainstorm.

Eden shook her head. "I can't believe they're still having people race."

"They stop after the fifty-year-olds, because anyone older than that ends up injuring themselves when they run." Scott gave a rueful smile, and Eden understood why her friend fell for the quiet, grumpy man. He was almost as attractive as Rudy when he smiled. He really should do it more often.

Eden looked around as the noise around them intensified.

The whole park was a hubbub of activity with a large blow-up slide and bouncy house, an obstacle course, and climbing wall. Pop-up canopies created improvised booths for carnival games, face painting, and a fortune teller. There was even a small petting zoo and a dunking booth. A variety of food trucks and other vendors filled one whole end of the park.

Families laid out blankets and camp chairs in every square inch of shade and set up additional pop-up canopies, intent on spending the whole day at the park.

The starting gun sounded yet again, and Eden jumped.

"Go Rudy!" Hearing one of his sisters call his name, Eden looked up to see Rudy sprinting down the field.

Her cheers joined that of his siblings as he pulled ahead of the other racers. He'd definitely been holding back the night they ran home in the rain.

The whole race was only fifty yards—it had grown longer as the age groups got older—and over in a matter of seconds, but Rudy beat the other six runners by at least five yards.

It seemed such a silly thing to be proud of him for winning a little race, but she hurried toward him and gave him a hug. "Way to go, Speedy!"

He'd shed his uniform shirt, gun belt, and Kevlar vest, leaving him in his tan pants and an olive-green t-shirt with a sheriff's department insignia on the chest that hugged his torso like a second skin. The color complimented his fair skin and auburn hair, making him look incredibly sexy.

Rudy hooked an arm around her waist and pulled her close. "Hey, gorgeous. If I'd known you were near the finish line, I would have run even faster."

"You won as it was."

"But it would have been more impressive if I'd won by a bigger margin."

"I'm plenty impressed." She smacked his shoulder before pulling away. "Why aren't you in uniform? Aren't you on duty all day?"

He wrapped and arm around her shoulders and led her away from his family. He leaned his head close to hers. "Don't tell anyone, but I think my boss is a romantic."

"The sheriff?"

"Yes. He saw me with you, obviously, and he told me to go win my girl over." Rudy's grin was so big it made Eden's heart stumble then race. Or maybe it was his words that made her heart race so fast it could beat all the women who were now racing.

Her mouth dropped open. "Your what?"

"Those were his words, not mine." Rudy held his hands up in surrender.

"Hey!" Eden elbowed him in the stomach.

"Make up your mind." Rudy grinned at her again. "First, you act offended that my boss calls you my girl, then you're upset when I don't?"

Eden elbowed him again. "You don't agree with him?"

Rudy pinned her arms to her sides by wrapping his arms around her. "Until we've had our talk, I don't dare think of you as my girl."

Eden stilled in his arms as desire lit in her. His strength and the warmth of his body surrounded her, making the simmering July day even hotter. And then there was the way he smelled...

Holy pheromones!

He should be sweating like a pig and smelling of body odor, but he didn't. He smelled nice—woodsy with a hint of spice.

She met his gaze as she clasped her hands around his waist. "Why don't you want to think of me as your girl?"

"I didn't say I don't want to. I said I don't dare." He caressed her cheek as he tucked a lock of hair behind her ear. "I don't want to get my hopes up if this isn't going to last."

Neither do I.

Eden was filled with equal parts dread and hope. She understood exactly how Rudy felt. She wanted a life here with him, but she couldn't get her hopes up without knowing if a happy-ever-after was guaranteed for them.

"Sounds like we need to have that talk then."

"Yes, we do." To her disappointment, he released her, taking her hand instead, and tugged her to walk beside him. "But first, I want you to spend the day with me. And please promise you'll keep an open mind while I show you all our little town has to offer."

"You're still set on convincing me to move to Providence permanently?" A grin pulled at Eden's lips.

She was already more than half convinced that she wanted to stay here forever, but she still feared that at some point, she'd want more than this little town could offer her.

Rudy stopped walking and stood in front of her. "I'm set on convincing you we belong together."

Eden's breath caught in her throat. The vehemence in his words resonated with something deep inside her. But it put added pressure on a relationship. It made her wish she could just move here and not feel like she was missing out on some opportunity that might come along for her.

All morning, Eden kept waiting for Rudy to find them a shady spot under a tree or suggest they take a drive so they could talk. But he seemed intent on showing her a good time. Hand in hand, they visited every booth, played every game, and talked to just about everyone in town.

When he handed over money and insisted she have her palm read by the fortune teller whose long wig, dangly jewelry, and tie-dye skirt made her look like an eccentric clairvoyant, Eden tried to refuse.

"Come on, it'll be fun." He nudged her toward the chair. "Esmeralda can be kind of accurate...sometimes."

"Esmeralda?" Even her name sounded mystical and exotic.

"What are you afraid of, dear?" Esmeralda asked.

Eden studied the woman seated at the small table. She looked a lot like the cashier at the grocery store last week who sold her the chocolate-covered gummy bears.

"Nothing." Eden dropped into the chair and laid her palm on the table, preparing to hear a bunch of generic mumbo jumbo that could be interpreted a dozen different ways.

Esmeralda ran her fingers over Eden's palm a few times then closed her eyes and hummed. Eden was aiming an eye roll at Rudy when the older woman spoke.

"You have a strong lifeline, but I sense conflict. In your past and your present." Esmeralda traced a crease across Eden's hand. "Conflict...with a loved one"

Almost everyone had conflict with a loved one at one point or another. It didn't mean anything. Eden couldn't help herself from shooting a glare in Rudy's direction.

He held up his hands, palms out. "Don't look at me. I didn't tell her anything."

"Shh!" Esmeralda directed a scowl at Rudy before turning her attention back to Eden's hand. "Tread lightly but be persistent in what you want. Conflicts often resolve themselves over time."

But I don't know what I want!

"The conflict in your present is trickier." Esmeralda looked at Eden with piercing pale blue eyes. "Don't make hasty decisions." Then she smiled. "But don't give up too easily either."

"Wh-what's that supposed to mean?"

Eden didn't believe in clairvoyancy. The woman had probably given dozens of customers the same advice today, but she couldn't help wishing someone could give her the answers as to what she was supposed to do with her life.

"It means your Heart Line and your Money Line may be at odds with one another."

Meaning my heart wants a life here with Rudy, but my head knows I need to leave Providence to find a job to support myself.

"Don't be afraid to take risks. In love and in business." Esmeralda reached across the table and grabbed Eden's other hand. She studied the palm. "Aha. Yes." The older woman nodded. "Just as I thought."

"What's just as you thought?" Eden leaned forward, searching the woman's face. If the eccentric woman had any words of wisdom for her that would make the decisions she faced easier to make, she'd love to hear them.

"You'll have to walk by faith for a time and follow your heart, but it will all work itself out."

Walk by faith? That doesn't sound like something a true clairvoyant would say.

But Eden liked the counsel to follow her heart.

Esmeralda released Eden's hands and sat back in her chair. "Phew! You creative types are exhausting sometimes."

Creative? Am I a creative type?

Was that why she hated analytics so much?

Eden stood, still staring at the woman, wondering how much stock she should put in her words.

"Oh," Esmeralda leaned forward again. "You should really think about starting your own business."

"What?" Eden stumbled into Rudy.

I don't want to own my own business. Do I?

"It will bring it all together for you."

"What business?" Eden's mind raced, trying to figure out what the woman could possibly mean. What kind of business?

Esmeralda waved her away. "Time will tell. You'll see."

"Come on." Rudy took her hand and started to lead her away.

"But what about you? You need to have your palm read."

"Ach! I've read his a dozen times." Esmeralda waved a hand in dismissal. "It will never change unless he starts living for himself, instead of trying to fulfill someone else's dreams."

"Love you too, Esmeralda." Rudy tugged Eden out from under the fortune teller's canopy.

Did Esmeralda mean the way Rudy followed Parker's life plan?

Of course, this was a small town. Everyone knew Rudy lost a buddy and made a lane change in his professional life. They had probably all heard about her conflict with her dad too.

She let him lead her to the car show where he became absorbed with inspecting every car. Classic cars, sports cars, jacked up trucks, and even a couple of vintage tractors. Each one was unique and fun to explore.

They munched on Italian ice, snow cones, and cotton candy all morning and into the afternoon before deciding they'd better eat something healthy. Sitting on a blanket under the tree near his family, they shared a plate full of street tacos.

Other than repeatedly checking the time on his phone, Rudy seemed content to stay by her side, holding her hand. She was equally glad to be by his. More than one resident of Providence gave them curious looks, often followed by a smile and a nod of approval. Each time this happened, Eden felt her grin grow. She liked being recognized as Rudy's girlfriend.

At his insistence, they'd bypassed the dunking booth that was run by the sheriff's office and the fire department, saying they'd come back to it later. Shortly before two, he left her standing under a tree, promising to be back in a few minutes.

When he returned, he wore shorts with his t-shirt.

She gave him a wide-eyed look. Was the heat finally getting to him?

"I have to take a turn in the dunking booth." He tilted his head toward the tub of water.

"Is that so?" A grin split her face. "Do I get to dunk you?"

"Depends, can you throw?"

"I guess we'll see, won't we?"

Eden stood to the side and watched another young deputy climb from the dunking booth before Rudy took his spot.

He immediately began to call out the throwers' names and egg them on. At one point, when there was no one else in line and Eden debated about stepping in, he cupped his hands around his mouth and called out to someone halfway across the park.

"Travis Butler!"

Half the park went quiet, searching for Travis, then somewhere in the middle, a group of teenagers—mostly girls—split and a lanky teenage boy stepped out.

"I bet you can't dunk me, Travis!" Rudy followed the jeer with a loud clucking sound.

Grinning, the lanky teen approached the booth and pulled money from his pocket. Several young men lined up behind him, and Eden grinned.

Rudy took his job of raising money for the sheriff's office and fire department seriously. Either that, or he loved the youth.

Probably both.

Rudy seemed to get along with everybody.

Travis's first throw went wide.

"Come on, Trav, you call yourself a quaterba—" And down Rudy went with Travis's next throw.

He surfaced with a grin and hopped back onto the seat. "Cheap shot! Let's see you do it again."

Each time Rudy went down, he came up with a grin and a smart comment that made the thrower eager to spend more money to dunk him again.

As the line continued to grow, Eden decided if she wanted a chance to dunk Rudy, she'd better claim a spot. When Chase rolled himself to the end of the line, she joined him. She was almost embarrassed to throw after these teenage athletes, but she couldn't pass up this chance to dunk Rudy.

Chase gave her a grin over his shoulder. "Is there a way to shut this guy up?"

Eden laughed. "Today? I don't think so."

She grew more and more nervous as she approached the front of the line, especially since a large crowd had grown around them. She leaned forward to whisper to Chase. "I don't actually know how to throw. I'll make a fool of myself if I can't dunk him."

"Just focus on the center of the bullseye. You can do it."

"Oh, ho ho, if it isn't Wonder Boy Williams." Rudy grinned when Chase pulled out his money. "You still got it, man?"

"You mean can I shut you up?" Chase tossed his first ball in the air then caught it. "No problem."

He let the first ball fly, but it glanced off the edge of the target.

Rudy made a clicking sound with his tongue. "I think you've gone soft." He barely got the words out before Chase threw again and dropped Rudy into the water.

As usual, he came up spouting a jab. "Lucky shot." He hadn't quite settled himself onto the seat before it dropped, and he fell again.

Chase handed over another dollar bill and dunked Rudy three more times.

After his fifth dunking at Chase's hands Rudy wiped the water from his face, making no move to get back on the bench. "Okay, Wonder Boy, you've still got it. How about we let the pretty lady have a chance?"

"I don't know," Eden raised her voice. "Maybe I should just pay for more balls for Chase to throw."

Rudy climbed onto the bench before calling back. "Nope. Everyone has to throw their own." He smiled at Eden. "Let's see if the city girl knows how to throw?"

Talk about pressure. If I fail, I make city people everywhere look bad.

Eden's hands grew clammy as the girl taking the money handed her the first baseball. It felt way too small and completely foreign in her hands.

Have I ever even held a baseball?

She must have a time or two back in her high school gym class, but that seemed like eons ago. She rolled the ball around in her hand for a moment, praying she wouldn't make a complete fool of herself, before letting it go.

It sailed over the bullseye and hit the backdrop.

A collective groan rippled through the surrounding crowd.

Chase rolled closer to her. "Keep your chin tucked, your gaze leveled on the target, and put some power behind that ball. Even if you hit the target, you won't knock him down with how softly you're throwing."

"Looks like she's all beauty and no brawn," Rudy called with a teasing grin.

A chuckle rippled through the crowd, and Eden glared at Rudy through the glass.

He stared right back, holding her gaze. Then he winked at her.

Rotating her body slightly to the right like she'd seen many of the teenage athletes do, she followed Chase's instructions, and threw another ball.

It glanced off the outside edge of the target.

"Good. Now more power on the next ball," Chase said.

"I'll make you a deal, DuPont," Rudy said, still grinning. "You dunk me, I'll give you a kiss."

The crowd hooted and hollered, and warmth that had nothing to do with the hot July day filled her cheeks. She'd been hoping all day that Rudy would pull her behind the city offices or under a low-hanging tree and kiss her. Every time he leaned in close, and she thought he might do just that, he ended up pulling away.

Chanting rose across the crowd that seemed to have multiplied. "Dunk him. Dunk him."

So much pressure.

Deciding not to let it get to her, but rather to just give it her best, she took the next ball and again followed Chase's instructions.

It hit the bullseye, and Rudy dropped with a splash.

The crowd cheered, many of them clapping her on the back.

Rudy emerged from the water wearing the biggest grin he had yet today. "That's my girl!"

Heat again filled Eden's cheeks, but she didn't mind this time. She liked being called Rudy's girl.

Several people closed in to congratulate her, and before she knew it, Rudy had emerged from the dunking booth and stood in front of her. Judging by the dangerous look in his eyes, he intended to kiss her. Right here, right now. In front of all these people.

"Rudy, no." She took a step back but found her retreat blocked by teenagers.

"Oh, yes." He continued to close in on her, the look in his eyes growing hungrier and darker by the second.

"Kiss her. Kiss her." The crowd chanted, growing louder by the second.

Hands behind her propelled her forward, right into Rudy.

Traitors!

He cupped her cheeks in a cold, wet grip that was both gentle and possessive.

"But I'm wearing a white shir—"

His mouth smothered her protest as he claimed her lips in a kiss that erased any doubt anyone might have—including her—about them being in a relationship. It was both possessive yet tender. Passionate yet gentle. It was the kiss she'd been waiting for all day.

She wanted this with him. Forever. So how did she reconcile that with the desire to still live the corporate life? And maybe even own her own business.

Darn Esmeralda and the power of suggestion.

Blocking the fortune teller from her mind, she slid her hands up Rudy's shoulders, losing herself in the kiss. She loved the feel of his muscles bunched beneath the wet cotton. Pleasure—pure and simple —filled her, making her forget they had an audience.

Rudy's cold, wet body enveloped her overheated one as he shifted his hands from her face to wrap around her, pulling her flush against him. Moisture seeped through her shirt as warmth built inside her.

Talk about a shock to the system!

Considering the urgency with which his lips moved against hers, she expected steam to start rising from their bodies soon. But cheers, catcalls, and jeers of "Get a room," surrounded them, and Rudy pulled back much sooner than she would have liked.

Eden clung to him. "Don't let go of me. I don't want everyone to see my pink bra through my now-wet t-shirt."

"The pink one, huh?" he asked with a chuckle.

She slapped the back of his head. "Have you been thinking about my bras?"

"Only when you wear a white t-shirt." Before Eden could stop to think about how often that was, Rudy raised his voice. "Sheriff Winters is up next! Ryan and Carson, didn't he write you both tickets last month?"

The crowd cheered and shifted to form a line again.

Rudy guided her across the park, keeping an arm around her

shoulders. When they reached the back of the city offices where the crowds had thinned, he relaxed his hold on her.

"Do you want to go home and change into dry clothes?"

Eden surveyed her shirt. Yes, it was wet and somewhat see-through, but the damp fabric also cooled her from the heat of the day.

"If you can keep from ogling my pink bra, I'll just let it dry. But you probably want dry clothes."

"I have a duffel bag with extra clothes in the car." He hooked a thumb over his shoulders. "Question is: do you want to keep hanging out here or go to the rodeo grounds?"

"Aren't we planning on going to the rodeo tomorrow night?"

"Yes, but this afternoon there are a bunch of activities going on over there."

"Like what?"

"Dog races, cow pie drop, mutton busting, and goat wrestling. Mostly little kids' stuff, but it's fun to watch."

Eden felt her brows inching a little higher with each thing he listed.

Cow Pie Drop? Mutton busting?

"I think I need to see these...*activities* for myself."

CHAPTER 19

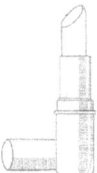

*a*nd that's how Eden found herself an hour later sitting in the shade of a wide umbrella that Rudy had the foresight to bring, waiting for a cow to poop in the rodeo arena. The crowds were not as plentiful here as at the park, but there were surprisingly still a lot of people.

"Explain to me what we're doing again." She looked at Rudy beside her.

"Remember that big board with the grid on it at the entrance?"

"The one where you handed over money to put our names on little squares?"

"Yes. Each of those little squares represents a square foot in the arena. They've fed this cow well all morning before releasing her into the arena. Now we wait for her to poop. If she poops in our square, we get the money."

Once again, Eden looked at him like was crazy. Just like she had when he handed over fifty dollars to put their names on ten squares. The dog races had been humorous to watch as some dogs refused to run, and others chased balls that didn't belong to them and still others enjoyed running so much they refused to let their owners leash them again.

But waiting for a cow to poop? This wasn't fun to watch.

"Don't cows have like four stomachs? It could be hours before it processes all the food they fed it this morning."

Rudy grinned. "Yes, but last night's food should be digested by now."

Eden just shook her head, still giving him a "you're-crazy" look. "What happens if the cow doesn't poop?"

"They'll let a second one into the arena, and eventually, a third, if necessary."

This would have been a good time for them to have their talk because nothing was happening! But Rudy didn't seem inclined to bring the subject up, so Eden didn't either. He did, however, hold her hand and tell her stories about how much he'd always enjoyed celebrating Independence Day with his family as a kid in this small town.

In some regards, Eden envied him. She usually traveled with her father around this holiday, often spending time with friends on a yacht or visiting places like New York City and the Bahamas. Those places were great, but with all the things they'd done over the years, they'd never celebrated their freedoms the way the people in this small town did.

While they waited for the cow to do its business, Eden couldn't help thinking about Esmeralda's words. She hoped the conflicts with her dad would resolve themselves in time, but she wasn't sure she could be so patient with her career and her personal life. Especially since the manager of her apartment building had insisted she pay three months' rent to keep her apartment.

And what did Esmeralda mean about me owning my own business?

The idea had never crossed her mind, but now she couldn't seem to get it out of her head.

The officiators finally turned a second cow loose in the arena, and ten minutes later, the first one decided to poop. Hearing everyone cheer for a bovine as it did its business was the oddest thing Eden had ever experienced. Then spectators held their breath as officials brought out a measuring tape.

The cow patty landed across the line of two different squares, but both contestants cheered when it was announced that the owners of each square won eighteen hundred dollars.

People accumulatively spent thirty-six hundred dollars to watch a cow poop?

Fortunately, the afternoon improved from there, and Eden found herself repeatedly laughing as she watched preschool age children chase a goat staked to a post in the middle of the arena with the goal of pulling the ribbon off its tail. Then slightly older children strapped on a helmet and rode sheep for as long as they could with nothing to hold on to except the sheep's wool.

Most of them didn't last very long but watching them get up and dust off their little chaps was the cutest thing Eden had ever seen.

She was ready for a nap by the time they left the rodeo grounds, but Rudy drove them back to the park where the crowds had thinned out some but began to grow again in anticipation of a live band and later on, fireworks. They joined most of his family who were gathered under a large oak tree and eventually made their way to the food trucks again for dinner.

She and Rudy bought an assortment of pizza, scones, chicken kabobs, more Italian ice, and more cotton candy. She'd feel horrible tomorrow, but she may as well enjoy herself tonight.

They all laughed, ate, visited, and played card games while listening to the country band that played. Eden didn't think she'd ever enjoyed herself so much or laughed so hard. That is until the bloated feeling hit her stomach much sooner than she expected.

As dusk settled in, Rudy excused himself and disappeared for a while. When he returned, he wore his full uniform again.

He took her hand and pulled her to her feet. "I have to be at the northwest corner of the park to direct traffic immediately after the fireworks. Would you like to watch them from there with me?"

"Sure." She'd been with him almost all day, but she liked the idea of spending even more time with him.

They packed up the blanket and camp chairs they'd been lounging on and made their way to the corner where Rudy's patrol car was parked. When they got there, Eden expected him to set the chairs up again, but instead, he dropped them on the ground and pulled her into his arms.

"Dance with me?"

Eden laughed. "Here? If you wanted to dance, why didn't you invite me to the dance floor in front of the bandstand?"

The closest group of people—the ones who planned to make a quick getaway after the fireworks—sat at least twenty feet away. This was the most privacy they'd had all day.

"It's less crowded here, but we can still hear the music." Rudy settled his hands on her hips. "And here, you can hear me when I whisper sweet nothings in your ear."

"Sweet nothings, huh?" She slid her arms around his neck. "What do those sound like?"

Rudy pulled her closer and began to slowly sway. He bent his head close to her ear. "I like you, Eden DuPont. I like you a lot."

His warm breath tickled her ear and a shiver of awareness shot through her.

She pulled back a little so she could see his face. "Are we finally having *the talk* now? Here?"

"We can wait and do it later if you want." He lifted one shoulder in a shrug. "Maybe under the stars, in the back of my truck." He pressed feather-light kisses to the hollow below her ear.

The thought of stargazing with him turned her insides to jelly and made her knees weak. It was tempting, but probably not a good idea, considering the electricity between them.

"No, this is as good of a time as any." She chewed on her bottom lip for a moment. "The problem is, I'm not sure what I'm supposed to say."

Rudy tightened his hold on her. "Me either, but I did tell you that I like you a lot. It's customary to tell the person whether you reciproc—"

"I like you too, Rudy. In fact..." She bit her bottom lip again.

"What? Please don't leave me hanging after that kind of declaration."

"I think I'm falling in love with you."

Eden thought the smile he gave her after she dunked him was big, but it was nothing compared to the one that covered his face now.

He lifted her up in his arms and swung her around. "Ditto!"

She pushed against his shoulders, and he released her, his smile fading faster than it had come. "It's not that simple though. Is it?"

He caught her hand before letting her slip away completely. "Love doesn't have to be complicated, Eden."

"Maybe not for most people, but nothing between us has been normal or easy."

"Are you still hung up on thinking God doesn't want us to be together?"

"No. Yes, maybe. I don't know." She used her free hand to flip her hair from one side of her head to the other. "You said it yourself this afternoon, I'm a city girl. Just because I like it here in Providence, that doesn't magically change who I am."

Rudy's posture stiffened as he released her hand. "Are you saying you'll never consider moving to Providence permanently?"

"Not necessarily." She flipped her hair again in an effort to curb the anxiety building in her. Even her stomach churned now. "I love it here, and I love working with Hattie, but..."

"But what?" Rudy's hands now rested on the gun belt at his hips.

"But I'm capable of so much more, Rudy. I'm smart and skilled. I have amazing talents that I've hardly used in over a month."

"The talents you used at Dupont Analytics? I thought you didn't like working for your father?"

"I didn't, but I can do so many other things too." She folded her arms across her chest. "I want to be more than a craft boutique assistant."

She bit her tongue before blurting out that she wanted to be a mother too. And maybe even own her own business.

Thanks a lot, Esmeralda.

She had so many dreams bottled up inside her, she wasn't sure she was ready to choose just one, even if that choice included Rudy. And that thought brought tears to her eyes. She wanted a future with Rudy, but she also wanted so much more.

Despite the near darkness, Rudy must have seen the moisture in her eyes, because he stepped close and pulled her into his arms again. "Hey, I know you're crazy smart and talented." He pressed a kiss to her temple. "I'm not trying to force you to choose something you don't want to do. I'm not like your dad."

"I want to choose Providence and you, but I worry it won't be enough."

"Me too." His arms tightened around her. "That's the one thing that's held me back this whole time."

"Same." Eden wrapped her arms around his waist and rested her forehead against his chest.

"But I'm tired of fighting how I feel about you, Eden."

His voice took on that husky tone again, and the way he said her name sent a shiver of warmth skittering down her spine.

"Promise me you won't give up on us yet. Let's see where this leads and work on a solution together." He lifted her chin and gazed into her eyes. "Will you promise me?"

Even though knots still filled her stomach, making her rather nauseous, she nodded.

Rudy's thumb shifted to stroke her bottom lip, and a spark of desire lit in her. He tilted his head a little then paused to search her face, then ever so slowly he closed the gap between his lips and hers.

They'd kissed enough times now that she should be used to the unexpected rush of giddiness that Rudy's kiss triggered in her, but she wasn't. She hoped she never got used to the feel of his mouth on hers, the taste of his kiss, his smell that drove her crazy each time he got close. She could easily become addicted to this; always searching for her next dopamine, serotonin, and oxytocin hit. He'd totally destroyed her for any other man.

A loud boom enveloped them, and the night sky lit up.

"There's something about kissing you..." Rudy said in that husky voice. "I swear I see fireworks whenever my lips touch yours."

Laughing, Eden poked him in the stomach and backed away. She turned her face toward the sky as fireworks exploded one after the other. They were beautiful, but they didn't compare to kissing Rudy. Not even close.

Instead of setting out their chairs, like Eden expected him to do, Rudy laid the blanket on the ground. He looked at her and lifted an eyebrow. When she nodded, he laid down and spread his arm out for her to lay her head on.

They were finally alone and able to kiss freely without an audience, yet Eden's stomach churned with anxiety. So much so, she had a hard time enjoying the fireworks and the occasional kiss that Rudy stole.

Had she made a mistake by agreeing to not give up on them?

He'd told her he was falling in love with her too, so she should feel ecstatic. But she didn't. She felt nauseous and agitated. Being in love only complicated the choices she needed to make.

Relief flooded over her when the fireworks finally ended. She was more than ready to go home and go to bed. Hopefully, she'd be able to shut her brain off and be able to sleep. That is if her roiling stomach would let her.

Rudy got up and helped her to her feet. "Want to go for a drive after I get done here?" When she didn't answer, he went on. "It'll be late, but...we could talk some more, or you know, make out a little?" He wiggled his eyebrows and gave her a wicked grin that normally turned her knees to jelly, but tonight, it only added to her anxiety.

She pressed a hand to her stomach that continued to churn. "Can I take a raincheck? My stomach's not feeling very good. I think I'd better just catch a ride home with Kennedy and Scott."

Rudy's brows dipped as he gave her a concerned look. "Why didn't you say something? I could have taken you home hours ago?"

"It really only hit a little while ago, but it has gotten steadily worse."

Eden's stomach bucked and convulsed. Watery saliva filled her mouth, and it was all she could do not to throw up at Rudy's feet again.

"Yeah, you don't look good. Why don't you sit in my car, and I'll call Scott to swing by and pick you up."

Too miserable to argue, Eden let him lead her to his car where she waited and wondered.

Was this a stomach bug? With all the kissing they'd done, Rudy would probably end up getting it too. Or was it something she ate?

She felt the blood drain from her face as she considered another possibility.

Is this punishment from God for kissing Rudy? For falling in love with a small-town boy whose world I don't belong in?

RUDY'S HAND paused as he reached to unlock the bathroom door on Eden's side. It was late, and he was ready for bed, but he wasn't tired. In fact, he felt wired.

Eden had told him she was falling in love with him, and like an idiot, he'd said, "Ditto."

He shook his head at himself. He should have told her the truth.

He was so far gone over her that he was questioning his ten-year and even his fifteen-year plans. Heck, he wanted to throw the plans out the window altogether. He wanted to make Eden his wife and start a family with her. He wanted her by his side forever.

But then reality hit him, like it had earlier this evening, and he remembered he didn't have a house to raise a family in. Not yet anyway. And even though Eden wasn't nearly as uppity as he had first thought, he still worried whether he could support her comfortably considering her upbringing.

Would she turn out like Austin's first wife, who was raised with money but left her parents to marry Austin only to be dissatisfied with their life together, no matter how hard Austin worked to provide for them?

He'd been hoping Eden would still be up when he got home so they could talk more, but no light came from under her door. Hopefully, they would get a chance to talk tomorrow.

He unlocked the door on her side and went to his own room. Lying in bed, staring at the ceiling, he couldn't help recalling Esmeralda's words. For fun, he'd had his fortune told many times in the past, and each time the pretend fortune teller told him he needed to start following his own dreams and stop living for Parker. But he enjoyed the life he was living. He enjoyed serving the people of his community, so it didn't feel like he was living someone else's dreams.

Sure, he could make more money in the computer field, doing programming or cyber security, but those jobs were often solitary, and he was not an introvert. He meant it when he told Oliver that he would become bored with the tedium of a programming job. He needed more interaction and excitement.

The sound of a door banging open and the toilet seat hitting the back of the toilet followed by the sound of gagging and coughing brought him upright in bed.

Is Eden throwing up?

She looked miserable after the fireworks, but he'd figured she'd asked for a raincheck on stargazing because she didn't want to discuss their relationship anymore tonight. She must have been sicker than he thought.

The retching sounds went on for a long time followed by a low moan, then he heard the toilet flushing and water running in the sink.

Climbing from his bed, he knocked softly on the bathroom door. "Eden, are you okay?"

Several long moments passed before the door opened to reveal a pale, miserable-looking Eden.

"Are you alright?"

"Not really, but I feel a little better now." She frowned and pressed a hand to her stomach. "I think."

"Do you think it was something you ate?"

"I don't know. Maybe." She slumped against the counter. "Or maybe it's..."

"What?"

"Never mind. It's dumb to even think it."

"Think what?" Rudy stepped a little closer.

The somber, dejected look on Eden's face made him want to know exactly what she thought.

"Nothing." She motioned to her room. "I'm fine, but I'd like to go back to bed."

"Okay, let me know if you need anything. Ginger ale or something."

"Thanks." She nodded then closed the door behind her.

Rudy went back to bed only to stare at the ceiling again. He hadn't heard of a stomach bug going around, so if it wasn't food poisoning, why was Eden so sick?

He was about to drift off when he again heard the bathroom door bang open followed by the sound of the toilet seat hitting the back of the toilet then more violent gagging and retching.

He was out of his bed in a heartbeat, feeling the need to help Eden. Without waiting for her to open the door after his soft knock, he poked his head into the bathroom.

"Is there anything I can do for you?"

Eden, still bent over the toilet, sniffled and shook her head. She tucked her hair behind her ear before feebly waving him away and heaving again. Her hair fell forward as she braced her hands on the back of the toilet.

Rudy searched the drawers until he found one of her hair elastics. He stepped close to her side. "Here, let me pull your hair back."

"It's okay. I can do it." Her voice sounded as weak as she looked. "In a minute."

"So can I."

She waited patiently for him to pull her hair back into a sloppy ponytail. Tendrils of damp hair clung to her neck where her skin felt flushed despite her paleness. She sank down onto the floor and leaned her back against the tub, letting out a heavy sigh.

Dampening a washcloth with cold water, he sat on the tub beside her and pressed the cloth to the side of her neck.

"That feels good." She took the cloth and alternately pressed it to the sides and back of her neck then to her forehead.

"Here let me cool it again." Rudy took the cloth and rinsed it out before returning to sit by her again. "Do you think it's food poisoning? The chicken kabobs perhaps?"

That was the only thing he could think of that she'd eaten that would make her this sick.

"Probably. Or maybe it's a combination of all the junk I ate."

"I ate all the same stuff and I feel fine. I only had a couple bites of the chicken though."

She gave a weak shrug and propped her elbows on her raised knees and dropped her head into her hands. Soft sniffles came from behind her hands.

"Hey, what's wrong?" He rubbed her shoulder.

"Nothing. I just get weepy when I'm sick."

She made no move to get up, so he stayed by her side with his hand on her shoulder, wishing he could take the pain and discomfort from her.

Finally, she lifted her head. "I should go back to bed."

Rudy sprang to his feet and helped her up. He watched as she washed her hands and rinsed her mouth. When she walked out of the bathroom without closing the door, he closed it part way, leaving only a crack. Then he turned off the lights over the vanity, and switched on the main light that was less bright.

Hopefully, now that her stomach was empty, she'd be able to sleep.

His hopes were in vain however, because thirty minutes later he woke up to the sound of her heaving again. He couldn't help himself; he rushed to her side. Only bile came up this time, but she dry-heaved long after anything ceased to come up.

An hour later, she did the same thing. Then again two more times during the early morning hours. And each time, he helped her back to bed, because she grew increasingly weaker.

Sometime around two in the morning, with tears in her eyes, she asked, "Do you think God is punishing me?"

Despite his own exhaustion, Rudy laughed. "Why would he punish you?"

"Because I fell in love with you." She rolled onto her side and closed her eyes. "But maybe I don't belong here." The last of her words were barely a whisper as she drifted off to sleep again.

He was glad she didn't expect an answer because he wasn't sure he could have spoken around the sharp twisting pain in his chest. God wasn't punishing Eden. He was sure of it. But he hated the fact that she'd had to work so hard for acceptance for every choice she made in her life that she doubted even deity.

Is that why she hadn't found a full-time job yet? Because she doubted herself and her choices? Would her doubts make a relationship between them impossible?

Somewhere around four in the morning, before he finally settled into a deep sleep, he decided maybe he needed to be the one to sacrifice and change lanes.

CHAPTER 20

"What do you mean you aren't going fishing?" Eden scowled at the phone on the bathroom counter while she braided her hair. "You're the one who convinced me to go and now you're bailing?"

Kennedy moaned. "I've thrown up three times since I got out of bed, and now all I want to do is sleep for the rest of the day."

"Oh no. Did you get what I had?" Eden had been certain she'd had food poisoning, especially when no one else got sick, but maybe it had been viral.

"Um... no, this hits every morning." Kennedy's voice was cautious.

Eden dropped her arms and stared at the phone. "Wait? Are you...pregnant?"

A lengthy silence filled the phone before Kennedy finally spoke. "Yes, but—"

"Seriously? That's so exciting! I can't believe you didn't tell me."

"We haven't told anyone yet, so you're actually the first to know. But don't tell anyone else, especially not Scott's family."

"Why not?"

"Well, everyone is so excited about Debbie's first pregnancy, and she has waited so long to have a baby, I didn't want to steal any of the attention."

"How far along are you? How long do you plan to hide it?"

"I'm three weeks behind Debbie. We plan to announce it next week on Alice's birthday."

"I'm so excited for you!" Eden squealed.

Her stomach did that funny clenching thing that it did when she heard Debbie was pregnant. The same powerful thing it did when she tended Debbie's kids for two days. The wave of longing that hit her made her nauseous and lightheaded.

She braced herself against the bathroom counter and stared at her reflection.

My biological clock is not ticking! I'm just disappointed Kennedy and I won't be raising babies together, that's all. I have plenty of years to have children.

After ending the call, she finished her braid and left the bathroom to finish getting ready.

Scott was good with his nieces and nephews, but Eden had a hard time picturing him as a dad. Rudy on the other hand, would be a great dad. He was great with kids of all ages. And he took such good care of her when she was sick.

Memories of him pulling her hair back into a ponytail and wiping her neck with a cool cloth filled her head. Every time she rushed to the bathroom to vomit, he joined her, patiently waiting to see if she needed anything. And every time, embarrassment—that he'd once again seen her at her worst—filled her. But he was so kind and gentle in helping her back to bed that she could only be grateful. In fact, she recalled him carrying her to her bed that last time.

Yes, he'd make a good dad, but...did he want kids?

RUDY KILLED the engine of his dad's fishing boat in their favorite fishing spot; a little alcove near the bend, just before the lake opened wider on the north end. Although there were several boats out on the lake today, nobody else fished in this alcove. Which was perfect because he liked the idea of having Eden all to himself.

"Why are we doing this again?" she asked.

Rudy studied her. She looked very stylish in bib overall shorts with a pink tank top and a white, long-sleeved shirt tied around her waist. If it wasn't for his mom's big, floppy brimmed hat on her head, she'd look like a model sitting there on the little bench.

"We're here because my dad insisted we couldn't miss our annual fishing trip. Even though he's laid up, the tradition must go on." Rudy held up a finger and mimicked his dad.

"I still think you and Scott should have gone by yourselves."

"Yeah, but he felt like he needed to stay with Kennedy while she wasn't feeling well."

A secretive smile covered Eden's face, but before he could question what it meant, she pointed a finger at him. "This makes us even. You helped me with my dad, now I'm helping you with yours.

"That's the only reason you came fishing with me? To please my dad?"

"That and to work on my tan." She gave a casual shrug.

"And here I thought you came because you overheard my mom telling me a day out on the lake with just the two of us would be romantic."

"I came because I heard her say she packed some of her homemade cream puffs and chocolate éclairs." Eden eyed the cooler behind him.

Rudy laughed and rolled his eyes. He pulled the fishing poles from their storage compartments and handed one to her.

She took it with two fingers and held it at arm's length.

"It's not going to bite you. It doesn't even have a hook on it yet."

"But I don't know what to do with it. I've never, and I mean *never*, been fishing before."

He opened his dad's tackle box and pulled out a hook.

"You're not going to make me touch worms, are you?"

"Nah, we'll use power bait today." He pulled a little jar of neon green bait from the box and tossed it to her.

She studied the jar. "Looks like play dough." Twisting off the lid, she lifted it up to examine it more closely. "Agh, that's disgusting!" She dropped the jar and leaned over the edge of the boat and gagged.

The small craft rocked precariously.

Rudy burst out laughing. "You're not supposed to sniff it."

"I didn't. It just attacked my nostrils." She gagged again. "Holy smokes! That's almost as bad as the skunks."

He rolled his eyes. "Now who's being dramatic?" He held her fishing pole out to her with the newly attached hook.

"Nope. No way. Not happening." She scowled and leaned away from him. She pointed down at the jar of power bait still lying on the floor of the boat. "There's no way I'm touching that stuff."

"Fine, I'll bait your hook, but it's going to cost you."

"Cost me? I'm already out here against my will."

"Against your will? I didn't force you to get on the boat."

"You literally lifted me right off the dock and deposited me in the boat when I questioned its safety."

When Eden said she'd never been on a boat this small, the image of her on a super yacht belonging to some billionaire filled his mind, triggering a blizzard of insecurities.

"You didn't exactly kick and scream. In fact, you looked like you enjoyed being in my arms." Rudy grinned. "Besides, you willingly got in my truck and drove up here with me."

"Fine." She grabbed the handle of the fishing rod as though she expected it to bite her. "Show me how to do this so I can cross fishing off my bucket list even though it isn't on there."

Rudy quickly tied his hook and put bait on both hooks, then he demonstrated how to cast the line and slowly reel it in. He made her practice casting several times. Her hook nearly caught his ear on one cast, and he decided it was best to just let her leave her line in the water.

"Now what?" She pushed her sunglasses up her nose and looked out across the lake from under the brim of his mom's hat.

She looked so ridiculous, yet sexy at the same time.

"Now we wait for the fish to bite."

Eden sat so close, their knees almost touched, and the electricity fairly crackled between them. His palm tingled as he recalled touching the bare skin of her thigh in the truck on the drive here. He fiddled with the little knob on his reel to keep from reaching out and touching her again.

"Does it always smell like this?"

"Like what?"

"Swampy and...fishy." Her nose wrinkled again, and Rudy couldn't help thinking how cute she looked when she did that.

"It's a lake. Lakes smell fishy."

She tapped her nails on the bench beside her. A sign of boredom.

Her acrylic nails were gone, but pale coral nail polish tipped her fingers. Evidently manicures were a luxury she decided she couldn't afford anymore.

His chest tightened as it did every time he thought about her paying rent on an apartment she didn't even live in anymore. Even though she seemed content to stay in Providence, it felt like she wasn't ready to let go of her life in Spokane.

Was she simply toying with him? Would she pick up and leave as soon as a job offer came her way? Or once she'd tired of this small town?

"Do you..." Eden hesitated. "Do you want children?"

Warmth filled Rudy's face. "We only just started dating and you're ready for that conversation already?"

She gave a nonchalant shrug, but her cheeks reddened. "It feels like something we should know about each other sooner rather than later."

"You're right." He nodded. "I do want kids. A bunch of them, but not for a few years."

"A few years?"

"Yes, I'd like to get my house built first, and make sure I'm financially stable."

Eden's face fell, and he was unsure what caused the change in her expression.

He took her hand. "What about you? Do you want kids?"

The smile she gave him looked forced and tense. "Yes, I'd like three or four."

"That's one or two less than a bunch, but I'd say we're compatible in that regard." He lifted her hand to his lips and pressed a kiss to her knuckles.

Her smile softened, but she pulled her hand from his and fiddled with her fishing pole.

Trying to ignore the tension that suddenly surrounded them, Rudy reeled his line in and cast it back out again.

Eden copied his actions, nearly taking his ear off again.

"So, what do you do while you wait for the fish to bite?"

"Enjoy nature." He shrugged. "When my dad is with us, we talk occasionally. If it's just me and Scott, I ramble on about anything and everything just to see how long it takes for his grunts to turn to growls."

Eden laughed. "I don't imagine it takes very long."

"No, it doesn't."

After a lengthy silence, she sighed. "Seriously, this is all you do? All day long?"

"This is it." He propped his rod into the holder so he could focus his attention on Eden. Bracing his elbows on his knees, he leaned toward her. "If you're bored, we can find something to entertain you."

"Oh yeah?" She propped her own rod in its holder and mimicked his posture. A small smile lifted the corners of her lips. "What might that be?"

He couldn't kiss her with his mom's monstrosity of a hat on her head. Reaching up, he pulled it off and dropped it on the bench beside Eden. It fell to the floor of the boat, but he didn't care.

"We could play...I Spy."

Eden looked around before looking back at him and smirking. "Pass."

"Twenty Questions?" He inched closer to her and reached out to caress her cheek.

"Maybe later." Her voice took on a husky quality, and the blood pumped a little harder in his veins.

"Do you have a better idea?" Grinning, he leaned a little closer still.
"Only one."

They were so close now that her breath tickled his cheek.

"Which is?" It was all Rudy could do not to close the gap between his lips and hers.

"Stop torturing me."

He wasn't sure who leaned that final inch; him or Eden. Maybe both. But when his lips met hers, it was pure pleasure. All his senses became instantly aware of every little thing. The birds in the trees on the shore sang a little louder. Gentle waves rocked the boat in a hypnotic rhythm. Eden's subtle, floral perfume overpowered the fishy smell of the lake, and his heart raced so fast he could power the boat with it, if he wanted to.

The taste and feel of her lips were pure perfection. Sweeter than his mom's cinnamon rolls and softer than his pillow where he dreamed about a life with Eden every night.

His sunglasses bumped against hers, so he pulled away and ripped them off, then he reached up for hers and paused. She gave a slight nod, so he lifted them off her face. His gaze went immediately to her mesmerizing brown eyes. Her dark lashes were as thick and as long as ever.

He'd been convinced she had fillers and extensions, but those should be long gone by now. He searched her eyes, trying to determine if she wanted to continue this kiss as much as he did.

He got his answer when she grabbed the front of his shirt and pulled him toward her.

He cupped her head as he lost himself in her kiss. He could do this forever and still never get enough of Eden DuPont.

A whirring sound had them both jerking back.

Eden's fishing rod bent in the holder. She caught it with an excited squeal. "Ah! Haha, I caught something!"

Rudy had the fleeting thought that Eden had caught a lot more than a fish today, but when she excitedly jumped to her feet and sent the boat lurching from side to side, he didn't have time to think about how tangled he was in her net.

"Calm down. And for Pete's sake, sit down before you tip us over."

"Sorry." She plopped back down onto the bench and jerked back on the fishing pole.

"Easy. Reel it in, nice and slow, like I showed you, so you don't break the pole."

Eden's excitement continued to grow as she slowly drew the fish closer to the boat. When it was almost there, Rudy stood and turned to grab the net behind him. His shoe caught in his mom's floppy sun hat that was now wedged under Eden's sandal.

His foot refused to move as he lifted it to step over the bench, but he had too much momentum to stop himself. Off balance and out of control, he flailed his arms as the boat rocked.

He fell, cracking his temple against the edge of the boat.

Acute pain pierced his skull, shooting stars through his vision. He was vaguely aware of Eden shrieking as spasms of agony ricocheted through his head.

"Rudy! Are you okay?"

Shadows hovered around the edges of his vision as he struggled to clear his head. He finally managed to upright himself and figure out what he was supposed to be doing. He grabbed the net and much more carefully this time, he slid himself back onto the seat and rotated his body until he faced Eden again.

"Holy smokes! You're bleeding!" She gasped and clapped a hand over her mouth.

Rudy registered the warmth trickling down his face as he processed her words. He reached up and touched a finger to his brow. Pain that had settled into a dull throb intensified at his touch. He pulled his hand away to find sticky, bright-red blood on his fingertips.

Eden's arm jerked, and she shrieked again as the fish she'd been reeling in tried to gain his freedom. The line suddenly snapped, and she fell back, rocking the boat and the world with it. Literally.

He closed his eyes waiting for everything to stop rocking and wishing the pain would subside already.

She set her fishing pole aside. "We'd better get you to the hospital."

"It's just a scratch." He waved away her concern. "I'll be fine."

"Seriously, Rudy. You need to go to the hospital." She pulled her phone from the front pocket of her bib overalls and snapped a quick picture. "Here, look at your face."

Blood covered the whole right side of his face and dripped onto his white T-shirt. He wasn't typically squeamish. He'd seen plenty of blood in the five years that he'd been in law enforcement, but he'd never seen that much blood on himself.

His vision blurred, and the boat rocked. Or maybe it was the rest of the world that tilted this time.

"Do you need me to drive the boat back to the dock?" Eden shifted as if she meant to stand up.

"No, sit down." He held out a hand. "I have a first aid kit somewhere."

Feeling more than a little light-headed, he rummaged around the cooler and other paraphernalia, searching for the little red and white box his dad always brought along.

But Dad isn't here today, and neither is the first aid kit.

He rotated. "I can't find it."

Eden untied the shirt she wore around her waist and twisted it to look like a rope. "Here, we need to stop the bleeding. This is going to need stitches."

"Head wounds tend to bleed a lot but they're rarely as bad as they look."

"I hope you're right, but you're going to the hospital regardless."

He leaned away as she reached toward him with her shirt. "You'll ruin your shirt."

"I don't care. We need to keep pressure on it to stop the bleeding. Now hold still."

Rudy clenched his teeth together while she wrapped her shirt around his head. He sucked in a sharp breath, then let it out in a hiss when she tied the knot over the wound.

"Sorry." Her voice was apologetic. "Now can you explain to me how to drive this thing back to the dock?"

"I got it." Rudy shifted to the back of the boat and grabbed the pull cord to start the engine.

They'd barely made it halfway across the lake before he regretted his decision to drive. It took forever to reach the dock, and the ache in his head pounded like a giant bass drum the whole time.

Eden was much more eager to help unload the boat than she had been to load it, and thanks to some good Samaritan fishermen, Rudy expended very little energy getting the boat loaded back on the trailer. He was more than a little embarrassed by his white turban, but he was in too much pain to truly care.

And he was utterly exhausted. When his vision blurred for the second time after getting behind the wheel, he brought the truck to a stop and turned to Eden. "I need you to drive."

"But I've never driven a truck before, let alone one pulling a boa—"

He must have looked as bad as he felt, because after taking one look at him, she unbuckled her seat belt and opened her door. Thank goodness, because he didn't have the energy to argue with her. Not did he want to admit how light-headed and shaky he felt.

Rudy did his best not to wince and hiss every time she hit a bump, but the thirty-minute drive back to Providence felt like an eternity.

Eden repeatedly mumbled under her breath. "I knew we shouldn't have kissed." And "That was stupid. I should have known better."

For once, Rudy didn't argue with her. Their kiss clearly hadn't caused his accident, but it happened so quickly afterward, that he feared Eden might be right.

God really is punishing us.

It wasn't until she said, "Of course, God is more powerful than Alice," that he finally spoke up.

"What did you say?"

"Nothing." She shook her head as she kept a tight grip on the steering wheel.

"Tell me what you meant about God being more powerful than my mom."

She huffed out a sigh. "Ever since I came to Providence, your mom has been pushing us together, but it seems like God doesn't want us to be together. Hence the reason all of these bad things keep happening."

Her cheeks took on a rosy tint. "I've kind of been keeping a tally in my head of Alice vs. God."

Rudy would have laughed out loud if he didn't think it would make his head hurt worse. "Who's winning?"

Eden barely spared him a glance. "God, of course."

Yeah, and he used my mom's ridiculous hat to chalk up this point.

CHAPTER 21

*E*den sent Kennedy another intense stare from across the kitchen.

This time, Kennedy met and held her gaze. She lifted a questioning brow and tilted her head toward the hall.

Eden nodded and made her way through the crowded dining and family rooms to her bedroom.

It was Alice's birthday and the whole family was at the Wheeler's house. The place was packed. Now that they'd sung "Happy Birthday" and eaten cake and ice cream, most of the kids had gone outside to play, but the noise level—with so many conversations going on at once—was almost deafening.

Scott and Kennedy had shared their good news, and Alice had acted as excited as though this were her first grandchild, not her fifteenth. And the rest of the family had congratulated Scott and Kennedy with hugs and back slaps. Debbie had been the most excited because it meant she and Kennedy could raise their little ones together.

Debbie's comment had caused a surge of envy in Eden and another wave of longing that she didn't know how to stop.

"What's going on between you and Rudy?" Kennedy asked as soon as they reached Eden's room.

Eden flopped onto the bed. "I don't know. He's hardly talked to me this week." She didn't blame him after everything that had happened, but it still felt personal.

"But you guys were practically joined at the hip on the Fourth."

"That was before I got food poisoning and he split his head open."

Kennedy sat on the bed by Eden. "All the more reason for you to shower each other with affection."

"Yeah, but every time we get close, we end up kissing." Before the smile on Kennedy's face could grow any bigger, Eden went on. "And every time we kiss, bad things happen."

Her friend burst out laughing. "That's the most ridiculous thing I've ever heard."

"If I wasn't living it, I would laugh too, but it's true. Almost every time we're around each other something horrible happens."

"They're just coincidences." Kennedy let out one final giggle. "Are you sure you're not just trying to find an excuse not to fall for Rudy because it means sticking around this small town."

"I've already fallen for him, and I'm not opposed to sticking around Providence."

Eden never thought she'd say those words, but they were true.

"I'm afraid one of us will end up dead or maimed before we find our happily ever after."

Kennedy laughed again. "You've been hanging out around the Wheelers too long. You're being overly dramatic."

Scowling, Eden sat up and grabbed a pillow. She smacked Kennedy on the head with it before wrapping her arms around it and hugging it to her chest. "What happened between me and Rudy at your wedding?"

"He gave you a bloody nose, trying to keep Violet from bowling you over when she dove for the bouquet. But that was totally an accide—"

Eden held up a hand and cut her off. "What happened to me the moment I hit the city limits when I moved here."

Kennedy rolled her eyes. "You got stung by a bee, but you can't blame that on Rudy. In fact, he saved your life that day."

"I know, but it doesn't negate the fact that bad things keep happening." Eden plumped the pillow in her arms, then hugged it again. "The first walk we took together, we got caught in a freak rainstorm." She started ticking things off with her fingers. "Then the first time he kissed me, I had an asthma attack because he had just eaten a cookie with walnuts in it."

"Wait, when was your first kiss?"

"A few weeks ago, when my dad showed up unannounced, remember? He didn't believe Rudy and I were in a relationship—"

"Which you weren't."

Eden waved away the interruption. "No, we weren't yet, but that's beside the point." She went back to ticking off disasters on her fingers. "The next time we went for a walk, we stopped to look up at the stars, and we ended up kissing." A warm flush enveloped Eden's body as she recalled that kiss. "But then we got sprayed by skunks."

Kennedy snorted as she tried to hold back the laughter this time. She wasn't successful and ended up giving into full-bodied belly laughter. "I didn't realize you were kissing when you got sprayed by the skunks."

"Well, we stopped right before, when the skunks appeared, obviously."

"Still." Kennedy chuckled again.

"Can I finish please?"

Kennedy waved a hand for Eden to continue. "One night, we kissed in the entryway." She motioned in the general direction of the front door. "And Alice turned the light on and caught us."

"Alice caught you?" Kennedy gave into the laughter again.

"She said it was about time then turned off the light and told us to carry on."

Kennedy snorted again, but Eden went on before her friend could interrupt. "After we kissed on Independence Day, I ended up with food poisoning."

Kennedy pointed a finger at Eden. "Again, not a direct correlation to kissing Rudy."

"I know, but it happened, nonetheless." Then she continued. "The next time we kissed he fell asleep afterward because he had been up all night with me while I was vomiting, then the following day, I couldn't find my phone for an hour after he kissed me goodbye." She was on a roll now and couldn't stop. "That night, he got called out on an emergency shortly after kissing me. And then last week, when we were fishing..." Eden was so worked up she needed to pause and take some deep breaths before continuing.

"Wait." Kennedy grabbed Eden's arm. "Were you guys kissing when he fell and hit his head?"

"No, but only moments before we were." Eden buried her face in her hands. "Rudy used to laugh every time I questioned whether God wants us to be together, but he's hardly come near me since he got eight stitches in his head."

Kennedy pulled Eden's hands away from her face. "You guys do seem to have had your share of bad luck, but that's all it is. Your luck will turn around."

"Will it? Love isn't supposed to be a series of mishaps and accidents. I want to be swept off my feet, not bathing in peroxide and baking soda and running to the hospital every time I turn around." Tears filled Eden's eyes. "Why does falling in love have to be so hard?"

"It's not hard, normally. For most people, it happens rather effortlessly. But anything worth having is worth working for." Kennedy shook Eden's shoulders. "Don't give up. Don't let your head look for reasons not to follow your heart."

"But Rudy has withdrawn now."

"Maybe he needs to know you're willing to fight for this too. He shouldn't be the only one to do all of the work." Kennedy leaned forward. "You lost your mom at a young age, and your father let you down in so many ways, but it doesn't mean you don't deserve love."

Warmth filled Eden's chest, and she threw her arms around Kennedy. As always, her best friend knew exactly what she needed to hear.

"Did you hear Alice offer to help me make some baby blankets and burp clothes?" Kennedy asked when the hug ended.

Eden still wanted to talk to Kennedy about her job, or lack thereof, especially since she had a virtual interview with Avant Garde Home Decor this week that went well, but she was also still considering starting her own business. But they could discuss all that later. Right now, her friend needed her attention.

"I still can't believe you're pregnant! Do you want a boy or a girl?"

"I'll be happy with either, but I can't help imagining Scott holding our baby girl."

"Oh, she would be so cute, I'm sure of it. I think you'd enjoy learning to sew with Alice. She started to teach me how to sew this week. We started off with straight lines, making square quilt blocks." Eden sprang off the bed. "Wait here, I'll go get the pieces I sewed together this week and show you."

Eden hurried past the crowd in the family room that had only thinned marginally and went downstairs. She was almost to the open door of the workout room when she heard Scott's gruff voice.

"So, what's going on between you and Eden?"

She skidded to a stop in the hall.

Would Rudy tell his brother the same things she'd just told Kennedy? Would Scott give him the same encouragement Kennedy had given her.

Rudy snorted, much like Kennedy had. "I don't know, man. Skunks and stitches aside, she's pretty and fun to hang out with. We always have a good time, but I'm not sure I should set my heart on more than that."

Fun to hang out with?

Was that all she was to him? Entertainment in this small town where there was nothing to do?

"Why not?" Scott said.

"It's beginning to feel like this is all bad timing." Rudy grunted under whatever weight he lifted. "Marriage isn't really part of my life plans right now."

Pain sharp and hot pierced Eden's chest as tears filled her eyes.

He'd asked her not to give up on them so they could look for a solution together, but he'd never had any intentions of changing his ten-year plan so they could be together?

That's why she'd withdrawn emotionally on the boat last week, but then he'd charmed her and kissed her, made her think that everything would be okay somehow. Had that just been for his own entertainment?

"Besides," Rudy's voice came through the door again. "I'm not sure I can support her in the kind of lifestyle she's accustomed to."

Eden's jaw dropped.

Does he still think I'm some spoiled debutante after all this time? Haven't I shown him that money doesn't matter to me?

Even as the thought filled her head, she recalled her frequent shopping trips over the past year.

Additional tears filled her eyes, and Eden spun and ran back up the stairs.

∼

"So, what's going on between you and Eden?"

Rudy froze at Scott's question. Kennedy must have put him up to this.

He snorted. "I don't know man. Skunks and stitches aside, she's pretty and fun to hang out with. We always have a good time, but I'm not sure I should set my heart on more than that."

Now, why did I say that? My heart is already set on so much more.

"Why not?" Scott said.

"It's beginning to feel like this is all bad timing."

He tried not to put any stock in Eden's fears about God not wanting them to be together, but he couldn't deny that bad stuff kept happening. That's why he'd backed off this week. He didn't want her to freak out over their relationship any more than she already was.

Rudy grunted as he continued his bench presses. "Marriage isn't really part of my life plans right now."

Another lie. Because he was definitely second guessing his life plans. He'd already imagined a dozen disastrous scenarios of asking Oliver DuPont for his blessing to propose to Eden. And wondered whether she'd mind living with his parents until he could build them a house. Both of those things caused more than a little anxiety.

But he couldn't bring himself to admit any of that to his brother who hid his emotions better than anyone Rudy knew.

"Besides, I'm not sure I can support her in the kind of lifestyle she's accustomed to."

And there was the real crux of his problem. His own freaking insecurities!

"Cut the crap, man!" Scott took the loaded barbell from Rudy's hands and set it in the rack on the bench press, then he circled around and sat on the low stool and waited for Rudy to sit up. "You like her, don't you?" He barely waited for Rudy to nod before continuing, "So what's holding you back?"

"I'm not sure I can support a woman with Eden's tastes. Besides, I'm not planning on getting married for at least another three years, and kids..." Rudy snorted. "They definitely aren't on the plan until after I get my house built."

"So what? You're going to let her walk out of your life just like what's her name did after high school? Because it doesn't fit into your 'ten-year plan'?" Scott made finger quotes when he said ten-year plan.

"Those weren't just my plans. Meredith and I made those plans together. We were going to go to college *together* and eventually get married. But she couldn't even wait for me to earn money for school by working a summer job. She took off three days after graduation and within three months, was married to some rich real estate developer."

"And you think Eden's the same as Meredith?"

"I don't know." Rudy let out a heavy sigh as he wiped the sweat from his brow. "She comes from a heck of a lot more money than Meredith did. So why should I think she'd be content sticking around this little town?"

"From what Kennedy tells me, Eden is pretty down to earth, despite coming from wealth."

"I know she is, but I still doubt Eden would be content to settle for this." He waved his arms in an arc, motioning to their parents' house.

"This," Scott mimicked Rudy's actions, "isn't all that bad. Yes, we lived modestly, but we were comfortable and happy. Shouldn't Eden be given a choice of whether she wants this?" He waved his arm again.

All the air whooshed from Rudy's lungs as Scott's final sentence hit him right in the chest, as swift as a punch.

His brother was right. Eden should be given the chance to choose this. But if she didn't choose him and this small town, was he willing to move to her world?

"What if..." He'd been thinking about this for a long time, so it shouldn't be so difficult to spit out. "What if she chooses me, but she doesn't choose Providence?"

"What do you mean?"

"Eden still wants a career, perhaps in the corporate world again. She can't have that here."

"Well then I guess Eden isn't the only one who has to make some hard choices."

You can say that again.

If Rudy decided to abandon his life plan, like he'd been considering, he'd also need to truly forgive himself for Parkers' death and start living for himself.

He wasn't sure he knew how to do that.

CHAPTER 22

*R*udy was surprised to see Eden loading a suitcase into the back of her BMW when he came home from work on Monday.

He knew from the cold shoulder she gave him yesterday that she was upset about something, but he wasn't sure what, and he didn't know how to fix it. He'd hoped to convince her to go for a walk with him tonight so they could talk. But now his stomach sank. And when he took in her red-rimmed eyes, his chest tightened.

"Where are you going?" He stepped up to her car as she closed the trunk.

"My dad's in the hospital." Tears filled her eyes again.

He pulled her into his arms. "Is he okay?"

"I don't know. Helen called a little while ago and said my Dad didn't want her to tell me, but she felt I should know that he's going into surgery to have an aneurysm repaired." She pulled away from him. "I need to go see him."

"Eden, wait. You shouldn't drive when you're so upset. Let me drive you."

"No!" She held up her hand. "I need to go alone."

"But..." Rudy wanted to argue that as her boyfriend he should go with her, but a hard glint filled her eyes, and the words stuck in his throat.

She opened the car door and slid into the driver's seat, but he grabbed it before she could close it. "When are you coming back?"

"I don't know. I need to make sure my dad's going to be okay. And I might need to help out at DuPont Analytics for a while."

If she went back to work for her dad, would she ever leave again?

"But...you're coming back...aren't you?"

She lowered her gaze and pressed a fingernail into the stitching on the steering wheel. "I don't know."

Rudy fell back a step as the air seized in his chest, and she used the opportunity to close the door. Before he could even swallow away the boulder-sized lump that blocked his throat, she started the car and backed out of the driveway.

"Eden, wait!"

But it was too late. She was gone.

Feeling like his boots were encased in concrete, he trudged into the house. Not even the familiar sight of his mom at the kitchen counter chopping vegetables was enough to calm the turmoil raging inside him.

"You just missed Eden. She's headed to Spokane. Her dad's having surgery today."

"I know. I saw her."

"I wouldn't worry too much. At least they caught the aneurysm before it ruptured."

Rudy stared at the knife that cut so effortlessly through the vegetables, feeling like his heart had just been chopped into tiny pieces.

"Is she...? Did she say when she was coming back?"

Or even if she plans to come back?

He prayed his mom would give him a different answer than Eden had.

"I don't know. She might have to stay in Spokane for a while to keep an eye on her father's business."

Will she be able to walk away from that again?

What if she decides she doesn't want to this time?

"Dinner will be ready in about thirty minutes. Why don't you go watch TV with your dad for a bit?"

Watch TV? The woman I love just walked out of my life, and you want me to watch golf like my world hasn't just fallen apart?

Okay, he was being dramatic, he knew that. But he couldn't seem to get his head and heart to accept that there was a happy ending for him and Eden with this new twist.

"I'm not hungry." He turned toward the hall. "I'm going for a run."

Rudy's racing thoughts kept pace with his feet as he ran mile after mile down dusty country roads. After his talk with Scott on Saturday, he'd been determined to find a way to make things work between him and Eden. That's why he'd looked for jobs in Spokane today. He had two in mind that he considered applying for; one in law enforcement and the other in computers.

About the time he hit five miles, he decided if Eden wanted to stay in Spokane, he would follow her.

EDEN BROUGHT her car to a stop in the hospital parking lot and looked up at the building where she said her final goodbyes to her mother before they unplugged the machines that kept her alive. And now her dad was here, facing his own mortality.

That's not totally true. He'd had a good scare, but Helen had assured Eden he would be okay.

She picked up her phone and noted the missed calls and texts from Rudy.

She'd been talking to Helen when he called the first time, so she ignored his call. And even though her car alerted her when he texted, she chose not to listen to them. Then when he called a few minutes ago, she couldn't bring herself to talk to him.

She read his first text: *I hope everything is okay with your father. Let me know if there is anything I can do.*

Then the next one read: *Please call me and let me know how your dad is doing. I want to be there for you.*

She listened to the voicemail he left. "I'm sorry, I'm too impatient to wait for you to call. I really hope your dad is okay. I'm praying for him. And I'm praying for you... For us. I know we've been a little distant lately, but... I want to fix that, Eden. Please call me as soon as you can."

Tears pricked her eyes at the sound of his voice. All day yesterday, she'd made it a point to avoid him, even to the extent of claiming to have a headache and going to her room at seven o'clock. He'd looked disappointed, but he hadn't pressed to spend time with her, which only discouraged her even more. And then this morning, she'd waited until she was sure he'd left for work before she came out of her room.

Does he mean it? Does he really want to fix things between us?

Does he have any idea what it would take to do that? Or does he just want to make sure she came back, so he'd continue to have a *fun* companion to do things with?

Opening her door, she decided the answers to her questions could wait. She needed to see how her dad was doing.

Helen called her half an hour ago and told her that her dad's surgery went well. He was now in the ICU where they would monitor him overnight. The doctor had said that he should make a full recovery, but that didn't keep Eden's hands from trembling as she pushed the button on the elevator. The same one she rode down with her father sixteen years ago, leaving her mother behind. She wrapped her arms around herself as the elevator doors closed, praying her father would indeed be okay.

She found the room number Helen had given her and paused outside the open door. Her father, clad in a blue hospital gown with a multitude of cords coming out of the top, lay flat on the bed, looking unusually pale, but otherwise fine.

Thank goodness!

Realizing Helen wasn't just standing close by, but rather, sitting on the edge of the bed, holding her dad's hand, Eden lingered in the doorway, giving herself a minute to get used to the idea of her dad dating his housekeeper and her former nanny.

A smile pushed up the corners of her lips. If anyone could keep her dad in his place, Helen could.

She stepped into the room. "You didn't have to go to such drastic lengths to get me to come visit you, Dad."

Helen sprang to her feet as though she'd been burned and stepped away from the bed.

Eden went to her dad's side and bent down to give him a hug.

He let out a little growl. "I told Helen not to worry you. I'm fine. It's not a big deal." Despite his words, her father's arms closed tighter around her than she could ever remember.

She inhaled his Old Spice scent.

"An aneurysm certainly is a big deal." She scowled at her dad before rounding the bed to give Helen a hug. "Thanks for calling me."

"He misses you so much even though he won't admit it," Helen whispered. "He talks about you every day."

"I've missed him too." Well, she missed the man who showed up at every dance recital and read her bedtime stories. Not so much the man who felt the need to dictate her life.

Eden released Helen and returned to the other side of the bed. Ignoring the oxygen sensor on his finger and the blood pressure cuff on his upper arm, she took his hand. "What did the doctor say?"

Helen did most of the talking as they explained how the doctor repaired the aneurysm by going in through the artery in the groin to place a coil and stent in the aneurysm at the base of his brain.

"How did they even discover that you had an aneurysm?" Eden hated to think how things might have ended if the aneurysm had ruptured.

"I've been having some pretty severe headaches for a while now," he said. "And when they started affecting my vision, my doctor decided I needed an MRI. The aneurysm was just over six millimeters."

"They often rupture when they hit seven," Helen interjected.

Thank goodness his didn't.

"And you're really going to be okay?" She squeezed his hand. "You're out of danger?"

"He has to lay flat for a few more hours before they'll let him sit up. Otherwise, he risks bleeding out in the artery in the groin. Then he needs to take it easy for the next two weeks."

Relieved that her father was mostly out of danger, she looked back and forth between him and Helen and grinned. "Now, tell me what's going on between you two."

Helen's face blanched and she fell back a step. "Nothing. We were...I was just...concerned about him, that's all."

Eden raised an eyebrow as she looked at her dad, daring him to deny there was something going on.

"Come now, Helen." He held his hand out to his housekeeper. "We've been talking about making our relationship public. No time like the present. Eden may as well be the first to know."

"I'd better be the first to know. How long has this been going on?"

Helen took her dad's hand and perched on the other side of the bed but didn't meet Eden's eyes.

Her dad was the one who spoke up. "For a number of years, I suppose."

"Years?"

"No, it hasn't." Helen gently slapped his shoulder. "I only went out with him for the first time eight months ago."

"But I'd been trying to get you to go out with me for years."

Eden couldn't believe what she was hearing. Her dad and Helen had been going out in public for months now? And he'd been interested in her for years?

She locked gazes with her dad. "So, do you plan to make this relationship permanent?"

"As a matter of fact, we were just talking about that before you arrived." He squeezed Helen's hand. "I've asked her to marry me, but she's concerned about how it might affect my business if I marry my housekeeper."

"And you're not?" Eden was careful to keep the censure out of her voice. She couldn't be happier for them, and she wanted them to know that.

Her father made a sound that was a cross between a growl and clearing his throat. "I'm tired of caring what all those pious, rich ba—"

"Uh-uh." Helen pointed a finger at him. "No swearing."

Eden bit back a smile.

Yep. She's good for him.

"I'm tired of living to someone else's standard."

Eden's eyebrows shot up and she inhaled so sharply she choked on her own spit.

He held up his hand. "I know, I'm one of those...idiots who think they have the right to dictate how everyone else lives. But I'm trying to change my ways." He squeezed Eden's hand and locked gazes with her. "Will you please forgive me for all the ridiculous demands I placed on you."

On any other day she wouldn't have been willing to forgive him so easily, but knowing how close she'd come to losing him, she wasn't willing to put off that task.

"Of course, I forgive you." Eden blinked back the tears that filled her eyes as she leaned in and gave him another hug.

"Pardon me for interrupting, but I need to do a quick assessment on your father." A tall, buff male nurse walked into the room.

Eden stood beside Helen while the nurse asked her dad a series of simple questions and checked the pulses in the tops of his feet.

"They have to check him often to make sure he doesn't have a stroke," Helen whispered.

A stroke!

So he's not totally out of danger yet.

When the nurse lifted the blanket to check the bandage near the groin where doctors had gone in to do the surgery, she and Helen turned their backs. Once the nurse was finished, Eden returned to the right side of the bed while Helen sat on the left.

She'd barely settled on the bed when her dad said, "How come Rudy didn't come with you? I'd like to talk stocks with him again."

Just the mention of Rudy's name was enough to make her heart beat a little faster. But then she reminded herself of what he said to Scott on Saturday, and her stomach hardened.

"No. He uh... he wanted to, but I'll probably stay for a while, and he couldn't afford to take the time off work."

"You're staying for a while?" Helen asked, hope lighting her eyes.

"Well, I figured I'd check in with Sam and make sure things don't fall to pieces while you're laid up."

Sam was her dad's second in command, and he was more than capable of running the company while her dad recuperated, but she needed to ensure she wasn't letting her dad down when he needed her most.

"You don't have to do that," her dad said. "I know you hate it there."

"I don't hate it. I just didn't...always enjoy it."

"I understand. It *will* give me a little peace of mind if you check in with Sam and Dirk. But you need to know...that I want you to be happy. Even if it's not with DuPont or...here in Spokane."

When Eden blinked back the tears again, he let out a sigh and closed his eyes for a long moment. Then he opened them again and smiled. "Tell me how things are going with you and Rudy. Are there going to be wedding bells in your future soon?"

I wish!

Tears flooded Eden's eyes, and her efforts to blink them away only succeeded in forcing them out.

"Hey, what's wrong?" Dad squeezed her hand while Helen leaned over and put an arm around Eden's shoulder.

"Rudy and I aren't...in a good place right now."

"What did he do?" Anger filled her dad's voice.

"Nothing."

That was the real crux of the problem. He wasn't ready to deviate from his plans and settle down.

"And everything."

So many sweet things that made me fall in love with him.

Eden didn't know how to tell her dad and Helen what was wrong without telling them the whole story. All of it. Including the part where she lied to her father.

She started by apologizing to him for deceiving him, then hesitantly began to tell them how Alice kept pushing her and Rudy together and how each interaction ended in disaster.

They laughed when she told them about the skunks and their subsequent tomato sauce then peroxide and baking soda baths. Then they grimaced when she mentioned her bout with food poisoning and gasped when she described Rudy's fishing accident. Of course, she left out the toe-curling, knee-weakening kisses that Rudy gave her each time, especially the one that Alice interrupted in the entryway.

Finally, she finished with, "I just can't help wondering if God doesn't want me to be with Rudy. And if that's the case, then why did he allow me to fall in love with him. The man is the epitome of a cinnamon roll hero."

"A what?" Dad and Helen asked in unison.

"He's an all-around good guy. The kind that takes a fresh loaf of bread to little old ladies who can't cook and takes time out of his busy day to play basketball with a struggling neighbor. He literally saved my life the first day I showed up in Providence, and he pulled my hair back and mopped my brow when I was vomiting."

Helen sighed. "He sounds perfect."

"He is. In every way. Except he has a plan for his life that he refuses to stray from. And it doesn't include marriage and a family for another three years."

Her dad's brow furrowed. "I understand wanting to have financial stability, but is he a big enough idiot to throw love away over a few life goals?"

Helen's arm tightened around Eden's shoulders. "Do you love him enough to fight for him?"

Didn't Kennedy say something similar a couple days ago?

When Eden didn't answer, Helen tried again. "You need to ask yourself what you want more than anything else. Then go for it. If it's meant to be, it'll work out. Just put your trust in God."

That's something I haven't done in a while. In fact, I've blamed him for every bit of bad luck that has happened to me and Rudy when I should have been thanking him for bringing Rudy into my life.

"Thanks for the reminder." Eden blinked back tears. "I want... I want to get married and have a family right away, but..."

"But what?" Dad and Helen said in unison again.

"Is it enough?" Eden bit her lip, half afraid of how her dad might respond. "Is being a mom enough?"

Could she trade in the power suits for baby bottles and diapers without feeling like she was letting people down or missing out on something in her life?

"It was enough for your mom." Dad sandwiched Eden's hand between his. "She was a high-powered attorney before she had you. But she gave it all up and never regretted it."

How had Eden forgotten that her mother used to be a lawyer? It must have been because she was simply always there. She never complained about being a mom, and her parents had rarely ever talked about the sacrifices she made.

"And let me tell you, honey," Dad patted her hand again. "After going through this..." He pointed to his head. "I realize there are much more important things in life than work."

"Your mother loved being a mom. You were her whole world." Helen stroked Eden's hair. "I think you'll make a great mom."

Me too.

Eden leaned into Helen's touch. The woman had been the only mother she'd known for the past sixteen years, and if all went well, she'd be Eden's stepmother soon.

Then there was Alice. She took Eden in and treated her like one of her own, teaching her all the things she'd taught her own daughters. Eden didn't want to lose that new mother figure in her life.

So how do I convince Rudy that love is worth altering his plans for?

CHAPTER 23

*E*den parked her car under the carport for 4-B and pulled her suitcase from the trunk.

Last night Helen had insisted she come spend the night with her in the apartment over the garage after treating her to a late dinner. But tonight, her former nanny encouraged her to return to her apartment.

Eden knew she needed to face the place at some point, but it had been so quiet after Kennedy moved out last year that she'd dreaded coming home to it in the evenings. She'd rarely bothered to cook, so she hadn't left much food in the fridge, but she hated to think what might be growing in there.

She stifled a yawn as she hefted her suitcase onto the sidewalk.

When she visited her father this morning, he'd had a lot more color and was eager to go home, so she'd left him with a very capable Helen while she visited DuPont Analytics. It had only taken four hours of impromptu meetings with Sam and Dirk and many of the department heads to remind her why she'd left the corporate world. She'd forgotten how much she hated meetings.

But I still like the idea of owning my own business. One that's not stuffy and boring.

Once again, she couldn't help but wonder what Esmeralda meant by her owning her own business. Especially since she got a job offer via email today from Avant Garde Home Decor. An offer that if it had come two weeks ago would have thrilled her. Now, she was just plain confused.

Why is God dangling this carrot in front of me when I've decided to do whatever it takes to make things work with Rudy.

After leaving work, she'd made the trip back to her dad's house to make sure he'd made it home from the hospital and was feeling okay. So of course, Helen insisted on feeding her again.

It was after seven now, and all she wanted to do was sink into a hot bubble bath.

She rounded the corner to her apartment and froze.

There on her front steps sat Rudy.

He was the last person she expected to see, so the sight of him took her breath away. It didn't help that he wore denim shorts and a light-blue polo shirt that hugged his biceps. He looked up, and eyes as blue as the Caribbean Ocean locked on her.

"What are you doing here?" Her voice squeaked.

He rose to his feet, all six foot-one of glorious perfection.

"You never called, so I had to come." He shrugged like it was no big deal, but the way he shoved his hands into his pockets reflected a hint of insecurity.

When Eden had finally checked her phone last night, she had two more messages from Rudy. Both asked her to call him. But she couldn't bring herself to do it. Instead, she'd finally sent him a text, saying her dad was going to be fine then turned her phone off.

Of course, there were another two messages and a missed call from him this morning, but she'd ignored them. If she was going to convince him to throw away his life plans and take a chance on her, she needed a game plan. She couldn't just race into this blindly and hope for the best.

Go for what you want. And put your trust in God.

Helen's words filled her head.

Eden took a deep breath and smiled as she approached Rudy. "How long have you been here?"

"Here on your doorstep? Or here in Spokane?"

She quirked an eyebrow. "Both."

"I've been sitting on your step for..." He checked his watch. "For about an hour and a half. And I've been in Spokane since about nine-thirty this morning."

She gasped. "You've been here all day? Why?"

"I told you. You never called. I had to come make sure your dad is okay." He pressed the toe of his tennis shoe into a crack in the sidewalk. "And I need to know if...we're okay."

The flutter of a thousand butterfly wings filled her stomach, and a lightness flooded her chest. Refusing to get her hopes up too soon, she mentally tamped down the flutters and said, "My dad is doing good. He's home now."

"I know." When she gave him a surprised look, he went on. "I showed up at the hospital this morning hoping to find you, but you'd just left. Your dad and Helen invited me to sit and visit for a while. Then when they discharged your dad, Helen insisted I follow them home so she could feed me lunch. I tried to refuse, but they told me you'd be busy all day at work, so I may as well hang out with them."

Rudy spent the day with Dad and Helen? She hated to think of the things they might have said to him.

"But I just came from there." And neither of them had let on that they'd spent the better part of the day with Rudy.

No wonder Helen wanted me to come back to my own apartment tonight.

"I got impatient waiting for you, so I finally left about four-thirty and drove to Dupont Analytics."

"Which is about the time I left. We must have just missed each other."

"Please tell me you're not planning on returning to work there full time." He stepped toward her.

"Good grief, no way!"

Relief covered his face as he nodded, then an uncomfortable silence settled between them.

She wanted to throw her arms around him and kiss him until she grew weak in the knees, but she needed to make sure her hopes for a relationship weren't in vain.

He cleared his throat. "So, uh... I've been waiting here for a while. Do you think I could come in?" He motioned to the door behind him.

"Yes. Of course. Absolutely." She pulled the keys from her purse and skirted around him.

He grabbed her suitcase as she prepared to lift it up the steps. "Allow me."

Sparks of electricity shot up her arm the moment his hand touched hers. She released the handle so fast he probably thought she was afraid of getting cooties or something. She rubbed the side of her hand against her thigh as she unlocked the door, once again tamping down the butterflies swarming her stomach.

Once inside, she looked around. A layer of dust coated everything, but otherwise it looked just like she'd left it. And that was rather depressing. It had been her home for almost seven years, but it didn't feel nearly as homey as the Wheeler's house.

"You can just leave the suitcase there." She pointed to the side of the entrance. "Can I offer you some..."

Do I have anything to offer him besides sour milk and spoiled orange juice?

"I um... Would you like a glass of water?"

"Water would be great."

He followed her to the kitchen where she was acutely aware of his presence. She filled a glass from the sink because the water in the fridge was probably stale after all this time.

When she handed it to him, he didn't drink it. He just stared at the glass in his hand.

"Is something wrong?" Eden asked.

"Yes." He set the glass on the counter. "Everything is wrong, and I'm not sure how to make it right. I only know I want to." He stepped closer, forcing her to look up at him.

Eden's lungs stalled, both from his words and his nearness. She turned and walked into the living room. If they were going to have this conversation, she needed to sit down. Forcing herself to breathe normally, she asked, "What is it you want to make right?"

He sat beside her then turned to face her. "This." He waved a hand back and forth between them. "Us."

Eden's heart pounded a little harder, and she struggled to draw sufficient air into her lungs. She wasn't sure what to say, so she remained quiet.

"After this happened..." he touched the fresh pink scar on his right eyebrow, "I decided to step back a little because you were so sure this was punishment for us kissing. I was afraid if I pushed you to continue our relationship, I'd drive you away." He shrugged one shoulder and gave her a sheepish look. "And I admit, I was a little spooked after requiring eight stitches."

He backed off because he was afraid of pushing me away?

To most people that wouldn't make sense, but Eden understood why he did it.

"Then when I made up my mind to keep fighting for us, you withdrew. Physically and emotionally." He scooted a little closer. "You hardly looked at me on Sunday. I don't know what I said or did to push you away, but I wish I could unsay or undo it."

Tears filled Eden's eyes. Did he really mean it? Or would he insist on sticking to his *plan* if she called him out on it?

She lowered her gaze and fiddled with the hem of her skirt. "I heard what you said to Scott in the weight room last Saturday." She lifted her gaze and made eye contact with him, daring him to deny his words.

His brow furrowed, and he looked sideways, deep in thought. Then his brow lifted, and he hung his head. "You heard me tell Scott I wasn't sure I could support you in the manner you were accustomed to."

"Do you honestly think I'm that hung up on material things? That money and status matter that much to me?"

"No, I've come to realize they don't, but my own insecurities kick in every once in a while, and I have a hard time believing that with your background, you'd be happy with a lowly sheriff's deputy." He looked around. "I mean, this is a really nice apartment."

"The only thing lowly about you is how you regard yourself and your abilities. And if you think I wouldn't be happy living the kind of life with you that I have had for the past couple months, then you don't know me at all."

"You're right." He grabbed her hand. "I judged you on a past experience with a former girlfriend and that was wrong."

This was the first time Rudy had mentioned a former girlfriend, and even though Eden was curious what happened between them, she didn't want to think about him with another woman right now.

"I also heard you say that I was fun to hang out with, but you weren't sure you should set your heart on more than a good time with me."

He grimaced. "That sounds a lot worse than what I meant, believe me. I was having a hard time being vulnerable in front of Scott. Lame, I know." He tugged at the collar of his t-shirt. "The truth is I already have my heart set on so much more with you, Eden." His voice dropped as he said her name, and a little shudder of warmth rippled through her.

"You do?" Eden's heart pounded against her ribcage. "But you said you weren't planning on getting married for another three years." Emotion clogged Eden's throat. "I don't want to wait that long, Rudy."

"Me either."

"What about your plan?"

Releasing her hand, he shifted on the sofa, facing forward with his elbows propped on his knees. He stared at his clasped hands. "I used to be that guy who flew by the seat of his pants, always looking for the next adventure. I never took life seriously. I was smart, so I aced school with minimal effort. But when...Parker died, I floundered for over a year. I kept asking God why Parker. He had it all together. He had a plan. He knew what he wanted to do with his life. He was going to help so many people." He popped his knuckles one by one now. "It should have been me."

"Rudy, no." She scooted closer and put an arm around his shoulders. "It shouldn't have been you, and you need to stop blaming yourself."

"No matter how many times people told me that, I couldn't." He shook his head and stared across the room. "Then one day, my dad told me if I didn't make good use of the second chance I was given, then two lives were lost in that accident. And I don't know what it was, but something hit me. I decided I needed to live the life Parker didn't get to." Rudy flexed his fingers. "Setting goals and following his plan was the only thing that gave my life direction for years. I eventually came to believe that I needed to stick to that plan to succeed. It has served me well, and I'm happy with where I'm at in my life." He gave her a rueful smile. "Well, I was until you moved to Providence."

"You're saying you're willing to deviate from your plan for me?"

Rudy took her hand. "I'm saying I choose you, Eden. Over my plan. Over my job, if necessary."

"Your job?"

"I'm willing to leave Providence, if need be, so we can be together."

Eden's chest expanded with a rush of emotions as tears pricked the back of her eyes. "But I don't want you to leave Providence. *I* don't want to leave Providence."

So why did I tell Rudy I wasn't sure if I'd be coming back to Providence when he asked?

"But you want a career that may not be an option in Providence."

"I know. I feel torn because I want this." She motioned back and forth between them. "But I also want something more. After all this time, I should understand what that is..." She lowered her gaze. "But I don't."

Rudy rubbed his thumb over her knuckles. "Can we figure it out together?"

"I'd like that." She pressed a hand to his chest as he leaned in for the kiss she desperately wanted. "There's something I need to tell you first. This morning I got a job offer from one of the home decor stores that I applied with a few weeks ago." She held up her hand. "I'm not sure I want to accept it, but I've been floundering for far too long now. I need to do something with my life."

Rudy acknowledged her words with barely a nod. "I applied for two jobs in Spokane myself last night. I'm not sure I want either of them, but I'm willing to move, if you decide you want to stay here."

"Seriously? Why would you do that?"

Eden had always had to fight to be able to make her own choices, and now, having Rudy offer this kind of support made her tear up again.

"I wanted you to know I'm committed to doing whatever it takes to make this work. It's silly to put so much stock in the words of a wannabe fortune teller, but I've thought a lot about Esmeralda's words, and I've decided I want to start living my own life and following my dreams. I'm still deciding what those dreams are, but I know they center around you."

"I'm happy for you. I wish I understood what dreams I'm supposed to follow." She lifted a hand to his cheek where her palm rasped against the stubble on his jaw, ramping up her attraction and the desire to have his lips on hers. "Other than you, of course. You're definitely in my dreams."

"I'm leaving it in God's hands," Rudy said.

"That's what I need to do. Although I've doubted God so much lately that I'm not sure He will guide me in this decision."

"He will, don't worry." Rudy caressed her cheek, slowly dragging a finger along her jaw. "Can I kiss you now?"

"Are you sure we dare?" Eden joked, even though she was still half serious.

"I have a plan to make sure nothing bad happens," he whispered as he leaned in.

"What's that?"

"We're safe here, right? No danger of something bad happening as long as we don't move from this spot." When Eden nodded, he went on. "So, my plan is that we kiss for a minute or five, then we don't move. You simply let me hold you for the next fifteen minutes."

"I like that plan." Eden tilted her head as she leaned toward him, ready for his kiss, but he spoke again.

"But we have to agree that if something bad happens within the next twenty-four hours, we won't blame it on the kiss."

"Okay." Eden agreed, for no other reason than to have him kiss her already.

Finally, he pressed his lips to hers. Feathery and hesitant at first, then more passionate and possessive.

She let out a sigh as she pushed her fingers into his hair. It had only been ten days since the last time they kissed, but she'd missed this. The feel of his lips on hers, his scent that drove her crazy, his strong arms around her. She loved it all. She loved him.

Kissing him felt like coming home. She didn't care what the future held as long as Rudy was in it.

When he gathered her into his embrace so he could deepen the kiss, she willingly scooted into his arms, her mouth keeping tempo with his the whole time. The kiss lasted much longer than a minute, but to Eden's disappointment, it didn't last five minutes.

They were both short of breath by the time he pulled his mouth from hers and pressed his forehead to hers. "I'll take all the bad luck in the world as long as I can do that with you every day."

Eden giggled. "Be careful or you'll jinx us."

She settled into his arms, relishing the feel of his muscled chest at her back. She could get used to this. Making a new resolve, she vowed to not blame any more of her bad luck on God. She would only praise him, like her mom and Helen had taught her.

A STRANGE SENSE of deja vu hit Eden as she spotted the roadside stand where she'd purchased strawberries seven weeks ago. The signs now touted raspberries and blackberries.

She thought about stopping, but she didn't want a repeat of the bee fiasco. Besides, the Wheelers had plenty of fresh berries in their garden.

She couldn't wait to get home.

She wasn't sure when she'd started to think of the Wheeler's house as home, but it was. And she couldn't wait to get there after this long, crazy week.

To keep her dad from stressing about work, she'd stuck around and assisted Sam and Dirk with some restructuring that would allow her dad to take it a little easier. They'd created two new positions, promoted a few people, and hired some more.

Then after dinner with her dad and Helen each evening, Eden spent her nights boxing up her apartment while she talked to Rudy on the phone. For now, she'd put all her stuff in storage until she solidified her plans for her future. Everything that is, except for the power suits and many of the expensive accessories she'd purchased over the past year. She'd taken those to a consignment shop that specialized in top quality, brand-name clothing.

After dropping them off, she'd found herself perusing the racks, even though she'd never bought anything second-hand before. She'd picked up a Louis Vuitton handbag before realizing that except for a handful of personal items and a few snacks and groceries, she hadn't been shopping for almost two months.

She didn't need to start now.

She had other more important things to focus on, like running her own business. Tired of trying to figure out what for Esmeralda meant, she'd developed a plan to go after what she wanted. Hopefully, things would play out the way she planned.

Excitement bubbled in her chest as she crested the hill just before Providence.

Only ten more minutes!

She pressed a little harder on the gas. Then out of nowhere, red and blue lights flashed in her rear-view mirror.

Frick!

She slowed and pulled her car over to the side of the road. Her hands grew sweaty as she waited for the officer to step out of his car. She'd never gotten a ticket before, and she couldn't afford one now. Not when she was about to risk everything she owned plus take out a hefty loan to follow her dreams.

When the tall, good-looking sheriff's deputy climbed from his car, a grin split her face. She lowered her window and watched in her rear-view mirror as the handsome officer sauntered forward.

"Do you have any idea how fast you were going ma'am?" Rudy's posture was stiff with his thumbs hanging off the front of his gun belt, but a hint of a smile teased at his lips.

"I'm so sorry, officer. I guess I was a little distracted. I was thinking about seeing my boyfriend again after being away forever."

"It has felt like forever." Rudy cleared his throat and deepened his voice. "I mean, driving while distracted is dangerous. You should be more careful about where you let your thoughts wander while you drive. But out of curiosity...what exactly do you plan to do when you see your boyfriend again?" His lips quirked as he continued to fight a smile.

She tapped her chin, pretending to contemplate her answer while her heart screamed, *"Kiss him until we're both breathless!"*

"You know, he insulted me a while back while I was in the hospital. I tried to start a pillow fight with him, but I didn't have enough strength to follow through." She winked at him. "I'm feeling much stronger now."

"A pillow fight?" All semblance of a smile fled. Then a gleam filled his eyes. "What would the winner of this pillow fight get?"

Now she was the one holding back a smile. "Hmm... I think three months of not having to clean the bathroom."

His brow furrowed. "May I suggest a better reward?"

"What's that?"

"A kiss."

She gave a dramatic grimace. "I'm not sure that's a good idea. Bad things always happen when we kiss."

Amusement filled his face. "Maybe the loser could rub the winner's shoulders."

"Ooh, that sounds good. I could use a massage after the week I've had."

"Confident you'll win, huh?"

"Absolutely!" Although she was having fun, Rudy needed to kiss her soon, or she might attack him, right here on the side of the highway. "So, uh...officer, do you intend to harass me all day? Because like I said, I'm kind of anxious to see my boy—"

"I'm not harassing you." Surprise filled Rudy's voice.

"Then what do you call this?" She motioned to his car then hers.

He crouched down and put his arms on her door.

Finally!

"This is me asking you to go out with me tomorrow."

Eden's eyebrows arched. "You pulled me over to ask me out on a date?"

"Well, I was anticipating having to save your life again. But since that wasn't necessary, I figured I may as well ask you out since you're really pretty and all." When she picked up her purse to swat at him, he blocked it and laughed.

"Why do we need to wait until tomorrow to go out? Won't you be off work..." She checked her watch. "In a couple hours?"

"Because Kennedy has unequivocally let me know that you're hers tonight."

Eden had talked to Kennedy on the phone a few times this week, but she'd missed her friend too. She couldn't wait to tell Kennedy her plans.

"Did you really have to pull me over to ask me out? You couldn't have called me?"

"It's just more fun this way."

She took another swing at him with her purse, but he blocked it again.

"I didn't want you to make any other plans. I want you to spend the whole day with me tomorrow."

"The whole day? You're not planning on taking me fishing again, are you?"

"No fishing. Although, I plan to take you back to the lake after we go horseback riding and hiking, where we'll have a campfire and—"

"Horseback riding, hiking, and a campfire? Sounds like lots of opportunities for things to go wrong. We'd better make sure we don't kiss."

"Oh, I plan to kiss you alright. A lot." He reached out and caressed her bottom lip with his thumb, making it difficult for her to breathe.

Her mouth moistened in anticipation of his kiss, and she leaned toward her open window.

Then he gave her a wink and a wicked grin before standing. "Drive safe now, ma'am. Don't drive distracted." He turned and walked back to his car.

Wait! What?

She couldn't possibly be more distracted.

"You'd better watch out, Officer Wheeler! I'll beat you home, and I'll be hiding where you least expect it with the biggest pillow from the downstairs sectional."

He slowed his walk and grinned over his shoulder. "Looking forward to it!"

She shook her head to clear it after shooting a scowl at Rudy's backside. She had more important things to worry about anyway. She needed to get her life in order before starting the next chapter with the handsome, teasing sheriff's deputy.

Ten minutes later, Eden's breathing sped up as she walked through the back door of Hattie's shop. She paused to control her excited breathing and sent up a little prayer for success.

When she stepped into the shop, Hattie was waving to customers who walked out the front door. Eden's gaze darted around the showroom.

No customers. Perfect.

Slow moments on Saturdays were rare nowadays.

"Eden? I didn't know you were back in town."

"I just got back."

Hattie walked over to the center of the store where the arrangement of furniture now sat. She sighed as she sank down onto the armchair. "Phew! It's been busy today. Lots of out-of-towners bringing in those coupons you asked Amy to give out at the diner."

Eden perched on the edge of the settee as though she feared it might collapse under her. She bit her lip and stared at Hattie.

"Is something wrong, sweetie?"

"Yes! No! Maybe." Eden shook her head to clear it of the dozens of ideas and plans that had filled it over the past week; a craft cottage as well as a gym and dance or gymnastics studio or maybe a spa or a tech shop, the possibilities were endless.

Still staring at Hattie, Eden leaned forward. "Everything in my life is either about to fall into place or fall apart. It all depends on you, Hattie."

The older woman's eyes grew wide as she pressed a hand to her chest. "What do you mean?"

"I want to buy your shop and the vacant space next to it." Eden held her breath for a split second before rushing on. "Or if you want to sell the whole row of buildings, I'm interested in buying it all."

BREATHE.

All day long, Rudy repeatedly caught himself holding his breath, waiting for something bad to happen.

But it didn't.

He and Eden had ridden horses at the Double Diamond, where they'd eaten a picnic lunch that his mom had been all too eager to fix. Then they hiked hand in hand, talking about anything and everything until the trail became too narrow to walk side by side. No one tripped and sprained an ankle. Nothing disastrous happened even though they shared several lingering kisses at the summit.

They skipped rocks on the lake without incident and even went wading and got in a water fight. They laughed and kissed some more. Neither of them fell into the water and got soaked or cut a foot on sharp rocks.

Rudy took extra care with the fire, using caution and practicing every fire safety skill he learned in Boy Scouts. No one tripped and fell into the flames. No errant ash landed on them. They didn't even burn their hot dogs.

Eden did burn her marshmallows, but only because she liked it that way.

They now sat curled up together in his dad's extra-large camp chair staring at the dancing flames, his fingers laced with hers. Again, they talked. This time about Eden's visions for Hattie's store that she planned to rename The Craft Cottage.

It didn't surprise Rudy that Hattie agreed to sell Eden the store. The woman was pushing eighty, after all. What surprised him was the phone call Eden received last night from Hattie.

After talking it over with her daughter, Naomi, Hattie decided to sell the entire row of buildings to Eden with the stipulation that Naomi and Susie could rent the salon space for reasonably low rent for as long as they wanted.

Rudy hadn't expected Naomi to agree to the sale, but she *had* just turned sixty. Maybe she figured she was too old to take on so much responsibility.

"So, what's your plan for the empty space next door to the boutique?"

"I'm thinking it would make a great dance and gymnastics studio with a gym in the back. Or a spa, but there may not be a big enough demand here in Providence for a spa. A computer repair shop might do well. Really, the possibilities are endless."

"They are." Rudy laughed.

He loved how excited Eden was about this new venture. She came alive last night after the phone call from Hattie, and she still glowed.

She had a lot of work ahead of her, including cashing in a few investments and securing funding, but he had no doubt she could do anything she set her mind to. And he looked forward to working alongside her.

His thoughts turned to the ring box in his glove compartment. Eden's mother's wedding ring. Oliver gave it to him on Tuesday when he asked for his permission to ask Eden to marry him. Rudy took the rings to have them cleaned before leaving Spokane on Wednesday, and they'd been burning a hole in his pocket ever since.

He'd planned to propose today, but a little voice in his head kept telling him he was rushing things. And it was right.

He didn't want to do anything to mess things up with Eden, so the ring had remained in his glove box all day. He'd move it to a safe place when they got home tonight, and when he felt like the time was right, he'd be ready.

He doubted he could wait much longer though, because he was eager to start his life with her.

When the fire died down and the night grew dark and chilly, he grabbed the blanket he'd brought along and pulled Eden into his arms again. For another hour, they talked, studied the stars, and kissed some more.

He hated to see the day end, but when she started to yawn, he decided they'd better head home. They had everything loaded back in the truck in no time, and Eden soon sat beside him tucked under his arm with her hand on his thigh.

He sucked in a deep breath and let it out in a lengthy sigh. The day couldn't have turned out any more perfect. He'd enjoyed every minute spent with this beautiful woman. And more importantly, nothing had gone wrong.

A loud pop sounded outside the truck, and the wheel jerked.

Oh snap!

After he brought the truck to a stop, Rudy closed his eyes and groaned. He'd spoken—or rather thought—too soon. Evidently something could still go wrong. And it had.

"What's the matter?" Eden asked, her voice tense.

Rudy was hesitant to tell her for fear she would think it was a sign that God didn't want them together. But he couldn't hide it from her either.

He cleared his throat. "We uh... We blew a tire."

"Of course we did. Because nothing can ever be simple with us." Then she surprised him by bursting into laughter.

Grateful she didn't blame this on God, he joined her.

They laughed long and hard until they had tears streaming down her face.

She was the first to sober up. "You know how to change a tire, right? You do that for little old ladies all the time, don't you?"

"Yes, I know how to change a tire." He reached for his door

handle. "Although, I've only ever had to do it twice for *stranded motorists.*" He grinned as he climbed out. "I call Scott to come help the little old ladies with their flat tires. They tend to get a little handsy sometimes."

Eden laughed as she scooted out behind him. "So you *have* helped the little old ladies."

"More times than I can count." He pulled his cell phone from his pocket. "Would you mind holding the light for me?"

"Sure."

Rudy did his best to focus on the job at hand and not Eden's shapely legs beside him. What should have only taken fifteen minutes took almost twice that because of a stubborn lug nut, but he accomplished the job.

He settled back into the driver's seat with Eden beside him, grateful tonight's bad luck didn't require a trip to the ER. Eager to get Eden home so he could give her a goodnight kiss, he turned the key in the ignition.

Click.

Stomach sinking, he turned it off and back on again.

Click.

No. No. No.

He tried again. Nothing but a click.

"Oh snap!" In his head he said much worse words.

"What's wrong with your truck?" Eden spoke slowly as though afraid to hear the answer.

"It won't start." He spoke through clenched teeth.

"Why?"

"I don't know. It could be a dozen different things." He pulled the handle to pop the hood. "Stay here and try starting it again when I tell you to."

Rudy lifted the hood and stared into the dark. He fished his phone out again for a flashlight and wiggled the battery cables.

"Okay, try it now."

Click.

He studied the area where the sound came from but couldn't

discern any issues. However, he had a sinking feeling it was the alternator.

I should have paid better attention when Scott talked about cars.

Not that knowledge would do him any good out here in the middle of nowhere with no tools.

He braced himself for Eden's anger and possible refusal to have anything more to do with him before he slammed the hood closed.

He tried to force a smile as he climbed back in the truck, but he must not have been convincing, because she said, "It's not fixable, is it?"

"Not at the moment."

She sank back against the seat and sighed. He expected her to shout or burst into tears. But she didn't. From what little he could see of her face in the moonlight, she didn't even look angry.

"It's okay, you can say it," he said.

"Say what?"

"I know we're both thinking it."

"I'm trying not to, because I don't want to believe that God is against us being together. If that was the case, then why did he allow you to save my life when I got stung by the bee?"

Rudy took her hand. "You're not angry?"

"Being angry at God won't help. It only hurts me. Helen taught me that after my mom died." Eden flipped her hair from one side of her head to the other. "So, what do we do now?"

He pulled out his phone yet again. "I'll call Scott to come tow my tru—" Rudy's mind shut down when he saw zero bars of service on his phone. His battery was almost dead, to boot, and of course he hadn't thought to bring a charger with him.

"Let me guess. No service."

"Yep."

Eden lifted her phone from her lap. "I checked mine while you were fiddling with the engine. I don't have any either."

"Eden, I am so sorry. This is all my fault. I take full responsibility. I won't blame you for hating me."

She clasped his hand and rotated toward him the best she could. "I don't hate you, Rudy. I love you. One more reason I can't blame this on God. If he didn't want me to fall in love with you, he wouldn't have allowed me to develop these feelings for you."

Rudy cupped her cheek. "Have I ever told you what an amazing woman you are?"

She grinned. "Not yet."

"You are amazing and beautiful. And I'm so in love with you."

He pressed his lips to hers. Rudy had never felt quite so complete and alive as when he kissed Eden. He hoped he got the chance to kiss this woman every day for the rest of his life.

When they finally broke apart, Eden sighed. "Okay, what are our options?"

"I can walk until I get service then call Scott and hope he's not dead to the world and will actually answer my call."

"How far would you have to walk?"

"Probably a couple miles."

"Should I come with you?"

"It'd probably be safer for you to stay here. You're less likely to twist an ankle on a rock or pothole."

She looked out the window into the darkness. "I don't want to stay here alone. Besides, what if something happens to you?" She chewed on her lip for a moment. "Are there skunks out there?"

"They're nocturnal, so probably." The thought of walking in the dark appealed less and less to Rudy.

"What are our other options?"

"We spend the night in the truck and start walking first thing in the morning."

Her nose wrinkled. "It doesn't sound very comfortable, but I think it's our safest option. So, how do we do this? You take the back seat and I take the front?"

"We could do that. Or..." He hesitated to finish the sentence because he didn't want her to think he was trying to take advantage of the situation, even though he kind of was.

"What?"

"Well, it's likely to get pretty chilly tonight, and we only have one blanket."

"Are you suggesting I sleep snuggled up with you?" Her voice was full of faux shock.

"Only if you want to."

"I want to stay warm and my chances of doing that are probably higher in your arms. So I guess a girl's gotta do what a girl's gotta do."

He reached over the seat and grabbed the blanket. "I see how it is. You just want me for my hot body."

"Definitely." There was a hint of huskiness in her voice that sent his hormones raging.

Laughter filled the cab of the truck as they repeatedly rearranged themselves for optimal comfort and snuggle capability. Finally, Rudy leaned back against the passenger door with one leg across the seat, and Eden sat in front of him with her back against his chest.

It wasn't comfortable by any means, but when she laid her head against his shoulder, he decided he could definitely think of worse ways to sleep.

"You know," she said, "we could totally consider this situation as more bad luck, but I feel pretty lucky right now."

"Me too." He tightened his arms around her.

I'm the luckiest man in the world.

Eden started giggling before he even had the chance to close his eyes.

"What's so funny?"

"If stuff like this continues to happen every time we're together, can you imagine what we're going to have to go through if we get married and start a family."

Rudy sucked in a sharp breath. He was having a hard enough time keeping his mind from traveling down roads it shouldn't go. He didn't need to be thinking about intimate activities that led to *starting a family*.

"Eden," he spoke through clenched teeth. "Please don't talk about us having kids."

She shifted to look at him, alarm on her face. "I thought you wanted kids."

"I do. I just can't imagine having them with you." Her mouth dropped open, and he realized how his words sounded. He rushed on. "I can't *let* myself imagine it *right now*. Not while I'm here with you. *Like this*." He put emphasis on his words hoping she would catch his meaning.

"Oh." Her lips pinched as though she bit back a smile. "Sorry." She shifted back to her original position and laid her head against him again.

Another little giggle escaped.

"Honey?" It was the first time he'd used the endearment. He loved how naturally it rolled off his tongue.

"Yeah?"

"Go to sleep or I'm going to throw you out to the wolves."

She bolted upright. "Are there really wolves out there?"

Rudy burst out laughing again as happiness bubbled up inside him. He looked forward to spending the rest of his life with this beautiful, spunky woman.

If you enjoyed Changing Lanes, please consider leaving a review on Amazon.

Have you read the Finding Providence series?

Be sure you join my newsletter, so you don't miss a new release.
jillburrell.com/newsletter

ABOUT THE AUTHOR

JILL HAS always been an avid reader, and romance has always been her favorite genre. If she's not writing or folding laundry her head is usually in a book.

When her father told her, "I've got a story I want you to write," she didn't think she'd ever actually do it.

But after twenty years of being a stay-at-home mom with seven children, the idea of writing and publishing a book sounded less terrifying than entering the workforce again. Boy, was she wrong!

Keep in touch with Jill Burrell
www.jillburrell.com

amazon.com/author/jillburrell

facebook.com/authorjillburrell

goodreads.com/authorjillburrell

bookbub.com/authors/jill-burrell

www.ingramcontent.com/pod-product-compliance
Lightning Source LLC
Chambersburg PA
CBHW070808180626
46818CB00001B/168